ALSO BY JENELLE LEANNE SCHMIDT

Turrim Archive

The Orb and the Airship

Mantles of Oak and Iron

Hearts of Stone and Steel

The Prisoner and the Pirate

Towers of Might and Memory

A Classic Retold

Steal the Morrow

The Minstrel's Song

King's Warrior

Second Son

Yorien's Hand

Minstrel's Call

The Faelands

An Echo of the Fae

Children's Picture Books

'Twas an Evening in Bethlehem

MANTLES OF OAK AND IRON

BOOK 2 OF THE TURRIM ARCHIVE

JENELLE LEANNE SCHMIDT

STORMCAVE

Mantles of Oak and Iron

Volume 2 of The Turrim Archive

By Jenelle Leanne Schmidt

Copyright 2023 by Jenelle Leanne Schmidt

Published by Stormcave

www.jenelleschmidt.com

Mantles of Oak and Iron

ISBN-13: 978-1-960357-00-7

Cover art by Dragonpen Designs

Book design and maps by Declan Rowe

To Grant: this series only continues because you were its first real fan.

THE WORLD OF TURRIM

Turrim is a single-continent world with six separate cultures and a calendar that looks slightly different from our own.

Turrim's year is only 336 days long, separated into twelve lunats (what we would call months) and each lunat is exactly 28 days long, separated into 4 sennights (what we would call weeks). Their seasons are much as our own, following the same pattern of fall, winter, spring, and summer.

Their new year begins on what would for us be September 21st, or the Fall Equinox.

The months of the year (starting at the beginning of their calendar year) are named thus:

Chanjar	October
Deepthen	November
Darkthen	December
Edrian	January
Tella	February
Malla	March
Urin	April
Paute	May
Avar	June
Mirad	July
Avest	August
Felling	September

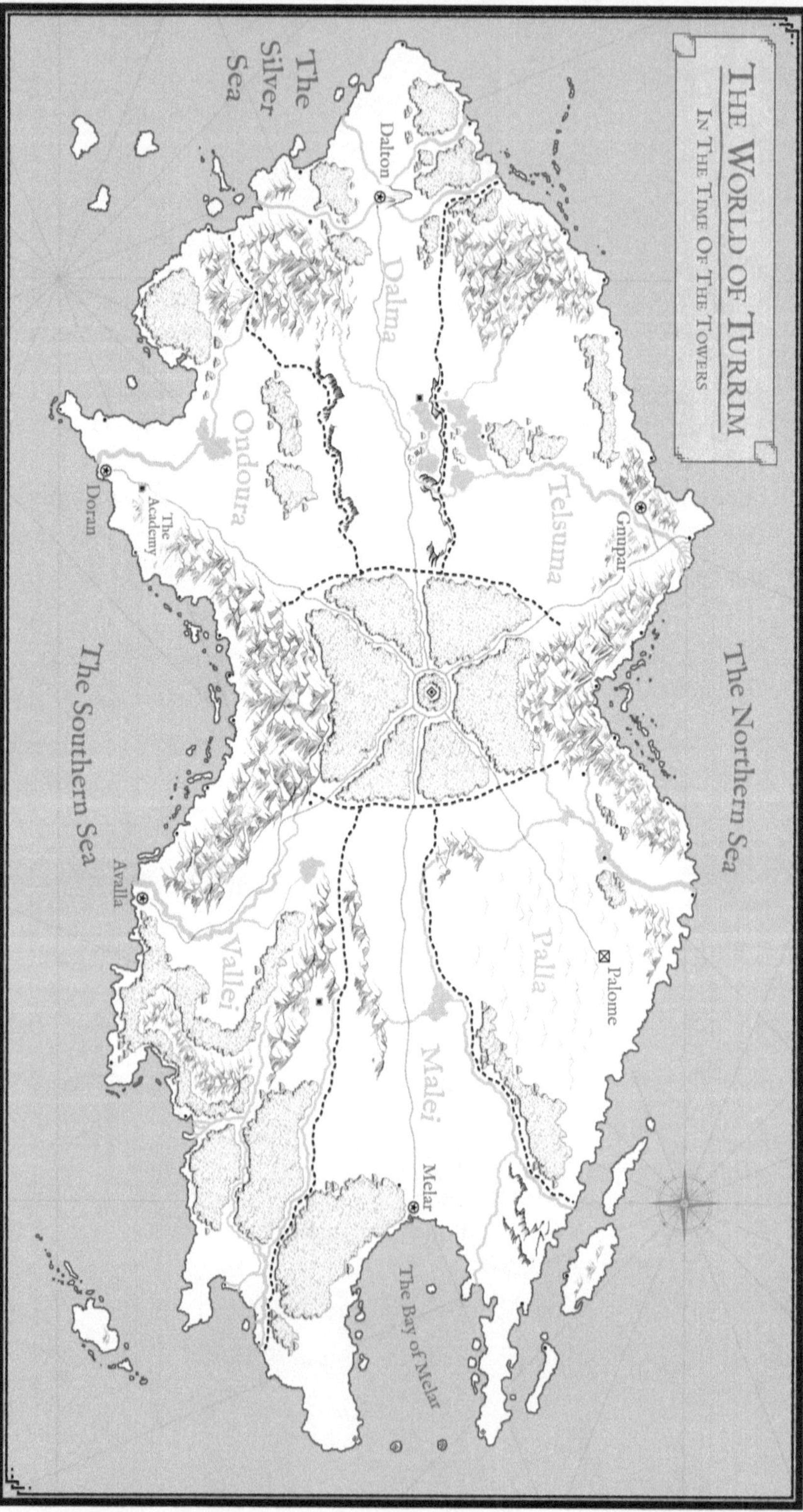

THE WORLD OF TURRIM
IN THE TIME OF THE TOWERS
The Silver Sea
Dalton
Dalma
Ondoura
Doran
The Academy
Telsuma
Gnupar
The Northern Sea
The Southern Sea
Avalla
Vallei
Palla
Palome
Malei
Melar
The Bay of Melar

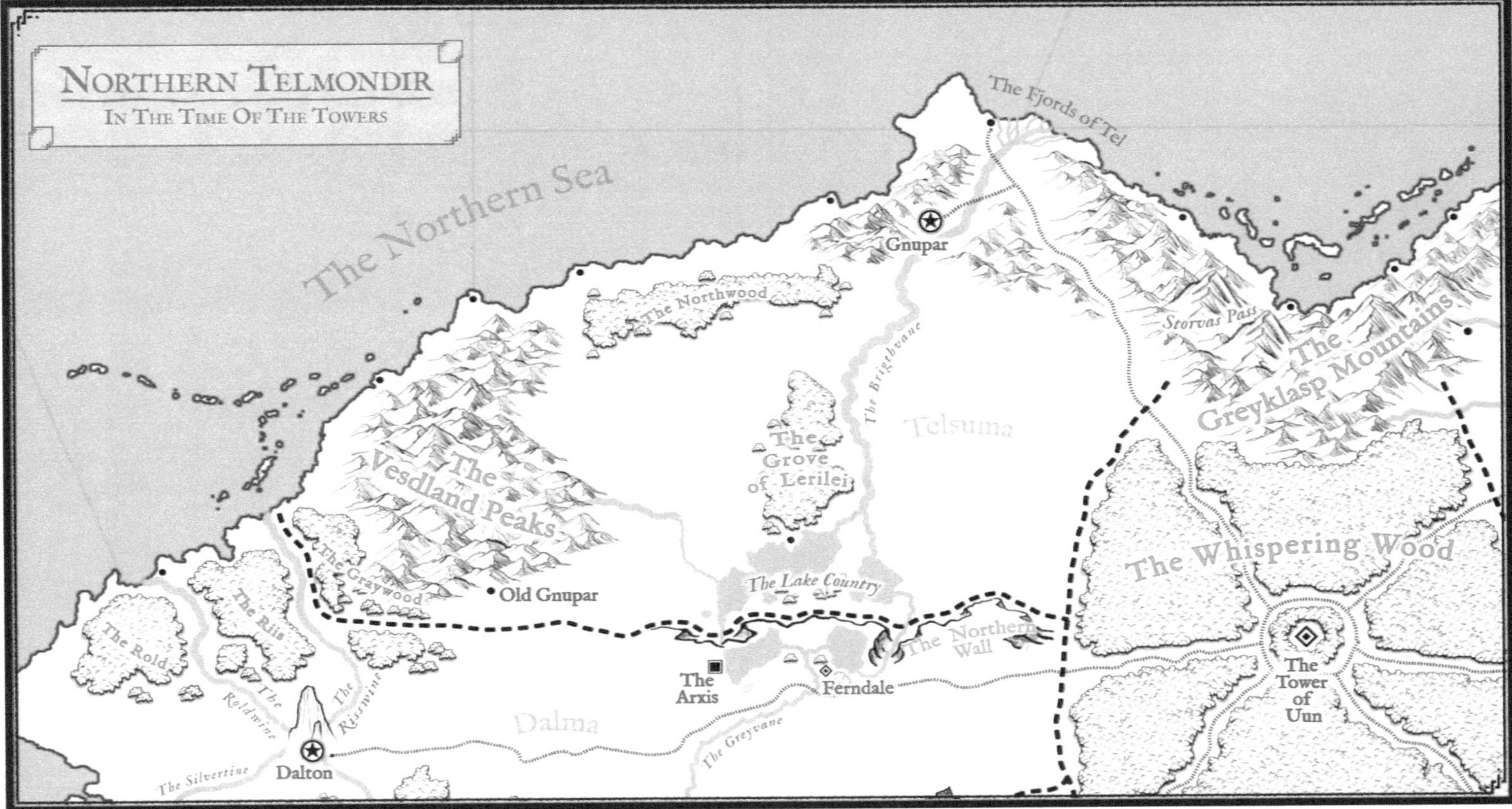

Northern Telmondir
In The Time Of The Towers
The Fjords of Tel
The Northern Sea
Gnupar
The Northwood
Storvas Pass
The Brigebvane
Telsuma
The Greyklasp Mountains
The Grove of Lerilei
The Vesdland Peaks
The Graywood
Old Gnupar
The Lake Country
The Whispering Wood
The Rold
The Riis
The Roldwine
The Risswine
The Northern Wall
The Arxis
Ferndale
The Tower of Uun
Dalma
The Greyvane
The Silvertine
Dalton

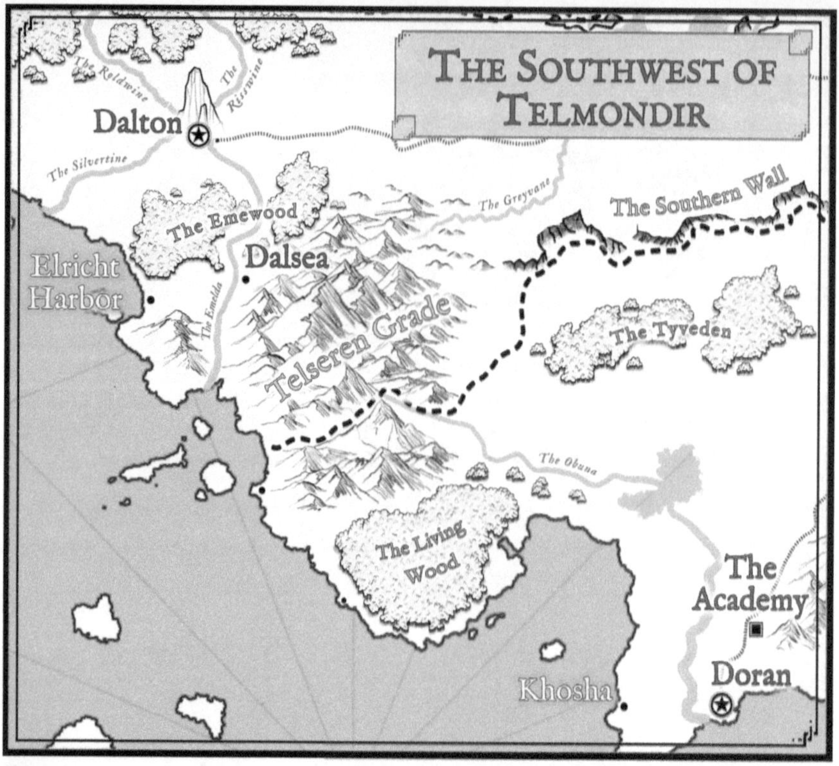

THE SOUTHWEST OF TELMONDIR
The Reldwine
The Risswine
Dalton
The Silvertine
The Emewood
Dalsea
Elricht Harbor
The Emelda
The Greyvane
The Southern Wall
The Tyveden
Telseren Grade
The Obuna
The Living Wood
The Academy
Doran
Khosha

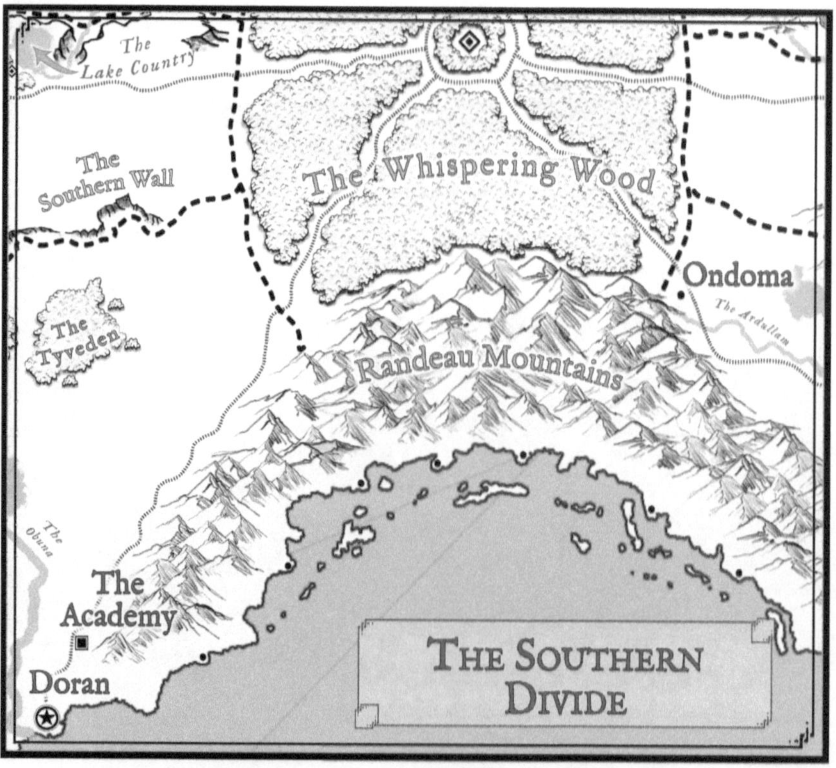

The Lake Country
The Southern Wall
The Whispering Wood
The Tyveden
Ondoma
The Ardullam
Randeau Mountains
The Obuna
The Academy
Doran
THE SOUTHERN DIVIDE

1

Dalmir stood on the deck of the airship, holding the sleeping girl in his arms. As the *Valdeun Hawk* alighted on the glistening surface of the large pond, he stared over the railing at their destination.

Across a grassy lawn, a solid, square building soared up several stories under a complicated and beautifully angled roof covered with fine wooden shingles. Myriad windows glinted in the sun, accompanied by overflowing flower boxes hanging from each sill. Thick beams painted in gentle blue supported the plaster walls and crisscrossed in a pleasing pattern.

"We've arrived," he whispered to the sleeping girl, but she did not waken. He frowned at her, worried. She had not stirred in the entire three-day journey from the Whispering Wood. She was such a tiny slip of a thing already; surely she needed to eat more than the little broth they forced her to swallow in her sleep.

"This is the healing center? The sychstal?" he called up to Marik, stumbling over the unfamiliar word.

"Ferndale is the best sychstal in Turrim," Marik replied, holding the wheel steady, a cascade of ripples emanating from the hull as Marik maneuvered closer to the sandy shore.

A man rushed out of the building waving his arms and shouting, but his words fluttered on the breeze, not reaching the ears of anyone on board the vessel. He waited on the shore, his face flushed an angry red, bordering on purple, and he shook his finger as Dalmir approached in the longboat.

"You can't just land in the Healer's Pool like that, do you hear me?" the man shouted out as Dalmir rose. "You—" Glimpsing the fragile burden Dalmir bore, the man's demeanor changed abruptly. "A patient for the healers?"

"Yes," Dalmir replied. "I was told the best physicians in the world reside here."

The man straightened, his manner now solicitous and concerned. "You were told truly. Right this way, sir. We will get her to a healer immediately."

He ushered Dalmir into the building and bade him wait in a pristine parlor. Sunshine sang in through the windows, casting a pleasant light throughout the sparsely decorated room. Dalmir sat on a leather sofa, the girl still cradled in his arms. As he waited for the healer, Dalmir contemplated his burden. Hers was a delicate face, tiny and heart-shaped. Despite her sunken cheeks and the furrow etched into her brow above her nose, it was a sweet face, possibly even pretty. Dalmir stared at her, willing her to wake. He had done what he could for her, treating her visible wounds, but something deeper, something he could not touch, ailed her. He could not erase the lunats she had spent as a prisoner, terrified and alone. He could do little to mend the bruises her heart and soul had sustained from her ordeal. It had been a long, long time since he had felt so helpless. Suddenly, he wondered if she had a family. Were they searching for her? How had she fallen into Uun's grasp? Questions and sorrow chased their way through his thoughts.

"How may I help you?" A business-like female voice spoke.

In the doorway stood an elderly woman. She wore her white hair bound back tightly, but wisps had come loose and stuck out in odd ways, making her appear scattered.

"This child needs care," he said.

She sat next to him. "May I?" she asked.

Dalmir nodded wordlessly as the woman pressed her hand across the girl's forehead. Then she raised one of the girl's arms and held her wrist with a faraway look of concentration. She gently lifted one eyelid and peered into the girl's eye. Heaving a sigh through her nose, the healer sat back.

"Besides being malnourished, this child has suffered a severe trauma," she said. "Is she your daughter? Can you tell me what happened to her? There is much here I have never seen before."

"I do not know her," Dalmir replied. "My companions and I found her where she was being held prisoner. I have no idea how long she was there."

"Where did you find her?"

"In the Whispering Wood."

The woman took a sharp breath at his words. "I believe we can help her. How much will be up to her. Follow me." She strode out of the room and down a long hallway, her soft soles padding over the wooden floorboards. She pushed open a door and held it for Dalmir. A bed adorned with white comfort greeted them. A simple table holding a basin and pitcher stood under a large window that opened to a view of the pond. The walls were white, but a faint painting of vines and flowers above the bed wound about in delicate swirls and added a spot of color and welcome in otherwise stark surroundings.

The woman glanced at Dalmir and smiled at his disappointed expression. "Do not worry. We keep these rooms undecorated until they hold a guest. Now that she is here, we will bring in some items to make her more comfortable. It works better if we can determine what her individual tastes are. We will give her the best care possible. Believe me... ah..." She reached up and smoothed her hair, which made no difference, as the strays sprang right back up once her hand was gone. "Forgive me, I seem to have neglected to ask your name."

"Dalmir," he supplied, setting the girl on the bed and covering her up with the blankets.

"Welcome, Dalmir." She extended her hand as he turned. "I am Healer Raffaela."

"I may want to check on her from time to time." Dalmir took the proffered hand. "Would that be acceptable?"

"Of course." Healer Raffaela gave her head a little shake. "We get this sort of situation more often than you might guess, unfortunately. It is quite normal that you would feel an attachment to this child you rescued. She owes you her life. She will want to thank you when she is better. It would be beneficial to her if you would return."

Dalmir's body grew stiff. "She owes me nothing. But I will try to return and check on her."

"Very well." Raffaela nodded. She put her hand on Dalmir's arm and ushered him out of the room. As they returned to the open entryway, Raffaela paused, her eyes sweeping over Dalmir. "We do not turn away any who need us," she said primly. "But there is the question of payment for our services..."

"How much for a lunat of care?"

She pursed her lips and gave a reluctant sigh. "Four sigyls. But we have other options if you can't afford such fare, or don't want to spend that kind of money on a stranger."

Dalmir extended his hand. In his outstretched palm rested three runes. "How long will this last?"

Raffaela stared at the coins. When she looked up, her face held a mixture of emotions. "That will last for more than a year," she replied in a gentle whisper. "But I doubt she will need that much time."

"She may," Dalmir said. "Waking is merely the first obstacle. The trauma she has suffered appears... severe. I suspect recovery will be slow. Will you keep her safe for me?"

"Of course." Raffaela drew herself up stiffly. "I would do so without the offer of such a sum."

Dalmir peered at her, his eyes sharp and discerning. "I intended no offense," he said. "You are well-suited to care for this precious child. My part is to keep you at that work. Will you deny me the opportunity to give what aid I can?"

She made a strange sound in her throat and gave a tiny shake of her head. "No." Her voice softened. "No, of course not. Your generosity is most appreciated. She will be well-cared-for here at Ferndale."

Dalmir deposited the runes in her hand, gently closing her fingers around them. "At present, I am needed elsewhere, but I will return to see your handiwork and I very much look forward to that day."

"I will tell her."

Dalmir left the building and wound his way to the pond where he boarded the airship. Marik greeted him with a nod.

"Well, Captain," Dalmir said as Oleck pulled in the gangplank, "you said you knew where these mysterious cynders are being created."

Marik gave a sideways tilt of his head. "I found a refinery, yes. I can take you there. The mine suffered an... accident a few lunats ago. I don't know if the Ar'Mol restored operations or moved to another location. If the refinery has moved, I could not tell you where."

Oleck muttered something under his breath. Marik fixed him with a glare and the man frowned narrowly, hunched his shoulders, and walked away. Dalmir watched him go.

"Anything I should be concerned about regarding your crew?" he asked.

"They're the truest friends I've ever had," Marik replied. "They just don't like not knowing the plan."

"Friends like that, you should take care of."

"Believe me, I know." Marik's eyes darkened as he stared out toward the horizon. Then he shook himself and leaped up the ladder to the steerage. The *Valdeun Hawk* slowly rose off the water, a cascade of droplets falling from her hull and sprinkling the surface of the pond with a sound like the start of a summer rain.

"Take me to this mine," Dalmir said.

2

"Now announcing Lord and Lady Petrahn," the footman bellowed into the grand room.

Regeont Roshana pasted a welcoming smile across her face as the two guests swept through the doors and past the footman and joined those gathered for the event. Noses in the air, they paused for a moment on the balcony, their exquisite clothing and poise capturing the attention of many who were already present in the ballroom. Then they glided down the stairs, nodding at many, casting lofty smiles at a few, until they finally made their way across the room to their hostess.

"Regeont Roshana," Lady Petrahn murmured in a voice that was all sweetness and courtesy, "thank you for inviting us to your beautiful home this evening. You are looking most well."

Lord Petrahn took Roshana's proffered hand and bent over it, kissing her gloved knuckles. Straightening, he leaned forward and asked in a low voice, "Have you heard anything more about the kidnapped students?"

Roshana fixed him with a polite smile that she knew appeared more amused than she felt. "Come now, Lord Petrahn, surely now is not the time to speak of such things. This is a party, not a political meeting."

"Those poor children." Lady Petrahn stepped closer, dabbing at her face with a lacy handkerchief, her gown swishing around her as she moved.

"They are hardly children," Roshana muttered drily.

"I heard they escaped the clutches of the Ar'Mol himself. Is this the prelude to the war we have been fearing for so many years?" Lord Petrahn whispered, still clutching her fingers in his own.

"There will be no whispers of war here in my home tonight," Roshana said, her voice low and cold. "We are here to celebrate my grandson's promotion. This is neither the time nor the place for such gossip. Now, if you will be so kind as to excuse me..."

"Has a meeting at the Arxis been called?" Lord Petrahn pressed, his tone urgent. "Will the Council convene to discuss what course of action Telmondir should take in response? What will Ondoura's role be in the coming war?"

Roshana's gaze turned icy. "That, my good sir, is frankly none of your business. I am the Regeont. Council member and representative of Ondoura's interests. If a meeting at the Arxis is called, I will attend and do what I can to represent our fair country well and give what support we may to our alliance. Since it was Lord Adelfried's son who was kidnapped, I believe it is Lord Adelfried's call. And that is all I shall say on the matter this evening. Your speculations on the political relations between Telmondir and Igyea are not welcome here tonight." Her jaw ached, but she held a wide smile fixed upon her lips. "Please, enjoy the party." With an imperious gesture, Roshana swept past the couple and walked with swift, tiny steps across the room toward a friendlier and far more welcome face.

"Nadia," she exclaimed, her smile turning warm and genuine as she drew closer to the woman who had just entered the house. The footman looked mildly confused at not getting a chance to introduce this newcomer, but he had many years of experience serving the Regeont and as she approached, he stepped back and allowed her to greet this latecomer personally. Roshana stepped forward and took hold of the woman's hands, clasping them together in her own. "How are you holding up? I did not think you would come, what with the recent events, and it is such a long journey for a mere party..." She trailed off, taking in Nadia's traveling cloak, the dust covering her tall boots, and the haunted look in her eyes. "You did not come for my Ioan's celebration, did you?"

A warm smile spread across Lady Nadia's weary expression and she squeezed Roshana's hands. "A happy, happy coincidence. I received your very generous invitation, but despaired of being able to attend. However, with the occurrence of recent events, my husband thought it best if I came personally."

Joy at seeing her friend mingled with a deep weariness—and a tiny flicker of disappointment—that crept over Roshana's shoulders, weighing them down. "This is not a social visit." It was not a question. She dropped her friend's hands and half-turned away.

"No, I am afraid not," Nadia replied softly. "But forgive me, I did not mean to dampen the celebration of Ioan's accomplishment. I truly did hurry specifically in order to arrive for this occasion. I promise not to speak of politics tonight, my friend, only of congratulations." As if to prove her veracity, Nadia craned her head. "Where is the mighty warrior? I even brought him a gift from Drengur, who was severely disappointed he could not accompany me on this visit."

A tendril of warmth crept back into Roshana's thoughts, pushing away the heavier emotions that clutched at her heart. "Dear Drengur. Does he feel terribly left out? He always has looked up to Ioan. Is he lonely now, without Beren around?"

"It's not as if there aren't others to keep him company," Nadia replied, a teasing note in her voice.

"True, but they aren't as close in age."

"He is a little forlorn these days. But he and Jonas are forming a deeper friendship. They are getting to the point where the age difference doesn't matter as much."

"That is good to hear." Roshana smiled. "Come, Ioan will be happy to see you and hear news of your boys."

She led her old friend over to the mass of well-wishers waiting in a cluster to see Ioan. "And how is Thorben?"

Nadia heaved a sigh and brushed aside a lock of brown hair that had snuck out of the thick braid hanging down her back. "He is well. Overburdened by worry lately, I fear."

"And yourself?"

Nadia gave a small laugh and plucked a pastry off the tray of a passing server. "I am happy to be here, helping celebrate your grandson's achievement. Captain! And so young, too." She leaned her head forward and raised her eyebrows, a grin spreading across her face. "You must be so proud. I'm surprised to see you walking around here with your feet on the floor." She took a dainty bite of the treat. "These are delicious."

"I am proud," Roshana replied. "I only wish his parents could have been here tonight."

Nadia placed a hand on her friend's shoulder. "You have done a wonderful job raising him."

"Thank you. Shavash deserves much of the credit, though."

"Forgive me," Nadia whispered. "I seem to be wrapped in a rain cloud tonight. Everything I say seems to bring sorrowful memories."

"No, no, it is not your fault." Roshana waved a hand, as if she could dispel sorrowful thoughts like clouds of smoke. "And they are not sorrowful memories. They are happy. The happiest memories of my life are of my dear Shavash, as well as those of my daughter and her husband, and of course of their son: my Ioan. It is because those memories are filled with such joy that thinking about them and missing them hurts. When you reach my age, even the good memories carry a certain sorrow with them. I am the one who should apologize. You are right; tonight is supposed to be a celebration."

"You are not so ancient as all that, my friend." Nadia gave her hand a gentle squeeze.

Roshana sighed. How could she explain that even on a joyous occasion such as this, she felt every one of her years keenly? "I fear I am feeling my age more and more these days. I used to look forward to our Council meetings, but now I face the prospect with weariness. Frankly, Nadia, I'm getting too old for this job."

"Nonsense."

"It's true. I may carry my years well, but I remember the time before they built the first airships."

Nadia raised an eyebrow. "Roshana, that is an outright lie. You were but a year old when the first airship was commissioned. You cannot possibly remember the time before that."

Heat flooded Roshana's cheeks, and she gave an embarrassed chuckle. "Well, I was born in the time before the airships... if only just. And they didn't become a normal sight in Telmondir skies until twenty years ago."

Nadia smiled warmly. "I am just teasing you, dear friend. I understand what you're trying to say. But Ondoura truly does need you."

Nadia finished her pastry as the people standing in front of her finished congratulating Ioan. He glanced up to see who was next, and his dark face split into a wide grin.

"Aunt Nadia! I did not know you were coming." He embraced her, lifting her off the ground and spinning her around once. "Is any of your family with you?"

"I'm afraid you only get me," Nadia said, regaining her feet and laughing. "But I'm sure Berenger would love for you to visit him once he's gotten a bit more settled at the Academy."

"I heard he was going to the Academy! Good for him."

"All your influence, I'm afraid." Nadia smiled. "You've been like an older cousin he always idolized."

Ioan winked, his green eyes twinkling with mischief. "Maybe he'll finally find a place that can put some meat on those bones of his."

"Hush now!" Nadia exclaimed. "He gets enough teasing about that from his brothers, thank you."

Ioan laughed.

"When do you leave to take your new post?" Nadia asked.

"Tomorrow morning, I must meet my company early."

"Perhaps I will see you before you leave." Nadia smiled. "I plan to be up early myself."

"That would be delightful. It's hard to have a quality conversation in scattered moments during a party one is hosting. I would enjoy hearing more about Beren's recent adventures, as well. I'm rather jealous that he's already gotten more actual combat experience than I, and he's only just an initiate at the Academy."

"I will tell him you said so when I visit him tomorrow. He will be disappointed he could not be here for your party."

Ioan waved a hand, white teeth gleaming. "I wish he could have been here, too. But I understand he's new, and still settling in. They don't give the students a lot of freedom until they've earned it, not even as a favor to the Regeont."

"A policy I support," Nadia said. "Well, congratulations, Ioan. We are all very proud of you, Captain." She pulled a small box out of a deep pocket on the inside of her cloak. "This is from all of us, but mostly from Drengur."

Ioan accepted the box and grinned. "Thank you, Aunt Nadia. And thank you for coming. It means the world to me."

"You are welcome." She tousled his dark hair playfully. "Now, go celebrate with your friends. No reason to stand around talking to your old aunt."

"You're hardly what any of us would call old, dear Aunt Nadia," Ioan corrected her.

"That is the right answer." Nadia raised her chin. "No wonder they promoted you so early." She turned to her friend. "Roshana, he's a smart one, your boy."

Roshana's heart felt as though it might burst with pride and love. "Yes, he is."

3

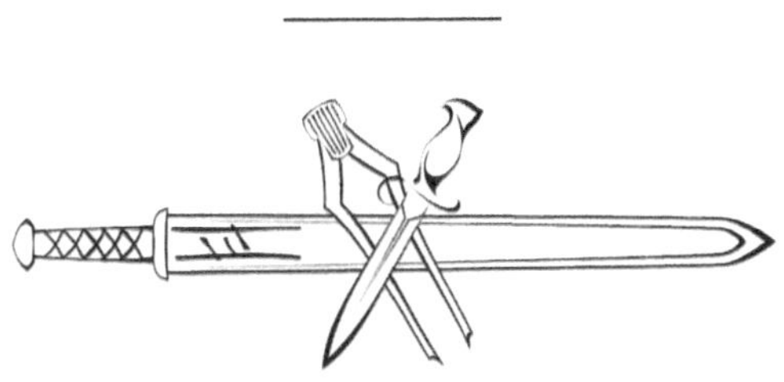

I t was hot. Hotter than Grayden felt it had any right to be for so late in the fall and so early in the morning, but he had been informed that the warm weather lasted much longer here than it did at home. It was just one of the many reasons that the Academy had been established in southern Ondoura where it stayed warm and temperate for most of the year. Even now, a full sennight into Chanjar, the days remained warm and humid. Back home in Dalsea, there might be a foot of snow covering everything already. Of course, the mountains had something to do with that.

Grayden stood near his friends in the large courtyard, waiting for Headmaster Freidzen to arrive. The entire school had been ordered to attend the assembly. Grayden looked around and saw his own curiosity and weariness reflected in the faces of his fellow students. Despite the heat, even the first-years stood at attention and restrained themselves from whispering to their comrades. The past lunat had taught them all a new level of discipline, and not one of them was willing to attract the disapproving glance of any of their instructors.

Orientation had been intense thus far. He had not known what to expect upon arriving at the Academy. Grayden had always assumed that he would arrive and immediately begin classes with his fellow students, but that had not been the case. Instead, he had spent the first two sennights being tested in every way imaginable including written examinations, oral recitations, challenging if not downright impossible physical tasks, and sparring with fellow students of every age and experience. He had handled every weapon he had a name for, and many more he had never heard of. And always the instructors were watching, scrutinizing, writing things down. Most of these tests had been individual, though the sparring had been done mostly in pairs. When he expressed his confusion to Beren, the young giant had merely shrugged.

"I don't know much more than you about the inner workings of the Academy. Headmaster Freidzen might be my uncle, but he has always been tight-lipped when it comes to the Academy. He's not just the headmaster here, he's the head of Telmondir's military, so he has to be careful about what he says. He understands his role and the grave importance he plays in preparing the students—which now includes us—to safeguard our lands. I imagine that actual warfare brings many surprises; perhaps this is part of the training for that."

Dalmir and the pirates had departed a sennight ago, but Grayden had barely noticed their absence. Weariness throbbed in every fiber of his being from the moment he awoke to the moment he crashed into his bunk at night. He felt that he was being squeezed through the rolling mill of a jewelry shop over and over again until every ounce of energy had been flattened out of him.

All around him, the students went rigid, cutting into Grayden's thoughts as Headmaster Freidzen strode up the stone steps to the raised platform at the far end of the courtyard. Every eye fixed on him as he turned to face the students.

"Good afternoon, students." The headmaster's voice rang out with the commanding tones of military authority. "I apologize for keeping you waiting. I have a few announcements; I will keep them short. First of all, to the first-year students, congratulations. You have completed your orientation."

There was a buzz of excited murmurs, which the headmaster allowed to rumble across the courtyard for a moment. Then he continued, "Older students will have noticed changes to our program. You are all aware of tensions with our eastern neighbors and talk of war has been ever-present these past many years. Recent events tell us that war is on our threshold. This Academy, you students, the defenders you will become, and the defenders you will join, are our greatest weapons in preventing war and likewise our greatest strength in waging war, should that be necessary. We always seek peace, but we always prepare for war. We need defenders, and that is why you are here. You may have noticed several new faces that arrived two sennights ago have already disappeared. We have no interest in wasting your time, or ours."

Grayden let his eyes dart about without turning his head. He saw a mixture of relief, confusion, and worry in the expressions of his fellow students.

Freidzen continued. "Your teachers will prepare you and your training will challenge you. Do not allow yourselves to hope otherwise. You will be pushed to achieve the next level as rapidly as possible. We have zero time to waste and your skills and talents and courage will be developed as quickly and fully as possible. Work hard, rest when you can, and know this: the finest men and the greatest hope of our people are those who train, grow, and graduate from this singular program. Our future is entrusted to your courage, strength, and care."

Silence lay across the courtyard embodied in hearts on fire.

Freidzen allowed himself a grim smile. "That is all, gentlemen!"

The courtyard churned in an orderly fashion as students relaxed and headed to their respective wings in the dormitory. Inside the halls once more, Grayden heard some of the older students begin shouting something about lists and waving pieces of paper above their heads.

Wynn turned a perplexed look at Grayden. "Lists?"

Grayden shrugged. But Beren, who had overheard the question, answered. "Our list of classes for the year. Usually first-years have a fairly basic set of classes."

"What do you think Headmaster Freidzen meant about changes?" Grayden asked. Excitement mounted within him. He had spent the past lunat listening to the older students reminisce about their first-year classes, bemoaning remembered boredom and the slow pace. Perhaps the changes that had been hinted at meant he would not have to endure such trials.

"I don't know," Wynn said.

"At least orientation is over," Beren said with a hearty sigh of relief.

"Words of truth," Wynn agreed.

Together, they mounted the steps into the dormitory, affectionately known by the cadets as the Horseshoe due to its unconventional shape. Like all the other buildings, it was constructed mainly of stone blocks, but coated with stucco to give everything a more uniform aesthetic and insulate against the heat of the baking sun. The two "arms" of the building stretched to the west, embracing the winds that tended to originate from that direction. Thus, despite the wretched heat that permeated the region, the dorm itself stayed bearable, even pleasant.

Grayden, Wynn, and Beren had been assigned a room on the second level at the heart of the horseshoe. Their window faced west, and often afforded them a cool breeze come evening. Climbing the stairs was often the last thing any of them wanted to do after the long hours of work and study, but that cool breeze was something Grayden looked forward to all day long.

They were laughing as they entered their quarters. Grayden was the first to notice the stranger in their room and he fell silent. A tall, slender woman stood inside their room, her back to the door, looking out the window. Her brown hair was streaked with gray and fell in a braid down her back nearly to her waist. She turned as they entered the room, a warm smile that was tinged with relief spreading across her dark face.

"Berenger." She spoke in a low, smooth voice, like warm honey. Her brown eyes lit with pleasure at the sight of the three young men.

"Mother." Beren sounded surprised.

They shared an embrace, and then Beren introduced her to his friends. "Mother, this is Wynn and Grayden. Wynn, Grayden, my mother, Lady Nadia Adelfried."

She smiled at all of them and then turned back to Beren, looking him over with a worried glint in her eyes as though searching for wounds or expecting to find scars.

"I am pleased to see you, Mother," Beren said. "But may I ask why you are here? Is everyone well at home? Father... is he...?"

"Your father is well, your brothers and sisters are well. They send their love. They wanted to be here, but you know how hard it is for all of us to get away at the same time."

"Then...?" His brow furrowed.

Lady Nadia's expression softened into one of fond exasperation. "You were abducted, and you are my son. I came to make sure that you are well, and to hear of the events from you so I can accurately relay them to your father. It will be his job to determine the next course of action."

Beren nodded seriously. "It is rather a long story."

Lady Nadia sat on one of the beds with regal grace, her presence instantly turning the small cot into a throne. She folded her hands in her lap and gestured at the other seats in the room.

"I have time, and you have the afternoon off. As I understand it, your new schedules begin tomorrow morning." She shot a curious glance at Wynn and Grayden. "And I would like to become better acquainted with your friends."

"Without them, I would never have made it to the Academy," Beren said.

"Then please, by all means, stay." Lady Nadia gestured for all three of them to sit. "I extend my household's thanks to you both for assisting in seeing my son safely to the Academy, and I would desire to hear any perspective you might be able to give on the events that occurred."

"It actually started before we even left Dalton," Beren began. "We were in the marketplace…"

Lady Nadia was an attentive listener. She did not interrupt throughout the entire story. She merely listened, taking it all in; even during the points of the story where all three of them were trying to talk at once, she did not grow impatient, she did not open her mouth, but waited until they sorted through which parts of the story to tell first. The telling took up most of the afternoon, and when they had finished, the sun was sinking low on the horizon. As they concluded their tale, Beren's mother sat very quietly for a moment. Then she rose and crossed the room to embrace Beren once again. She held him tightly, then pushed him back to arm's length and looked him over once more. She turned and embraced first Grayden and then Wynn, both of whom received her hugs with stiff awkwardness that melted in her warm, motherly embrace.

"I should like to meet this Dalmir," she announced when she had finished hugging all of them. "Is he still here?"

"No, ma'am," Beren replied. "He left with Captain Marik. I'm not sure where they were headed."

"I see." Lady Nadia's expression grew disappointed. "I owe him a debt of gratitude for seeing my son to safety. Perhaps he will return?"

"He came and found me to say goodbye before they left," Grayden said. "But he did not mention whether he would return. He seemed worried and distracted, like he had important business to attend to, but wasn't sure how it would turn out."

Lady Nadia nodded thoughtfully. "In any case, I will be here in Ondoura for a few lunats. Beren, your father is planning to call a meeting at the Arxis, and I must meet with Regeont Roshana to inform her of the events that are unfolding. The Igyeum grows bold, and we fear what they may be plotting."

"An Arxis meeting?" Beren asked. "Am I required to attend?"

"No, classes here at the Academy will still be in session when the meeting occurs. Drengur will go in your stead."

"Good, I am glad. And Drengur will be pleased that father is including him," Beren replied. "You will be staying with Regeont Roshana, then?"

"I am not sure. I came to deliver her the summons, but your father and I had hoped I might be able to stay here for a few sennights. I will send word to let you know my plans. If I remain in Doran for a time, once you have earned a free day, you and your friends are welcome to visit me wherever I am staying." She stood.

"I will escort you to the gate." Beren rose as well, but Lady Nadia stopped him with a regal wave of her hand.

"No, my son. I have seen that you are well, and my mother's heart is laid at peace. I interrupted you and your friends." Her lips curved into an impish grin. "Besides, I've seen you casting glances at those papers on your table. I'm sure they hold important information pertaining to your immediate future. I am impressed with your patience. I have imposed upon you for long enough. I will see you again soon, my son." She paused. "Berenger Adelfried—" She shook her head and closed her eyes. "I am extremely relieved to see you all in one piece. I assume I cannot talk you out of this foolishness of becoming a defender?"

Beren flushed and shook his head.

"I thought not." Her stern demeanor faded slightly as she embraced him once more. "I am very proud of you, my son. And I love you," she whispered fiercely. Then, in a swishing of light fabric, she left.

After she departed, the three young men retrieved the slips of paper and perused them eagerly. Grayden read over his list of courses. His breath caught at the title of the first class on the list: Airmanship. His heart pounded with excitement. It was the one course he had desperately longed for, and the one he had not dared to hope for.

"What's on your schedule?" Wynn asked, peering over Grayden's shoulder to compare their lists.

Grayden shook his head and read further down the schedule. His remaining hours after the morning Airmanship class would be filled with Wilderness Survival, Military History, Military Strategic Studies, Combat Skills, and a course labeled simply: Leadership.

The three of them were delighted to discover that they had been placed in many of the same time slots, though there were a few differences. Wynn was not taking Leadership, instead his schedule had Fundamentals of Aeronautics Engineering during that time slot. Beren was not taking Military History, but was enrolled in a course labelled Current Politics. All three of them had Airmanship, Wilderness Survival, and Combat Skills together.

"After what the headmaster said, I didn't think we'd have so many classes together at the same time," Wynn commented.

"In spite of what he indicated," Beren replied, "it makes sense that many of the first-year students would still be placed together at the start. I'll bet most of us have nearly identical schedules, with just a few variations based on our individual evaluations and assessments, as well as from the original results they received from the scouts. The combining of skill levels most likely occurred primarily among the older students."

Grayden stood and stretched. "Well, I'm feeling a little cooped up. Anyone up for a bit of a run before dinner?"

4

"You have done well, Lorcan," Roald said. He stared up in awe at the immense jungle surrounding them.

"Just done what was asked, what was asked, that is all," Lorcan mumbled, caressing the green gemstone in his hand.

Roald wondered about the gem. Lorcan was always holding it, touching it, talking to it. There was something a bit off about Lorcan. Most of the troops referred to him as "the madman" behind his back, though Roald wasn't certain that the nickname would actually bother Lorcan. However, despite his obvious instability, no one could deny that the man had a gift when it came to growing things. When the Ar'Mol had announced his decision to house his growing army in the inhospitable Plains of Temnia in the northern reaches of Palla, Roald was not the only one who had been skeptical. But then Lord Uun had produced the madman.

Thin to the point of emaciated, the madman unsettled anyone who had to spend more than a few minutes with him. Sometimes just a single sentence emanating from Lorcan's mouth could produce nightmares in even the staunchest soldier's dreams. Despite his slight frame, the man had wiry muscles and Roald had seen him perform feats of sudden, animalistic strength and violence, enough to make him step cautiously around the man. White hair stood out in unruly tufts from his sunken face, and dark eyes glimmered deep in their sockets, revealing an intense insanity that studied and watched everything.

Roald turned his attention away from the madman, repressing a shudder, and back to the jungle. Anyone unfamiliar with this region would never believe it had once been a harsh desert. Streams of water burbled along between lush green banks and rolling hills. The entire oasis spanned eighty acres, surrounded by a thick ring of tall trees that had not been present less than a year ago. Roald shook his head. However it had been accomplished, the results were impressive, and it was a power he wished neither to question nor challenge.

Lorcan had worked alongside the Ar'Molon for decades, even longer than Roald had been in service to him, but their meetings had before always been brief. Roald knew that he did not see the entire map of Lord Uun's vision for the future. Such a vast and complex plan was not for the likes of him. He was merely proud to have his own small part to play, even if at times his role might seem distasteful. As it did now.

"What have you come for, come for?" Lorcan asked, his gaze abruptly clear and piercing.

"The Ar'Mol has sent me to fetch you, Lorcan," Roald said, repressing a shudder. "Your work here is done; you are to move on to the next phase. I have an airship and a regiment of guards waiting to take you to a location where you will be able to focus on your experiments with no distractions and no one to disturb you."

For the first time, Lorcan brightened. "The next phase, yes. The work I truly wish to do. Lead the way, lead the way, Captain. I go to my task eagerly. Eagerly!" The man capered a bit around him, his eagerness sending shivers up Roald's spine.

"Do you need to gather any supplies? Any belongings?" Roald asked.

Lorcan looked at him oddly, then held out the green gem. "I

have all I need. All. Let us go. Let me work. The next phase! Lead the way. Lead!" His crackling voice turned solid and impenetrable as he delivered the final word as a command that nearly spun Roald about and sent him marching toward the airship. Roald frowned as they climbed aboard; had he purposed to board the airship just now on his own? Why did he suddenly feel loose and empty, like a puppet whose strings had been cut?

Irritably, he barked the orders to cast off. Lorcan hunkered down between some barrels and the railing. He sat there staring at the orb in his hands and muttering to it. Roald watched him for a bit through narrow eyes. It was hard not to be wary around Lorcan. He tried to shake away the discomfort that prickled across the back of his neck at the thought of being in such close proximity to the strangeness that was Lorcan for an extended journey. At least it was only his task to fly the man to the drop-off point. He did not envy the guards who were to escort the madman on foot to his final destination hidden high in the mountains. It was not even Roald's business to know that spot's precise location. He was merely a ferry. Under normal conditions, the ignoble assignment might have grated on the assassin's nerves, but this time he accepted it with gratitude. The sooner he and Lorcan parted ways, the better.

Roald stared at the madman for another long moment, then shook off the unease that had settled around his shoulders. Lorcan was harmless, if a bit eccentric; good with plants, as evidenced by the beautiful oasis he had created. Roald did not want to know how he had managed such a feat. He did not want to know what this "next phase" was at which Lord Uun had hinted. He did not have any desire to know what other things Lorcan had done for the Ar'Molon in the past.

Roald turned away, determined to ignore Lorcan as best he could. He had duties to attend to, and another mission once they had transported the botanist to the drop-off point. That location was another sore subject for Roald. He did not like the idea of

Lorcan being in enemy territory, but Lord Uun had assured him that the man would be well hidden.

"Nobody will discover him," Uun had said when Roald raised his objections. "We need him positioned there specifically. He will be invaluable to us once we begin the Ar'Mol's campaign to conquer Telmondir."

Roald glanced over at Lorcan and found that the madman was staring at him. Something about his unwavering, penetrating gaze sent a chill sweeping through Roald. He strode down the steps of the airship as though he had some purpose belowdecks. In truth, he just wanted to get away from that unnerving, unblinking scrutiny. Roald frowned and reprimanded himself sternly. It was unlike him to get jittery. This was just another assignment, like any other assignment.

Even so, he could not help but think that he would much prefer assassinating the madman to transporting him.

5

From his vantage point at the top of the ridge, Ettore Niveya felt a grim streak of satisfaction at the havoc he had caused below. The rockslide had not been his intention, but it was covering his retreat nicely. And it took the edge off of the itch he felt to act, to do. He chafed at this waiting game his father played. Though he understood the need for stealth and secrecy, he ached to take direct action, to engage in the conflict stirring all around him. The air thickened with political tension as nations gathered to either side of the Niveyan stronghold and prepared for war that threatened to break across the continent like a tidal wave. He could taste the strong, bitter flavor of hatred that permeated the Igyeum forces he had infiltrated and spied upon. He could smell the loathing rising up from the acrimonious gossip that the troops planted within the markets and among the homesteads throughout the countryside. The Ar'Mol's men were working hard to stir up resentment of their western neighbors among the natives of the Igyeum.

Tasked with watching and listening, Ettore fidgeted on the back of his giant gray malkyn and strained against the invisible bonds his father had wrapped around him, binding his hands and stopping his voice. It was clear that the Ar'Mol was readying his regiments to invade Telmondir in force, and soon. Had it not been for the accident at the cynder refinery some lunats before, the Ar'Mol would have already marched his armies into Telmondir. It was certain he was merely biding his time until the cynder supply had been recovered somewhat. Ettore had not been able to ascertain the actual timetable, but invasion was imminent. Perhaps it had already begun. He squeezed his hands into fists on the reins of his mount and growled under his breath. The enormous beast turned a lazy eye on its rider and raised a massive, yet delicate paw to swipe across its face as if to say that it found their current task boring, as well. He smiled and patted the creature's soft fur.

Ettore gritted his teeth, remembering the messenger from the Ar'Mol. He had brought Arrio's body home, at least, but it chafed like burrs against his skin that they could take no direct retaliation.

Yet. He reminded himself. They could take no direct retaliation yet. Surely his father had a plan to make the Ar'Mol regret his hasty actions. Though there had been little love lost between him and Arrio as cousins, Arrio had been family. He had been blood. And blood meant everything to the Niveyas.

"Certainly Arrio had no head for business or stealth. Whatever were he and Father thinking, actively thwarting the Ar'Mol?" Ettore muttered. The malkyn shifted uneasily beneath him, as though picking up on his irritation. "Father knows what he is doing. I would like nothing better than to ride down there and attack, to tell Aunt Nira that we've begun avenging our cousin, but then I know what Father would say. To act now could jeopardize everything my family has worked to build. And it wouldn't avenge Arrio, not really. To avenge him properly, we need to know more. We know who gave the order, but we must discover who carried it out. Then we will make our move. And then they will regret ever having crossed the Niveya Family."

The gray cat tossed its head with an imperious gesture, its ears flicking back and forth between its master's voice and the sounds coming from the caravan and its leaders as they shouted and worked to dig the road clear of the rubble now blocking their path.

"I know," Ettore muttered. "Understanding doesn't make this assignment feel any more productive. But we have learned some information that I believe my father will find intriguing, and he will know how to use it." He turned the reins and directed the cat up the mountain. "And at least we slowed down this caravan, even if it wasn't on purpose."

The malkyn leaped up the rocky face of the cliffs and crags, following an invisible path. Ettore gave the creature its head. His mount knew the way home, and it was past time to relay to his father the things he had learned while spying upon the caravan as it traveled toward Melar.

6

Daegan sat hunched over his desk, straining his already weak eyes in the flickering lamplight. Papers, books, bits of charcoal, and a spreading ink stain from where he had jostled his inkwell were strewn across the table in a haphazard frenzy, but the clutter did not bother him. He pored over his current schematic with single-minded purpose. His quill scratched across the paper as he put down his notes with precise strokes. He jotted down measurements neatly in the space around the drawing, measuring everything twice to make certain the scale was correct.

The door behind him opened and a much younger woman entered the room. She carried a stack of papers carefully in her arms.

"Daegan, where do you want me to put these?" she asked, glancing about the room with an expression of defeat in her eyes.

"Just... wherever they fit." Daegan waved a hand at her, but did not look up.

"Daegan, these are the latest schematics from the rest of the department, based on the criteria you outlined in the last meeting. You're the head of the Artificineers, you need to be coordinating our efforts, not working on the problem all by yourself." Her tone was frustrated.

Daegan sat up and stared at her. "We are so very close, Molly. Your own designs are brilliant, as are the others', but I'm the only one who can make the pieces all fit together. I can't be holding everyone's hands and doling out platitudes right now. Haven't you heard? The Igyeum attempted to kidnap the young Adelfried heir... or assassinate him... or both..." He paused. What had the reports said about it? He decided it didn't matter and shook his head. "It's a bit muddled, but either way, it means the impending war is nearly upon us, and we must be ready."

"I know all that, Daegan, but..."

"Not now, Molly. Just set the schematics on the table somewhere, I'll look over them when I've finished these notes. I don't want to stop in the middle of a thought, I may never be able to remember where it was going. I'm so close, I can feel it, we're on the cusp of something great. This could be our salvation when the war comes."

Molly muttered something under her breath, but Daegan had no focus to spare. He did not look up even when she had left his workshop, so intent was he on his latest idea. At some point, he began pulling the new schematics from the stack Molly had brought in, perusing them to see if they held the answer he was looking for. He scribbled down notes and took measurements and completed equations long into the night.

At long last, he sat back and studied his work. It was finally complete, his life's work. It had taken nearly five decades, but he was confident in the solution he and his team had designed. He ran a hand over his head, unwittingly leaving streaks of black ink as it rubbed off his fingers onto his unruly white hair. It should work. It had to work. It would work. It must. But could it be built?

He got up and puttered about the small room, putting on a kettle for tea. His eyes widened as his gaze fell upon the chaos his desk had erupted into and he began straightening papers and placing the various instruments into their proper places while he waited for the water to boil. Just as the kettle began to sing, his workspace was once more neat and tidy. The spilled ink had been mopped up, and the plans and sketches it had threatened had been whisked to safety.

Daegan sipped his tea and relaxed in front of his fire. The rest and the hot drink produced the desired effect of calming his whirling thoughts. He glanced across the room at the finished drawing and a flutter of excitement stirred in his heart. With a weary groan, he pushed himself out of his comfortable chair and retrieved the precious drawing. With a critical eye he went over every detail yet again. He could not bring this before the Council until he was certain there were no mistakes, no errors in judgment, no leaps of whimsy. It was not the time to hope for success, it was time to find the flaws, the weaknesses in his latest design. He was sure he would find them, he always did, and those flaws always tossed a bucket of icy disappointment across his rising excitement and sent him back to his desk.

Several hours later, Daegan mopped his forehead with a clean handkerchief and for the first time in many lunats he allowed himself to feel the deep satisfaction of being finished. His work was complete. He allowed himself another moment to bask in the feeling of having reached the finish line. But there was little time for reveling in this accomplishment, for more work loomed ahead. The plans were complete, the schematics were as nearly perfect as he could make them. But now his machine needed to be built, and he would entrust no other with the onerous duty of overseeing that effort. It was not hubris that brought him to this decision, but merely fact. Of all the people in his department, he was the smartest, the quickest-thinking. The task of building this contraption had to be carefully detailed. The smallest mistake could not be allowed. And he was the only one who could guarantee the kind of close attention to detail that was required. Never mind that the honor should belong to him anyway as head of the department.

With a burst of energy, Daegan rose from his worktable and crashed through his door. "Molly! Molly!" he shouted as he raced down the hall to his room, gathering instruments and rolls of paper as he went. "I need to be in Telsuma as quickly as it can be arranged! Molly! Where are you?"

"I'm right here." Molly emerged from a side room and peered at him, a concerned expression on her heart-shaped face. "You need to travel to Telsuma? But your work here..." She trailed off as understanding gripped her. "You finished it?"

"Yes, I need to get to Telsuma right away," Daegan replied irritably. "Haven't you been listening to a word I've said? I need to go to Keene's forge, he's the best in his trade and nobody else can be trusted. Will you make the arrangements? I have to pack." He continued down the hall, but paused, swinging around to stare at the young woman. "What are you standing there for?" he demanded. "Didn't you hear me? This is urgent!"

"You finished it," she breathed again. "Please, Daegan, can I see it?"

Her words halted his mad dashing about and a pleased smile spread itself across his lips. "I suppose I can spare a moment to show it to you."

7

"Good morning," Regeont Roshana said, looking up from the book she was reading as Nadia entered the room. "You spoke truly when you said you were getting up early. I barely managed to pull myself out of bed to bid Ioan goodbye, and he said you had gotten up with him for breakfast and had a nice chat. You came back late last night. Did you see Berenger yesterday?"

"Yes."

"All his limbs still attached, I take it?" Roshana raised an eyebrow.

Nadia chuckled. "My worry was that obvious at the party?"

"Not really," Roshana admitted. "But it was the kind of worry one mother can easily spot in another."

"You always could read me like a newly penned scroll. He is fine. He seems... older."

"You say that as though it were a bad thing." Roshana eyed her friend, noting a sadness about the corners of her friend's eyes.

"No, not really. I just... I'm so proud of him. I thought perhaps he might need to see me, somehow. But he didn't. If I'm honest, I just needed to see him, to make certain he was well. It's humbling, for a parent to realize they are not as necessary as they once were."

Something tightened in Roshana's chest, an empathetic sort of sadness. "He still needs you, he will always need you. It's simply different."

"I know that."

Roshana reached over and put a hand on top of Nadia's. "Everyone has an opinion on the most difficult stages of parenting. But I don't think anything is harder than doing all you can to raise them to be independent, and then having to let them go. But it is necessary. And it is beautiful, in its way. It allows your relationship to grow, to turn into a friendship, and I promise you, that is worth the pain of letting go."

Nadia heaved a sigh and gave a small, watery smile.

Roshana was silent for a long moment, letting her friend have this small reprieve from duty. Unfortunately, she could give Nadia no more than a few minutes. When Nadia had finished wiping her eyes on a handkerchief, Roshana cocked an eyebrow. "Well? Are you going to tell me why you are really here?"

Nadia dropped her eyes and fidgeted with the handkerchief. "I came to personally deliver your summons to an emergency Arxis meeting one sennight hence."

"I thought as much." Roshana swept her hands across her lap. "With what happened to Berenger it was only a matter of time, really. Unsettling, for sure." Roshana let out the tiniest sigh. "I fear I am getting far too old for this. Perhaps it is time to step down from my seat on the Council, let younger hands hold the reins."

"No, don't say that. You have much to offer," Nadia replied. "Your wisdom and experience would be missed most sorely, were you to leave now, especially now, when our relations with the Igyeum are so strained. You have always been a voice of restraint on the Council."

"A kind way of acknowledging my age." Roshana smirked. "But not an argument against it, I notice."

"As my husband is fond of saying, 'If you want to catch a bigger fish, best bring bigger bait.'" Nadia's eyes twinkled.

Roshana could not hold back her laughter at that. She did love the blunt way Telsumans had with words. "He's not wrong," Roshana replied wryly when she had regained her composure. "By the way, I have not said it yet—I think because I feared giving it voice would make it suddenly far too real—but I am truly sorry about the ordeal your Beren suffered through, and I am sincerely glad that he is safe at the Academy."

"Thank you. He weathered it well. I think he saw it as a grand adventure and my fear is that it taught him nothing of caution, but then, that's my Beren. He also seems to have made a few quality friends, albeit unlikely ones, according to his tale, though that remains to be seen."

"Yes, that sounds like him." Roshana stood abruptly. "Your husband is quite right to call the Council to the Arxis after such an affront. I shall begin making ready for the journey at once. It will take time to make the necessary arrangements." She crossed to Nadia, laying a hand on her shoulder, a sudden idea occurring to her. "My dear, is there any pressing need for you to return home presently?"

Nadia thought and shook her head slowly. "No. In fact, I had hoped to stay in Doran for a few sennights, perhaps even rent a house for a few lunats to give Beren someone familiar nearby, though I'm sure he doesn't need it. Why do you ask?"

"I was wondering if I might impose upon your time?"

"What were you thinking?"

"My cousin's granddaughter and grandson are planning to visit and I would hate for them to come to an empty house. They will be staying for a lengthy visit. It is imperative that I attend the Council Meeting," Roshana replied. "But, given the short notice, it would not be right to ask my guests to change their plans and come later, especially since I will be returning well before their visit is over. Would it be terribly improper of me to request your assistance? Though, after what you just said, perhaps this arrangement will help us both. If you could stay and watch over my home and attend to my guests in my absence, just until I return, I would be most grateful."

"Are you sure I wouldn't be in the way?" Nadia asked. "I don't want your family members to feel awkward, having a stranger about."

Roshana waved a graceful hand. "They have always tended to keep to themselves, even when they are visiting me. I think they just enjoy getting a change of scenery. You will not be a bother to them in the slightest, and it would make me feel better if I knew someone were here to stand in for me as a gracious host. It chafes a bit, the idea of them coming to visit a house with darkened windows."

"I would be happy to assist you in this matter, of course."

"Excellent." Roshana beamed. "Now, tell me what the weather is like further north so I can plan my wardrobe accordingly."

8

"Kiefer, can I trouble you for a moment of your time?"

Kiefer looked up from his desk and nodded at his colleague. "Come in, sit, I just have one last paper to grade."

Mathis entered the room and sat, waiting patiently for Kiefer to finish his work. After a few minutes, Kiefer scrawled a note at the bottom of the page he had been looking at and set it aside. He rolled his shoulders and stretched his neck then looked up expectantly.

"What can I do for you?"

"I was wondering, are Wynn Drexel, Grayden Ormond, and Berenger Adelfried all taking your class on Military Strategic Studies?"

Kiefer squinted. "Not all at the same time, but yes, I do have all three of them."

"And what is your assessment of their abilities?"

"Extremely bright young men, all three of them. I'd say they are the most promising recruits I've ever had the pleasure of teaching. Why do you ask?"

"I have Mister Drexel in my Fundamentals of Aeronautics Engineering class, and the other two in Leadership. I have been extremely impressed by all three of them, though Mister Drexel is far and away the most intelligent person I have ever encountered."

Kiefer's expression became one of disbelief. "Surely you are exaggerating. You cannot mean that seriously."

"I do." Mathis spoke in a low, deliberate tone. "I have had bright students before, but Wynn Drexel makes them all look like simpletons. I honestly believe that I lack the ability to teach him anything."

"Mathis," Kiefer scoffed, "the boy may be brilliant, but yours is one of the most intelligent minds in the world. Do you truly expect me to believe that an initiate is smarter than you?"

"Just take a look at this." Mathis shoved a folder into Kiefer's hand. "Their assignment was to come up with a solution to an enemy having the advantage of air power in an all-out assault. It's one of the first things I do to assess where my students land on the spectrum so I can better know where to begin teaching them. I usually get the same general mix of ideas: weapons that can hurl projectiles with enough force to reach the airships, armored vehicles that can lumber along the ground and withstand the assault of the airships, a theoretical schematic for creating our own cynders, but... well, just look at it and tell me what you think."

Kiefer opened the folder and began to read. After a moment his eyebrows shot up and he glanced at Mathis.

"Keep reading," Mathis urged.

Kiefer continued reading. The only sound was the rustle of paper when he moved to the next page. When he was finished, he set the stack neatly back on the desk and cleared his throat.

"Well!"

"That is what I said when I finished reading."

"This is very close to some of Daegan's first drafts."

"I know. I saw that immediately."

"There's no way he could know about that?"

"None."

"Have you shown this to the headmaster?"

"I plan to; he and the Board of Instructors are being summoned to an emergency meeting at the Arxis. I thought I would give it to him with my full report and recommendation. Hopefully the Council will consider it."

"And what is your recommendation?"

"That these three young men be promoted through the ranks as swiftly as possible. I think they should be included on the Storvas Mission this spring."

"The Storvas Mission?" Kiefer looked aghast. "I don't care how brilliant they are, that is a graduating requirement! You are talking about cadets who have been here less than a full lunat. You cannot possibly believe they are ready for such a challenge."

"I do believe it. I firmly believe it. I have talked with all of their instructors. They aren't just excelling in their academics—but in every area of their training."

Kiefer furrowed his brow, then glanced at the report still sitting on his desk. At length, he nodded. "Mathis, you're one of the most brilliant, meticulous people I know. We've been friends a long time, and I know you would never intentionally put a recruit in danger. If you say these three young men are ready and should be included on the Storvas Mission, I believe you."

"Then I can add your name to the list of instructors who recommend this course of action?"

"Yes."

"Thank you."

Kiefer hesitated. "You're welcome. But, Mathis, one thing."

"Yes?"

"What if you're wrong? What if academic brilliance and expertise isn't enough? What if there is something to be said for the two years our recruits spend training with us before they advance to Experyus-level? If we are all wrong about this experiment..."

"If we're wrong, I honestly don't think it's a problem we'll have long to worry about," Mathis replied, his voice grim. "We'll be in the middle of a war we can't hope to win."

Kiefer's lower jaw jutted off to one side as he puffed out a pent-up breath. "Words of truth, my friend." He turned back to the papers on his desk. "Talk to Syrus. If he agrees with your assessment, I will stand with you and support your recommendation."

9

Vallei had always been the most beautiful of the lands, Dalmir reflected. Forests spread below them, separating pastures of emerald and gold. Food grew here year round, in this, the southernmost region of Turrim. Air currents sweeping in from the south-eastern ocean brought warm breezes and a thick humidity. Even from his vantage point far above the earth, Dalmir could smell the sweet, tangy scent of citrus trees.

Avaleun, your realm is still the jewel you wished it to be, Dalmir thought wistfully. He reached into the deep pocket inside his robe, his fingers brushing across the orbs within. The purple one he had taken from around Aubri Niveya's neck lay dormant, its dull surface a painful reminder of all he had lost.

He stared down at the land below; the treetops and rocky crags passed swiftly beneath them. How strange to be traveling in such a way, sailing through the air. Events had been moving so fast, he had barely even acknowledged it, but truly, these airships were marvelous contraptions. Though he disapproved greatly of the power holding them aloft, Dalmir could appreciate the elegance of the design. He was used to the sensation of flying by now. How had it been accomplished? Palte's power lifted these great ships, held them aloft, but Palte had died hundreds of years ago. He pulled his hand out of his pocket and gripped the rail of the airship fiercely, anger blossoming. Was it not enough that the others were dead? Must Uun trespass over their graves, as well? Was there nothing sacred to him?

"We're nearly there." Marik's voice pulled Dalmir out of his contemplation of the landscape below.

"Ah." Dalmir nodded. "Thank you."

Marik started to turn, then he hesitated. "I do not know what you are hoping to find down there," he said. "But I want you to know that there may not be much left to examine."

"Why do you say that?" Dalmir asked.

"I was here several lunats ago," Marik admitted. "I stumbled upon it rather by accident."

Dalmir waited.

A strange expression passed across the pirate's face. "There was an explosion. I barely escaped in one piece. I just thought you ought to know."

"An explosion? How is that possible?"

"I had grabbed one of the cynders. Everyone knows they can be dangerous, but I had no idea it would... do that."

Dalmir pulled at his lower lip and scowled down at the fast-approaching mountain range. These mountains were part of the enormous Randeau chain in which the Niveyan Fortress was hidden far to the north, but here the peaks were much smaller and farther apart, and few of them rose high enough to be capped with snow. The tops and sides of these mountains were covered in green, matching the verdant lowlands of Vallei.

"Interesting," Dalmir finally replied.

The *Valdeun Hawk* soared on, entering the mountain range and descending between two peaks. Marik returned to the steering deck to help guide his airship to a safe landing place, from which they would approach the cynder-manufacturing facility on foot. Dalmir remained at the railing, pondering what Marik had told him. He did not know much about these cynders, though he had spent a little time pondering them in the engine room at various times throughout their trip, but he had gleaned little from his observation.

A few moments later, the airship was hovering above the ground in a shallow, hidden valley. Raisa and Oleck lowered the "stilts" as they liked to call them, attaching them expertly so that the airship could land and power down, but also be ready to take off at a moment's notice. When this was accomplished, Marik came up and clapped Dalmir on the shoulder.

"Ready?"

Dalmir nodded and they disembarked, Marik leading the way.

It was not a long hike or climb to the entrance, but it was a strenuous one. Both men were breathing hard and covered in a grimy, dusty sweat by the time they reached the yawning aperture. Dalmir wiped his brow on the sleeve of his shirt. He accepted Marik's offer of water from the flask he carried, and took a long swig of the refreshing liquid, then handed it back and waited while the pirate did the same. Marik wiped his mouth, capped the canteen, and nodded.

"Right, this is a sort of side entrance. I'll go ahead and see if it is guarded." He moved away stealthily, his boots barely making a sound on the rocky mountainside. A moment later he returned.

"The passage is clear, and there's no sign that any of the Ar'Mol's men have returned here."

Marik led the way, and Dalmir followed close behind into the cavern, clambering over the enormous chunks of rock that partially blocked the entrance. Neither man spoke as they ventured further into the side of the mountain, picking their way over rubble and past large, fallen rocks. Eventually they reached a section of the tunnel that was completely blocked, and they could go no farther.

"We can try one of the side passages," Marik offered.

They retraced their steps and sought a way around the obstruction. After a few false starts and a dead-end, they found a tunnel that led into a large, open area.

"This must be where they brought the finished cynders to load onto carts," Marik muttered.

The room bore the obvious signs of mining. The floor had been polished smooth, presumably so that crates filled with cynders could be loaded on wheeled carts and easily transported outside. The remains of smashed crates were piled on the floor, as well as several abandoned tools and a few overturned chairs and tables. Other than that, the chamber appeared to have escaped the explosion Marik had spoken of largely unscathed.

Dalmir traversed the room, his fingers trailing along the walls. His eyes closed, he stood in silence. Marik waited, not wanting to disturb Dalmir's concentration.

Frowning, Dalmir ground his teeth together and opened his eyes. "There are traces here, but I cannot believe it, and I cannot be sure..."

"Traces of what?"

Dalmir did not answer.

"Can't you just unblock the tunnel?" Marik asked. "If you can lift an entire airship with... whatever power is at your disposal..."

"If I use that much power, it will alert Uun to my whereabouts. I would prefer to keep my movements concealed from him for the time being." Dalmir crouched down near the smashed crates and began sorting through the wreckage. "Especially now that he has been released from the last of his chains."

"This Uun... Ar'Molon Uun," Marik said. "Is he like you?"

Dalmir growled, "He is nothing like me."

"But does he have the kind of power you have?"

Dalmir nodded reluctantly, not looking up from his search. "We are evenly matched."

Marik let out a low whistle. "The world just became a rather terrifying place."

"It already was. You were simply unaware of it."

"Thanks." Marik's voice was wry. "Do you want to check out any more of the side tunnels?"

"No," Dalmir said, his attention fixated on something besides Marik's words. "I think I found what I need." He rose, holding two objects in his hands.

"What have you got there?"

"I'm not sure." Dalmir held out a cylindrical gray stone for Marik's inspection.

"That's one of the unrefined cynders," Marik said, taking it and rotating it in his hands. "Did you find any more of them?"

"I thought that might be what it was," Dalmir replied and gave a jerk of his head. "There are several crates of them down that tunnel." He held up the other object. "This looks like something Palte would create. I think I even remember seeing a drawing of his that this resembles. Any ideas as to what it does?"

Marik glanced up and then froze, staring. "I thought those were myths."

"What is it?"

Marik scratched the back of his head and took a deep breath. "Well, based on the descriptions, my best guess is that the object you're holding is a refiner. It's the thing they use to create the cynders. Though that one looks a mite too small for the quantities that were coming through this mine. I would guess what you are holding is a prototype. I'm pretty sure I saw a much bigger version last time I was here. Before the"—he glanced away—"the accident."

Dalmir studied the object in his hands: a small, but deep bowl. The bowl was vaguely flower-shaped, with multiple spouts. Its rough, gray exterior bore little interest, but the interior of the bowl captured Dalmir's attention. A delicate working of silver filigree, blooming into a small half-sphere, like a second cup sprang up from the center of the object. At first glance, the bowl appeared to be empty, but as one gazed further into the bowl, it became apparent that it contained something: a murky darkness that rippled like liquid. As Dalmir stared into the darkness, he noticed tiny pinpoints of light within the liquid, like miniature stars. Frowning, he held up the unrefined cynder and stared at it contemplatively.

"I wonder..."

Marik watched in curious silence.

Dalmir reached into his pocket and retrieved his orb. He held it for a moment, then he placed the orb within the silver cup. It fit perfectly. The dark liquid within the bowl flared with light and turned a deep sapphire. The liquid bubbled and began to rise toward the rim. Swiftly, Dalmir held the unrefined cynder under one of the spouts as the liquid spilled out onto the rough cylinder; the gray stone absorbed the liquid and began to glow with an azure light. Marik's eyes widened and he and Dalmir shared a startled glance. Dalmir handed the cynder to Marik and then swiftly removed the orb from its place. The liquid diminished immediately and returned to its darkened state.

Marik held the blue cynder gingerly, staring at it in confusion. "It's blue. They're usually a kind of yellow-orange."

Dalmir nodded. "Because I used my orb. I was afraid of this." He rubbed his fingers between his eyes.

"Afraid of what?"

Dalmir pressed a finger to his lips thoughtfully, but said nothing.

"Listen," Marik said after a moment, his tone slightly exasperated, "I have my own affairs and I know what it means to lead. There are things you have to keep to yourself. You don't have to tell me anything, you're paying my crew enough to ferry you about with no questions asked. You don't owe me..."

Dalmir turned his blue eyes on Marik and raised an eyebrow. "But?"

Marik pressed his lips together, his expression angry. "But after what I witnessed in that tower... catching just a glimpse of the evil at work there... I thought... no, that's not right. I want to be included. I want to know what's going on. You don't have to tell me who you are, or how you can do any of the things you do, but tell me something."

"Or you walk away?"

Marik made a growling noise deep in his throat. "It's been known to happen."

Dalmir's lips twitched upwards at the corners. "I am sorry. I am not concealing things from you on purpose. You have to understand, I haven't spoken regularly with anyone in two hundred and eighty-nine years; I have grown accustomed to keeping my own council. You say I do not need to tell you about myself or my abilities, but it is all linked, and there are things I am not yet ready to share. If I am silent, it is for your own protection, and perhaps, for mine, as well."

Marik contemplated him for a long moment, his expression a strange mixture of skepticism and awe. Then he gave a short nod. "I can understand that. And maybe I don't really want to know what you're up to. But"—he hesitated then plowed on—"but I want to be part of this great purpose that surrounds you and that binds you. I am not unaware. I have seen first-hand the great evil you speak of for which I have no answer. If you have the answer, I want in. I want to earn your trust. Our ways and stories are different, but my vision shares a glimpse—perhaps a tiny glimpse—of your own. I may be foolish, but I am no fool."

"No, indeed you are not. We may not be privileged to walk the same path, but we will walk the same purpose." Dalmir thrust the little device into a pocket inside his cloak and straightened. "I think I've learned all I can from this place. We should return to your ship."

"Where to next?"

"Palla, I think."

Marik wrinkled his nose. "Not much in Palla."

"I want to visit a few villages."

"Which ones?"

"That's where I'm going to have to start exercising some of that trust you just spoke of," Dalmir said, a smile in his voice. "I don't know. I want to see for myself what is going on in Turrim, how the people are living, what this Ar'Mol and his soldiers are up to. Where do you suggest I go to get a look at those things? I'd also like to stay clear of any of the Igyeum soldiers and beneath the notice of the Ar'Mol."

Marik's lips twitched as he contemplated Dalmir's question. "That's a bit of a tall order... for most people." He gave an easy grin. "But if you're traveling with me, you have a few more options. Most of our safe houses are near villages such as what you just described..." He trailed off and eyed Dalmir through narrowed eyes, a sudden suspicious glint in his expression.

Dalmir gave a beatific smile. "Trust goes both ways, Captain."

Marik shook his head. "The crew won't like it. We don't usually hand out our address to strangers."

"Then take me somewhere else." Dalmir shrugged. "I didn't ask to see your safe houses."

"I'll talk with the crew about it. In the meantime, we'll head north toward Arva. It's a small village on the southern border between Malei and Vallei. Then perhaps we can go further toward Palla if you wish."

"I assume the Igyeum has some form of air patrols?"

Marik nodded. "Yes, but I know how to avoid them. Besides, they're spread a little thin since the cynder shortage, though I'm sure they'll be back up to their regular strength in a few lunats when they've got their new refinery up and running."

"Their new refinery?" Surprise made Dalmir pause. "You know where it is?"

"No."

"Then..."

Marik waved a hand aimlessly. "They have a new cynder refinery, trust me. It may not be working at peak efficiency yet, but the Ar'Mol will have a secondary site picked and crews mining as quickly as they can. I know the way the Igyeum works. There's no way they'll let this slow them down for long. Since they clearly don't really need any kind of special ore for the cynders, they'll just find a new mine—if they haven't already—and get back to work. There are plenty of people needing work."

"Even after what happened here?"

"Most of them won't know about it. And the ones who do will be so desperate to put food in front of their families they won't care. Come on." With a grim set to his jaw, Marik led the way back out of the mine and up to where they had left the *Hawk*.

10

Major Syrus carefully placed a large envelope on Headmaster Freidzen's desk. "The reports you requested for the information you intend to deliver to the Council on our preliminary assessments of the accelerated program. Is there anything else you need before you leave for the Arxis?"

"Thank you, Syrus." Freidzen picked up the stack. "You are just in time, my carriage will be arriving any minute to take me to the docks. Are there any points of concern?"

"Not at this time, Headmaster."

"Excellent. Anything I should take special note of?"

"There is one thing. I took the liberty of placing it at the top. The masters have made a recommendation they would like you to present to the Council and the Board of Instructors. I looked over what they presented and determined it should be brought to your attention. I think Daegan will be most interested to see this student's work."

"Really?" Freidzen resisted the urge to open the envelope immediately. "Did someone solve Daegan's problem?"

Syrus's lips twitched. "You'll have to read it for yourself. It's fascinating."

Freidzen patted the envelope. "Anything else?"

"Not for the Council. But I did include some reading material for you. Several of the first-year initiates are exceeding all expectations. The masters would like your approval to move these few names up through the ranks even more swiftly."

"Excellent. This is precisely why we have been working so hard," Freidzen said. "Are there any concerns about pushing too hard?"

"Not with these young men. The masters are more concerned about them growing bored."

"Bored? I find that hard to believe," Freidzen scoffed. "It has only been three sennights since the beginning of the semester. How can they possibly have determined so quickly what these young men are capable of in so short a time?"

"Sir, you asked us to push these young men to the limit, and that necessarily means that we are pushing ourselves to the limit as well as we test them and evaluate their readiness to move forward. Your challenge did not fall on deaf ears," Syrus replied. "Nor did the spark you ignited fall only on the students."

Freidzen leaned back in his chair. "Who made the recommendation?"

"Colonel Mathis, I believe."

"Mathis," Freidzen mused. "That is... unexpected. He does not usually instigate endorsements, and he isn't a fan of initiates in general."

"No, sir."

"But he believes there is something special about these new recruits?"

"Read the report and the recommendation, sir. He's gotten every instructor in the Academy to agree to his proposed course of action. If you disagree, you have the final say. I have included all of the masters' notes. You can read them on the way to the docks."

"Very well. Thank you, Syrus. Is there anything else you needed before I leave?"

"No, sir. And you are welcome. I hope the Arxis meeting goes well."

"I do not know how it could go well." Freidzen felt a weariness all the way into the marrow of his bones. "I fear it is a council of war."

The major left and Freidzen tucked the envelope under his arm. He wanted to begin reading the contents right away. He strode through the halls of the Academy—his Academy, he called it fondly in the privacy of his own thoughts. Exiting the building into the chillier winds of Deepthen, he saw the carriage waiting for him. Freidzen hauled himself into the coach and the driver shouted a command to the horses, causing the carriage to rumble up the gravel path and out onto the cobblestone street.

The Academy stood on the outskirts of Doran, the seaport capital of Ondoura. Doran boasted no enormous hangar in the side of a mountain for the airships to rest in while they awaited their passengers, but that was no problem. The harbor worked just as well. The airships, constructed in the fashion of their seafaring ancestors, floated in the water without difficulty.

As he rode, the horse's hooves clopping against the cobblestones of the street and the carriage wheels providing a steady background rumble, Freidzen perused the report that Syrus had brought him. It was mostly good news, as he had hoped. Although the accelerated program had only been approved by the Board of Instructors after they had heard Berenger Adelfried's story about his attempted kidnapping, the plan itself was solid. Headmaster Freidzen himself had been working on it for several years, hoping to bring it to light and shorten the time recruits needed for training in the event that the Igyeum ever attacked and the need for defenders became urgent. He reached the final page. Frowning slightly, Freidzen read the page three times to be certain he had not missed anything, then he neatly placed the stack of papers inside his pack.

He sat back and gazed out the window. His eyes barely registered the tall buildings as the carriage swept past them; they were familiar sights by now. Freidzen remembered his first visit to Ondoura when he was just an initiate himself. The bustling seaport cities and green, rolling plains dotted with olive groves, and the deep, dense, ancient forests were vastly different from the sparkling crystal lakes and mountains of Telsuma, his homeland. The buildings were different, as well. Tall, stone buildings featuring short, thick columns and shallow arches made the city of Doran appear both beautiful and sturdy, though the sea winds and salt left their mark on the finish of many of the homes and buildings as one ventured further toward the harbor.

Shaking himself out of his reverie, Freidzen patted the packet of papers now resting on his lap.

"Well!" he said quietly. "Well!"

The tip of Raisa's nose was cold. She wrinkled it a few times trying to warm it back up. Despite the fact that they were in the southern reaches of Turrim, and although winter had not yet descended upon the world in full force, this high up in the mountains there was always snow on the ground. They had stopped for the night in a shallow depression between two cliffs where the *Valdeun Hawk* would be safe from prying eyes. The wind whipped her cloak about and she pulled it tightly around her body as she paced back and forth in front of the only viable entrance to their shelter, her knee-high black boots sinking down through at least eight inches of frozen, crusty snow with every step.

Not a glimmer of stars peeked through the clouds to shed their light on Raisa's pacing as she waited for her watch to be over, her breath puffing out in impatient little clouds of mist. However, as always seemed to be the case when snow blanketed the ground, a pale light glimmered as though emanating from the snow itself. It was eerie, how much lighter the world was, even on the blackest night, when snow was present.

She shivered. Unbidden, the ghosts of Raisa's past rose up to haunt her.

A dusty background, tinged with crimson. Her father kneeling in their parched front yard as the Ar'Mol's men whipped him mercilessly, demanding answers that he refused to give. Fireflies dancing with a light all their own around the soldier's cookfires drew the scene in soft strokes, illuminating it for everyone in the village to see. Tears pricked at Raisa's eyes and trailed down her cheeks as she watched from the woodshed, her hiding place, where her father had urged her to run when they heard the tromp of the soldiers' feet coming through the village to their door. Terror welled in her heart as she watched through the crack in the door: fear that she would be discovered underscored by a simmering anger that wanted nothing more than to leap out and attack these men who dared harm her father.

He had been a good man, her father. He had provided for her well, and cared for her with kindness and love. She could still remember him dancing with her at the village festival when she was small, his delighted smile when she won first place for her stitching, the strength of his arms holding her and comforting her when she was sick or woke with a bad dream. He could not compensate fully for the loss of her mother, but he had certainly tried. A lump welled up in Raisa's throat as she struggled to pull her thoughts back under control. She rubbed her arms and stamped her feet. It did not do to dwell on these sorts of musings. She would only work herself into a frenzy as the terror and rage returned, undimmed in their force despite the years that had passed since that horrible night. The soft crunch of another's footsteps helped distract her.

"Ray?" Marik's whispered voice floated to her ears.

"Here, Marik."

He trudged over to her and stood with his back to the cliff. "Beautiful night for scheming," he commented.

"Marik—" Raisa hesitated. "What are we doing? Did the old man find what he was looking for in the abandoned refinery? Where are we going next?"

"He wants to go to Palla."

"Palla? What could he possibly want in Palla?"

Marik shrugged. "I'm not sure. He says he wants to see for himself what is happening all across Turrim."

"What about the air patrols?"

Marik gave her a cocky grin that looked shadowed and spooky in the ethereal gleam. "They've never managed to bother us before."

Raisa bit her lip and studied him. What had happened to her captain? Where was the man she had joined, the one who had a fire of vengeance burning in his soul? True, Marik often joked and threw around that cocky grin... but always a shadow underscored it. Always a dark defiance gleamed in the back of his gaze. Her captain always had a constant, ever-present driving force moving him forward. This Marik seemed almost... carefree. This Marik was strange and foreign, and a shrill terror she had never felt in his presence shivered through her.

"What did you see in that tower?" The words slipped out in a strangled whisper before she realized she meant to even say them. "What happened to that girl you brought back? How did she get there?"

"I know you have questions, Ray. I have questions, too. But we are going to have to be a little patient this time. Dalmir doesn't trust me yet, and I don't want to press him."

"What about your mission? Our mission?" Raisa demanded. "Ever since we took that job from Arrio it's like we're not ourselves anymore. You're not yourself. Something changed you on that last job, and something changed you even more in that tower; I want to know what it was. What is the plan? Don't you think it's about time you tell me what we're doing? We are your crew, we deserve to know where you're taking us."

"Or what?" Marik's voice was soft.

"Or nothing," Raisa spat. "You're our captain and we'll follow you anywhere, you know that. But we aren't used to being kept in the dark. We don't like it, Marik."

"Are you speaking for Oleck and Mouse, too? Or just yourself?"

Raisa scowled and kicked at the snow. She hadn't spoken to Mouse or Oleck about her own misgivings, but she knew what they would say, especially Oleck.

"You're just going to have to trust me. Oleck trusts me."

Fury and sorrow mingled together in Raisa's mind. Surely he couldn't have known her thoughts. "That's dirty, Marik, and you know it. Using Oleck against me..." She stopped, staring as Marik chuckled. "What?" she demanded.

"I've been doing it for years," Marik replied. "It's just that usually I do it the other way 'round."

Raisa glared at him. "We both trust you, you know that, right?"

"I know." Marik sobered. "Please trust me now when I say that what we're doing right now is crucial."

"What about the Ar'Mol? What about our reputation as pirates and smugglers? We're going to lose everything that's important if you're not careful."

"No, Raisa, that's where you're wrong. We just might win the only important thing... if I'm careful."

"I don't understand what you're talking about. It's like you're a different person these days."

"Maybe I am. Would that really be so bad?"

"So, what, you're just going to forget whatever it was that the Ar'Mol did to you? To me? To our families?"

"That's not fair, Ray," Marik growled. He passed a hand across his eyes. "And, no. I'll never forget, and I'll never stop fighting him. But I realize now I've been thinking too small."

Raisa heaved a sigh. "And what about Shaesta?"

"What about her?"

"Are we going to keep her locked up in the hold of the *Hawk* forever? What are you going to do about her, Marik?"

"I haven't decided just yet," Marik growled. "We've been a little busy the last few sennights, Ray."

In the snow-lit darkness, Raisa studied Marik's face. It was the same face it had always been. Thin, with a strong jaw and dark eyebrows over deep hazel eyes, that sometimes gleamed brown and sometimes held hints of green, that stared at her with the same cunning they always had. Stern eyes that held just a touch of craziness, the kind of crazy that always made her feel as though Marik was invincible. There was also determination in his expression, a stubborn set to his jaw that said he would see any plan through to the bitter end. But there was something new now, as well. It was something she had been trying to put a name to for sennights, a glimmer of something she had never seen before now smoldered in the depths of his eyes. Perhaps it was resolve, or courage, or something else entirely, but it had appeared when he and Dalmir returned from the tower, carrying that bone-thin child, and it had remained throughout the ensuing sennights, growing stronger every day.

"I trust you," Raisa whispered at last. "I've always trusted you, Marik. Oleck, Mouse, and I will follow you anywhere, even if your chart makes no sense to us. So don't worry about that. We might ask questions, but we trust you. You're our captain."

Marik swallowed hard and nodded once. "Thank you, Raisa. I'll take the next watch. You go on inside and get warm."

12

Dianira Torin's brown eyes stared up at her brother accusingly from within their sunken, reddened lids.

"I came here to find out what steps you are taking to avenge the murder of my son and what do I find?" She thrust the open letter into his face with an angry gesture.

"Nira, it isn't what it seems," Ericole Niveya replied, raising his hands defensively.

"How can it be other than what it seems?" Dianira hissed. "You were working with the men who slaughtered my son. They must be punished, they must be crushed. My Arrio, my Arrio!" Her voice broke off, rising into a high-pitched wail.

"Nira, Nira, please, you mustn't do this to yourself." Ericole took a step forward, pulling his sister into his arms where she sobbed loudly into his chest. "I promised you Arrio would be avenged, and he will. Look at me." He pushed her away so he could meet her eyes directly. "I am not an honest man, but have I ever lied to you?"

She sniffled a bit but shook her head.

"There." He took the letter from her hand with gentle fingers. "For Arrio to be avenged, we must first know who is responsible, no?"

"Yes," Dianira whispered.

"I have my suspicions, but would you want me to go after the wrong man and allow Arrio's true murderer to walk free?"

"No." She sagged limply in his arms, her fighting spirit dying a temporary death.

"Good, I am glad you understand. Now, listen to me, Nira, the ones responsible... they are powerful. If we are to bring them to justice, we cannot act rashly. We must be patient. We must be cautious. It would dishonor Arrio's memory to be anything else, yes?"

Dianira merely nodded, her face pale and devoid of expression. She wilted into a nearby chair, and sat, absently rubbing one arm and staring blankly at the wall behind Ericole. He frowned and knelt before her, looking up into her face, but she refused to meet his gaze.

"Nira..."

"Husband!" Aubri Niveya's smooth voice carried down the hall and Ericole rose, turning, as his wife glided toward them with swift, sure steps.

"Yes?"

"Ettore has arrived."

"Very good. Tell him I will see him in a moment."

Dianira waved a limp hand, shooing him away. "No, go now. You are busy, and my son must be avenged. I will not keep you from that important work. Tell your Ettore that his cousin's blood is restless, my boy is unable to lie in peace while his murderer walks free." She rose from her seat and drifted listlessly down the hall in the opposite direction from where Aubri had appeared.

Aubri watched her go and shook her head, but did not utter a word. Ericole admired her restraint. His wife and sister had a professional respect for each other, though no sisterly feelings of affection were wasted between them. But that was as much as he had ever hoped for in finding a woman with whom he could oversee the family business in a true partnership. And while Arrio had made his share of mistakes, he was still family, and family was everything. Ericole clenched his fists and turned his face slightly toward the east. Ar'Molon Uun would soon discover the severe error of crossing a Niveya. It was only how such a thing could be accomplished that troubled him.

Though he had no proof, Ericole was certain Uun's power was more than just influence. It wasn't merely that he had the Ar'Mol's ear and trust. There was a presence about the man, a confidence that was more than simple authority. No. Ar'Molon Uun was a dangerous foe. In order to deliver the revenge he had promised to his sister, Ericole knew he would have to be cunning and wary. Thankfully, events in the world were unfurling swiftly. Events that, if handled correctly, would afford an intelligent man plenty of opportunities. A war was coming, and a war always had the potential to be extremely profitable for a man who had the wits to use both sides of the conflict to his own advantage.

Ericole licked his lips. He was just such a man.

With a confident smirk, he followed his wife to where their son was waiting. Ettore had been spying in the Igyeum, and Ericole was eager to hear what news he had brought home.

A few minutes later, Ettore stood before his father and looked him in the eye. "Ar'Molon Uun gave the order to have Arrio killed." He brushed a hand through his dark, longish hair, the dust from the long road he had traveled likely making his scalp itch. "The Ar'Molon has done nothing to hide his part in the murder. The order came from his lips."

Ericole Niveya gazed down from where he sat in his favorite chair. The seat was not quite a throne, but not quite anything else, either. He wondered suddenly just when this young man before him had grown so tall and confident. Ettore had been taking on more and more responsibility over the past year or two, and would soon know all the delicate workings of the Niveya Syndicate. Despite his youth, he already demonstrated in full measure that he would make a capable heir. The stare Ericole directed at his son now was pensive and troubled. "The Ar'Molon is not to be crossed lightly."

"You do not seem surprised at this news." Ettore scowled. "I followed that caravan for nearly a lunat, infiltrated the ranks of the army, and all for what? To discover something you already knew?"

"I did not know, I guessed." Ericole rose from his chair and faced his son, putting both hands on the young man's shoulders. "The Ar'Molon was suspicious that I had crossed him in the matter of kidnapping young Adelfried, but I did not believe he could know for sure. I underestimated him. It was a mistake to have Arrio deal with him directly for the original information. I should have made sure he covered his tracks better. I suspected his involvement in your cousin's death, but I did not know for certain. Now, whether he discovered our duplicity, or he murdered Arrio as a warning, or out of simple frustration at losing his prize, I do not know. His reasons are not as important as the message itself. Did you learn anything else?" He dropped his hands to his sides and paced over to stare out a window.

"The Ar'Molon has in his employ a small team of assassins. They report directly to him and often carry out his orders. I was able to determine that they were responsible for Arrio's death"—Ettore hesitated—"but that isn't the interesting part."

"Oh?" Ericole turned back toward his son, his own interest piqued.

"The Ar'Mol himself has no knowledge of these assassins."

Ericole let out a hissing breath from between clenched teeth, a feral grin tugging at the corners of his lips. "Now that is intriguing. Do these assassins know that they work solely for the Ar'Molon?"

"They are fiercely loyal to Ar'Molon Uun only. So long as he is loyal to the Ar'Mol, they remain so, as well."

Ericole strode over and clapped his son on the back. "Well done, my boy. That is information we can put to use. To very good use, indeed." He wrinkled his nose and swiped his hand at the mud encrusting Ettore's sleeve. "You should go bathe yourself and change into fresh clothes before dinner. If she sees you looking like this, your mother will not be pleased."

Ettore chuckled and gave a weary nod. "Perhaps a nap, as well. Sleeping on the road is not exactly comfortable." He strode out of the room.

Lord Niveya returned to the window. It was a large, plate-glass window, facing east. He gazed through it now, his eyes unseeing as his mind churned over the discoveries his son had made. There were many possible routes he could go with this information, but which one would be the most advantageous? Dianira and Kale must be considered, of course. Their sole desire was to seek retribution for the murder of their only son. And there remained the issue of the pride of his family name. No matter how he had felt about the boy personally, Arrio had been family. That still counted for something if you were a Niveya. Ericole's fingers drummed on the sill. But vengeance did not have to be the only priority. There was the war to think of now. The first jabs had been quiet and subtle, but they had been thrust, and the stage upon which the next events unfolded was going to be very interesting. Ericole had not spent his entire life building his own personal empire just to get shoved to the sidelines now. There was a profit to be made in the coming lunats, and if he was clever, it was a profit that could be doubled, as both sides were going to need that all-important currency that he happened to have plenty of—and if he didn't have it, he had cultivated a special talent for acquiring more of it over the course of his entire life: information.

Ericole bared his teeth in what might have been a snarl, or perhaps a grin. He felt confident of his position. The trick mostly lay in convincing his sister to be patient. Nira tended toward action without thought, a trait her son had inherited, to his eventual detriment. Kale would understand, though. He was a patient, more thoughtful man. Biding their time was the best course of action for now. But it did not mean a reprieve for the Ar'Molon. No, justice was inevitable for Lord Uun. He would soon regret the day he had given the order that had led to the death of a Niveya, Ericole would make certain of that.

13

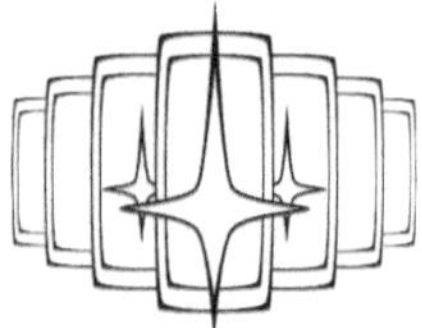

The heavy cedar gates swung open at the end of one long journey. Duke Langston took a deep breath as he stepped through them, beginning an altogether different sort of venture. His footsteps were slow and his heart was filled with trepidation. The Duke of Dalma took his time as he entered the grounds of the Arxis.

In days gone by, the Council had alternated meeting places between their nations, each governor hosting a summit in his own home in turn. However, as the years of cooperation restored trust between nations, and the West grew accustomed to its chosen government, the need for this caution had been outgrown. Thus the Arxis had been constructed. It had stood for nearly a hundred years now, but it remained unchanged in that time except for minor repairs.

Duke Langston always felt a certain sense of peace descend upon him whenever he entered the Arxis grounds. Even now, despite the urgency of his summons, he took the time to truly study his surroundings. The Arxis stood as near the center of Telmondir as possible. It could not inhabit the exact center, as that point lay in the middle of a lake. The lake in question sat just north of the main lodge. The path that led from the main road to the front door was a wide, cobblestone walkway that ran straight as an arrow to its destination. The lawn at the front and southern side of the main building was large and grassy, with little decoration other than the path itself. However, if one wished for more variety there were many other smaller, gravel paths that could be explored, each meandering its way amongst the beautiful garden to the west of the building. The area to the east of the building held a forest of many different varieties of ancient trees: oak, maple, willow, and sycamore. The forest had been tamed a bit, but not completely domesticated. Deep, dark places and tangles of undergrowth still remained, though tended well to prevent wild-fires from racing unchecked toward the prairie that bordered the forest or the village beyond. Few intentional paths wound through the forested area, though occasional benches had been strategically placed for any who wished to sit and think in peace. The entire design of the Arxis lent itself to a peaceful atmosphere in which members of the Council could interact and have weighty discussions, but also get away to think through various proposals in uninterrupted contemplation.

An intricately designed, arched pergola covered the latter half of the walkway leading to the main building. As Langston's steps brought him beneath the walkway, he paused. Vines grew thickly on the trellises, turning this part of the path into a tunnel. Langston always felt a bit uncomfortable when he reached this area, as if entering the arbor caused him to step briefly into some other world. However, he could not come up with any good reason to walk around the structure, and so he plunged ahead.

Despite his discomfort at being within the confines of the arbor, Langston could not hasten his steps. The same aspects of this path that caused him disquiet, also caused a certain sense of solemnity and reverence to settle upon him. A great responsibility graced his shoulders as the representative and governor of Dalma, and in no other place did he feel that responsibility more keenly than when he walked up the path to enter the Arxis.

At long last, he reached the other end of the arbor and made his way up the stone steps at the front of the cedar lodge. Two guards stood at attention on either side of the massive doorway. They were dressed in the traditional green and gray garb of the defenders, and they saluted him as he approached. Langston nodded and smiled to himself. Four guards were visible. Any intruder might look at the Arxis and think it unprotected, but that intruder would be wrong. Dozens of guards lurked unseen about the grounds. His own personal guards were included in that number, though they did not visibly accompany him.

He entered the lodge, removed his light traveling cloak, and strode into the large meeting room where the others waited. The normally spacious, open area now felt cluttered and claustrophobic as Langston noted that more people than usual had joined them. Lord Thorben Adelfried stood before the hearth speaking with Regeont Roshana Petrescu. His eyes flicked about the room. Adelfried's second-oldest son, Drengur, stood near a window talking to Headmaster Freidzen. The entire Board of Instructors were crowded inside as well, seated around the edges of the room and looking slightly uncomfortable. The Master of the Dalton Docks stood awkwardly near the corner, as well as several other faces that Langston did not recognize.

The room was furnished in the styles of all three countries that made up the Western Accord. Large windows overlooked the lake for the Ondourans, who did not enjoy being cooped up inside and were partial to large bodies of water. Rustic, comfortable furniture set in earthy hues of browns and dark greens represented the Dalman folk, who preferred to live simply and by the work of their hands and sweat of their brows. The massive fireplace on the western wall was built entirely from the stones of the Telsuma mountains—the livelihood of its people. Upon the eastern wall hung tapestries depicting all three lands, as well as the story of how the Council of Three had begun.

"Ah, Duke Langston," Adelfried hailed him. "I believe we are all assembled, now."

"I came as quickly as I could," Langston replied, taking a seat.

"I will not mince words," Thorben Adelfried began. "I am certain that you are all aware by now of what has happened, but for any who might not know, on his way to the Academy, my oldest son Beren was abducted. The ship he was on was commandeered by pirates and subsequently crashed. The entire crew and the new initiates were spared."

Lord Adelfried's words were met with stoic grimness. All those present had already been apprised of the situation, and they were well aware of the events that had transpired. They were also aware that Berenger Adelfried had, indeed, managed to outwit his abductors and make his way safely to the Academy, where he was currently enrolled in classes and had so far excelled in his orientation. The young man was a person of interest, and Langston was certain that he was not the only one in the room who had informants dedicated to keeping an eye on the young lord's whereabouts.

Adelfried continued, "My wife is currently visiting Ondoura, as it is a mother's prerogative to make certain her children are well. Needless to say, this abduction attempt is not simply about myself and my family. Unfortunately, it appears that the Igyeum is escalating matters and the war we have been hoping to avoid these past several years is now upon us. I would have your advice and counsel, my friends, on how we should proceed. Headmaster Freidzen is here to apprise us of how the Academy will be implementing a new and accelerated program, but I also wish to hear what your counselors and informants have to say about these incidents."

Duke Langston stood. "May I be the first to offer my official and heartfelt condolences that a member of your family was in danger, as well as a common rejoicing with you that this affair has ended happily. For my part, I do not have much more information about the events surrounding young Adelfried's abduction, or who, ultimately, was responsible."

Thorben nodded. "According to my son, we believe that there were at least two factions involved in the attempt, and perhaps part of the reason they failed was that they were not working together."

"Why do you believe they were not working together?" Langston asked.

"Because one group clearly wanted to assassinate him, while Ericole Niveya simply seemed interested in a ransom, though he was clever enough to never use the word," Thorben replied.

Regeont Roshana stood next. She was older than either Adelfried or Langston, but she spoke in a clear voice, her back straight as an iron rod, her hands steady as she also voiced her sympathy and relief. The older woman paused a moment, and then lowered her head. "My sources do tell of one point of interest that seems to not have yet been told." She spoke softly. "They tell me of a man traveling with young Berenger, a man of indeterminate age, who wielded a power unlike anything they had ever seen before."

"Not this legend again," Langston scoffed, but Adelfried held up a hand, stopping the Duke of Dalma from saying more.

"Your source within the Niveyan stronghold?" Adelfried asked eagerly. "After reading Beren's account of the matter I had hoped for your insight most particularly."

Roshana nodded gravely. "As you are all well aware, we in Ondoura are uncomfortably close neighbors to the Randeau Mountains where it is reported that the Niveyan family syndicate has made their home. My predecessor spent many long years attempting to get a source inside their walls. It was not easy, but at long last we succeeded. My informant is in constant danger, but manages to get small pieces of crucial information out to me from time to time. When I learned that young Berenger had been taken there, I sent word asking for whatever illumination my informant could offer. His reply was not at all what I had expected. It seems that Beren was accompanied not only by a band of pirates and the other young men who were also Academy-bound, but also a tall man with white hair and a youthful face. This man demonstrated a power they had never seen before and it was by this power that young Adelfried was rescued from the clutches of Ericole Niveya."

"Lord Adelfried, you cannot possibly believe..." Langston began.

"There are stories," Adelfried cut him off. "Stories and legends of men who wielded a power unlike anything ever seen before or since. Men with lives that seemed never to end, who used their power to build cities and spread knowledge."

"Fairy tales." Langston's voice was scornful. "Children's nursery rhymes. Not true history."

"Perhaps," Adelfried replied. "But this informant's account matches exactly what was in the private letter my son sent upon reaching the Academy, a letter that only myself and my wife have laid eyes upon. How do you explain such a phenomenon?"

Langston frowned. "Trickery of some kind. Fear of the unknown is a powerful weapon, and one that pirates and villains use often. I do not doubt that your son and this informant saw something strange, but to attribute it to some sort of mystical power... no, there must be some other explanation."

Roshana took her seat quietly, moving with elegant grace, and folded her hands in her lap. "Either way, it seems to me that the matter bears looking into. Perhaps we can find this mysterious figure, perhaps he does have a power he can lend to our cause. Or perhaps it was all mere illusion created by these pirates. If that is the case, they seem a capable force, one to be reckoned with, or perhaps bargained with to join our cause against the Igyeum."

Langston's mouth snapped shut and he sat down, shaking his head with a wry smile playing about his lips. After all these years, he should know better. Roshana was excellent at making her case in multiple directions at once.

"Agreed," Adelfried replied. "Now, I would like you all to hear from Headmaster Freidzen on his update from the Academy: the accelerated program and this year's new recruits."

14

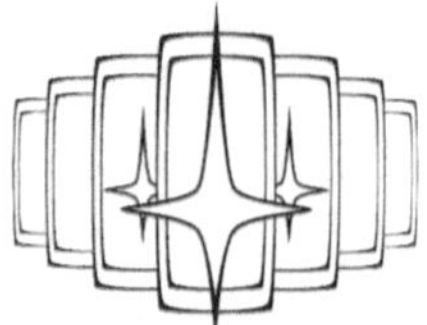

Standing before his peers, Headmaster Freidzen spoke at length about how well the new program at the Academy was working. For the most part it was all good news. The recruits were handling the accelerated courses well, and though some of the teachers had expressed concern about pushing the young men too hard, there were no signs yet of the type of fatigue and stress that had been feared.

"Of course, it is early days yet," Freidzen concluded. "But the students are handling the increased pressure and pace better than expected."

"Thank you, Freidzen," Lord Adelfried said at the end of the headmaster's presentation. "Is there anything else?"

"Only that one of our first-year students has solved Daegan's puzzle."

"A first-year?" Duke Langston asked in a tone of disbelief.

"I have brought his work to show you," Freidzen said. He pulled out the stack of papers that Syrus had given him and passed it around.

There was a shuffling of papers as everyone leafed through the pages.

Langston broke the silence first. "Do you realize what this looks like?" He whispered the question.

"Indeed, I do," Freidzen replied. "Syrus gave it to me just before I left the Academy. The similarities are astounding."

"Daegan worked on this problem for years. Are you saying this is... that this is truly the work of a first-year cadet?" Langston asked.

"I am."

"Who is this young man?" Lord Adelfried asked.

"You might be familiar with his name," Freidzen replied. "Wynn Drexel."

"One of the students who helped rescue my son?" Adelfried looked up sharply.

"The same," Freidzen confirmed. "And there are several others who show similar promise in various subjects. The masters have requested that I consider moving them through the curriculum even more swiftly than we had planned."

A thoughtful silence lay over the room.

Roshana was the first to speak. "We bow to you on this decision, Headmaster. As the one who has been presiding over the affairs of the Academy and our military for a decade, and doing a fine job, it is yours to determine such courses of action. The Council will abide by your decision and trust your judgment."

The rest of the Council members nodded their agreement.

"Thank you for bringing us this update, Freidzen," Adelfried said. "I know it was a long journey, but we have full confidence in you and the graduates you produce to defend our alliance."

Freidzen bowed and exited the room.

When he had gone, Adelfried turned to those who were left in the room. "Now, to the business of defending ourselves," he said calmly. "We must secure our borders, and begin to limit trade with the Imperium."

"Has any thought been given to the airship situation?" Roshana asked.

Adelfried's face darkened. "It is a primary concern."

"Despite our best intentions, we have grown far too reliant upon the trade they allow, and the ease of travel they provide." Roshana gave voice to the heart of the matter, as was her wont. "Am I correct in assuming that we have made little progress in discovering a way to replicate the power source?"

"Yes." Adelfried sighed. "We are no closer to learning the secret of the cynders than we were when the airships first began arriving from the Igyeum. We have managed to store some cynders away for emergency use over the years, but our supply is yet limited. With the recent shortage, we have not been able to store further cynders in almost a year, and we have even been forced to use some of our stockpile in order to keep certain promises. It is a valid concern that you raise, Regeont Roshana, and one that is felt most keenly by my people. Telsumans rely far more than they should on the shipments of food and livestock that are provided by Dalma and Ondoura."

"We may be able to feed and clothe ourselves without the airships"—Langston's voice was gruff—"but we rely on the ore from your mines and the coin that we receive from Telsuma every bit as much as you rely on our farms."

Adelfried nodded. "I did not mean to imply that was not the case," he murmured. "I merely wished to acknowledge that I am as guilty of allowing my country to fall into deeper reliance on the airships throughout the years as anyone else."

"This is ridiculous," Regeont Roshana said. "The airships have been around for less than a century. Most of us in this room are old enough to remember a time when they were not so common. Our three nations can provide for themselves in the eventuality that we lose the power of flight."

"This is true," Adelfried replied quietly. "But you have to admit that we have become accustomed to their convenience. What about the floods you suffered last year, the ones that ruined a large part of your fields and crops? Without the airships your people would have had to wait lunats for the supplies and grain that Dalma and Telsuma sent. Many lives would have been lost, and more would have gone hungry. And five years ago, when the drought fell upon my own lands and my people could not coax life into their crops and the rivers dried up, so many more would have died if we had not had the airships to swiftly bring us water and food."

"I agree with both of you," Duke Langston added. "And I, myself, remember ten years ago when the giant storms swept across the plains of Dalma and both of your nations sent us tools and supplies to rebuild houses and barns. But the loss of trade we might suffer if we cannot power the airships is not my greatest concern. We have managed without the airships in the past, and I am confident we can do so once again if the need arises. But how can we defend against an enemy that has the advantage of flight? And how can we be certain that the shortage of cynders is truly a shortage and not just the Imperium readying its troops for a full-scale assault on our lands? If I was the Ar'Mol, planning to attack us, the first thing I would do is make up a story about a cynder shortage so I could cut off my enemy's supply of power for their own airships."

Adelfried's face was grim. "Believe me, you are not the only one to raise such a concern; it has weighed heavy on my mind as well. We must treat these matters in earnest if we are to be prepared when the war we have been hoping to avoid falls upon us. Speaking of which, Daegan arrived in Telsuma about a sennight ago with a completed design that he believes could solve at least some of our problems when it comes to the Igyeum's superior air power."

Langston felt a ripple of displeasure at this news. "He did? Why did he not inform me of this before he left Dalma?"

Adelfried looked surprised. "I assumed he had."

Langston scowled. "This is the first I've heard of it."

"You know how Daegan is," Roshana soothed. "He probably finished the design and his only thought was getting it to Keene. Daegan is a genius, but the finer points of hierarchy and the etiquette of informing his superiors in the proper order tend to escape him."

Langston grudgingly had to admit the truth of this. "I should like to see these schematics, Thorben, did you bring them?"

"I did, indeed," Thorben replied. He gestured and one of his aides hurried forward with a thick set of rolled papers. "I will also be taking Master Drexel's papers to Daegan. The artificineer may be taking on a new apprentice sooner than we thought."

15

Wynn turned in his report and left the training room. He had some free time before his next class, so he wandered down to the lake where Marik had landed the *Valdeun Hawk*. The pirate and his crew had only left a few sennights ago, but Wynn felt like the ordeal he and his friends had gone through to reach the Academy had happened in another lifetime. He picked up one of the numerous smooth pebbles that lay scattered around the lake and tossed it. The pebble skipped several times before it sank out of sight below the water and Wynn blew out his breath in a dissatisfied puff of air.

Everything was different than he had expected. He had studied so hard, trained for so many hours, worked harder than ever before, and wanted this more than anything in his entire life. He had wanted to prove he could get here, to show everyone in Dalsea that Wynn Drexel was not just the village oddity. To show his family that he could accomplish something they could grasp. He knew his family loved him, but he also knew they often had no idea what to do with him. His thoughts moved so much more swiftly than theirs, and so differently. They could not keep up, and he did not fault them for it, but he also could not find a way to bridge the gap and help them understand. The Academy had been his shining light, something to work toward that they could approve, that they could be excited about, that they could help him achieve. But now that he had arrived, little had changed.

He did not belong here. Even among the other students, he stood apart. He had hoped it would be different: that here, among others who stood apart, he might finally fit in.

Fingers tapping against his leg in the familiar pattern that helped him organize his thoughts when he didn't have a pen in hand, he found another pebble and tossed it out over the lake, as well. It skipped six times before sinking. Wynn watched the ripples spread across the surface of the water and then bent down, searching for another flat stone.

His body moved of its own accord, a pattern emerging without any thought, without any intent from him. Bend down; brush the sand lightly with his fingertips; lift a stone; weigh it in his hand: once, twice, three times; arm back, arm forward, arm back, arm forward; release! Stone after stone skipped across the pond, but they barely registered. His body continued what he had told it to do, uncontrolled by his mind, settling into the soothing rhythm he had found.

His thoughts troubled him, and he wished he could toss them into the lake along with the rocks he so easily sent down into the watery depths. He missed his workshop. The snug four walls that hemmed him in, the little room, bursting with his drawings and schematics, the tiny stove his father had installed for him. He missed counting his steps from his little shop to the back door of his house, fifty-nine paces, a prime number. Prime numbers were pure, unsullied, separate, like him. He missed his books. Oh, the library here had plenty of books and scrolls he could peruse to his heart's content, and he had books for his classes of course, but it was not the same as the books he had carefully collected, the ones that were so well-known and beloved that he could open any one of them to the exact page he needed at any given moment. His heart ached for the books that had crashed to the ground in the *Crimson Eagle*.

But more than anything, what Wynn wanted to do was build the things that crowded together within his brain and demanded to be let out. The ones he couldn't contain. The ones he had to put down on paper lest they tear their way out of him. He held a secret horror that if he did not at least put his ideas down on paper—or at the very least scratch them in the dust—they would manifest physically, ripping their way through his skin and leaving him filled with holes. His hands itched to build something, or to take something apart. Working with his father had always helped keep that itch at bay. He had always enjoyed helping his father repair things the villagers had brought and paid for him to fix. The more difficult projects had always been his favorites: the ones his father had to admit he needed Wynn's help with.

Wynn scowled at the water, then squeezed his eyes shut, forcing his body back under his control. He counted to eleven. Slowly, reluctantly, his fingers uncurled from the stone and dropped it to the ground. To break the rhythm in the middle like that felt unnatural, but Wynn kept his eyes shut, taking deep breaths until he felt himself relax. There was no real end to skipping rocks, and if he didn't break the rhythm somewhere, he would probably just stay here, skipping rocks until he died.

That thought frightened him. It always frightened him, how focused he got. How difficult it was to tear himself away from anything that caught his attention.

Opening his eyes, Wynn turned his back on the lake and began walking back to the dormitory, his thoughts still awhirl.

The town had thrown a party for Grayden, knowing how hard he had worked. Everyone just assumed Wynn had gotten accepted by a horse's whisker. The question of why the Academy would admit such an odd lad had crossed more than one mind, though Wynn had never heard it cross any lips. Nobody except Grayden knew how easily the knowledge came to him, how swiftly he had finished the written exams. None of them knew how badly he had wanted that acceptance letter. And nobody knew that Wynn had secretly been terrified that he would get accepted instead of his best friend. The last thing he had wanted was to stand in Grayden's way. The day the scout had returned and given them the news that they had both made it in, and that the Academy was waiving half of their tuition fees... it had been better than anything Wynn could have hoped for.

To study at the Academy; to have space for his thoughts beyond the cramped shed his parents had given him—not that he wished to complain, it had been all the space they could afford to build for a luxury—had been all he ever wanted. He had hoped his classwork here would challenge him, push him beyond his own small thoughts into greater designs, higher artistry, or perhaps finally provide thoughts that would force his brain to slow down and take its time examining new and more difficult concepts.

But now... now he was not so sure. He had expected to struggle with his assignments, to slog through difficult ideas and problems. The Academy had grown in his imagination to a place where he would finally be tested to the point where he would have to toil and strain simply to keep up. It was a challenge he had looked forward to with eager anticipation. He had known he would be defeated in the training ring. Physically, he was not as adept as Grayden. And there, he had been correct in his estimation. He was by no means at the bottom of the lists, but he hovered in the middle.

What he had never expected was to find himself growing bored, to find his classes dull and his assignments easy. Wynn had been so certain that, once he was placed amongst the top recruits in Telmondir, he would find himself outmatched and near the bottom of the stack. The disappointment stung. Since arriving at the Academy, nothing had come close to demanding his full attention.

Wynn scowled and stopped. He turned and jogged back to the shore. Stooping, he searched briefly before picking up the pebble he had dropped. He flung it out across the lake, watching it skip away until it sank into its watery grave. Then he chuckled; only he could be disappointed by the fact that he was excelling in such a highly respected institution. Grayden would tell him he was being ridiculous. He squatted down and washed the sand and grit off his hands. Grayden would be right. With a rueful grin, he turned and headed back toward the main building. He had one more class before lunch.

16

Grayden sat at one of the long tables in his Military Strategic Studies class, his pencil frantically racing along his slate as he took notes. Tonight, he would take the slate and commit every word to memory before he wiped it clean for the next day's lessons. He counted himself lucky that he only had three classes where he needed to take notes; the other classes were far more hands-on. Thankfully, this was his last academic class of the day, and he still had a little space on his slate. The masters had explained the use of the slates during the first true sennight of classes, reminding them that on a battlefield or some other assignment, they would not have the luxury of looking through their notes or finding a book with the answer, but would be expected to make split-second decisions that could mean the lives of their fellow defenders. Thus, they would not keep vast notebooks, but rather were expected to store what knowledge they gained inside their own heads.

Grayden didn't mind the work, though he felt like he was struggling to keep up in most of his classes. All except for Airmanship, which was his favorite, and the one that he felt the most natural with. His only disappointment was that it only met two days each sennight, instead of three, or five, as most of his classes did. He also liked the daily combat training sessions. And his Leadership class, while challenging, was extremely interesting.

As the bell sounded to end the class, they stood and saluted Master Kiefer, who informed them that there would be a test in three days.

Grayden filed out with the rest of his class, catching up with Wynn as they reached the hall. Together they made their way out to the training ring.

"Six sennights," Wynn commented.

"What?" Grayden looked up from his slate.

"We've been here exactly six sennights tomorrow, a lunat and a half," Wynn said.

"Oh." Grayden paused as he tried to summon up the date. "I guess you're right."

"Are you still glad we were chosen?"

Grayden thought about the long hours in the practice ring, and how his muscles screamed at him each evening when he tried to relax. He thought about how at night his brain kept spinning over the previous day's lessons, preventing him from falling asleep easily. Six sennights. Including the ordeal it had taken to get them to the Academy, he had endured two lunats of constant weariness, constant challenge, and a neverending ache throughout his entire body. He grinned. "Yes."

Wynn shook his head.

"Aren't you?" Grayden asked.

Wynn gave a non-committal shrug.

"Wynn?"

His friend mumbled something he didn't quite catch.

"What?"

"I miss my workshop," Wynn said.

Grayden felt his brain pause. He swung himself around in front of his friend, causing Wynn to stutter to a stop himself. "Wynn, you're not saying you want to go home?"

Wynn shook his head. "Not really. I just... it's not what I expected, that's all."

"What do you mean?"

"My friends!" Beren's voice boomed around them as he came bounding across the yard from his own class. "Are you ready for combat training?"

Wynn's expression changed, turning blank and stony. Grayden gave him a searching glance, but he could tell that his friend did not wish to continue the conversation in front of Beren. He thought he understood. Wynn had always found it as difficult to make friends as Grayden found it easy. But in spite of their personality differences, they had been friends for as long as either of them could remember.

Together, they continued to the training ring, the conversation revolving around their classwork.

"Six sennights!" Beren suddenly said, his face beaming.

"Yes, that's how long we've been at the Academy," Grayden said, wondering why everyone had suddenly become obsessed with tracking time.

"Words of truth," Beren replied. "But it also means that in one more sennight we'll have earned our first free day."

Wynn and Grayden stared at him.

"Remember what Koen told us on our first day?" Beren reminded them. "In another seven days we can take an entire day away from campus."

"Really?" Wynn asked, suddenly sounding more alert.

"Truthfully, I would not lie to my best friends!" Beren grinned. "And I have an idea. Why not accompany me to visit my mother at Regeont Roshana's home and let us show you around Doran?"

"That sounds excellent," Grayden said. He glanced at Wynn and raised his eyebrows.

Wynn nodded, his expression turning more cheerful.

"A plan it is, then!" Beren roared, clapping them both around the shoulders with his huge arms. "I will send word to my mother this evening and tell her to expect all three of us."

"It won't be a bother to her if we all come?" Grayden asked.

"Not at all!" Beren assured him. "She invited us, if you remember. My mother enjoys hosting, and Doran is one of her favorite places to visit. She knows of all the best spots. I am sure she would be displeased with me if I did not bring you."

"Very well then," Grayden agreed. His heart lightened. A day of rest away from the training and the furious pace of their classes sounded glorious. He glanced at Wynn, whose lips curved up in a slight smile, and he relaxed. Surely his friend just needed a break. The classes had been grueling and they had been going non-stop for almost two lunats now. He knew that the coursework came more easily for Wynn, but even he had to be feeling the strain. A day off would be something to look forward to for the next several days, and give them something pleasant to look back on when they returned to the Academy.

GRAYDEN AND WYNN trailed behind Beren as he mounted the short, circular steps and approached the tall mansion of the Regeont. Walls of white stones, perfectly aligned, soared above their heads. Tall windows stared down at them with complete disinterest, each one adorned with a golden corbel. A balcony protruded in a half circle above the dark entryway, a yawning mouth into which they must enter in order to gain the door.

A servant opened the door before Beren had even raised a hand to knock. She greeted them with quiet sincerity and led them into an elegant, but not overbearing, room. Everything within the great manor bespoke elegance, and yet, nothing about the decor could be considered ostentatious. Understated was perhaps more accurate, or even austere.

Nadia Adelfried looked up from her breakfast tray at their entrance and rose gracefully with a delighted smile. "Berenger! You have earned a free day at last." She crossed the room and took her son's hands in her own, pulling him into a motherly embrace.

She then greeted Wynn and Grayden, bidding them welcome and gesturing for them to sit.

"Have you eaten?" she asked, returning to her own seat and her breakfast.

"We had a light breakfast," Beren replied. "But we would not turn away the offer of something better than Commons fare."

Lady Nadia chuckled delicately and gestured to the servant, who nodded and disappeared through the doorway. "Did you have any specific plans for your day off?" she asked, picking up a bite of yellow fruit Grayden had never seen before.

Beren shook his head. "I had hoped that you might be willing to take us on a tour of Doran. Grayden and Wynn haven't traveled much—except to get to the Academy—and I wanted to show them around. But you know the area better than I do."

"That sounds lovely," Nadia replied. The maid returned carrying a large tray covered in glistening cut-up fruit, octagonally-shaped crackers, and various cubes of cheese in an array of colors. "Why don't you join me for breakfast. Lord Elan and Lady Ilya should be up soon. I do not wish to leave without informing them of our plans."

"When did they arrive?" Beren asked. Grayden wondered at his friend's suddenly flat tone.

"Beren, be nice." Lady Nadia's voice held a note of warning. "They arrived about a sennight ago. Roshana asked me to act as hostess for her while she is gone. It would not be a good hostess who simply disappears before her guests rise for the day."

Beren ducked his head and put a slice of fruit into his mouth, accepting his mother's mild rebuke. Grayden wondered what his friend disliked about the lord and lady who had come to visit, but it did not seem like a good time to ask.

They had nearly finished the food when Ilya and Elan swept into the room.

"Lord Elan, Lady Ilya, good morning," Nadia welcomed them. Her voice remained warm but her tone grew more formal. "I would like to present my son, whom you may remember, Lord

Berenger Adelfried, and his friends, Grayden Ormond and Wynn Drexel. They are all Academy initiates this year and have come to visit Doran for their first free day."

Lady Ilya floated over to a settee next to Beren's chair and alighted on it, her gold and red dress draped over a single shoulder. A gauzy veil surrounded her shoulders. "Initiates at the Academy," Ilya gushed, fluttering her eyelashes at each of the young men. "My brother would have gone last year if he had been accepted." Her mouth dropped open in surprise as her gaze came to rest on Beren. "Why, Beren, I almost didn't recognize you!"

Beren shifted his weight in his chair and looked as though he wished to jump to his feet and run.

"The Academy tests are difficult," Grayden said, trying to break through the awkwardness for his friend.

"What?" Ilya gave him a distracted little smile and then burst into a tittering little laugh. "Oh, Elan didn't even apply." She cast her brother a sly glance. "He says there are more important things to be done than swing a sword all day. Of course, swordplay does have some benefits." She touched Beren's muscled arm lightly and gave him a brilliant smile.

Beren rose from his seat as though he'd been stung and crossed the room, where he crouched down and stirred at the logs in the hearth. Ilya followed him, keeping up a stream of inane conversation. Elan, tall and imposing with a thin, dark beard outlining his mouth and the lower half of his face, bowed to each of them.

"Sister." Elan's voice cut through the room. "We have an appointment to keep."

Ilya sighed prettily and shook her head so that two dark tendrils of hair framed her face elegantly. She stared up at Beren hopefully. "Will you be joining us for dinner this evening?"

Beren put on an exaggerated expression of regret. "I am afraid not."

Ilya's lips turned down in a pout. "Oh dear. And Elan and I have a pressing engagement we cannot miss just now. There just isn't enough time. I had so hoped to spend a few hours catching up with you. When I learned that your mother had come for a visit I did so hope that dear Cathrine would be with her; we were close when we were younger. How is she? I heard she opened a little school in Gnupar."

"She is doing well," Beren replied stiffly. "This year she had over thirty students apply and is considering expanding the school next year and hiring at least one more teacher."

"Maybe she should hire more than one, and then she could get away to see neglected old friends once in a while," Ilya pouted.

"Ilya." Elan's tone grew sharper. "We will be late."

Ilya made a shushing motion with her hand before resting it on Beren's arm. "It was good to see you, Berenger." She fluttered her eyelashes at him. "But far too short of a visit. Oh!" She gasped as though something had just occurred to her. "Berenger, you must come visit again before my brother and I depart for home. We are expecting Auntie back any day now, and I was hoping to convince your mother to help me throw a party for her. You must come for that." Ilya's gaze included Grayden and Wynn. "All three of you are invited, of course."

She went up on tiptoe and kissed the air next to Beren's jaw.

Beren bowed his head slightly and politely freed himself from Ilya's grasp. "If we are allowed another free day so soon, we will make our best effort to attend."

"So formal." Ilya giggled and batted her eyelashes. "I do love that about your nation."

Grayden nearly choked as he attempted to conceal his amusement. Beren shot him a glare, which only made Grayden want to laugh even more.

Elan made a sound in his throat and stalked out of the room.

"I must be off," Ilya continued. "It was so nice meeting all of you." She spun away in a flutter of golden veil and breezed through the door after her brother. When she was gone, Nadia smiled at the three men and invited them to sit with her.

"At last, a bit of peace," she said. "Now, Beren, your friends were just starting to tell me more about your coursework at the Academy. How is your training progressing?" Nadia looked at each of them, her attention complete and sincere.

"Very well, ma'am," Wynn replied.

"Excellent," Nadia said. "The work is challenging?"

Wynn scratched his head and gave a rueful grimace.

Grayden watched his friend with a bemused expression on his face. He had gotten Wynn to speak more openly about what was bothering him in the past several days. "Wynn's too humble to say anything, and we know the headmaster is your brother, so he doesn't wish to offend..."

"You may speak openly," Nadia said, looking intrigued.

"Well, ma'am, like I was saying, Wynn would never say so, but he's actually getting a bit bored," Grayden continued. "Everyone back home would be shocked, probably. Everyone in town knew how hard I was studying to get accepted into the Academy. It's all I talked about to anyone who would listen. But Wynn stayed quiet about it. He kind of surprised everyone by doing so well on the tests—better than me, actually—but that's just because he's so smart already, and because he didn't make a big fuss about it, but I never could keep up with him, even in primary school."

Wynn shook his head. "I can't match you in the training ring, though."

"Nobody can," Beren rumbled. "Grayden is undefeated in the arena."

"Only because you've never been matched against me." Grayden grinned. He paused. "In fact, I haven't seen you in the combat ring at all."

"You are only competing against other first-year recruits, are you not?" Lady Nadia asked before Beren could reply.

"At first that was true," Wynn admitted, "but lately Grayden has been assigned to spar with quite a few second-years, as well."

"I see." Beren's mother gave them a wry smile. "If that is the case, I would not worry about being bored for much longer. It sounds as though your instructors are aware of the situation, else they would not be pairing you against older recruits. I believe they are testing the limits of your abilities so as to better know where to place you in the next stage of your training. I would assume they are doing the same evaluation of your coursework."

"I suppose that makes sense," Wynn said, perking up a bit.

"But enough about your training," Nadia said, turning to catch her son's eye. "Beren says that you two have never been to Doran before, is this true?"

"Yes, ma'am," Grayden and Wynn replied.

"Then it is settled, I shall call for a carriage and the four of us will spend the day touring the city. Dalton is impressive, but Doran has some truly marvelous wonders of its own."

Together, they exited the Regeont's mansion and climbed into the stately carriage which then clattered down the cobble-stone streets into the heart of the city.

Grayden wasn't sure what he had expected, but Doran was nothing like any place he had ever been. He had half assumed the capital of Ondoura would be a kind of mixture of Elricht Harbor and Dalton, but he was wrong. The first thing he noticed was the heat. Even though it was late autumn, the air blowing in from the sea was warm and sticky, and carried a scent of spices on its back; he couldn't begin to identify them all, though he caught hints of cloves and something tangy and a little sharp that seemed familiar but he couldn't place. He knew they were much farther south than Elricht Harbor, or Dalsea, but it was still difficult to truly grasp how different the weather was here on the southern border of Ondoura. The sun beat down on his head and the trees they passed retained their lush, green leaves... though many of them seemed to have fronds rather than leaves.

As they rumbled over the cobblestones, he noticed that the gaps between the cobbles were wide and filled with yellow sand. When they reached the outskirts of the city, the stone buildings were another new sight. The small village of Dalsea was comprised of either log cabins or huts made from wattle and plaster with large timbers helping keep everything together. Some of the houses had wooden shingles, though most were thatched. But here in Doran every building boasted slate tiles for their roofs. Every building was made from a gray or reddish-hued stone and covered in elaborate carvings. Many of the structures were supported by various columns, all of them short and squat. Grayden had to admit that the city was impressive, but he secretly preferred the white stone and soaring arches of Dalton that drew one's eyes up toward the mountain-top.

The buildings drew closer together as they ventured closer to the harbor. When the streets grew too narrow for the carriage, they disembarked and continued on foot. Grayden found it hard to keep his eyes on where they were going, as there were so many interesting things to look at. Lady Nadia, who was leading them, stopped abruptly.

"This is the Doran Market," she said, sweeping her hand out in front of her.

Grayden stared. It was so different from the Dalton marketplace, which had been set up in a huge courtyard, with all the sellers at tables or booths that were open to the sky above. Here, the booths appeared to be attached to the outsides of the buildings, though upon closer inspection Grayden realized that they were separate, but so heavily decorated with each seller's wares it was impossible to see where the booth ended and the building began. Glowing lanterns hung down on either side of the path, illuminating the various items for sale, and casting eerie shadows on the faces of the merchants gathered there. Above them, large, colorful fabrics stretched between the buildings overhead, creating a false ceiling for the entire marketplace where daylight trickled through, glowing in varied hues depending on the color of the fabric they were beneath.

The noise, at least, was familiar. Everyone was shouting. Bells chimed, animals whinnied, brayed, and bleated, while sellers called out the items they had for sale as Grayden and his friends passed by. Grayden felt as though a war was being waged on his senses. As if the brilliant colors and cacophony were not enough, the smell of fish and herd animals mingled with scents of perfume and spices in a strange, but not unpleasant way. Various entertainers were situated throughout the crisscrossing streets of the market, showing off their talents and begging for coppers from anyone who lingered to watch. It was at once overwhelming and amusing.

"Come along," Lady Nadia urged. "I sent word ahead."

They finally emerged from the long, narrow road out into the open air. The cobblestone path ended abruptly and gave way to a wooden bridge extending out over the water beyond the wide sandy shoreline that stretched out toward the horizon on either side. The breeze picked up, dancing around them with playful abandon. All the scents that had assaulted their nostrils in the market streets were swept away and replaced by the strong, briny, fishy smell of the ocean.

Lady Nadia pointed.

The three boys grinned at each other as they saw that she was gesturing at a large, floating structure moored to the end of the long dock on which they were now standing. It could not rightly be called a ship, for Grayden had a feeling that the vessel would be impossible to steer, and would most likely tip over with only a little encouragement from the waves. As they drew closer, it became apparent that the floating structure was not built for sailing at all. Instead, it appeared to be a series of seven decks all built atop one another, completely open to the sea and sky, with just a railing surrounding each deck. Within each of these decks were low tables for dining, drinking, and conversation.

"What is it?" Wynn asked.

"That is where we will be having luncheon today," Lady Nadia replied. "In addition to being a truly unique location, the food is the best Doran has to offer. Also, it's a little bit quieter, and you can gaze at the city and take it in from a distance. Your first visit to Doran can be a little overwhelming."

Wynn and Grayden grinned at her in relieved gratitude and they followed her out across the dock. They entered the structure and a man dressed in pristine clothes greeted them. "Welcome to the Salla Batayloc. We have tables available on every deck; do you have a preference?"

"Top deck, please," Lady Nadia replied, handing him a small card.

They followed the man up the six flights of wooden stairs and toward the railing where he left them at a low table surrounded by large, comfortable pillows upon which Lady Nadia invited them to recline. Their location at the corner of the deck had an unobstructed view of the ocean. In one direction, water stretched off to the horizon as far as the eye could see: a myriad of blues, greens, grays, and a series of ever-changing pinpoints of white where the waves rose, crested, and fell. In the other direction, they could now see a large portion of Doran, the buildings rising up out of the sand, the tunnel-like roads that all emptied out onto the shore, the bustling of people in and out of shops and up and down streets. The distant cries of sellers and the squawk of gulls wheeling over-head mingled in a strange way like discordant, but not unpleas-ant, music.

The meal itself far surpassed anything the young men had tasted since starting at the Academy. Their plates were filled with slices of various kinds of meat that had been cooked with onions and tomatoes, a delicious cornmeal pudding, and stewed vegeta-bles. When their plates were empty, their server brought them each a large slice of bread that Grayden and Wynn did not recog-nize. Tasting it, they discovered that it was dense and moist and filled with nuts and chopped dates that exploded with sweet flavors in their mouths.

They exclaimed their gratitude to Beren's mother as they ate and talked. But at length, the sun began to fall lower in the sky.

"We need to get you back to the Academy before sunset, am I correct?" Lady Nadia asked.

Reluctantly, the three young men nodded.

"Breakfast tomorrow is going to taste like wood shavings

compared to this," Wynn said, wiping up a few remaining crumbs from his sweetbread and licking them from his finger.

"You always say breakfast tastes like wood shavings," Beren teased.

"Well, not much tastes good before dawn," Wynn shot back.

"And to think, you used to live on a farm," Grayden chuckled.

"Don't remind me," Wynn groaned. "Morning routine makes me miss the luxury of sleeping in and the life of ease I used to enjoy."

Lady Nadia listened quietly, a contented smile on her face as they made their way back to the Regeont's estate, where she insisted on lending them the carriage for their return to the Academy. When they were settled, she stepped up and gave Beren a final hug.

"Come back and visit me on your next free day," she instructed. "I should be here for another several sennights." She looked at them each in turn. "You have made some fine friends, my son."

She stepped down and the coachman urged the horses into a swift trot.

17

In the crisp morning air, high above the clouds, Marik called his crew to the fo'c'sle. He kept his expression placid, but inside his thoughts were in a turmoil. How would they react to his decision? Should he have discussed it with the crew first? But no, he was their leader, he should bear the weight of these kinds of worries. Perhaps they would see the benefit of their current situation. He hoped they would.

"We'll be making a quick stop in Arva for a few minor repairs," he began. "Most of you signed on for a job we didn't complete and didn't get paid for. I can't pay you what was promised, but I can pay every one of you ten tavs for your time. I know it's not what you signed up for, but it's all I can offer."

"Ten tavs?" Raisa arched an eyebrow. "Captain, where did you get that kind of money?"

Marik jerked his head at Dalmir, standing above them at the wheel, holding the *Hawk* steady. "I told you we've got a paying client. It's a bit different than our usual fare, but easier to spend without raising eyebrows. But with the cynders you each have from our last job, none of you will walk away poor."

"Where are we letting him off?" Mouse piped up.

Marik took a deep breath. He had been dreading this conversation, but he knew he couldn't put it off any longer. "We aren't letting him off just yet," he admitted.

Yefrem squinted in curiosity. "Captain, what are we doing?"

Marik kept his gaze steady. "We are transporting a paying customer wherever he wants to go."

"Marik," Raisa began, her voice cautious. "We've been talking a bit..."

"Talking?" Marik's tone deepened.

"Just talking, Cap'n," Raisa said hurriedly. "We've been a bit worried, see."

"Being a ferryboat isn't what we're used to," Oleck muttered, though he looked uncomfortable being the one to say it.

"I see." Marik glanced around. "And you've all been talking about this, have you? When I'm not around? Voicing your concerns about your captain, perhaps? Talking about how he must be addled in some way? Muttering in darkened corners, maybe? Perhaps plotting a quiet little take-over of his ship to get us all back on track?"

"Captain, it weren't nothin' like that!" Mouse exclaimed, his tone horrified.

"No, Mouse? Then what was it like?" Marik growled. "Because it sounds a lot like mutiny to me."

Oleck shifted. "Not a mutiny, just voicing our concerns."

"Behind closed doors, that kind of talk is usually the precursor to mutiny."

"Captain, you know we would never..."

"I know?" Marik cut Oleck's argument short, then his shoulders slumped. "You're right, Oleck. I know." He rubbed the back of his neck and gave a shame-faced chuckle. "I don't know what has come over me. But I've been doing some hard looking in the mirror and I find myself lacking."

"Captain!" Mouse's denial, so filled with certainty, warmed Marik's heart, but he shook his head at the youth sadly.

"I'm no hero, Mouse," he said. "But the truth is, I want to be one. Those young men at the Academy, Dalmir..." He sighed.

"Somewhere along the way, I lost what they have. Decency and virtue: these are things I used to prize. Things I used to have. And I want them back. I don't know if being a transport for the old man will get me those things, but I think he could teach me something. Something I want to learn." He mustered the courage to look up and meet the eyes of his crew. One by one, they met his gaze, and he was surprised at what he found there.

"Captain!" Mouse suddenly exclaimed. "We weren't discussing no mutiny, I swear. We just want to understand. We're crew, Captain. That means... well, it means... you know... it's more like..." Mouse's eyes darted to Raisa and the words faltered on his lips. "Well... it just means something important, that's all. We're with you to the end, no matter what."

Marik gave the boy a tight-lipped smile.

"The lad's right," Oleck rumbled. "We're not questioning your decision, Captain." Oleck scratched at his short beard.

"We'd just like to know why," Raisa burst out. "Like Mouse said, we're with you. But can we at least know what it is we're doing and why we're doing it? We've always known that before."

Yefrem scowled. "No mutiny here, Captain. But I'd still like to be let off in Arva, if it's all the same to you. I didn't sign on to be a full-time member of your crew, and the last job cost my brother his life." He paused. "Maybe I need to learn some of what you're looking for, too. But I don't think I can find it here."

"That's fair, Yefrem," Marik said softly.

The red-bearded man gave Marik a respectful nod and stumped off, his shoulders slumped a little. Marik turned back to his crew.

"It's what you saw in that tower, isn't it?" Raisa asked in a whisper.

Marik's throat threatened to seize up and for a long moment he couldn't say a word. In his mind, he suddenly stood in that awful, bone-filled room once more, smelled the stench of death and decay, heard the agonized pleading of the young girl... He blinked furiously, trying to clear the memories from his mind.

"Yes," he managed to choke out. "I don't know how long Dalmir will need the services of the *Hawk*, or of our crew, but I have bound my purpose to his. At least for the moment. I do not ask the same of you. You're a good crew, the best, and more than that, you are my friends." He did not look at Mouse as he said these words. He couldn't say the word Mouse wanted to hear. There were too many painful memories associated with that word for Marik. "I will not order you to join me in this. But I will tell you that I have seen evidence of evil beyond anything I had imagined. We've been less than angels, I know that, but I like to think we've done good where we could—and now we have a chance to do more, without doing any harm in return. Men like me don't always get that kind of opportunity, and I'm guessing it won't be offered twice." He gazed at the others, his eyes roving across each of their faces, searching for their answer.

"I'm with you wherever you go, Cap'n," Oleck rumbled gruffly. "You should know that by now. If you have to ask..."

"I do know that, Oleck. Under ordinary circumstances, of course I know that. But nothing about these days is ordinary."

"Words of truth." Oleck grimaced. He puckered his mouth like he wanted to spit, but refrained. "I'm with you," he said simply.

"And me," Raisa added.

"And me," Mouse squeaked, sounding as though the words had gotten stuck in his throat.

Marik gazed around at the three faces he cared most about in the world and gave a small smile. "Thank you."

Oleck and Mouse dispersed, leaving to attend their respective duties, but Raisa hung back, a strange look on her face.

"Yes?" Marik asked.

"What about Shaesta?"

"What about her?"

"Without Yefrem, we're a hand short."

"Short?" Marik eyed her. "What do you mean? We've never

needed more than the three of us and Mouse before, and we have Dalmir, who seems to pick things up fairly quickly."

"True." Raisa leaned against the railing and folded her arms.

"Last I checked, you weren't too happy with her. You've avoided being the one to take her food, you've glowered every time anyone mentioned her name, and even stormed out on me when I tried to talk to you about her situation a few days ago. And now... what? You want to make her crew again?"

"No!" The word burst from her lips. "No," she repeated, her tone calmer the second time. "I'm not saying we should trust her, but I am saying that we can't keep her locked up in her cabin forever."

"I figured we'd leave her in Arva," Marik said.

Raisa nodded slowly. "Perhaps that would be for the best."

"Talk to me." Marik's tone was quiet and even, but Raisa wouldn't meet his gaze.

"I..." She didn't continue immediately, but paused and took a deep breath. Then she plunged on. "I'm not sure what I want. I want to hate her, but I can't. She was my friend, almost like... crew. She betrayed me, betrayed all of us. And yet... I've been thinking about my father. If someone told me today I could have him back, but I had to betray everyone I loved just to see him one more time"—Raisa looked up at Marik, her face filled with anguish—"I'd do it. I wouldn't hesitate. I wouldn't even stop to think. Would you?"

Marik stared out at the horizon, the white of his knuckles gripping the hilt of his sword the only indication he had even heard her. The question rang in his thoughts. If he could see his father again... what he would do. Angry flames flickered in his mind's eye as hurt and betrayal he had thought long buried surged to the surface. He licked his lips slowly. "If we give her this chance..."

"We never let her out of our sight."

"If she even wants a chance."

"And Oleck has to be all right with it," Raisa added.

Marik nodded. "If he says she's off the *Hawk*, we leave her behind in Arva."

"She might prefer that. She might want to go back to her family."

Marik gave her a long, thoughtful look. "She might."

18

Lorcan stood in the small, hidden valley and stared up at the soaring cliffs and rocky parapets all about him. It had taken them many days to hike to this location, almost a sennight since they had departed the airship and De'Anan Roald's company. He wiggled his bare toes into the earth, shuddering at the memory of the flight. He did not enjoy the feeling of air beneath his toes; he liked dirt. Plants were easy and orderly. They could be controlled and manipulated as the gardener saw fit. Air flitted about, untrustworthy and unhelpful. Lord Uun did not often require him to fly; the Ar'Molon was a considerate benefactor, he knew of Lorcan's distaste for airships. And Lorcan had proved useful in the past. Yes. There had been many experiments. Not all of them successes... Lorcan pulled at a tuft of his white hair and scowled, remembering one of his less successful endeavors. That experiment had failed miserably. Not only had all his subjects wilted, but he had not found the cure. Not completely, anyway. He scowled. It had been that experiment that had lost him favor with the Ar'Mol.

Then he grinned to himself and gave a gleeful little cackle. Despite the failure, he had gained much from that endeavor. Not all he hoped, but enough to grant him many more years of trying. The Ar'Molon understood.

"Are you pleased with the location?" One of the guards pulled Lorcan out of his memories.

Lorcan gazed about once more. Mountains, gleaming and white-capped, encircled the valley protectively. Greenery stretched about the shallow bowl in which they stood, bordered by a thick ring of ancient trees. It was perfect.

"Yes." His voice faltered with disuse even as the words tumbled out of his mouth like the steam of his breath. "Yes, this will do nicely." He glanced sideways at the squad of soldiers that had been assigned to bring him to this place. "You are dismissed. Dismissed!" he barked hoarsely.

"We were instructed to assist you in any way you saw fit," one of the guards began to protest.

"Your assistance was needed only to bring me here in safety and secrecy," the madman snapped. "You have achieved that goal. Now, leave."

"We had thought to construct a shelter for you before we left. The Ar'Molon will not be pleased if we leave you like this."

"I am perfectly capable of providing shelter for myself," Lorcan snarled, enraged by the thought that this lowly servant should question him. He focused on the emerald orb in his hand. The gemstone grew warm and began to glow with a ghastly, unhealthy gleam.

"Sir," the guard began to protest once more.

He never finished. The madman screamed out a wordless cry of fury. The guards clapped their hands to their ears, cowering before his high, animalistic wail of power. Lorcan clenched his fist and called to the orb's power. Thick roots sprang from beneath the rocky ground, winding their way swiftly around the guard's legs, wrapping him in a rough embrace. Up his body the roots wrapped and grew, faster and thicker and tighter, encasing his form in thick bands of a twisting, spiraling prison. From the middle of the newly sprouted growth, the former guard's face filled with terror as his eyes darted to his companions. He let out a startled cry and struggled—too late—the roots wrapped around him held him fast.

"What... what are you doing to me?" the guard demanded, breathing hard, his eyes wide with terror.

"Making you into a more pleasant companion," the madman crooned. "Fear not, I am granting you a great boon in return for the courage you have shown by questioning me. You are a guard, are you not? I am making you more perfect in your duties. You will be a perfect sentry, standing guard here at my threshold." He paused, then hissed, "And you will never question me again!"

"But"—the man's voice came out in a wail of strangled desperation—"but what have you done to me?"

"You are the first of my experiments here in this valley. You should be honored. It is a great honor, yes, you are the first to be chosen. Lord Uun wants an army, and an army I shall grant him. You will be my captain, my general. My very own Ar'Molon." He turned a vacant gaze on the other soldiers who stood staring at their captain in horror.

"Do any of the rest of you wish to stay and assist me?"

Without a word, the remaining soldiers turned and fled without a backward glance for their doomed captain. The madman watched them go, his lips curved into a mocking smile.

"So few are willing to commit everything, Captain. But you, you understand our cause. You know what we're up against. I thank you for volunteering."

"I can't move." The guard's eyes widened frantically. "I can't... I can't get out! I can't move!"

"You have no need of such banalities any longer," the madman snapped irritably. "You are going to be transformed. Movement will eventually be restored. Soldiers who cannot move are of no use on the battlefield. No. When we leave here, you will follow. It is a good bargain. You gain the tree's strength and ability to survive off sunshine and the soil, the tree gains your intelligence, awareness, and mobility. It will be better, you will see."

The guard made a pathetic whimpering sound that was part sob, part scream as the roots writhed up his body, now encasing him all the way up to his chin.

The madman sighed in disgust. "Now I see why Lord Uun suggested I experiment with animals; they are less bothersome and don't panic like humans do. But on the other hand, they are not so intelligent, either. And intelligence is not to be discarded so lightly. I need minds that can solve problems with creativity and cunning for my generals. The foot soldiers can be lesser beasts, perhaps, but my generals, ah, my generals shall be magnificent. This time, I shall not fail."

The guard emitted one last scream of terror that was cut off mid-wail as the madman squeezed his fist around the glowing orb in his hand and the bands of the prison thickened and drew closer together, sealing off the chrysalis and its occupant.

The madman surveyed his handiwork for a moment. Then, cocking his head to one side, he gave a tiny flick of his wrist. Vines slithered through the grass after the rustling sounds of the fleeing guards. Startled cries of terror rose up into the air as the madman held up the glowing green orb and gazed into it thoughtfully. Moments later, the vines retracted, pulling seven new wooden chrysalides into the clearing.

"My generals. The first glimmerings of my army. Sleep here for a time," Lorcan whispered softly. Then he turned and strode deeper into the hidden valley without a backward glance.

19

Wynn and Beren stood at the edge of the practice ring, watching as Grayden mopped his forehead with his sleeve and faced Arven, his latest opponent. Combat training was a grueling affair, but every student at the Academy agreed it was their favorite class. The older student eyed him warily, circling with the caution that the first- and second-year students had learned after a few rounds in the sparring ring with Grayden. A third-year, Arven had volunteered to test his mettle against the undefeated first-year, claiming that three lunats was more than long enough for such success and that it was time someone taught the pup a lesson.

"It's not too late to forfeit honorably," Arven offered, his voice carrying to those standing around the ring.

"Not a chance," Grayden retorted.

The rest of their classmates were gathered around the ring, watching with eager anticipation. Grayden's feats in the sparring ring had quickly grown legendary, as he defeated challenger after challenger. The battle master had put him up against all of his fellow initiates, and then had begun allowing him to take on students in their second year. Arven was the first third-year to be allowed in the ring with him, though, and Wynn couldn't help but feel a little nervous on behalf of his friend.

Across the ring, watching intently, stood the masters. Headmaster Freidzen was also present, having returned from the Arxis a few days ago. They stood silent, taking in everything, but betraying no emotion.

Grayden gripped his staff, his stance low. Arven had won the coin-toss and chosen the weapon he was best at. Of course, everyone in the class knew that they would be fighting with staves even if Grayden had won the choice. That was just how Grayden operated, and in the lunats since the semester started, it had become common knowledge that Grayden would always choose to spar using his opponent's weapon of choice, if he knew it. If he did not know his opponent's strength, he would ask—which had more than once resulted in a humorous match, at least in the first few sennights. One time, Grayden's opponent, thinking Grayden was attempting to trick him, had replied to the question by naming the weapon he was least skilled in. Grayden had, of course, chosen it, thinking to give his opponent an advantage. That match had quickly become Academy legend, and no one made that mistake again.

Not everyone realized why Grayden was doing this, though Wynn had figured it out right away, and he and Grayden had explained it to Beren. These tactics had helped Grayden quickly familiarize himself with every weapon in the armory.

The other result of his choice to use his opponent's favored weapon was that not one of his classmates knew which weapon Grayden preferred. A few had asked Wynn, knowing that the two of them had been friends before the Academy, but Wynn always gave a jaunty grin and a shrug and that was the end of that line of conversation. He grinned, wondering what they'd say if they knew the truth: Grayden didn't really have a preferred weapon. He had trained hard with Master Farley in many different modes of combat, even before leaving their little village of Dalsea.

Arven attacked with sudden ferocity that forced Grayden

back a few steps, and Wynn's knuckles whitened as he gripped the side-rail tightly. Grayden whirled and parried, and the dance began in earnest.

"Think he'll win?" Wynn asked.

"I do believe our friend will defend his record on the field today," Beren replied formally.

"You know, I don't think Gray even knows that he's got the top score." Wynn's tone was offhand. "He never looks at the standings."

"That is not why he is here," Beren agreed.

Wynn craned his neck to stare up at his friend. "That reminds me. Why isn't your name ever in the lists? I haven't seen you spar once since getting here. I figured you'd be at the top of all the standings. Grayden and I still talk about how you dispatched those assassins in Dalton. Like it was easy."

Beren did not look away from the ring. "Well, that is not why I am here," he replied.

Wynn frowned, wanting to press the question, but he was distracted by Arven delivering a particularly painful sounding blow to Grayden's shoulder. "Ouch!" Wynn winced in sympathy.

Grayden allowed himself to drop beneath the blow and twist away. He lunged back in and delivered his own rap to Arven's wrist, causing the other young man to momentarily lose his grip on his stave. Arven shook his hand and backed away warily, readjusting his hold on the weapon.

"I shall enjoy watching Grayden in the Trials," Beren commented.

"The what?"

"The Trials," Beren repeated. At Wynn's blank look, he grimaced. "Exams that we take at the end of each semester before moving on to the next class."

"What kind of exams?"

"Ah..." Beren hesitated. "Perhaps I should not say. My position as Headmaster Freidzen's nephew perhaps gives me an unfair advantage and foreknowledge of such things."

Wynn made a face. "Come on."

"It is a test where we must use what we have learned. We are given a scenario and must use whatever is at hand to complete the assignment. There is usually a combat section, which is the aspect of the test to which I was referring just now. You do not take your own weapons into the Trials, only using what has been provided in the scenario."

"I see." Wynn's eyes lit with amusement. "I'm guessing they omit the student's weapon of strength?"

"At least one of them, yes."

"They may have some difficulty with setting up Grayden's Trial, then."

"Words of truth." Beren's voice rumbled with laughter.

"That will be inter... ah, there we go."

Arven had fallen to his knees as Grayden's staff found its mark across the backs of Arven's wrists, rapping them sharply and causing his opponent to drop his weapon. Grayden swung the tip of his staff up under Arven's chin, stopping at the last second as they had been taught for sparring. Arven winced and rubbed his wrists, then grinned up at Grayden.

"Good match," he said, taking Grayden's offered hand and rising to his feet. He bowed slightly. "I beg forgiveness for my arrogant mouth."

Grayden gave a sudden laugh. "Granted," he said, leaning on his staff and breathing hard. "I thought you almost had me with that last move."

"As did I," Arven replied. "I can see that I will have to practice twice as hard before we have a rematch." He strode away.

Wynn thumped his friend on the back. "We all have to practice twice as hard to keep up with Grayden."

"Verily," Beren thundered.

Grayden ducked his head. "Stop it," he protested.

"It's truth we speak, my friend," Beren replied staunchly. "Your name tops the lists in the sparring ring."

Grayden smirked. "Only because I've never had to face you."

LATE THAT NIGHT in his room, Grayden stared at the words he had just written and felt a fog descend upon his brain. He was tired. The Academy seemed determined to break him into pieces, and though he had held his ground and given a good battle, he could feel himself beginning to crumble, like one of the rocky arches his father had shown him during one of their visits to Elricht Harbor. The arches were formed far out in the harbor by the waves breaking against the base of cliffs. But some of the arches had lost their structural integrity and fallen into the sea, leaving only sad pillars where once they had been things of glory.

He had been here for three and a half lunats. The last day of the semester approached with ominous speed. In just a few days, it would end, on the shortest day of the year, and with it, his first term at the Academy. All through the past sennight he had been thoroughly tested in his knowledge from every master, and he felt he could hold no more information in his brain or it would burst. With a heavy sigh, Grayden leaned forward and laid his head down on the table next to his papers. The candlelight flickered softly, mesmerizing him with its steady glow. His eyelids drooped closed. He was so tired.

A loud crashing brought Grayden to instant wakefulness. He leapt from his chair and spun around to see the door to his shared room being flung open.

"Hey, Wy..." His friend's name died on his lips.

Before him stood a tall figure, hooded and masked. Memories of the pirates surged through him and he grabbed the only weapon available to him: his chair. Heaving it up with a strangled cry, he rushed at the intruder. Brandishing the chair like a shield or a battering ram, he pushed his would-be assailant out into the hallway with a force born of desperation and fear. The intruder stumbled back, grabbing Grayden's arm and causing him to drop the chair. Grayden spun, levering himself off the chair back, and aimed a kick at the man's knee, throwing him further off balance.

Grayden followed him to the ground, pressing his knee into the assailant's sternum, his fist raised.

"Wai..."

A punch ended the attacker's shout mid-word.

"Grayden! Stop!" A voice from a bit further down the hall made Grayden pause. He looked up and saw Koen trotting toward him, a look of true alarm on his face. He looked down to see his attacker wrestling the mask off his face. Without the mask, Grayden recognized the man as one of the older students, though he could not remember his name. Grayden scrambled back, confused, as his attacker sat up and stared around a little blearily.

Koen knelt next to the other student. "You all right, Enric?"

Enric blinked a few times and then nodded. A dark circle was already spreading under his right eye.

"I'm... I'm sorry..." Grayden gasped, still unsure what was happening.

"Guess we should have known better than to try to sneak up on this one," Koen barked with a wry chuckle, thumping Enric on the shoulder and then helping him to his feet. "Or at least we should have made sure nobody tried it alone!"

"What is going on?" Grayden asked.

"I apologize for startling you, Grayden," Koen continued. "It's a tradition, that's all. Usually at the end of the first year, the oldest recruits pretend to kidnap the initiates and make them march into the woods. When we get there, we take off the masks and congratulate them on the accomplishment of lasting through the year and present them with the Academy scroll, entrusting it to their care. Then we have a bonfire and eat and share stories about what the initiates can expect from their next level classes."

"Sounds... like a pretty nice tradition," Grayden admitted. "Except for the kidnapping part."

"The initiates aren't usually quite so... aggressive," Enric said, wincing.

"Sorry about that." Grayden shrugged.

"My own fault," the other replied. "I may not have faced you in the sparring ring yet, but it's not like I didn't know you were a good fighter."

"We should have at least guessed you might be a bit jumpy after that whole mess with the pirates," Koen added.

"I know I would be," Enric said. "But Wynn and Beren didn't seem bothered, so we just didn't think. Sorry, friend."

"Beren's uncle is the headmaster; he probably already knew a little bit about the tradition. And Wynn's not much of a fighter," Grayden said.

"Didn't think of that," Enric mused. "Probably should have."

"Most of the others are on their way already," Koen said. "We decided to move the tradition up to the end of the first semester because of the new accelerated program. Most of us aren't even sure that we'll be here at the start of next term. If the war is as close to breaking as the rumors say... But the tradition is a good one, even if it is a bit early. Usually it's fun for everyone."

"You think they might call some of you up as full-fledged defenders halfway through the term?" Grayden stared at Koen, his interest piqued.

The older recruit shrugged. "Who knows what they'll do, now? But if the rumors are to be believed, that war we're training for is on our doorstep."

Grayden nodded.

"Anyway, you willing to come with us?" Koen asked. He turned and looked at Enric with a questioning glance. "You're supposed to be blindfolded, but I think you earned the right to walk out there without it."

Enric grinned and nodded his assent with a chuckle and Grayden felt his face grow warm. He nodded wordlessly and allowed the older students to lead him outside. A thin new layer of snow crunched beneath his boots. The air was crisp and his breath steamed in front of his face. Soon he could hear voices raised in amicable laughter. Just inside the woods, in one of the clearings, a large bonfire danced, its flames licking at the sky, sparks rising up to meet the stars.

"Grayden!" Wynn and Beren spotted him and ambled over, large grins on their faces and mugs of spiced ale in their hands.

Grayden felt the last of the tension fade from his shoulders. With a shake of his head he accepted an offered mug and allowed himself to be pulled inside the circle of brothers.

20

The repairs needed to the airship were minor, and so the detour in Arva only took a few days. Raisa and Oleck went into the town and bought the supplies they needed to restock their stores aboard the *Hawk*. Yefrem took his ten tavs and departed with little more than a cursory nod of farewell. Dalmir spent a little time wandering around the town. He purchased a meat stick and a few trinkets from various vendors in the tiny marketplace, using his status as a paying customer as an excuse to speak with the men and women selling their wares about their town and the state of the world in general. What he learned worried him. The war that Grayden and Wynn had spoken of in light terms along their journey seemed far closer and more tangible here on the western border of the Igyeum. The villagers spoke with grim belief that the war had already begun. Combat had not yet broken out, of course, but the war with Telmondir was a matter of common knowledge. Everyone felt the pinch of it as the Ar'Mol demanded more and more taxes and sent more and more of his troops through the countryside to commandeer leythan and malkyns for transport, as well as grain and other goods. Leather was also in short supply, and this seemed to worry the villagers the most.

Dalmir returned to the *Hawk* with a sense of unease roiling in his heart. Clearly, Uun had been wriggling out of his bonds for many years. Of course, he had only recently gained his full power, thanks to Dalmir's actions in his tower releasing the young girl trapped there. Most of his power and influence seemed to be political so far.

"What can I do against him?" Dalmir muttered to himself in self-berating frustration. "I should have paid better attention. If I had been doing my duty, Uun never would have been able to gain such power." He thought about everything he had seen since leaving his tower and cursed himself roundly. How could he have been so blind? How could he have allowed Uun to gain such a foothold in the world, the world Dalmir had sworn to protect from his machinations? "How did I miss everything?"

He thought of the enormous, abandoned train roads he had seen on the way to Dalton, appalled that he could have been so exceedingly negligent as to not notice such a construction taking place in his own yard. But then, he had been keeping a close watch on Uun's use of his own power: the threads of scarlet. He had not thought to keep watch for other colors.

"How has he managed to harness Palte's power?" Dalmir muttered to himself, perplexity taking the place of self-flagellation. "The cynders clearly hold Palte's signature, and the train roads themselves must be some of his designs; I would recognize his genius anywhere. These are not the ideas of Uun. How has he managed such a feat?"

Dalmir reached the airship and climbed aboard, lost in thought. He paused, seeing the crew congregating in the middle of the deck. Shaesta stood in the center of the group. Curious, Dalmir abandoned his wonderings and edged toward them.

"I don't think you do." There was a hard edge to Marik's voice as he replied to something Shaesta had said.

Shaesta dropped her gaze. "I know what it's like to be betrayed."

"That's just it, Shay, it's not the betrayal I actually care about," Marik growled. "Well, all right, I do care about that, but it's that you didn't trust us enough to tell us what was going on with your family, or who you were. You didn't just lie about one thing, you lied to us about everything. And you wonder why we never accepted you as fully part of the crew in the first place. I knew you were holding us at arm's length, but tattered sails, Shay! I didn't think you'd jam a sword into our backs!"

Shaesta cleared her throat. "I can see how you would think that."

Silence stretched between them. Oleck, Raisa, and Mouse stood like statues around the captain and the traitor.

"So... have you decided what to do with me, then?" Shaesta asked.

"Yes, actually. We have need of you on deck. Yefrem has disembarked and as a result we're a hand short."

Shaesta's head turned slightly, though she did not look directly at him. "Oh?"

Dalmir thought he detected a glimmer of hope in her tone.

"We're all in agreement about it. Raisa's idea, actually." He nodded at Raisa, who stood at his side with Oleck and Mouse. "Not sure I like it, but my crew wants to give you another chance... a chance to do what, I can't say exactly. But a chance. Or we can leave you here in Arva and you promise we never see you again. Those are your options."

Shaesta did look at him now, her lips parted slightly as her eyes darted to each face. "I don't know what to say."

"I'd just as soon have you out of my sight," Marik growled. "This isn't charity. But I need another set of hands and at the very least I know you're up to the task. Finding a replacement for Yefrem could prove tricky, and you're already here."

"I see." Shaesta's shoulders slumped. "So this is just a matter of convenience."

"Nothing convenient about it."

"No. No, I suppose there's not." Her voice lowered to a despairing whisper.

"Well? If you're leaving I need to know so we can find someone else."

Shaesta straightened, a slight spark returning to her eyes. She turned and took in each of the crew members standing around her, and something of iron appeared to strengthen her jaw. "Thank you, Captain." She said the words primly. "I would be glad to accept your generous offer of work."

"The job doesn't pay much."

"Money isn't the currency I'm interested in at the moment."

Marik made a disgusted sound deep in his throat. "And you'll be confined to quarters when you're not on duty."

"I understand, Captain."

"Don't expect it to be easy," Marik warned.

"I don't."

"Or even possible," Oleck muttered from where he stood off to one side. He turned his back and began to stride away. Behind him, Shaesta appeared to wilt, all the strength in her bones abandoning her. Raisa took her by the elbow and escorted her back belowdecks as Marik caught sight of Dalmir.

"Captain," Dalmir greeted him. "How are the repairs coming?"

"Almost finished," Marik replied with an easy smile. "We should be able to get back in the air in about an hour."

"Have you decided where we will go next?" Dalmir asked.

Marik nodded. "The crew has agreed to let you accompany us to one of our less-used hideouts in Palla. It's near a village where you can visit and ask whatever questions you want." Marik paused and eyed Dalmir. "Who's Palte?"

Dalmir froze. "What?"

"Back in the collapsed tunnels, you said that the refiner looked like something Palte would have built."

Dalmir mentally kicked himself. "I did."

"Who is Palte?"

"It doesn't matter," Dalmir replied.

"It might matter," Marik insisted. "I'm asking you to trust me. Just a little. Just enough to let me help you."

"It doesn't matter because Palte is dead."

Marik strode across the deck and began adjusting the tension on the sails. "You know, there's a legend about a man named Palte who founded and built the country of Palla," he said in an offhand sort of tone. "I didn't put it together at first, but that's who you meant, isn't it? You don't think he's just a legend. You think he actually lived." Marik tied off the rope and swung around to face Dalmir. "And you think he has something to do with the cynders."

Dalmir sighed. "You're right. I do."

"And that's what you want to investigate?"

Dalmir nodded wearily.

"Then we should go to Ebrim," Marik said abruptly.

"Ebrim?"

"It's the village in Palla that the first Shipwright came from," Marik explained.

Dalmir felt as though he were wading through mental quicksand. "Shipwright?"

Marik gave a tight grin. "The first man to build the airships. He came from Ebrim in Palla. Apparently he was already some sort of savant when it came to contraptions, but after the Ar'Molon hired him about eighty years ago..." Marik gestured expansively at the airship on which they stood. "Flying ships."

Dalmir's breath caught. "What about the trains?"

Marik raised an eyebrow. "Those relics? What about them?"

"Where did they come from? Who built them?"

Marik paused, his expression turning thoughtful. "Interesting. Some rumors say that 'Shipwright' is a title many have held over the years. Maybe the Ar'Molon has cultivated a few of them. You think one of them built the trains?" He paused. "But the trains first started running almost two centuries ago. That would make Lord Uun..." He stared at Dalmir as the implications sank in. "Just how old is the Ar'Molon?"

"A few years older than myself," Dalmir replied, keeping his voice light.

"And how old are you?" Marik asked, his words coming slowly from his mouth as though reluctant to ask the question.

"Now that is a rude thing to ask a man of my mature standing," Dalmir said, indicating his white hair. "I believe I see the workmen heading this way, Captain. You'd best pay them and we can be on our way. I suddenly have a powerful need to visit Ebrim. I believe I shall find that village... enlightening. But for now, I am growing tired. A man of my advanced years often finds himself in need of a nap. Wake me when we're aloft." Dalmir did his best to hide his amusement at Marik's confounded expression. He strode across the deck of the ship and swung himself down the ladder as nimbly as a child, chuckling to himself the entire way.

———

THE VILLAGE of Ebrim did not extend welcoming arms to strangers, nor did any of the other villages situated in the Temin River Valley. Every time they moved on to a new town, the villagers eyed Dalmir suspiciously and gave noncommittal grunts in reply to his queries about the Shipwright. Yes, he had originally been from Ebrim. Yes, he had designed the first airships. No, he had not been the first to bear that title, but nobody knew anything about the very first Shipwright. Even his name had been lost to history.

The towns began to blur together in Dalmir's thoughts, one endless road lined with shabby, rundown structures that looked as though a breath of wind might fell them, dirty-faced townspeople with untrusting eyes and close-lipped mouths, and the scent of sulphur. Always the reek of sulphur. Dalmir wanted to weep for what Palla had become.

"Palte," he muttered to himself. "I am glad you are not here to see this."

Doggedly, he continued to ask his questions of anyone who

would give him any hint or clue as to the nature of the Ship-wright, but the people mostly just answered him in monosyllabic grunts, pulled their tattered cloaks closer, and hurried on their way.

"The current Shipwright has been at his post for two decades," one older man in the seventh such village supplied when Dalmir bought him a drink at the tavern. "Maybe a bit more." The man scratched behind his ear thoughtfully. "Not sure."

"Do you know where he came from?"

The man took a long drink. "Nope."

"His name?"

"Nobody knows. You go to work for the Ar'Molon, word is, you leave everything behind. Even your name." The older man gave Dalmir an apologetic shrug and drained his tumbler. "My thanks." He grunted, then exited the structure.

Dalmir leaned his head into his hands and tried to figure out what to do next. He had learned much in these travels. Every-where they went in the Igyeum, they saw healthy flocks, working mills and lumber yards, and dirty, sick, and starving people. The Ar'Mol had enslaved his own people, turning them into a machine that supplied his army.

It appeared that Uun had been working behind the scenes for many years, though nobody said so outright. Dalmir was able to put together the pieces inside the tidbits of information and stories. The Igyeum had once been a constant battleground, scarred by the fighting of various tribes and warlords. But then, one warlord managed more success than his predecessors. He rose to power, conquering several tribes before he was assassinated. Then, another warlord in a different tribe also managed to amass a small kingdom before he had an unfortunate accident. One after another, these tales continued until finally the first Ar'Mol emerged on the scene, the first to unite all the factions into a single Igyeum.

He had ruled with an iron fist for forty-eight years, to be succeeded by his son, a far weaker ruler, who had only managed to stay in power for four years before a rival had risen up and defeated him. That rival had ruled for twenty-seven years before suffering a suspicious accident, leaving the scepter to his only surviving heir, a nephew named Eyvind, who now ruled as the current Ar'Mol.

Behind it all, Dalmir could imagine the shadowy presence of Uun. Always working in the dark, behind the throne. Working at the top, giving advice, plotting and planning all the strategies. Uun had picked who would be successful and who would die, careful never to use his own power, never to do anything that would alert Dalmir to the fact that he had slipped his bonds and was at work in the world once more.

And now he had his power back, and hundreds of years of work to rely on, while he, Dalmir, had been sulking in his tower. He felt overwhelmed at how much catching up he had to do. If only Shiori were here, he thought, she would know what to do, how to help. A pang of longing shot through him. With a small shake of his head, he banished the thought of her before it could fully form. Shiori would not help him. She had abandoned him long ago. Even if she were to appear, Dalmir would not want her to see him like this... so helpless and... guilt raged in his blood, heating his face with shame. He had shirked his duties. The knowledge plagued him, though he tried to ignore it and push it away. If Shiori were here now, she would shun him, and she would be right to do so. Awareness of how completely he had failed welled up within him. He had turned his back on the world and hidden in his tower. And he had done worse even than that. He should just... But no, he had no wish to return to the darkness that had engulfed him throughout those long, lonely years. Even now, the darkness threatened to pull him back down into its embrace. It whispered in his ear, reminding him of his worth-lessness.

"Any luck?" Marik's voice at his elbow made Dalmir jump in surprise.

"No," he muttered.

Marik did not reply, just waved at the bartender and received a tumbler of ale in response. The pirate took a slow sip and made a face. He turned to Dalmir. "Why does it matter so much?"

Taken aback, Dalmir frowned. "What?"

"The Shipwright. Why do you care? How does knowing more about him help you?"

"It matters because it should not be possible." Dalmir snapped the words before he thought to restrain them. He clamped his mouth shut, holding back the flood of words that came bubbling to the surface.

Marik's face betrayed no emotion at the sudden outburst. "What shouldn't be possible?"

Dalmir heaved a sigh. "The cynders."

Marik nodded slowly. "They aren't just technology that Telmondir hasn't figured out yet, are they? Whatever powers the orbs is like what you did when the *Hawk* was falling out of the sky, isn't it?"

Dalmir closed his eyes.

"I don't need to know."

Dalmir opened his eyes. "Captain..."

"No." Marik held up a hand. "I'm not even sure I want to know. Just tell me where you want me to fly."

Dalmir ran a hand across his eyes. "I'm not even sure I know the answer to that," he admitted, echoing Marik's own words. "I've learned nothing I hoped to learn."

"I tried to warn you," Marik said.

"I know. I just hoped you were exaggerating." Dalmir's shoulders slumped. "I had no idea things had gotten so bad." Fear filled the air with a palpable throbbing. It lined every face. It weighted down shoulders. The fear these people bore seemed beyond measure. It had beaten them down so far that they no longer noticed the constant companion it had become. They no longer fought it. Hopelessness and despair had won in this part of the world. Dalmir recognized it all, for he had battled the same for so many years. Perhaps it was time to trust someone again.

"There were seven of us." Dalmir's voice sounded empty and hollow to his own ears.

"Huh?" Marik gave him a sidelong glance.

"We were seven brothers. Edoran, the twins Telsume and Mulemo, Uun, Palte, Avaleun, and I." Dalmir found his voice gaining strength as he gathered up his courage to tell the story at last. Perhaps it was unwise to trust a pirate like Marik with the tale, but he had been alone for so long, his past eating away at him from the inside. "Seven brothers. Seven princes of a small nation beset on all sides by stronger kingdoms bent on conquering us and taking our land. Our father sent us to the great Library. This was many years ago, so long ago that the Library has sunk into the shadows of the past and been completely forgotten by all but two, myself and Uun. It was there that Emri granted us a great gift, or perhaps it was as Uun believed, a curse. Emri gave us knowledge and power and immortality."

"Emri?" Marik asked.

"The Builder," Dalmir replied.

"The one the Maleians believe in?" Marik asked.

Dalmir felt his eyes widen in surprise. "Perhaps," he murmured. "So something of our efforts survived..." He shook himself and returned to the story. "In those days, men called us grammaryans and came to us for our advice and aid. We each had our own interests, and as more and more people looked to us for leadership, we eventually divided up Turrim into seven parts, each of us taking responsibility for our own section. Across the years, we built things that we hoped would benefit the people of the world."

"What sorts of things did you build?" Marik asked, taking another sip from his mug.

"You've seen the city of Dalton."

"Yes."

"I built the tower upon which all of Dalton now rests."

Marik's eyes widened slightly and he let out a long whistle. "That was a tower? Truly? I thought it was just a mountain."

"No, it is a tower, with halls and rooms inside enough for the entire population of the city to live comfortably within. They have only discovered the room in the very top turret, of course; they are using it as a hangar for their airships; but the entire construction was my doing. It is really quite nice inside, though I am sure it is rather dusty by now."

Marik made an impressed noise. "Quite an undertaking. How long did you have to work on its construction?"

Dalmir shrugged modestly. "The better part of a day, give or take."

Marik's face paled visibly. There was a long pause, and then he cleared his throat with obvious effort. "The Crystal Domes of Adamal?" he asked slowly.

Dalmir's eyes softened. "The work of my brother, Avaleun. He loved all things beautiful and growing. You have seen them?"

"They are the jewel of Vallei, though nobody knows where they came from or who is responsible for their construction. We're not even sure how they were created."

"Ah. Well, Avaleun took a bit more time with his projects." Dalmir's face took on a knowing expression, but he said no more.

The weight of expectation hung between them, heavy as a full-laden warrior's pack. Marik's voice, soft as a whisper, broke the silence like a trumpet call. "So, what happened to them?"

Dalmir heaved a great sigh and his eyes grew sad. "Betrayal." His voice was dark and soft. "Uun was always pushing the limits, trying to come up with ever more impressive feats that he could perform. He convinced us that he had discovered a way to restore..." Dalmir's expression grew guarded and his eyes shadowed.

Marik raised his eyebrows. "A way to restore what?"

Dalmir scowled. "That is a long story, and not relevant. Suffice to say that he convinced us to combine our power. He was our brother, you have to understand; not one of us would have believed him capable of..." Dalmir sagged in his chair, feeling every day of his long life pressing down upon him. "He turned our power against us." The words whispered from his lips. "He murdered them all."

"How did you survive?"

"I never actually figured that out." Dalmir shook his head, as though reliving the moment of betrayal and disbelief. "I don't know how he managed to use our power against us in the first place. It should not have been possible. I don't know how I managed to pull away before he finished his strike. All I know is that I felt something was wrong, horribly wrong, and I... flinched. I pulled back. Perhaps I was not as trusting of Uun as I thought, after all. I remember the sensation of falling, all turning to blackness; when I once again was master of my senses I saw that my brothers were dead and that Uun and I were all that remained."

Memory, unbidden, unwanted, swept through Dalmir's mind, flooding his thoughts, pulling him back into the horror of that moment, that single moment he had tried to forget, but never could.

———

"WHAT HAVE YOU DONE?" Dalmir demanded, his mind reeling with horror. His brothers! What had happened? They lay, fallen from where they had been standing as they joined their power. He faced Uun across the circle, and stared into his brother's eyes. They were filled with cruelty; how had he never noticed that before? And they were devoid of emotion. There was no concern in his face for their fallen brothers, only hatred and pride as he gazed around impassively.

As Dalmir's words reached his ears Uun whirled to stare at him, his eyes wide with surprise. "How?"

"What have you done?" Dalmir's repeated question rose into an agonized scream.

"I did what had to be done." Uun had recovered from his surprise. "You all saw it as a gift," he sneered. "A gift and a mission.

I ever saw it only for what it truly was: a curse and an undeserved punishment."

"Uun... our brothers... how could you?" Sorrow—such sorrow—churned within the very depths of Dalmir's soul. His thoughts recoiled from the scene before him. Uun couldn't have done this! How could he be capable of such hatred, such evil?

"I had to! I want my life back! I'm done with our mission. I am sick and tired of catering to these pathetic humans. They are beneath us. I was meant to rule, and now I shall!" Uun's voice turned into an angry snarl. Without warning, he leapt at Dalmir.

Dalmir held up his orb in a reflexive motion of defense. The orb blazed with light, arcing to each of the other orbs that lay on the floor where they had fallen from his brothers' lifeless hands. Uun screamed in pain and terror as the light caught him.

Dalmir had no idea what happened next, and no idea how or why the orbs had connected, but he knew instinctively that this was the only chance he would ever get to stop Uun. Focusing his will, he poured every bit of power he could muster into the light, directing it, focusing on what he wanted. Uun screamed in rage again and again. He raised his arms and clawed at the air around him, but the light had become as solid as iron bars, creating a prison. It was the most difficult undertaking Dalmir had ever attempted, but at long last it was finished. The light faded and he slumped to the ground, but the prison remained, invisible but unbreakable. Long chains snaked out of the wall and solid manacles that looked like they were made of black iron wrapped themselves around Uun's wrists. Uun would remain trapped in this room, at the top of his tower. The prison would sustain him, but it would also contain him. Wearily, Dalmir stood and retrieved his brothers' orbs, one by one. Each one glimmered softly with an inner light.

When he had finished, Dalmir spared one last glance at his brother. The prison kept even the sound of Uun's voice contained, but Dalmir could tell that his brother was roaring and bellowing in rage as he paced the tiny confines of his cell. Dalmir's jaw tightened as he dropped his gaze to the forms of his fallen brothers and his eyes welled with tears.

"Forgive me, my brothers," he whispered to the nearly empty room. "Forgive me for my part in this curse." He glanced one last time at Uun, then turned and strode out of the tower.

———

"Dalmir?" Marik's voice cut through the memory, pulling Dalmir back to the present.

"Forgive me." Dalmir shook himself and took a deep breath. He rubbed a hand across his face and rose from his seat. He suddenly knew exactly what he had to do next.

"Are you well?"

"Yes. Yes, I am. Come along."

Marik drained his drink and set it on the bar. He stood. "Do you mind if I ask where we are going now?"

"We must return to the Academy."

"The..." Marik pressed his lips into a hard line, his face growing dark with a mixture of frustration and anger. "May I ask why?"

"The cynders were not made by Uun's magic. They were made by Palte's."

"And that means what?"

"That my brother has learned how to use an orb and a power that does not belong to him... that, or someone else has." Dalmir spoke the words with dark intensity.

Marik gritted his teeth. "And the reason we have to return to the Academy is...?"

"The young man, Grayden," Dalmir replied. "When I first met him, he somehow managed to activate my orb. That should not be possible. It has never been possible before. But I believe he holds the key to understanding how Uun managed to work in secret for so long without alerting me. Clearly, he has been limiting the use of his own power, and has discovered a way to harness the power of our brothers' orbs. I must figure out how he is doing it and defeat him before he grows too powerful to stop."

Marik growled deep in his throat. "I don't relish the idea of putting myself and my crew in the middle of a camp of defenders again. The headmaster was none too subtle about ordering us off the Academy premises, and he made it clear we weren't welcome to return."

"I am welcome," Dalmir replied. "I will personally guarantee the safety of you and your crew. But I must warn you, Captain, that I intend to do more than this. I must also find a way to address the Council of Telmondir. If that is asking too much, then we can part ways in Ondoura and I will find other means of transportation."

Marik's face paled at this declaration, but after a long, thoughtful moment, he straightened his shoulders. "Into the leythan's mouth we go, then."

21

Nervous tension and a bit of worry tangled together in the pit of Grayden's stomach as he jogged across the training grounds to the East Gate where he had been ordered to report just a few moments earlier. The order had come straight from the headmaster himself with no explanation, just instructions to grab his empty pack and one weapon of choice and make his way to the specified location where he would receive additional instructions. It was not uncommon for a recruit to receive a summons like this, but usually it meant some sort of disciplinary action. Grayden could not think of any rule he had broken recently. What made it all the more strange was that the summons had arrived just after the mid-day meal, which would make him late for his Military Strategies class.

He jogged across the fields, his pack feeling strange and loose on his back, flapping uselessly with nothing in it. His feet left imprints in the dusting of snow, about as much snow as this area ever experienced, his fellow students had assured him. The fog of his breath blew out around his face, steaming in the crisp air. The comforting presence of his dagger, strapped firmly to his upper arm, reminded him of home. A tiny amount of anger chewed its way around his anxiety and worry as he made his way toward the appointed destination. It had been a long day of classes and training. His instructors had pushed him harder than usual and he was tired. To top it all off, Grayden did not like being caught off-guard.

The older recruit who had handed him the message had also imparted a meaningful look that Grayden could not decipher. In any case, he was getting tired of being treated differently. He saw it often in the eyes of the older recruits who stopped what they were doing to watch him spar. It was in the calculating gazes of his instructors whenever he performed a task they set before him. It was in the whispered conversations that fell silent when he approached. He could not figure out why he was being singled out for such treatment. Unlike Wynn, his marks in most of his classes were fairly average and he worried that his performance was not meeting expectations. But then there were the lists and his name, still near the top. Even though he was no longer undefeated in the ring, he still managed to hold his own against most of his opponents, even the ones several years older than himself.

He enjoyed the sparring matches and the weaponry lessons, but his favorite part of being at the Academy were his flight and navigation classes. Being up in an airship still sent a thrill through him every time he took the wheel and lifted off from the ground.

As he approached the East Gate, his questions and worries subsided. Waiting for him was a group of half a dozen figures. As he drew nearer, he recognized them. Wynn and Beren were there, as well as Koen. The fourth figure was a second-year Grayden knew by sight, though he could not recall his name. The fifth he recognized as Enric, and gave him a cheerful nod. And the final figure was none other than Arven. The others all nodded their acknowledgment of Grayden's arrival.

"What's going on?" he asked as he jogged up to join them.

Beren nodded at Koen. "He would not tell us until you arrived."

They all turned questioning eyes on Koen.

"You six have been excelling beyond expectations in your classes and training," Koen explained.

The young men exchanged questioning looks.

"What does that mean?" Grayden asked.

"You are, of course, aware that many of the students at the Academy are being placed in accelerated programs this year," Koen stated.

They all nodded. The older students had suspected something in the first few sennights, but it had become common knowledge after Headmaster Freidzen returned from the Council meeting at the Arxis.

"The Igyeum has been preparing for war. We have been preparing for this for many years, but now the first advances have been made. Because of this, we need defenders more than ever before."

The young men looked at each other, and Grayden saw his own confusion reflected in their faces.

"What are you saying?" Grayden asked.

"I am saying that as candidates for even further acceleration through the program, you are all being tested. Do not worry about your classes, you have all been excused from your regular work for the rest of the sennight," Koen explained. "It is the opinion of Headmaster Freidzen, with unanimous support from your instructors, that you are indeed up to the challenge." Koen smiled tightly. "Congratulations." The older student pulled back a piece of canvas that had been resting on the ground next to him. Beneath it lay an assortment of food, canteens, blankets, and various other items. "The next stage of your training begins with a survival exercise that will help prepare you for future training. You will each fill your pack with the items I have assembled here. You have five minutes."

"What kind of future training?" Beren asked.

"Less than five minutes," Koen replied as he studied some notes.

There was an uncomfortable silence as the young men eyed

one another. Grayden nodded at the recruit whose name he could not remember.

"I'm Grayden."

"Zarek," the other replied shortly. "I know who you are."

Grayden was not sure how to interpret Zarek's expression. He busied himself sifting through the items that had been laid out. There were canteens of water, ropes, flint and steel, blankets, and other essentials. When everything had been transferred into their packs, Koen returned.

"Well done," he announced, after inspecting their gear. "Now, as the oldest among you, Enric will be the leader of this expedition." He handed Enric a large rolled-up piece of leather. "This is your guide. The six of you will navigate to the first location on the map. You will find your way to each subsequent location and retrieve the item that has been left there. When you have collected all ten items, you will make your way back here. If you complete the mission within six days, you will have succeeded. Any questions?"

"Does today count as day one?" Zarek asked.

"Yes," Koen replied.

"But the day is already half over!" Zarek argued.

Koen stared at him. "Any other questions?"

Zarek's expression was still hard to decipher, some mixture of eager, bored, and sullen. He glanced up and met Grayden's gaze and his expression hardened into one of angry hostility. Grayden looked away, confused and wondering what he had done to earn the other man's dislike. Enric and Arven, on the other hand, looked excited and determined. They grinned eagerly and shouldered their packs with enthusiasm.

Koen clapped his hands together. "The headmaster instructed me to give you a bit of advice."

They looked at him expectantly.

"Don't get lost. Don't get separated. Don't die." He turned and strode away.

"Not the most inspirational speech I've ever heard," Wynn muttered.

Zarek cracked a slight smile at that, but then rolled his eyes and lifted his pack. "Well, fearless leader?" He directed his words at Enric, a slight hint of mockery in his tone. "Where are we headed first?"

Enric studied the map and the clues for a long moment. "Looks like our first location is on the other side of the forest." He peered up at the darkening sky. "It's staying light out longer, now that we've passed the last day of Darkthen, but it's still going to be full dark before we reach the site."

Grayden blew into his fingers to warm them. "What say we get inside the forest and set up camp before we lose all the light, then we can start at first light tomorrow."

"What, are you scared of a little dark?" Zarek sneered.

"No," Grayden replied, confused by the other's derision. "But I don't want to spend hours searching in the dark for something that might be found quicker and more easily by morning light."

"That's a good point," Arven said. "I vote we go with Grayden's plan."

Wynn and Beren nodded. Zarek scowled and crossed his arms over his chest.

"Right." Enric folded up the map and then pointed east. "That way."

The trees cast long shadows across the forest floor by the time that Grayden and his companions had their camp set up in a suitable clearing. Wynn knelt by the pile of sticks they had gathered and struck his flint against his dagger, scattering a shower of sparks over the kindling that he gently coaxed to life. The ground here bore no layer of snow, protected as it was by the canopy of branches, but the wind whistled through the trees with a chill hiss that nearly blew out the fledgling fire.

"Darkened cynders!" Zarek shouted, leaping to shield the flames with his body. "You left a corridor wide open! Do you want to spend the entire night getting the fire going? You have to keep your body between the wind and the fire or you'll never get anywhere." He wrenched the flint and dagger from Wynn's astonished hands and set to the task with a will.

Acting purely on instinct, Grayden yanked Zarek back by the collar and had him shoved up against a tree before he could even think about what he planned to do. "What is your problem?" he demanded of the older student.

Dimly, he heard someone shouting at him, but the blood pounded angrily in his ears and he could not make out the words.

"Best let me down like Enric says." Zarek smiled smugly at him, then shifted his eyes down. Grayden followed his gaze and saw the dagger's point leveled at his own stomach. Cold fury washed through him.

"You wouldn't dare," he whispered.

Zarek's eyes turned hard. "I'll defend myself. Nobody would say I was out of line."

Slowly, Grayden released the handful of Zarek's collar and stepped back. A heartbeat later, Enric stood between them, thrusting Grayden farther away and glaring at them both.

"We're supposed to be working together," Enric growled. "I don't know what the problem is here, but get over it. Now! There's no room in the defenders for personal feuds. And no room for it at the Academy, either. That doesn't mean you have to be friends, but it does mean that you work together and get along. That kind of behavior will get you expelled quicker than blinking."

Zarek opened his eyes wide. "He just went crazy."

Enric pinned him with a hard stare. "He was defending his brother. I saw the whole thing."

"They're not brothers," Zarek muttered in a sulky tone.

"Yes, they are," Enric insisted. Grayden opened his mouth to set the older student straight, but Enric stopped him with an abrupt motion of his hand. "And they are your brothers, too, Zarek. We are all brothers. All of us. We all get here for different reasons, but at the end of the day, we're here to defend Telmondir.

When you stand beside someone and face the enemy together, you become brothers. When you train together to defend our nations, you become brothers. The second you stepped across the Academy threshold, you became a part of this family. Don't either of you forget it again."

Enric stepped back. "Now. It seems you've both volunteered for the middle watch. We, your brothers, thank you for your sacrifice."

Grayden and Zarek both groaned at this.

"Zarek, give the flint and dagger back to Wynn, and then go help Arven set up the shelter. Grayden, you and Beren go get some more firewood. It's going to be cold tonight, and we are going to want a good supply. Wynn and I will get supper going."

Zarek shot Grayden a murderous look and then stomped across the clearing, tossing the flint and dagger to the ground next to Wynn. Grayden strode over to join Beren on the outskirts of their little campsite, and together the two of them plunged into the darkening woods. They foraged for dry, fallen branches, each gathering a great armful. As the daylight waned, Grayden found himself unable to keep his thoughts from swirling around Zarek and his difficult attitude.

"What is his problem?" Grayden asked, stepping on a large branch and snapping it with more force than completely necessary.

"Zarek?" Beren asked. He shrugged. "Some cadets are like that."

"No, they're not," Grayden retorted. "I haven't met anyone at the Academy as interested in picking a fight as Zarek, and I only just met him today. Why does he have such an issue with Wynn?"

Beren broke off another stick and added it to his bundle. "I don't think it's Wynn he has the problem with."

"What do you mean?" Grayden demanded, tugging at a branch that refused to come up. "You saw the way he treated him, picking on him for one little mistake with the fire." Grayden frowned at the branch and pulled harder.

"He has a short temper," Beren admitted. "But I think it's you he dislikes."

"What? Why?" Grayden set down his bundle of sticks and took the branch in both hands, bracing himself and giving a mighty tug.

"I'm not sure," Beren said. "But he's been glaring at the back of your head all day."

The stick began to come up from the ground, but the more Grayden pulled, the longer it seemed to get. He gritted his teeth and pulled even harder. "Well. Whatever it is. He's just... going... to have to... stop!" Perspiration dripped down his forehead and dirt erupted from the forest floor in a long, snaking line, but the branch still refused to come free.

"Grayden?" Beren's voice rumbled with laughter.

"What?"

"That's a root."

Grayden stared down at the long, trailing branch he had been wrestling with and laughter bubbled up within him. Pulling out his dagger, he sliced the root into manageable segments and added it to his already large bundle of firewood. "I knew that." Chuckling at his own foolishness, he peered at Beren through the gloom of twilight. "Think we've got enough here?"

"Just about," Beren agreed. "We should head back."

They returned to the campsite to find a warm fire going and a sheltering canvas strung up in the trees above their blankets. Enric had a pot of stew hanging over the fire and bubbling merrily. The others sat around the fire already eating, Zarek noticeably separated from the others by a large space. Grayden grimaced. He took his bundle of sticks and carefully laid them down to one side of the fire, then he grabbed one of the tin bowls and ladled himself some dinner. He took a seat near Zarek.

The older student scowled darkly at him, but said nothing. Grayden took a spoonful of stew and blew on it for a minute before tasting it. A savory mixture of salted beef, potatoes, and beans greeted his taste buds.

"Nice job on the stew," Grayden called out across the fire to Enric.

"Could use some salt," Zarek grumbled.

Grayden turned to Zarek. "Did I do something to offend you?" he asked in a low voice.

Zarek eyed him. "No," he said shortly, scraping up the last bits of his stew.

"Then..." Grayden began, but Zarek abruptly got to his feet.

"I'm turning in. Wake me for the middle watch." The older student tossed his bowl and spoon to one side and stomped off to the shelter.

Grayden heaved a sigh and wondered if the whole sennight would be like this. He should turn in, as well. The middle watch meant the most broken sleep, but he had no interest in following Zarek at the moment. "I'll take the dishes down to the stream and wash them when everyone's done," he volunteered.

———

IT FELT as though he had just closed his eyes when Grayden felt himself being shaken awake. He blinked groggily in the darkness and it took him a minute to remember where he was. Awareness flooded through him and he grew more alert, nodding to Enric, who had wakened him. Grayden slipped his feet into his boots then grabbed his cloak and wrapped it tightly about his shoulders before crawling out from under the sheltering canvas and into the blackness of the night.

Zarek emerged a minute later, stomping his feet and rubbing at his eyes. Grayden tossed a few more sticks on the fire and stood near the warmth of the flames, coaxing his mind to alertness. Zarek joined him at the fire without a word, holding his hands out to the flames. Their breath fogged in the chill night air, and the leaves crackled with frost beneath their feet.

"We should make a few rounds about the perimeter,"

Grayden offered cautiously, making his voice as calm and emotionless as possible.

Zarek nodded. "I'll go first." He rubbed his hands together and then set off into the darkness without another word. Grayden watched him go, wondering what he had done to so irritate the other student. He pulled his dagger from its sheath and practiced twirling it about his fingers, enjoying the way it caught and reflected the firelight. He kept an ear attentive to the sounds of Zarek stomping around the camp.

The crackling of the fire and the dancing flames grew mesmerizing and Grayden pulled his attention away, turning his back to the fire and facing out into the looming trees. Something gentle and cold whispered a caress about his face and he realized that it had begun snowing. He stamped his feet and swung his arms, more to stay awake than to stave off the cold. The fire held plenty of warmth, and the air did not bite through his cloak nearly as hard as it did back home. He shuddered, his body yearning for sleep. Then, suddenly, a tingling sensation crept along the back of his neck and Grayden realized that he could no longer hear Zarek's footsteps. He stood still, straining his ears, but he heard no crunch of leaves, no snapping of twigs.

"Zarek?" he hissed through his teeth, hoping that the other student was simply playing a trick. He didn't want to call out louder, so as not to wake their sleeping companions.

A sound came to his ears that he could not quite identify. A hissing of breath, perhaps? A muffled cry? He determined the direction from which it had emanated and suddenly he was running, swift and silent, toward the sound.

He was not sure how far he had run when he saw a silhouette ahead.

"Zarek?" he called in a low voice.

The figure made a frantic signal with its arms and Grayden froze in his tracks. He strained his eyes, trying to see whatever it was that had caused his companion to warn him away. A loud snarl drew his eyes up into the trees. Framed by the moonlight, he could just make out a large shape up in the dark branches. A grymstalker! Grayden eyed the creature. The feral cousin to the great malkyns used as mounts in the east, this creature held the title of largest land predator in the west. He and his father had hunted a few of them back home. Grymstalkers were often a problem in areas where livestock were tended, and could pose a threat to human children, as well. The men of Dalsea often had to battle the enormous cats and kill them or drive them back into the mountains to protect the village. The creature snarled again, a challenge this time, its voice echoing through the frigid air.

Grayden fingered his dagger, wondering if he had a clear enough path to the animal for a throw. The heart of a grymstalker was a small target, but he had no doubts about his ability to hit it, if he could get a clear line. But it still wouldn't guarantee a kill. With only a knife, it would be better if he could get closer. Better still would be a spear, or a crossbow. There was a crossbow back in the camp, but Grayden could not be sure of making it there and back before the grymstalker struck. Why hadn't he thought to pick it up? He glanced at Zarek, wondering why the older student remained where he was; why hadn't he fled? Grayden edged a step closer to Zarek, but the older cadet was still making motions to warn him away.

The cat snarled again, and Grayden froze. No matter how many times he heard it, that eerie scream would never fail to turn his blood to ice. Had the grymstalker seen or scented him? He couldn't be sure. His position was far too exposed, but the few steps he had taken had given him a better line of sight to the animal. His heart pounded in his ears as he readied his dagger and gauged the distance for the throw.

The dagger gleamed faintly in the moonlight. He hefted it, taking a few slow, deep breaths to relax his body. Unconsciously, he shifted into the correct position, his muscles and body responding to the countless hours of practice. Grayden grimaced and hesitated. A miss—extremely likely in this lighting and at this angle and distance—would be fatal, though not for his intended target. It would also leave him without a weapon.

Click.

THADUNK!

The grymstalker screamed—an angry sound rife with pain—then leaped straight into the air, twisting once, before falling to the ground, crashing limply through the branches on the way down.

Grayden turned to see Enric standing behind him, lowering the crossbow he had just fired. He could not quite make out the other's face in the darkness.

"Thanks," he breathed.

Enric shrugged.

"Can someone give me a hand?" Zarek's voice rose across the darkness and Grayden and Enric hurried over to him.

When they reached him, Grayden discovered why Zarek had not moved from his spot. Upon seeing the grymstalker, Zarek had backed into a mass of nightvine and gotten himself tangled in the thorny branches. He now stood scowling as Grayden and Enric gingerly used their daggers to free him. Several of the thorns had pricked him about the neck and face, and a few more were embedded deeply in his shoulders and arms.

"Come on, come on," Zarek growled at them.

"Almost done," Enric said, his voice calm. "We'll have to get you back to the fire before we try to extract the deep ones. I want to make sure we've got clean water and some of that ointment on hand."

"Are the thorns poisonous?" Zarek asked, his voice sounding strained.

"Not exactly," Grayden replied, cutting away the last of the vines. "The sap inside the vines is, though, which is why we're being so careful getting them off you. You'll be uncomfortable for a few days, and we'll have to keep an eye out to make sure none of these punctures gets infected."

Zarek remained tense, staring off into the darkness as Grayden and Enric finished.

"You're free," Enric said.

Zarek took a few deep breaths before moving, his wince of pain visible even in the dim light of the moon.

Together, they returned to the fire, which glowed red and black. With the firewood they had gathered, Grayden got it going again until the flames shed enough light for them to treat the rest of Zarek's wounds.

"Get some rest," Enric directed after they washed the last puncture.

"What about the rest of our watch?" Zarek asked.

"The rest of us can split it," Enric replied. "You've been through enough."

It spoke to Zarek's weariness that he didn't argue, just crawled into his bedroll.

"I'm glad you showed up when you did," Grayden said. "How did you know to come after us?"

"That grymstalker's shriek would have woken the dead." Enric shrugged. "I just followed the sound."

"But how did you know we were in trouble?" Grayden pressed.

"I didn't. But I knew the stalker was too close to our camp for comfort. And when I saw the crossbow still sitting by the fire, I realized that someone could be in danger."

"Well, thanks. I'm not sure my dagger would have done any good."

Enric's teeth flashed white in the firelight. "I would have liked to see you make that throw."

The adrenaline pumping through his body had worn itself out and Grayden suddenly felt as though his entire body was made of stone. He bade Enric a good night and crawled into his blankets where he promptly fell into a deep sleep and didn't wake until morning.

22

Grayden awoke to find the roof of their shelter caved in by the weight of several inches of snow. He crawled out and grinned at the sight of Wynn stamping his feet and looking miserable. Enric, Arven, and Zarek stood huddled around the fire, their cloaks and coats pulled tightly around their shoulders. Beren was nowhere to be seen.

"Morning!" Grayden greeted the others. They grunted at him. He grinned and began brushing the snow away from the shelter, pulling the canvas up and folding the stiff fabric as best he could. "It helps if you get moving," he called to the others. "Wynn, you know better than to stand around, you'll never get warm that way."

Wynn made a face at him, but resumed stomping in place before joining the others in their efforts to pack up their gear.

Before Grayden could ask about their companion, Beren returned, a boar slung over his shoulder. The others brightened at the offering and erupted into motion as they helped the hunter carve up the meat and begin preparing breakfast.

After breakfast, the mood of the camp improved enough to begin considering the map and their first destination.

"This snow won't make it any easier," Zarek muttered.

"This is Ondoura," Enric replied, "by midday it will all have melted."

The air had already grown warmer, giving strength to Enric's words. They put out their fire, shouldered their packs, and began trudging through the wet snow. By the time they reached the edge of the forest, the terrain had turned more to a muddy slush than snow, and their boots squelched in puddles of muck.

"Fan out," Enric directed. "We should be close, but the map doesn't give any clue as to what we're looking for."

After a few minutes of searching, Grayden noticed something sticking out from beneath a fallen log. He drew closer, squinting. Suddenly, Zarek darted in front of him and snatched up the object.

"Found it!" The older cadet held up a small, oiled canvas bag covered in a layer of frost and mud.

"Good work, Zarek," Enric praised, taking the bag and opening it. He pulled out another map and a black stone.

Grayden gritted his teeth, but gave Zarek a nod. He figured it didn't matter who found the items first. This was a team exercise, after all. Nonetheless, he was determined not to let Zarek get the best of him like that again. "Where to next?" he asked.

Enric studied the map. "Looks like we need to find the river. The next location is here at this bend south of the Academy." He pulled out his compass and held it to the map, getting the correct orientation. "That way."

Shouldering their packs, they set their faces south-east and began the next leg of their trek.

It took them several hours to reach the river. They filled their canteens and Arven spotted some fish, but Enric argued against taking the time to hunt. "We have our rations," he insisted. "And we only have four and a half days left to find all nine locations and make it back."

They dug into their rations as they followed the river south, searching for the bend indicated on the map. When they found it, their hearts sank. Here the river widened and their prize sat floating in the middle of the bend in a tiny boat tethered in place. The water was ice-cold and moving fast.

Beren searched around until he found a sturdy stick about as tall as himself. He poked it into the water. The branch plunged down all the way to his fingers and he pulled it back up, shaking his head. "Too deep to wade," he said. "And swimming is definitely out of the question. We might last ten seconds before the cold overpowers us, and rescue would be impossible."

"If we made a hook of some sort, perhaps we could pull the boat toward us," Wynn suggested.

"Or we could build a raft," Zarek said.

"A raft would take too long and is more dangerous," Enric said. "We'll try Wynn's hook idea first."

Zarek pressed his lips together into a straight line, but did not argue.

They scoured the side of the riverbank for long sticks, and Grayden even found one that had a good curve to it. Lashing the branches together with a spool of twine Wynn had stuffed into his pack, they carefully extended the makeshift hook out over the rushing water.

It took several tries, but eventually they managed to hook the curved branch around the little boat. However, here they ran into a new problem. Their hook was not strong enough to pull the boat free of its tether.

"How did they even get it out there in the first place?" Grayden wondered.

"I still think we should make a raft," Zarek growled.

"Instead of trying to pull the craft all the way in to shore, perhaps we could hook just the bag?" Beren suggested, ignoring Zarek.

Enric shook his head. "I don't want to risk dropping it in the water and losing it."

"That risk might be our only option," Arven said.

"If we drop the bag and it floats away, we fail the mission automatically," Enric argued.

"This isn't going to work," Zarek muttered.

Grayden picked up the branch. "Let's try again," he said.

Zarek whirled on him, snatching the branch from his hands and catching him by surprise. Grayden let go of the hook, but the motion unbalanced him and he could feel himself losing his balance. He teetered on the edge of the bank for a moment, then plunged forward, his arms flailing before him. The icy shock of the water struck him as his arms sank beneath the surface, followed by his head and shoulders. His breath bubbled out of his mouth in a gasp as the frigid water numbed his skin instantly, shocking the air from his lungs. Distantly, he felt hands grabbing at him, and a moment later he lay on the bank, gasping for air and shivering. Shouts reached his ears, but he couldn't spare the energy to identify their meaning.

Rough hands dragged him into a sitting position. There was a ripping sound and he felt his shirt being torn from him; he heard more than felt the wet sleeves slapping against his skin as someone peeled the wet fabric off his body. Then a blanket wrapped around him, and another. Inside the blanket, his arms were drawn against his torso, causing him to wince at the coldness of his own skin. Nearby, someone coaxed a fire to life. Something rough rubbed fiercely at his head; it hurt, but he couldn't muster the energy to move away. Flames flickered to life nearby and his teeth chattered. Warmth seeped into him once more, and with the warmth came pain. He groaned and shivered convulsively.

"Grayden?"

He looked up, comprehension returning slowly.

"Grayden, try to relax." Enric's voice drifted to his ears. "I don't think he's in any danger now, but we need to keep him warm for a while."

Beren stepped nearer, relief and a twinkle in his eye. "I told you swimming was out of the question."

Grayden coughed. "Well, now we believe you."

Everyone laughed.

Gradually, the shivering eased, replaced by warmth from the

blanket and the fire. Grayden's thoughts grew clearer until he finally felt up to asking a question.

"What about the next map?"

Five sets of eyes stared at him.

"The map. We still need to get it." He repeated himself in case they hadn't heard him the first time.

"We were a little preoccupied trying to keep you from freezing to death," Wynn said. "You all right?"

"A little tired, but not so cold anymore," Grayden replied. "I have a dry shirt in my pack."

Enric handed him his pack and Grayden dug through it for his other shirt. His cloak was still damp, so he kept the blankets wrapped about him. He grimaced at the state of the shirt he had gone into the river with: still sopping wet, the back had been sliced open by a knife in his friends' haste to get him out of it. He fingered the fabric, ruing its destruction. He didn't have many clothes to spare.

"It can be stitched back together," Beren reassured him, seeing his grimace. "You'll barely notice."

He nodded, trying to remain positive. As he did so, Grayden caught Zarek's eye. The other man scowled and averted his gaze instantly, but not before Grayden saw the flash of regret.

"Zarek," he called out.

Zarek looked up, his expression wary.

"You mentioned building a raft."

Zarek peered at him questioningly, but gave a slow nod.

"Well, I suppose that now is a good time to give that a try. What do you need?"

Zarek offered detailed instructions. The raft came together quickly under Zarek's watchful eye. They built it a ways upstream from their intended target so that they could use the current to their advantage instead of fighting it the whole way. The raft was small, but sturdy, and when they set it in the water, it bobbed lightly as though eager to get going.

"Here." Grayden held out a crude paddle he had whittled. "Think it'll bear weight?"

Zarek nodded confidently. "It should. But I won't ask anyone else to take the risk," he said. "It's my idea, so I should be the one to take the ducking if it doesn't work."

Grayden shivered, his bones still retaining the chill from his own brief encounter with the icy water. He understood the other man's bravado, but he also knew from experience that going into the river was no joke. "Someone should keep the fire going. And we should tie a rope to Zarek, just in case."

The others agreed, and it was several minutes before Zarek was able to take up the paddle. He crawled out onto the raft carefully, spreading his weight across it. The platform wobbled, but not even a drop of water splashed up over the surface.

On his knees, Zarek paddled his way out to the middle of the river. Grayden and the others watched him as he steered the little craft out to the waiting prize, the rope tied around his waist played out from Beren's hands, while the others stood by, ready to help pull Zarek back if need be. He made it to the little boat and lifted another oiled canvas bag up and held it high for them to see. Then, he turned and began paddling back to shore, the current sweeping him farther downriver with every stroke. The raft sped up, and Zarek's face betrayed his exhaustion, though not any fear. Grim determination furrowed his brow.

Beren strained with the rope, and the others joined him, but they could not counter the might of the river, and they did not wish to pull Zarek off the raft and into the water.

"He's not going to make it before the rapids," Wynn shouted. "Hold him, Beren!" He snatched up the long pole and began racing down the riverbank.

Grayden followed, running as fast as he could to try to get ahead of the raft. Stumbling and slipping on the icy shore, they watched as the raft spun around. Zarek's tanned face bobbed out of sight for a moment behind a rock and then reappeared. He had lost his oar, and they could see him sprawled out on hands and knees, clinging to the raft and trying to spread his weight out evenly so it wouldn't tip him off.

Grayden pushed himself even faster, his legs pumping and his chest heaving as he kept pace with Wynn. "Here!" he gasped out, wrapping one arm around a tree growing up from the side of the riverbank. "We're ahead of him, but not for long. Now's our only chance before he hits those rocks."

With one arm looped through Wynn's, Grayden held tightly to the tree while Wynn stretched the pole out across the river. The raft bobbed furiously, speeding along as though dragged by some unseen hand below the water. Zarek saw the pole and made a grab for it. His hands found purchase and he clung to it. Wynn and Grayden pulled, but the force of the river held him fast. Grayden felt his grip on the tree slipping.

Then the others caught up. Beren still stood where they had left him, straining with the rope to keep Zarek and the raft from hitting the rocks. Enric grabbed the pole next to Wynn. Arven joined Grayden, using their own bodies as anchors while Wynn and Enric steadily pulled Zarek to shore.

Slowly, the raft floated closer to the bank. When it was within a few feet, Zarek sprang onto land, his weight pushing the raft back as he leaped onto the solid earth where his companions caught him and held him steady. The raft slipped on down the river, crashing into the rocks just a few yards further on. The little ship caromed off a boulder, tipped up, and crashed down, the force of the rapids ripping the fastenings apart until nothing remained of their creation except individual logs floating down the river, free and unbound.

They stared after the pieces for a long moment. Wordlessly, Zarek held up the canvas bag, a triumphant grin on his face. A great guffaw that started almost down at his toes bubbled out of Grayden as he slapped Zarek on the back. They all began to laugh, then took turns shouting and slamming their fists into each other's backs and shoulders in a friendly celebration of their delight at having faced down the might of the river. Grayden felt a surge of life and energy wash through him and he punched Zarek in the arm, congratulating him on his courage and survival. Zarek grinned back and shouted about Wynn's quick thinking.

Laughing and recounting the tale of daring, they hiked back upstream to their fire to chart the path to their next objective.

———

"Enric says it's time to get moving."

Grayden groaned as Beren shook him awake on the sixth morning of their mission. Every part of him ached. His stomach growled in protest, gnawing at him with hunger. The last time they had eaten had been breakfast the previous morning, as none of them had enjoyed any sort of success in hunting the day before. They had been far too busy scrambling over enormous boulders, slick with ice, to get to the ninth location before dark. In the end, they had found the last map and a pebble with a greenish hue and deep veins of olive running through it, but Wynn had twisted his ankle badly in the dark as they had searched for a suitable place to make camp.

"How's Wynn?" Grayden asked through a mouth that felt as though it had been filled with cotton. The deep purple sky above him still held faint stars dotting its canopy. A faint gleam of gold far behind the mountains was the only hint of morning.

"His ankle is swollen," Beren replied, his expression sober. "He said the snow we managed to pack around it last night helped, but he will need help walking."

Grayden grimaced.

"The good news, however," Beren continued, "is that we aren't far from the river. Arven went to try his hand at fishing."

At the thought of food, Grayden felt his spirits rise. His stomach rumbled its complaint, but he assured it that he would feed it soon. As he set to work packing up his bedroll he noticed Enric sitting near the campfire, the last map in his hand.

"Where to?" Grayden asked.

Enric looked up, his expression bleak. "Further into the mountains," he said. "And we'd better find the last satchel quick or we're going to have to run all the way back to the Academy to make it by sundown. According to this map, we're already a good ten miles from home."

Grayden couldn't keep his eyes from flitting over to where Wynn sat on the other side of the camp, chatting with Zarek. He caught Enric's gaze and understood the dilemma. While each of them could probably run the entire ten miles in under three hours under normal conditions—they all ran two or more miles multiple times a sennight as part of their regular routine—Wynn's swollen ankle would make a normal pace impossible.

Before either of them could say more, Arven returned carrying a string of fish. They cooked the catch on skewers to save time and gulped the food down before hefting their packs and setting out.

Enric and Grayden propped Wynn between them, helping him navigate the uneven terrain. The far horizon was awash with pink and gold as the sun emerged from its slumber. Daylight limned the mountains, turning them into stark silhouettes against the pale sky. Suddenly, the ravine they were following rang with a familiar sound that caused the hair on the back of Grayden's neck to stand on end. The yowling cry of a grymstalker rebounded off the rocks around them. Grayden glanced up and around, his eyes automatically finding the likely spots where the predators would be hiding.

There! The hint of a tail flicking back and forth. And there! The shadow of the giant cat slinking just out of view behind that rock. Two of them at least, maybe three.

Without a word, the cadets joined together, turning their backs and forming an outward-facing circle. Enric held the crossbow ready, and the rest of them drew their swords. Grayden pulled out his dagger. It would serve him better than a sword for now.

"They must be having as hard a time finding game as we did," Wynn muttered.

Grayden nodded. It was rare to find a grymstalker willing to hunt humans in daylight, and full-grown humans at that. Hunger and desperation had driven them out. Grayden's stomach clenched. Desperate grymstalkers would be unpredictable and relentless.

One of the cats screamed again, and then a dark shape pounced toward them. Grayden heard the click of Enric's crossbow, and then the clatter of the bolt hitting stone as it missed. In the next instant, the great cat had landed on top of Beren.

Beren rolled on the ground, scrabbling with the enormous beast. They were a flurry of claws and fur cloak, snarling and shouting. Grayden ran to his friend and attacked the creature with his dagger, but he could tell that the blade missed its mark. Then the cat went limp, but before Grayden could question his aim or haul the bulky carcass off Beren, a shout made him spin around.

Wynn had flung himself on the back of the second beast, his arms wrapped around its enormous neck. He clung there, a wild look of terror and determination in his eyes. Zarek shouted something and fended the creature off with his sword, maneuvering to avoid the sweeping strikes from the massive paws. Arven stood alone against the third creature, his own sword keeping it at bay.

Enric had managed to reload his crossbow, and this time, his arrow found its mark. Wynn's mount screamed and twisted, throwing Wynn from its back before collapsing in the icy mud.

Grayden flung his dagger at the third beast. The dagger spun through the morning air, glinting brightly before burying itself in the grymstalker's side. The cat snarled and spun toward him, giving Arven the opening he needed to finish it off.

Grayden helped push the heavy carcass off of Beren and then offered a hand to pull him up. The six men stood together, gulping down air and staring at the aftermath of the battle. Wynn limped closer.

"What were you thinking?" Zarek demanded as Wynn seated himself on a nearby boulder.

Wynn shrugged. "It seemed like the best way to distract it," he said. "I couldn't help much with my ankle in its current condition."

"So you jumped on a grymstalker's back." Zarek's voice filled with disbelief.

Grayden chuckled. "Sounds like Wynn. Thinks through every angle of a problem and acts before anyone else has even said good morning."

"You do not lack courage," Arven said. "But your actions may not have been completely wise."

Wynn shrugged again. "I figured that I'd be safer as a distraction and annoyance than as the lame part of our little herd. If our group had to spend energy protecting me, the battle would have taken longer and might not have turned out in our favor. It was a fairly simple equation."

Zarek stared at Wynn. Then he chuckled, his voice barking out into the air. "I've been stewing all year about you three, coming in and being accelerated through the program, being assigned to missions like this one that most students don't even get to go on until their third year if they're lucky. But I wouldn't have wanted to face those monsters with anyone else at my side today."

"You all right, Beren?" Enric turned to the Telsuman.

Beren grinned. "It managed to land a few scratches before Grayden struck a blow to its heart," he admitted, showing them a bloody smear across his left shoulder. "But nothing too deep. I'm glad we encountered these foes in winter when we were bundled against the cold. Lighter clothes would not have offered such protection."

They helped Beren clean and bandage his scratches. Grayden sat next to his friend and gazed at him thoughtfully as the others scouted around to make sure no other grymstalkers were near.

"What?" Beren asked.

"I didn't kill that grymstalker," Grayden said. "My knife didn't get anywhere near its heart."

Beren shrugged. "You hit something, then."

"Pretty sure it died from a snapped neck," Grayden replied.

Beren busied himself with his bandages, not meeting Grayden's gaze.

"Beren..."

"Let it rest, my friend." Beren did not raise his voice, but he spoke with a deep intensity that brooked no further argument.

The others returned and declared that the way forward appeared to be clear of danger for the moment. Beren packed up the bandages, and then Zarek and Grayden each stood on either side of Wynn, helping him along.

In another mile, they found the final satchel hidden in a cleft of rock. Enric tucked the final stone into his pack. Triumphant, they turned their faces west.

"I'd say it's about twelve miles," Enric said. He glanced at Wynn. "It will probably take us every minute of eight hours to get back to the Academy."

"And we have until sunset?" Beren queried. "When will that be?"

"About nine hours," Enric replied.

"Plenty of time," Beren rumbled.

Enric nodded, rolling up the map. "Very well, let's get moving."

***

THE SIX YOUNG men trudged out of the woods and crossed the archery range just as the last glimmers of sunlight gleamed gold on the horizon ahead of them. Wynn limped, his face set in a permanent grimace, his comrades supporting him on either side. Koen stood waiting at the East Gate where he had left them. His eyes swept over them as they came to stand before him, appraising their appearance. Grayden took a moment to gauge each of the members of their team as well.

Wynn's foot had swollen so much they had needed to remove his boot and wrap his ankle, and the rags were now gray and ragged from traversing the last several miles. Zarek's neck and arms were still covered in the red puncture wounds from the nightvines. Beren's shirt hung from one shoulder in tatters, blood seeping through the hasty bandages they had applied after the grymstalker attack. They were all dirty and exhausted.

"Well?" Koen asked, his expression giving away no hint of his thoughts about their appearance or their arrival.

Enric pulled his pack from his shoulder and slung it at Koen's feet. "Reporting as ordered, sir," he said, his voice raspy.

Koen picked up the pack and inspected the contents. All ten shining rocks and the maps to each location lay nestled within the sack. He nodded briskly, his expression softening to one of approval. "Very good. Did you run into any trouble?"

Grayden opened his mouth to give a report, but Wynn beat him to it.

"No issues, sir."

Koen frowned, his eyes narrowing as he directed his gaze first to Wynn's bandaged and bootless foot, then flicking to the wounds he could see on the others. "None?"

"Most boring sennight I've ever experienced, sir," Zarek replied, his face giving no hint of a smile.

Koen's lips twitched. "I see you found your way around nicely, and made it back within the allotted time. I apologize for your boredom. I will have to make sure your instructors give you plenty of work to make up for the sennight of excitement you missed here." Then Koen's face split into a full grin. "You've done well! Get cleaned up, grab some dinner, and then hit the sack. Tomorrow is yours."

Wynn let out a whoop that turned into a yelp of pain as he put too much weight on his injured foot.

Concern flashed on Koen's face. "Best have the physician look at that."

Wynn nodded and they all turned to head back to their rooms.

"That's something to be proud of," Enric informed them. "We accomplished our task within the deadline, and Koen said we passed. He's not stingy with praise, but he doesn't give false compliments, either."

The glow of their accomplishment washed over each of them as they ambled across the Academy grounds together. They continued along, an easy camaraderie settling over their group. They needed no words, and they needed no applause or recognition for the task they had accomplished. They had done their duty, they had survived nightvines, frigid rivers, hungry grymstalkers, and deadlier yet, warring personalities. They had climbed mountains and pushed through their own exhaustion. They had not come through the fire unscathed, but they had come through. And more than all they had endured, they had shared the ordeal together and become brothers.

23

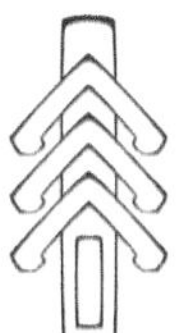

"How did it go?" Headmaster Freidzen asked as Major Syrus entered his office and closed the door behind him.

"It seems to have gone better than we hoped," Syrus replied. "The six young men that you selected for the exercise not only managed to find all ten checkpoints, but they made it back to the Academy by the deadline."

"I heard that there were injuries."

"Nothing too serious. A bruised and twisted ankle and a few scratches. From what I heard in the full debriefing, the group performed admirably and overcame some unexpected challenges."

"Good, good." Freidzen steepled his fingers and stared at them thoughtfully.

"Headmaster?"

"Yes?"

"May I ask, why did you select these six in particular? Such a mission is usually reserved for those in Experyus levels."

"Yes, I know." Freidzen nodded. "But these are uncertain times we traverse, Syrus. And war with the Igyeum has already broken out in remote locations along the Telsuman border. I have been looking at the records of all the students and have decided to accelerate some of them to defender before the end of this year."

"These six?"

"These six. They have all caught the attention of their instructors in some way or another. Even Master Drexel, Master Ormond, and Master Adelfried have managed to outperform cadets three or four years their senior. We cannot afford to bring them along gently or cultivate their talent, we must hone it now, turn them into blades we can use. Believe me, Syrus, I wish we did not have to, but we will need every blade we have, and soon. Within the year, I am certain."

"That soon?" Major Syrus' face paled.

"Sadly, yes."

"Where will you station them first?"

Headmaster Freidzen handed over a piece of paper. "The Storvas Outpost. I want them ready to man the outpost by mid-spring. It will be a good preparation for them, and will free up the current defenders there to be transferred to other locations of more import."

Syrus perused the list for a long moment. When he looked up, Freidzen's sharp eyes caught his troubled gaze.

"You disapprove?"

"Not of the students you've chosen," Syrus said hastily.

"Anything you care to discuss?"

"Captain Tomasson? He is your choice of their commanding officer?"

Freidzen eyed his subordinate. "You do not think he is up to the challenge? He has acquitted himself well and risen swiftly to the rank he now holds."

"It's not that." Syrus paused. "He is not the... kindest of teachers. And he is young for his rank."

Freidzen paced across the small office and stared out the window for a long moment. The trees outside had lost their leaves, and stood barren and stark on a grassy lawn that had lost its lustrous green of summer. The sky stood blue and clear, belying the chill that was noticeably present in the air. A great weariness pressed down upon the headmaster's shoulders as he turned to face his old friend.

"Syrus, the ones I have chosen for this posting, tell me truthfully: is kindness what they will most need in order to be equipped for the challenges they will face up in those mountains? Or the ones they will shortly encounter when they are called to our borders to fight the Igyèum soldiers? I know they are young. I am not blind to the fact that we will soon be sending boys to do men's work. But our time is short, and we will need them now. War is already upon us. They will be the difference for our side— not just these six, but all our cadets, all our young defenders. I must do what I can to prepare them for war. Difficulty is precisely what they will encounter, and it would be a disservice to equip them any less. Captain Tomasson will ensure that they are fully prepared for what is to come. He may be a poor choice for many things, but for this task, I would choose no other."

Syrus nodded sharply once. "Very well, I will send for him."

24

———

U un stood before Ar'Mol Eyvind. Despite standing on the floor and the necessity of looking up at the throne on the raised dais, Uun still gave the impression somehow that he towered over the Ar'Mol. The Ar'Mol leaned his chin on his hand and waited. Uun chafed inwardly at the need to stand before another and give a report. The day would come when he would no longer need this puppet, but for now the man was useful. The throne was not synonymous with power, and Uun preferred his freedom. For now.

"The secondary refinery is complete and operating well," he said. "We did lose a bit more time than I would have liked, but in the end, the destruction of the primary location has only delayed your plans, not impeded them. Production levels are almost back to normal already."

"Good. And the oasis?"

"Is everything we hoped."

"Excellent. What of Lorcan?" The Ar'Mol shifted, giving the appearance of lounging on the great throne. Uun would have preferred the man be less comfortable in his presence, but he could wait.

"Once he finished his work on the oasis project, I sent him on to a new task. The man is a great asset, but he needs to have his creativity constantly challenged or he grows... intractable."

"I have noticed." The Ar'Mol's lip curled ever so slightly in distaste. "And what is his new task?"

"Something I think you will appreciate. An assignment that should hold his interest and all his attention until the incursion begins. When it does, we can retrieve him and his new creations. If he is successful, I believe you will find them to be fascinating additions to your army."

"So you say, though I have yet to see the amazing feats you promised from Lorcan. A few trees and a pond in the desert may be impressive and useful for hiding my armies, but I don't see how it hurts my enemies. He has failed in this assignment before, remember."

"Which is exactly why I had to send him somewhere isolated," Uun replied, keeping his tone even and patient. "In the past his genius has been fettered, as I needed him to be careful around populated areas. In the mountains, he will be able to cultivate his weapons without endangering your own subjects."

The Ar'Mol drummed his fingers on the arm of his elaborate throne. "I am beginning to wonder if your pet project is worth the expense and irritation."

"He will be."

"He'd better be."

"Is that a threat, my lord?" Uun's voice was soft, but there was a hard glint in his eyes. "Perhaps you've forgotten who cleared the way for you to take the mantle of Ar'Mol when your uncle died?"

The Ar'Mol stopped his drumming and sat up, his back rigid, his expression filled with fury. Uun allowed himself a slight shiver of satisfaction. "You swore an oath to me that you would never whisper a word of that, either in public or private."

"And you pledged an oath to me, as well, Eyvind." He relished the moment, unleashing the Ar'Mol's name with casual familiarity, using every sound of it to remind him of the true nature of their relationship. Uun pulled a piece of cloth from a pocket in his robes and held it up, studying it intently, as if the conversation at hand did not interest him at all. "Do you remember? You swore to make me your right hand, to heed my counsel, and to expand your borders under my direction. You swore it because you knew I was the power behind your uncle's throne... and your own."

"All of which I have kept," Eyvind snarled. "I have broken no word of my pledge."

"But you threaten to abandon that pledge when you question my advice. You threaten my position when you question my methods. If I have in some way not delivered the aid I promised, or you have ceased to trust me, then perhaps it is time I find someone who will value my counsel more." The threat hung in the air between them, tangible as a coiled snake.

The Ar'Mol's face paled visibly and he ran nervous fingers through his curly hair. He rose and descended from his throne, his steps stumbling and uncertain. He reached out, his hands gripping Uun's forearms.

"Forgive me, I intended no disrespect..." He trailed off, staring up into Uun's face, his own visage awash with pleading. "I have not forgotten our accord, nor what you did to bring me to this position. Please, I trust you. I trust your methods. I did not mean to question your authority in these matters I have entrusted to you. If you say Lorcan will be a valuable asset, I believe you. Only do not..." He swallowed visibly, and Uun gloried in the fear he saw in the younger man's face. Eyvind knew. He knew just how easily Uun could depose him and set another on the throne. Uun did not need much, someone with a malleable temperament, who would do and say what he was told.

Staring down at the face of the most powerful man in the world, Uun's lip curled in a sneer. It was easy to forget just how young the Ar'Mol really was. He wore his authority well, with a casual arrogance that made people defer to him. Most of his people had no idea that the leader they feared and respected was little more than a puppet. It was only because of Uun's iron fist behind the throne that any of these warlords gained the power they did.

For four centuries he had been cultivating this position of power in the east, readying himself to attack the west, to control the known world. At first he had tried brute force and impatience, as was his wont, but over time he had adapted to methods that worked better. His machinations had grown more subtle, his hold on the reins more deft. He had eventually discovered that the lighter his touch, the more power he gained. It went against his nature, but he was nothing if not determined.

The grip on his forearms tightened, drawing Uun out of his thoughts. No. Cultivating another Ar'Mol would take too much time. Usually, Eyvind was the perfect puppet. Perhaps Uun had been growing lax in his oversight, giving the man too much authority. Distressingly, Eyvind had been showing flickers of ambition lately, and Uun hoped that his threat had sufficiently squashed such delusions of grandeur. With an imperious shudder he shrugged off the Ar'Mol's grasp on him and stepped back, staring regally down his nose at the young man. Such a weak thing, this emperor he had set up to hold the nations in his hands. All his years of planning, of plotting, of carefully maneuvering warring tribes into warring nations, into a single warlord over all three of the eastern nations, into the strong seat that was now called the "Ar'Mol" had come down to this man. This child. It was what he himself had wanted. But sometimes he wondered if it would have been better to take the throne himself. No. He shook his head firmly. It was better this way. The man he had picked was beholden to him, but he was also skilled in his own right and could keep certain aspects of the Igyeum running smoothly. This was just a minor stumble, not an egregious error. Uun was certain he had chosen well. He had manipulated this ending with every skill in his possession.

Still, it would not do to let his creation believe it did not need him. So he stared down now at Eyvind with pitiless disdain for a moment longer. The younger man cringed, then straightened, his spine stiffening beneath that cruel gaze. His jaw tightened and he stared back, a glimmer of defiance in his dark eyes.

"I have broken no accord with you, Ar'Molon Uun," the man said, his cowering replaced with a confidence that Uun admired, in spite of himself. "To question your methods is not to abandon your advice. It is no less than the lessons you taught me yourself: to question, to listen, to delve into, to define, to discover the heart of a matter and parse it until I can fully understand its worth." He raised his chin. "Thus it is you, and not I, who has taken a step toward breaking faith this day by speaking things you promised would remain silent."

A glow of pride warmed the cold within Uun's chest, but he concealed it. "Was there something you wished to keep hidden about my part in stepping forward and vouching for you before the Tu'Anan and De'Anan of your uncle's court? Nothing about that meeting is secret. I have broken nothing, not a single letter of our agreement."

The Ar'Mol glared at him, but the anger was fading. Understanding that this had been a test, and one that he had almost failed, dawned in his expression. He turned with a whirl of his royal robes and ascended the dais once more. "Your counsel is, as always, most appreciated. Please keep me informed of any further developments in these matters."

<h1 style="text-align:center">25</h1>

"Grayden." The gruff voice made Grayden jerk his head and look up from the papers he had been studying with focused intensity.

"Dalmir!" Grayden rose from his seat, delight at seeing the older man once more vying with confusion. "I did not think to see you again soon, though, I guess it has been quite a few lunats, hasn't it? It seems like you were just here. Do you want to get some food? I want to hear all about your travels with Captain Marik."

"No, no, sit, I will join you." Dalmir waved a hand and took the chair on the opposite side of the table.

The older man's eyes darted around the room, taking in the shelves filled with books and scrolls, the tables and chairs scattered throughout the aisles, and the numerous occupants of the room engaged in quiet study. "It is truly a beautiful thing."

Grayden wondered at the sadness in the older man's eyes and his wistful tone. "What are you doing here?" Grayden leaned across his books and papers, resting on his elbows, oblivious to the smudges he was creating on his newly penned notes. "Was your journey successful? Have you heard any news about what the Igyeans are planning to do next?"

Dalmir gave a low chuckle. "The young always have so many questions. My journey was"—he hesitated—"well, let us simply say that it had unexpected results. I knew very little of the Ar'Mol's plans; though from what Marik has told me of the man I can surmise rather a lot, especially in light of recent events. He has a close advisor who will certainly be urging him to action and war in the coming lunats. However, that is not why I am here. I need your help."

"My help?" Grayden sat back. "With what?"

"Not here." Dalmir's demeanor suddenly changed. He threw a cautious glance at the shelves containing numerous precious documents. "Somewhere perhaps a bit more... sturdy?"

Grayden narrowed his eyes, giving the older man a hard and thoughtful stare. "One of the practice arenas?" Grayden stood and began collecting his papers, leaving the books and scrolls he had been perusing to be re-shelved by the archivists.

"Lead the way."

It was a short walk to the training yards. Grayden stopped in one of the smaller rings. A noticeable crispness tinged the air, and a light layer of snow covered the ground. Grayden's boots crunched through it and he thought with an aching wave of homesickness that the snow back home was probably knee-deep by now. Seren would be building sculptures and forts, and Mother would be baking constantly as she seemed to think that fresh bread and pastries were the only proven method to get through the coldest lunats safely. He grinned, then felt worry creep into his musings. He hoped his father had found someone reliable to help him ready the orchards for the cold bite of winter.

"Well? Will this do?" he asked, stopping in the center of the ring and turning to Dalmir.

"Yes, this should be fine." Dalmir sat down on the cold ground and beckoned for Grayden to join him.

Mystified, Grayden sat, feeling the cold wetness of the frost seeping through his breeches. He wrinkled his nose, but said nothing. If the Academy had taught him nothing else, it had taught him to bear discomfort without comment.

Dalmir drew an object from a pocket hidden within his cloak and held it out to Grayden, who blinked. It was not what he had expected. In Dalmir's hand rested the dusky purple jewel he had taken from Aubri Niveya's necklace.

"Hold this."

Eyes wide, Grayden held out his hand for the spherical stone. It rested in his hand, glittering like a dull amethyst in the morning sunlight. Grayden glanced up at Dalmir, questions burning in his mind.

"Just focus on it with all your concentration," Dalmir muttered. "I just need to understand..." He trailed off.

Obediently, Grayden stared at the stone, trying to concentrate. It was difficult. A thousand thoughts and questions danced through his mind. The sun's pale warmth on his head mixed with the frosty air kissing his face and the incongruous sound of birds chirping so late in the winter was immensely distracting.

Dalmir snatched the stone from his palm. "I thought that might be the case." He shook his head. "Curious, though. I wonder why..."

"You thought what might be..." Grayden did not have time to finish his question before Dalmir slapped a different object into his still outstretched palm. This time the gem was blue, and slightly larger. It was familiar, both because he had seen it before, and because it felt right, resting there in his grasp.

Grayden stared, transfixed. All the rest of the world—his questions, his confusion, the sun and the birds—faded into the background as the stone began to gleam with a brilliant sapphire light from within. Its surface turned cold in his hand, icy, but not in an unpleasant or painful way. This time no strange, ugly streaks of red marred the stone's surface; it shimmered a clear blue like the waves of the ocean. With an effort, Grayden pulled his gaze from the gem and stared up at Dalmir.

"Why is it doing that?" he asked.

Dalmir's face was alight with wonder and triumph, but also a hint of confusion. Their eyes met and Dalmir squinted. Instead of answering, he asked, "Are you willing to try something a bit more difficult?"

Grayden nodded slowly, biting back his questions. He could be patient. The Academy had taught him that, as well.

Dalmir opened the canteen that hung at his side and produced a small bowl from somewhere within his cloak. He poured a bit of water into the bowl.

"Try to freeze the water," he commanded.

Grayden cleared his throat and gave Dalmir an incredulous glance. Had the man gone mad? "Freeze the..."

"Water." Dalmir's voice was kind. "Trust me, it is the simplest command you can give. Focus on the orb and freeze the water."

"Er... very well."

Grayden stared down at the glowing gem, one eye on the bowl of water. He could hear his blood pounding in his ears, aware of every breath that passed as nothing happened. He squeezed his hand around the gem, thinking of ice covering the pond back home, of the skates he and his friends would strap to their feet every winter when the cold returned to Dalsea. Images of fruit trees, encased in glittering ice swirled in his thoughts, the way the sun glinted on them and made the whole world look as though it were sheathed in glass. Unconsciously, he let his eyes flutter closed as his mind summoned up images of winter nestled in his family's cozy cabin. Suddenly the orb grew hot in his palm, so hot he was sure it would burn him. Grayden yelped and nearly dropped the stone, clenching his fist around it reflexively as he simultaneously grew aware of what Dalmir might do to him if he broke this precious object. Dalmir's sharp intake of breath startled him and he opened his eyes. The heat of the orb faded and he stared at the bowl of water, his mouth agape. The water had not turned to ice, but there was a thick ring of frost surrounding the lip of the bowl where some of the water had crystallized.

"What..." Grayden's mouth was dry. "What just happened?"

"You accessed the power of my orb," Dalmir replied. "But do not ask me how. This should not be possible."

"What do you mean don't ask you how? This was your idea but you don't know why it worked?"

"It shouldn't be possible," Dalmir repeated. "But with the help of the orb, you have managed to access a portion of my power. Just a fragment, really, but if you can do that, then my guess would be that you could do much more with the right training."

"You mean, I could do the things you can do?" Grayden asked.

"Theoretically, as long as you are touching the orb, yes. Or maybe you just need to be near it? I'm not sure," Dalmir replied. "I still do not understand. I will need to study this more fully."

"So... why can't I use the other one, then?"

"I am not sure of that, either, though I have a few guesses. Possibly for the same reason Aubri Niveya could wear it around her neck for years without awakening it."

"And that reason would be...?"

"That she is not native to Ondoura."

Grayden stared, uncomprehending. His mind reeled as he tried to sort out everything Dalmir was saying. Possibilities and excitement underscored by a thick vein of terror coursed through his thoughts as quick as blinking.

"It is just a theory." Dalmir shrugged. He held out his hand and Grayden deposited the blue orb into the man's palm. "This will definitely require more investigation. But I have other, more pressing matters to attend to first." He put the orbs away.

"That reminds me." Grayden dipped his finger into the frigid water and stirred it a bit. "Beren's mother was hoping to meet you if you returned. I think she wants to thank you for helping save Beren's life. She's been staying with the Regeont for the past several lunats, and we visit her whenever we have a rest day. She's been mentioning her need to return home to Gnupar for the past several visits, but I think she's afraid to let Beren out of her sight again."

"I would be most pleased to make the acquaintance of Lady Adelfried."

"We can probably take you there after classes today, if you like," Grayden offered. "It's not a rest day, but I'm sure Headmaster Freidzen will make an exception in this case."

"I would appreciate that." Dalmir overturned the bowl and rose from the ground. "I will meet you on the front lawn when you are ready."

———

It was twilight as the carriage rumbled over the cobblestones, carrying its passengers toward the heart of Doran. Beren had sent word ahead of their arrival and Lady Nadia was at the front gates waiting for them when the carriage came to a stop before the Regeont's manor. Nadia embraced her son and his friends, then clasped Dalmir's hand warmly between her own.

"Dalmir," she said, her voice a little choked. "My eternal gratitude is yours for saving my son from his abductors. I only wish I could have thanked you sooner."

"My dear lady"—Dalmir looked down at the slight woman, her small frame belying the strength of character and heart that shone through her eyes—"you are most welcome."

"If there is anything I can ever do to repay your kindness, please, all you have to do is say the word. You have done my family a great service as protector, and we of Telsuma do not forget such debts easily. And personally, as a mother..." Lady Nadia faltered, her eyes suddenly welling with more than just tears. Though she had known nothing of her son's peril during the events of their journey, the terror of what might have been clearly plagued her still.

Dalmir straightened, tightening his grip on her fingers as though he might be able to impart comfort through such a simple gesture. "Speak nothing more of it. Your son stands here with us, safe and whole, and in many ways, better for his adventures, I am sure." He gave her an amused smile and Nadia chuckled through her tears, then pulled her hand away and wiped the mistiness from her eyes.

"Mother," Beren mumbled, clearly uncomfortable with her display of emotion.

Lady Nadia took in a deep breath and dabbed at her eyes with the corner of a handkerchief. Then she smiled brightly. "Forgive my melancholy. This is a joyous occasion, the chance to meet and thank the man who helped save my son and his friends. I did not mean to make such a scene here at the end of the drive. Please, come in. I have had the chef prepare a banquet for us."

Dalmir hesitated, his conscience pricking him. "My dear lady, I must confess, when Grayden told me you wished to meet me, I agreed to come for motives of my own. Please understand that I do not feel you owe me anything, but I do fear that I must now beg your aid."

Nadia's smile blossomed in response. "If it is within my power, you shall have it. But please, do come inside and we can discuss your request."

She led the way into the palatial structure and bade them sit in one of the dining halls. The room was lavishly decorated. Tiles filled with intricate paintings within them covered the floor all around the room, and even the walls. The paintings mostly depicted birds and other small animals, surrounded by colorful flowers. In the center of the room, a large rug covered the tiled floor, boasting an intricate, flowery pattern in reds and blues. A large, ornate table stood in the center of the room, covered in platters of food. The younger men grinned appreciatively and took their seats, eager to participate in the feast.

On a side table against the far wall from the door stood a golden statue around which were placed various flowers and pieces of fruit. Dalmir recognized it as one of the Ondouran house shrines to Vera. Discomfort prickled through him, but he tried to ignore it. He had abandoned Emri long ago. If these people wanted to worship false gods, who was he to stop them—he, Dalmir, who had turned away from the Builder and sat in idle despair for so many years? Surely Emri had no further use for him. Anger snaked through his thoughts. Emri had abandoned him, first. Why should he care whether anyone in Turrim remembered their Creator?

"We shall not be disturbed in here," Nadia assured them, startling Dalmir out of his darkly spiraling thoughts. "Dalmir, please sit here next to me so we can talk more easily."

Dalmir sat down in one of the chairs and shifted around in an attempt to get comfortable. The furniture was ornate, wrought from wood that had been cleverly and intricately carved into various depictions of creatures. Unfortunately, though the carvings were interesting and beautiful to look upon, they were uncomfortable to rest against. Grayden and his friends sat on the edges of their chairs and watched in poorly concealed amusement as Dalmir adjusted a few times and then gave up and sat forward like the rest of them.

Once they had filled up their plates, Dalmir turned to Lady Adelfried. "I have important information for the leaders of Telmondir. Beren informed me on the way over that they will be holding another Council meeting in the near future?"

"In a day or two, actually," Nadia replied. "Regeont Roshana began her journey to the Arxis a few days ago. The Council members always meet in the first sennights of Edrian to discuss the previous year and plan for the one ahead."

"It is imperative that I gain access to that meeting."

Nadia tilted her chin to one side. "Normally that wouldn't be too difficult; petitioners often come before the Council when they are in session. From what the boys have told me, you are a citizen of Telmondir, and as such, you have a right to be heard by the Council. I would be happy to introduce you myself, but I fear we would never make it before they conclude the Arxis. All the airships in the docks at the moment are cargo cruisers, and they can only dock at the big city ports. You'd need a small schooner to get to the Arxis. But if it isn't too urgent, they meet three times a year—can you wait until Urin?"

"No. It cannot wait."

Nadia's expression turned down in pensive consideration.

"What if I told you that I have a very fast airship at my disposal?" Dalmir ventured. Inwardly he winced. He was not at all sure that Marik would be willing to fly even further into "enemy" territory, but the man had surprised him before.

"Ah, truly?" Nadia raised an eyebrow. "Well, that changes matters. If your information is as urgent as you say, we can leave tomorrow morning and be there in a day. Lady Ilya and Lord Elan are well settled in here and my need to remain has passed. In truth, I should have returned home long since, but I couldn't quite make myself." She smiled warmly at her son. "But I fear I have outstayed my usefulness."

"Mother," Beren began, but Nadia raised a hand to forestall his words.

"I merely jest, my son. I have enjoyed being able to visit with you and your friends these past lunats. But your schedule is getting busier and you cannot afford distractions. And I have duties at home, and other children to tend to. Escorting Dalmir to the Arxis on my way home gives me something useful to do."

"Thank you, my lady," Dalmir said.

"That's settled then." Nadia's demeanor became brusque. "You will spend the night here and in the morning we will begin our travels. May I ask where this airship of yours is?"

"In the Academy lake." Beren grinned, his expression impish as he joined the conversation. "Dalmir, were you planning to inform my mother that she has just agreed to travel with pirates?"

Lady Nadia drew in a sharp breath. "Not the same pirates who attempted to abduct my son?"

"No, dear lady, but rather, the ones who helped to save his life. I have traveled with them these past several lunats, and though they are pirates and a tad unpolished, a nobler group you will never find. I have been completely at ease in their care."

Nadia rose from her seat in a fluid motion, smoothing her long skirts. "It has been too long since I had an adventure. If you vouch for them, Sir Dalmir, then I shall trust you. But in the future be warned: I greatly dislike surprises."

"I will endeavor to remember." Dalmir spoke the words solemnly, but his eyes sparkled with mischief.

26

The *Valdeun Hawk* landed gently on the waters of the pond behind the Arxis building. As Marik's crew lowered the docking boat over the side of the airship, they could see a group of people gathering on the shore. Marik also noted that many of the onlookers were well-armed. How had he let the old man talk him into this madness? He didn't have to look at his crew to know they were wondering the same thing. It would be a miracle if they weren't all in chains by the end of the day.

"I think it would be prudent for you to ride at the front of the boat, my lady," Marik muttered to Lady Nadia, unease gripping him at the thought of willingly standing before the Council. "A familiar face should help ease our welcome here."

"I was just about to suggest that very course of action," Nadia replied, her demeanor unruffled.

As they glided across the still water of the pond, tension built in Marik's shoulders and his fingers itched to draw his sword. What had he been thinking? Dalmir had spun a beautiful dream for him, but he now had a sinking suspicion that was all it was: a dream. Could these rulers be any less corrupt than the Ar'Mol? Was he making the right decision, throwing his lot in with any governing body? Experience shouted, "No!" and yet, here he was.

Across the water, getting nearer by the second, the faces awaiting them were hard and guarded. However, as they drew closer, several of the onlookers recognized Lady Adelfried and the tension in their expressions faded. Lord Adelfried stood nearest the water; his eyes held a mixture of quizzical curiosity and concern. As Marik and Oleck rowed across the water and drove the small boat up onto the grassy bank, Nadia stood and stepped gracefully into her husband's arms.

"My love, this is unexpected," Lord Adelfried murmured into her ear. "Is everything well with you? Our son?"

"Quite well," Nadia assured him. "Has the meeting started?"

"Just this morning," he replied.

Nadia smiled and turned to the men behind her as they stepped out of the small boat. "May I introduce two of the men who aided in rescuing our son. This is Dalmir, a learned and wise man from Dalma. And this is Captain Marik, commander of the fine vessel that carried me here. Gentlemen, my husband, Thorben Adelfried."

Lord Adelfried clasped hands with each man in turn. "I am quite pleased to make your acquaintance," he assured them, "but this is not an ideal time. We of the Council have many important matters to discuss..."

"Husband," Nadia interrupted smoothly, "you know I would never interrupt you in the middle of an Arxis without good reason. These men have information you will want to hear."

"Ah." Lord Adelfried eyed the two men with renewed interest. "Then by all means, please come inside. Food will be brought out shortly to your crew, unless they also wish to disembark?"

"No," Marik replied. "They will stay with the airship, but they will surely appreciate something warm to eat. The weather is a bit chilly this far north. Oleck can wait here with the longboat and take the food out to them."

Oleck gave a gruff nod.

"Very good. If you will please follow me." Lord Adelfried

turned and led them toward the large, lodge-like building as the rest of the onlookers began to quietly disperse.

"When can we speak to the Council?" Dalmir pressed, his long legs keeping step with Lord Adelfried.

"Right away, if you wish. We were about to break for a light refreshment, but we can wait if the matter is urgent."

"It is," Dalmir replied.

"Perhaps we should let them eat first." Marik's voice held a bit of a lazy drawl. He clasped Dalmir's shoulder with a friendly hand and pulled him back slightly. "I'm not as wise or as powerful as you, but I do know people, and they are more likely to listen closely when their empty stomachs aren't complaining."

Dalmir nodded. "Very well."

———

THE COUNCIL RECONVENED after an abbreviated lunch at Lord Adelfried's insistence. A fire crackled in the enormous hearth behind Nadia as she stood and introduced the two newcomers.

"May it please the Council to hear the words of Dalmir and Captain Marik. They were instrumental in the rescue of my son when he was abducted by the Niveyan Syndicate several lunats ago, an event you are familiar with. Please hear them."

She stepped away and seated herself next to her husband, leaving the two men to speak before the Council.

Dalmir stepped forward. "War is upon you, as you well know," he began in a quiet tone. "Your preparations have been thoughtful and thorough even as you seek peace. Your warriors are well-trained, but they are overmatched."

Marik shifted uneasily, sensing a protest erupting, but Dalmir held up a hand.

"Please, hear me. They are overmatched because the Igyeum owns the sky. They control the power supply for all airships. This is not by accident, this is by design. Your artificineers are unable to replicate this power supply, the Ar'Mol has made certain of this. If you will allow me, I am here to help level the playing field, as it were."

He pulled the refiner they had found in the collapsed tunnels out of a large satchel, and Marik drew in his breath sharply. Surely Dalmir was not going to just hand it over? Years of experience screamed at him to intervene, to stop the older man, to tell him that he couldn't make a deal with someone by giving them everything they could ever hope for with no bargaining for some kind of return. The refiner was the largest bargaining chip Marik had ever held and now it would gain him nothing.

Even as these thoughts raced through his mind, Marik straightened, hardening his jaw and banishing the temptation to fall into his old habits. The refiner was not his to withhold or use, anyway. Even the Council could not use the refiner without the one card that only Dalmir could play. His own course was fixed to Dalmir's path, and he would see it through.

"What is that?" Duke Langston asked.

"It is a refiner." Next, Dalmir set a glowing blue object on the table and waited.

"Is that a cynder?" one of the aides asked in a hushed voice.

"It is," Dalmir replied.

Regeont Roshana stood and approached warily. "May I?" she asked.

Dalmir nodded and the older woman lifted the cynder carefully in her hands. She turned it over, examining it closely. Then she put it down.

"We would need to perform some tests," she declared to the rest of the Council, "but this does indeed appear to be a functional cynder." She gazed up at him with narrowed eyes. "It is the wrong color. I assume you are about to tell us that it functions the same as the ones we've been using?"

"It does," Dalmir confirmed.

"And what is this refiner?" The Regeont gestured at the other object on the table.

"That is the device that turns regular stone into cynders," Dalmir replied calmly.

The Council members shook their heads, their faces full of mingled awe and trepidation. Marik could see that they understood the value of what had been laid before them. They knew this technology stood far outside their reach without Dalmir's device. But he could also see their reluctance to trust a new player in this game.

Finally, Lord Adelfried rose and stepped forward. His voice was quiet and subdued. "What are your terms for such a marvel?"

"It is a gift," Dalmir said. "No bargain is intended. The refiner is yours, freely given for the simple purpose of safeguarding your free lands."

Marik tried not to let his own dismay show at this declaration.

Adelfried steepled his fingers together over his nose and stared penetratingly into the middle distance, looking at nothing, weighing everything. At long last he cleared his throat. "Can we see a demonstration of this... refiner, as you call it?"

"Certainly." Dalmir took another roughly cylindrical piece of stone out of the satchel and placed it under the spout of the strangely-shaped bowl and dipper device. Then he brought forth his orb, gently gleaming the same color as the already-full cynder. He placed the small blue gem into the small bowl of the refiner. Instantly, a stream of shimmering blue liquid poured out of the dipper and onto the cylinder, turning it from cold, lifeless rock into a transparent, shining blue crystal.

Everyone in the room suddenly burst into applause and several people rose and surged forward to express their gratitude and examine the marvel more closely. Marik found his hand being shaken warmly by Lord Adelfried, and then someone was slapping him on the back, and someone called for wine to celebrate this new weapon in their arsenal.

Marik stood there numbly, unable to find an appropriate response to this sudden change in the room. Thorben poured wine into goblets and toasts were made. Marik raised his glass and drank, but he barely tasted the liquid. Discussion began about how best to put this new device to use, and the implications of Telmondir's release from dependence on the Igyeum for power.

Adelfried turned to Dalmir and raised an eyebrow. "Can you teach us how to use this device?"

Dalmir shook his head. "I cannot. It requires the use of my orb, which is not part of the bargain. However, I believe that I—with the help of your artificineers—might be able to create a device that will store enough energy to fill a thousand cynders before it runs out and needs to be recharged. I would be more than willing to return to the device and do so whenever necessary."

"A thousand cynders," Duke Langston breathed.

"I will need access to a workshop and a forge," Dalmir said.

"They are yours to command," Lord Adelfried replied. "If you are willing to travel to my home in Gnupar I can get you access to both."

Dalmir inclined his head.

Thorben eyed him. "I have heard the story of your part in the rescue of my son. I must confess, before now I was not sure how much of it to believe. The Igyeum is a powerful foe, and already they trespass on our borders. You spoke of returning at need, which means you will eventually be departing from the workshop. Are you willing to stay your travels and help us in the war that pounds upon our door?"

Dalmir gave a mirthless smile. "As a weapon, I suppose you mean?"

Thorben's lips thinned. "Yes."

"Not as you might wish," Dalmir replied softly. "So long as Ar'Molon Uun stands behind the Igyeum throne, I cannot risk a direct confrontation. These cynders, the airships that soar through your sky, they are no technological achievement. Perhaps in another several hundred years your people might have been able to come up with a way to make air travel possible, but what Uun has done is... well, I suppose I consider it cheating."

"Cheating?" Duke Langston asked.

"He has used his power to advance the Igyeum's capabilities beyond what they could do on their own."

"And you are telling us that his power exceeds your own?" Roshana asked, an ashen horror in her voice.

"Uun and I are evenly matched," Dalmir replied. "If I face him directly, everyone will lose. A battle between us would tear Turrim apart and ultimately solve nothing. I do not have the power to destroy him, and he cannot destroy me. I kept him imprisoned for nearly a thousand years, but he has escaped that prison. I do not even know if I can chain him again."

"Are you saying our cause is hopeless?" Langston asked. "That no matter what we do, we will face eventual defeat?"

"No." Dalmir shook his head. "I am telling you that I cannot act as a weapon against Uun. I am telling you what you are up against. And I am telling you that I honestly do not know how to win. Yet. But I will not simply lie down and let Uun enslave this world. You will not see me on the battlefield in command of soldiers, or in your strategy sessions, but I am pledged to defeat Uun or die in the attempt. Whatever help I can bring, it is yours."

Marik's heart soared at these words. Could he believe it? Could he claim this purpose as his own? Could he move beyond the doubt and suspicion that had sharpened and clouded his own understanding of justice for so many years?

Dalmir continued speaking. "I can give you thousands of cynders. I can help you develop weapons and defenses against Uun and his Igyeum. But in the end, it will be your soldiers and your leaders, the people of Telmondir who will wage this actual war, who will determine the outcome. What you really need are the young men currently at your Academy, the defenders already patrolling your borders..." Dalmir paused and looked sharply at Marik, then returned his gaze to the Council. "You have good men in good measure, and that is a testament to your diligent leadership. You will also need those rare individuals who make the difference in most great purposes. Fortunately, one of those men stands before you now. Captain Marik has not studied at your Academy, but I am certain he could teach your professors a thing or two about your enemy and how to defeat him."

All eyes in the room turned to Marik and he resisted the urge to do anything other than meet their eyes with as much confidence as he could muster. The praise that had come from Dalmir —so unexpected, so unlooked for—settled like a heavy yoke across his shoulders. He had a sudden, desperate desire to be worthy of those words.

"Captain Marik?" Thorben said his name like it was a question.

"Sir," Marik replied, just barely keeping himself from saluting in the fashion of Igyeum soldiers. "It would be my honor to assist Telmondir in the coming war."

"But if I'm not mistaken," Regeont Roshana cut in smoothly, "your accent is Valleian."

He allowed a small upward quirk of his lips. "You have a good ear, Regeont."

"Why would you be interested in helping us fight the Igyeum?" Duke Langston asked.

"Sirs, Madam, I have been working against the Ar'Mol for years. Undoubtedly you have heard me and my crew described as pirates. I think 'survivors' is a more accurate term, but I am not ashamed of either label. I would not have chosen piracy, but when it was thrust upon me I embraced it. I used to be a soldier in the Ar'Mol's army, many years ago." His throat tightened at the sudden looks of horror on the faces before him but he plowed on. "It wasn't my choice to be there, my family sold me to the Igyeum in exchange for a certain level of status." He did his best not to growl out the words as old bitterness threatened to overwhelm him. "I saw first-hand the atrocities the Ar'Mol was willing to subject his own people to, had to participate in some of it. Finally, it turned my stomach too much to stand silently by any longer. In short, I'm a wanted man in the Igyeum: both for desertion and for my crimes as a pirate. I have nothing to go back to, and I bear nothing but hatred for the Ar'Mol and his ilk. Whether or not you good people accept my help, I aim to follow Dalmir here in whatever moves he makes next. I am so tired of pecking at the Ar'Mol's boots. If Dalmir says we can rid Turrim of this evil, this tyranny, this suffering that the people in the Igyeum have to endure on a daily basis, then I want to be there by his side, helping to make it happen."

Silence filled the room. After a long moment, Thorben Adelfried gave a nod.

"Gentlemen, give us a moment. Cathrine will show you to the parlor where I believe there are some refreshments waiting."

A young woman stepped demurely out of the corner. By her striking resemblance to Lady Nadia, Marik guessed that this must be a daughter. Surely she was too young to be a sister? Her soft, dark skin was a few shades lighter than her mother's, but her hair exhibited the same dark, tight ringlets as Lady Nadia's. She wore the traditional female trappings of Telsuma: a warm leather jerkin atop a long-sleeved tunic. Soft trousers that looked to be some sort of animal hide covered her legs and high boots came up to her knees. Her face was wholly ordinary, plain, even, but her brown eyes held a thoughtful expression that promised a swift intellect and a small gleam that indicated a sense of humor. Her lips quirked as she caught him staring at her. With a demure nod of her head, she directed them to follow her out of the central meeting chamber. They turned a corner, traversed a hall, and finally ended in a smaller room. The woman turned to Marik, her lips still holding a sly curl.

"My father will not thank you for staring so at his oldest daughter," she admonished, but her tone sounded more teasing than sincere.

"Forgive me, lady," Marik said. "I did not mean to stare. I was merely comparing you to your mother; you take after her quite strongly. Lady Cathrine, I believe your father called you?"

She let out a slight laugh and offered him a tray of biscuits.

"Just Cathrine, please. My students call me 'Lady,' but you are too old to be one of them."

"You are a teacher, then?" Marik selected a biscuit.

Cathrine nodded. "I have thirty-three students of varying ages in my school at the moment. I worry that they are not behaving for my substitute, but my father insisted that Drengur and I accompany him to the Arxis in Berenger's place."

"I am sure that they will want to please such a lovely teacher as yourself with a good report."

Cathrine rolled her eyes. "Please, Captain Marik, deception does not become you."

Marik frowned. "Excuse me?"

"I am no beauty," Cathrine said, her tone dismissive. "There is no need to flatter with such talk."

Puzzled, Marik studied her expression, searching for a hint of what he should say next. "I meant no offense," he said at length.

"None taken." She tossed her head with a light chuckle. "Jam?" She offered him a crystal bowl.

Marik surveyed the offering with distaste. "Do you have anything other than orange marmalade?"

"I'm sorry," Cathrine replied. "Not your favorite?"

"I'd rather eat canvas," Marik replied. "Just the plain biscuit is fine." He bit into the pastry and savored the buttery flavor.

Cathrine watched him eat, a speculative look in her eyes. "Are you truly a pirate?"

"My lady wounds me, seeing deception in my every word."

Cathrine made an exasperated sound in her throat.

"I am what I say I am," Marik said.

Dalmir made a sound that was half-harrumph, half-chuckle and made his way over to a table where he poured himself a glass of water.

"I hope my father accepts your offer of help," Cathrine said.

"Why?" Marik asked.

"Because we need men with your skills in the battles to come." She stared thoughtfully into his eyes and Marik found he could not hold her gaze. Suddenly, he did not want her to see who he had been, the scars and the wounds that still bled in his soul, the bitterness and the hatred he had carried for so long; she should not see such things. He dropped his eyes and hurried to the table to get some water for himself.

Dalmir studied him out of the corner of one eye as Marik poured the glass and immediately began guzzling it. Was it his imagination, or could he feel Cathrine's eyes behind him, boring into the back of his head? He resisted the urge to glance over his shoulder. Instead, he focused on Dalmir.

"If you return to Gnupar with Lord Adelfried, you won't be needing the *Hawk* for a while."

Dalmir gazed at Marik and tapped his tumbler. "You have somewhere pressing to be?"

Marik shrugged, trying to keep his expression bland. "Time on the ground is a waste of money in my line of work. I was thinking I could take the *Hawk* and do a little reconnaissance with her, see if I can't make myself useful. I'll be back to pick you up on any day you name, though."

Dalmir's hand swiped through the air under his chin and he winced. "Confounded beard. I'm not used to its absence yet. That is a very altruistic offer, Captain." He narrowed his gaze at Marik.

"I want to help, too. I'm not in this fight for myself, you know. Never have been."

"Never?"

Marik thought about throwing a quick retort, but the look on Dalmir's face stopped him. "I can't say the money wasn't a nice perk," he admitted. "But piracy wasn't the life I would have chosen."

"So you said," Dalmir replied. "And after hearing more of your story, I begin to believe you."

Marik paced across the room a few times with a jaunty but restless swagger. Dalmir's words had prompted a slew of unpleasant memories to unroll in his mind, memories he did not wish to revisit. He turned his thoughts forward, focusing on the

Council, on the words he had said, on the way that Cathrine's brown eyes gleamed with amusement when he had tried to compliment her appearance... he frowned. What? Why did her face suddenly float in his mind? His gaze flicked to where she stood by the doorway, observing all and saying nothing.

Marik sighed. "I meant what I said in there." He waved a hand at the closed door to the Council chambers across the hall. He wasn't sure whom his words were directed to, Dalmir or the young woman. But he needed to say them. Needed someone to know what was in his heart and mind.

"I know." Dalmir's tone had a wondering quality to it.

"You sound surprised." Marik glanced at him.

"I am."

Marik couldn't help the laugh that boiled up out of him. Shaking his head, he turned back to Cathrine. "How long do you think they'll be?"

She tilted her head to one side. "Not long, I expect. You both surprised them, and they're wise enough to be wary. But you also seem sincere. We need friends. What you offer is too valuable to ignore."

Marik nodded. He understood the need to step back and look at a thing from every angle. He had learned the hard way that most things seeming too good to be true probably were. But now that he had faced the Council, his feet itched to be back in the air, to be on his way, to be doing something useful. Standing still never sat well with him. Standing still on the ground was like trying to tell a bird it had to learn how to breathe water. His gaze flicked to Cathrine and then away.

The door across the hall opened. "Please rejoin the Council, now," said a young man, popping his head inside the room. From the time he had spent with Beren and, having now met Lord and Lady Adelfried, Marik knew instantly that this was one of Beren's younger brothers.

They followed the young man to the large meeting room. The Council rose as they entered. Cathrine swept over to her father and bent down to whisper something in his ear. He nodded, and she faded back to her original place.

"We are grateful to you both and gladly accept whatever help you can provide," Lord Adelfried said as they took their places.

Marik felt his breath catch in his throat. He couldn't go back now.

"In return, you have whatever we are able to provide in order to help you carry out your work and your purposes. For Captain Marik and his crew, we extend Telmondir citizenship."

Marik stared, uncertain what Lord Adelfried had said. Uncertain he meant it. Unsure of exactly what it meant at all.

"What?" he asked thickly.

"You said that you are a wanted man in the Igyeum," Langston supplied. "Consider this your sanctuary. You and your crew become citizens of Telmondir and thus fall under the protection of this Council."

"Provided you do not break any of our laws or practice any piracy on our citizens," Roshana said, her voice dry as burning paper.

Marik could not speak for a long moment. The gesture had stunned him. At length, he nodded. "I thank you. On behalf of my crew, I thank you. We will not take this generous gift for granted."

"See that you don't," Langston said.

"Ah, Langston," Roshana chided. "If we are to be friends, we must act more friendly."

Dalmir met her gaze across the room, his lips quirked. "Ever the diplomats, Ondourans. Edoran would be proud of you."

"You know of Edoran?" For the first time, Roshana appeared flustered. "He is a legendary figure not generally known outside our own borders."

"Yes, I know," Dalmir replied. "But I am more widely traveled than most of my fellow countrymen." His eyes danced as with a private joke.

Lord Adelfried rose and brought Marik a rolled-up tube of

thick paper wrapped in a thin chain with a small pendant attached to it. "This writ gives you the blessing of the Council and states that you, your crew, and ship are in our employ."

Marik accepted the paper solemnly. "Thank you, sir."

Adelfried nodded, then raised his voice. "It grows late, so let us adjourn. Dalmir, as you will be accompanying us back to Gnupar, I am certain that you will wish to gather your belongings from Captain Marik's airship."

Dalmir nodded.

Adelfried fixed Marik with a look. "My daughter says that you are eager for an assignment to help our cause. Return in the morning and we may have something for you."

27

It was dark by the time Marik returned to the *Hawk*. But he felt lighter and more awake than he had in years. He swung up the rope ladder from the docking boat and vaulted up and over the railing, landing on the deck with a solid thump. None of his crew were on the deck, and so he bounded over to the hatch and stuck his head down the ladder.

"Raisa? Oleck? Mouse? Where is everybody hiding? I have news!"

Oleck's face appeared as his door opened and Marik caught a glimpse of shadows inside the room. He swung himself easily down the ladder and landed on the floorboards with a thud.

"Oleck? What's going on?"

The big man loomed into the hall. His eyes darted about and finally settled on the floorboards directly in front of his toes.

"Oleck?" Marik straightened, his shoulders turning slightly in a defensive motion. Beyond the doorway he could see the rest of his crew gathered in Oleck's quarters.

"Nothing serious, Cap'n," Oleck mumbled. "We were just... waiting for you to get back."

Marik gave his crewman a calculating look. "You were planning a rescue?"

Oleck's eyes narrowed and he stared fixedly at the floorboards for a long moment before giving a single nod.

Marik grinned. "Nobody needs rescuing tonight. But I have good news, and I'm glad you're all still up."

Oleck stepped back to let Marik in. "What's your news?" he asked.

Marik held up the document Thorben had given him. "We have been granted citizenship here in Telmondir." Unwilling to quite meet their eyes, he hurried on. "I know it's not exactly what any of us anticipated. But I believe this will be a good thing. They might even have paying jobs for us. If you think about it for just a minute, I think you'll see that this will enable us to..."

"Captain," Oleck interrupted him and Marik looked up at his first mate. "We're with you."

Marik paused, completely at a loss for words for the second time that day. "All of you?" he asked thickly.

Raisa nodded. "Where else would we go?"

"What does Telmondir cit-citen-zenship mean?" Mouse asked.

"It means, little man," Oleck rumbled, "that we have a safe haven here in Telmondir. We abide by their laws, and they protect us."

"Oh," Mouse replied. He seemed to ponder this for a moment. "I guess that's all right, then."

"Glad you approve." Marik chuckled, tousling the boy's wildly curly blond hair. Kid needed a haircut, he thought idly. His gaze swept over the faces of his crew, and he found that he could even include Shaesta in his joy at the moment. He still found it hard to trust her, but he was learning to be comfortable with her as part of his crew once more, and that was a nice feeling.

———

As Marik strode into the Arxis building the next morning, he was greeted by the Council members and Dalmir, who had stayed ashore to speak privately with Lord Adelfried and discuss the best place to set up the refiner so that it could benefit Telmondir.

"Ah, Marik." Lord Adelfried welcomed him with a broad smile and a wave.

Marik nodded his head in acknowledgment. "Have you decided upon a mission for me and my crew?"

"I believe we have." Adelfried's brow furrowed a bit. "We are grateful for the refiner, and for your offer to add your unique talents to our arsenal. I am, however, loath to disclose any of our plans or purposes to anyone, let alone those who are new to our cause. However, our cause would be lost without the help that Dalmir has provided. He trusts you, as does Lady Nadia, though for the life of me I cannot understand why." Adelfried gave Marik a hard look. "But I am overruled. Your mission will send you into the heart of the Ar'Mol's territories, which will certainly put you and your crew in harm's way should anything go awry. We pay our soldiers well, and you will be well compensated for the risk you undertake with this mission, but there is grave risk. I wanted you to understand that."

Marik did not reply immediately. Instead he walked over to the large table in the center of the room and leaned his elbows upon it. The surface of the table was covered in a map of Turrim that had various symbols depicting troop placement and outposts, as well as a few words written on it in several locations. He studied it for a moment.

"I am well aware of the terms of our agreement." Marik picked up a pencil and idly made a few markings of his own on the map. "I can't remember life without risk. We are grateful for the compensation and the opportunity to continue my own commitment to aiding Dalmir on his mission. If it strikes a blow to the Ar'Mol while I'm at it, then so much the better."

"What are you marking there?" Duke Langston came over and peered over Marik's shoulder, a note of suspicion in his tone.

"Just a few outposts near your borders you don't seem to

know about, and a notation on the routes the army often uses in their supply lines." Marik squinted and made another few marks. "And the location of the ruined refinery. I doubt the Ar'Mol will return to it, but in a conflict like this knowledge is power."

"Words of truth," Langston muttered. He perused the marks Marik had made and his eyebrows shot up a bit. "Are those new outposts?"

"Fairly recent," Marik replied. "Maybe a few lunats old."

"How could we not have known about them?" Langston gestured to his fellow Councilors and pointed out the places Marik had indicated on the map. "If this is accurate, the Ar'Mol is growing bold ahead of the schedule we predicted."

"Or there is a new factor at play," Dalmir said.

"Such as?" Roshana asked, her keen ears catching Dalmir's whispered mutter.

Dalmir fixed her with a steady and implacable gaze. "The restoration of Uun's full power."

The wrinkles that layered themselves across the elderly Regeont's face bunched together as she peered at Dalmir with piercingly perceptive eyes. "What do you mean by that?"

Dalmir sighed. "Uun has been bound for hundreds of years, or at least, I thought he was. But I recently discovered that he found a way to wriggle through the bars by transferring another's life into his own manacles. In order to rescue the innocent he had trapped there, I had to open the prison door completely."

"Ah." Roshana frowned. "I see." She opened her mouth, then hesitated.

"You have other questions. Please feel free to ask them," Dalmir said.

"What is that orb you carry, and how does it work? How can such a small, simple thing produce something as complex as a cynder—able to power an entire airship—within moments? We have never been privileged enough to catch a glimpse of the Ar'Mol's technology before, and though we have tried to replicate it, our efforts have been in vain. Can you teach our engineers what they need to know in order to build our own refinery?" The Regeont's questions were delivered rapid-fire.

"I am afraid I cannot," Dalmir replied. "And as for what the orb itself is, I can only say that it is complicated to explain. I can, however, help set up the refiner that we brought to you and engineer something to allow it to run for a while on its own before I would need to refill it." He fell silent. Roshana waited for him to continue, but Dalmir merely turned his gaze to the map upon the table. "If you believe that the mines of Telsuma are the best place for me to set up the refiner, then how quickly can you get me there? I have other business to be about and thus I would prefer to get started immediately."

Roshana's lips parted as if she wished to protest, but she caught a look from Adelfried and kept her words unspoken, a deep wrinkle creasing her forehead above her nose.

"Yes, I believe the mines are the most convenient location," Adelfried said. "And if I am not mistaken, Daegan is there right now. Which brings me to the final item of note I had wanted to discuss here. A few sennights ago, Daegan sent word that at long last he has completed his design for a machine that can help us in the war with the Igyeum."

There was a collective intake of breath. Dalmir and Marik exchanged a puzzled glance.

Langston stared. "He has accomplished the task he told us not three lunats ago he was ready to give up as impossible? Even after completing the designs, he and Keene seemed unsure that they could actually build the thing."

"It seems they have solved the problem," Adelfried replied. "He had every intention of being here at this meeting with a working prototype, but was not sure it was possible in such a short amount of time. Clearly, it was not. However, I think it would behoove us to extend our time in order to visit Keene's forge and see what our master engineer has created."

"That is a very good idea," Langston agreed. "I, for one, am eager to see what this device is and how it works."

Roshana cleared her throat and stared pointedly at Marik. "Perhaps we should get back to the matter at hand? I believe we were about to tell Captain Marik about the assignment we have for him."

"Yes." Marik straightened. "My crew and I are eager for our first assignment."

"We have been attempting to get close to the Ar'Mol's inner circle for some time." Adelfried marched over to the map-covered table. "We know that this is his main stronghold"—he indicated a location in Malei—"but our attempts to gain access have been largely unsuccessful."

"You want me to infiltrate the Ar'Mol's palace?" Marik felt a thrill of terror mixed with elation. He narrowed his eyes and tried to think through the difficulties such a task might entail.

"Of course not," Roshana said, her tone harsh. "We barely know you."

"No." Adelfried shook his head. "You misunderstand me. It would be nice to have someone inside the palace, of course, but what we really need is information on the Ar'Mol's plan. Having the troop movements and the locations of outposts can only tell us so much. We are hoping to discover where his first attack will be made. Through our own sources, we have been carefully monitoring troop movements. However, a large force of Igyeum soldiers has suddenly disappeared."

"Disappeared?" Marik raised a skeptical eyebrow.

"I know what it sounds like, but we have our own network of informants, and a few lunats ago we were made aware of the fact that a large portion of the Ar'Mol's military had vanished. The numbers we had no longer matched up with the numbers we were seeing. Even with the new outposts you have made us aware of, the numbers do not match up. Now, either there was a mass defection, or a natural disaster we are unaware of, or..." Adelfried trailed off.

"Or he's moved them to a secret location and is preparing to strike from the shadows," Marik finished the thought.

"That is our concern," Langston confirmed.

"We need to find those missing troops, or, if we cannot do that, at least discover where the Ar'Mol intends to make his first move against Telmondir." Marik did not phrase it as a question.

"Precisely." Adelfried fixed him with an appraising stare. "Both pieces of information are critical. We know that keeping an airship aloft is no small feat, and the time table for this mission is undetermined. I wish we could offer you more to better compensate for the risk involved. Every resource we have is needed elsewhere at the moment. However, we can keep you at your work and cover your expenses for this assignment. Lady Roshana has one hundred runes to get you started, if you are amenable to this mission." Adelfried turned to his fellow Councilors to address other pressing concerns.

The weight of such an offer was not lost on Marik. The danger was as real as the compensation. A promise of wealth did not accompany this assignment, but a worthy purpose did. Marik paused and then replied, "Can you give me time to discuss this with my crew?"

Langston and Roshana held a whispered conference with Adelfried, who then turned to Marik. "Of course, you must include them in this decision. Regardless of your answer, you depart with our goodwill and the already offered citizenship."

Marik strode out of the room and returned to his ship. After detailing the parameters of their assignment, he waited, eyebrows raised to hear his crew's response. They each took a moment to think through what he had said, but in the end, each gave him a firm nod. He felt a flicker of tension settle in the pit of his stomach, the good kind of tension that preceded every mission. It was a mounting desire to return to the sky, to get underway.

When Marik returned, he stood before the Council one last time. "We accept the mission," he informed them.

Roshana approached and took Marik by the shoulders. She kissed the air on either side of his face with grace and then slung the strap of a satchel over his shoulder. "A small token of our appreciation. We walk on your hands. May success greet you like a field of flowers in spring."

Langston did not approach or speak, but gave him a firm nod.

Marik found himself swallowing past a sudden tightness in his throat. That these worthy, powerful people should look to him with trust in their eyes was at once overwhelming and strangely unbearable. It was a sensation he was not sure he liked, and one he was not eager to dwell upon. He gave them each a polite nod and left the Arxis building with swift, sure steps. He did not give in to the temptation to flee, but when his boots were once again solidly set on the deck of the *Hawk* there was no denying that he felt a certain measure of relief sweep through him.

28

Dalmir tried to overcome the uneasy quiver in his chest that made breathing difficult. He chafed at this delay to his plans. And yet, he believed it was necessary. He was glad he had been able to talk to the entire ruling body of Telmondir at once, which had saved him much unwelcome traveling and time. Still, time was passing, and with each moment, Dalmir feared that Uun's advantage grew.

As he stepped off the small airship that had carried him and the Adelfrieds across the miles from the Arxis into Telsuma, his unease subsided. The vast mountain ranges rising up all around him and the crisp, cold air penetrating his lungs soothed him. The majesty of this land made him feel strangely revitalized. This had always been one of his favorite places to visit. Telsume had always welcomed him and made him feel wanted.

"Even now, you comfort me, Tel," Dalmir whispered. "Yours was always the steady hand, the patient attention to detail. Never getting ahead of yourself, never rushing."

Lord Adelfried descended the gangplank before Dalmir. He led the way down the great stairs that formed the base of the docks where the airship hovered. These were far smaller than the great docks in Dalton, but so were the airships moored here. This was not the hub of trade for Telsuma, then, Dalmir surmised. No, of course not. Such activity would more likely be found in Telos, several miles farther east. But Chieftain Adelfried preferred to remain here in Gnupar on his family estate. Dalmir followed along, picking his way carefully down the wooden steps.

Adelfried led Dalmir along a well-worn dirt path until they reached a sprawling house. Some sort of commotion appeared to be reigning as loud shouts rang out and figures burst from the door. Then they were surrounded by the rest of the Adelfried family, which seemed to consist mainly of a group of children of varying ages, all jumping and running and shouting at once. Thorben and Nadia smiled and hugged each of their children, answering the many questions they asked as they made their way up to the house. Cathrine took over when they reached the door, shepherding the children inside and setting them to various tasks of getting ready for bed.

"Tomorrow, I will take you to the forge," Thorben said to Dalmir, blinking his eyes wearily. "Keene and Daegan will be eager to meet you and get to work on your device. You will be our guest here, of course."

"My thanks," Dalmir said, his head still reeling from the onslaught of children.

Thorben gave him a true smile. "Drengur, please show Dalmir to the guest quarters. Do you need anything before you turn in for the night?"

"The repast we had on the airship was plenty," Dalmir replied. "What I need right now is a bed. Or at least a place where I can be horizontal."

Thorben nodded. "I know what you mean. I will see you in the morning, then."

DALMIR EMERGED from his room the next morning feeling mildly refreshed. The sun had barely risen and the household remained in slumber. He wandered down the hall in the direction he thought the main rooms might be and soon found a large room filled with comfortable-looking furniture and a massive stone fireplace. Sitting on the floor near the hearth, a small child was studiously building something out of blocks. His dark head bent down over his work and small sounds emanated from his mouth as he placed one block on top of another. He glanced up as though sensing Dalmir's presence.

"Want to play with me?" the child asked.

Dalmir blinked. He looked around, wondering if the child had truly been speaking to him, but nobody else seemed to be awake yet. "Me?"

The child nodded.

Feeling a bit trapped, Dalmir stepped forward. "All right. I suppose."

"You have to come down here," the child said.

Dalmir dropped to the floor a few feet away from the boy, who promptly handed him a block.

"You build a castle," the boy instructed. "And I'll build a castle. And then our castles will have a fight!"

Nonplussed, Dalmir did as he was told. He selected blocks with care, watching the child out of the corner of his eye.

"What's your name?" the boy asked after a few minutes.

"Dalmir. And yours?" Dalmir placed a base layer of blocks in a rectangle.

"Hubert," the boy replied. "I'm the littlest."

"How old are you?"

Hubert scrunched up his nose. "Five. But I'm almost six."

"Really? When do you turn six?"

"Second day of Edrian!"

Dalmir could not contain the delighted laugh that sprang to his lips. The first sennight of Edrian had only just finished, meaning that the child had turned five a few days ago. "Are you the only one awake yet?" Dalmir asked as he stood some blocks on end and created walls.

Hubert nodded. "Momma doesn't like it when I wake her up before the sun."

Dalmir grinned. "She doesn't? That's strange." He used longer blocks to create a roof for his construction.

Hubert shook his head seriously. "That's a good castle," he said appreciatively. "Now let's fight!" He picked up a small block and tossed it at one of Dalmir's walls. It crashed through the structure, knocking part of it over. Dalmir stared for a moment, once again unsure of how to react. The boy stared up at him with wide, dark eyes. He seemed to be waiting for something. Dalmir picked up a block of his own and hesitantly tossed it at Hubert's castle, knocking part of it over. He braced himself, waiting for the child to burst into tears, but instead, Hubert's eyes danced with mischief and he tossed another block at Dalmir's castle. Within moments, they were both chuckling and tossing blocks softly, doing their best to demolish each other's creations.

"What is going on out here?" A feminine voice broke through their shouts of laughter—that had grown louder and more raucous without their realizing it—causing both Dalmir and Hubert to pause and look up guiltily.

Lady Nadia stood over them, her eyes tired and her hair messy from sleep. "Hubert, did you wake up our guest?"

"No, Momma," he said.

Dalmir scrambled to his feet. "Forgive me, madam, I have always been an early riser. I was wandering through your lovely home and happened upon your son. He graciously invited me to play blocks with him to pass the time before breakfast and I accepted. I apologize if our battle for the honor of Turrim woke you."

Nadia stared at him for a long moment, then she blinked and her lips curved up. "I thought our home had been invaded by Igyeum warriors," she teased. "I am glad to know that you and Hubert were up and ready to defend us had that been the case." She yawned. "Let me get dressed and I can start on breakfast. The rest of the family will be waking soon."

AFTER BREAKFAST, Lord Adelfried, Lady Nadia, and Drengur ushered Dalmir outside and down the path a bit further. The path came to a dead-end at a door carved directly into the face of a cliff that soared high above them.

"Come," Adelfried said. "Keene and Daegan will be eager to meet you. They're both a little eccentric, but you'll not find more steadfast, loyal hearts anywhere."

Adelfried approached the enormous door and pulled a metal lever sticking out of the wall. A loud jangling of bells sounded from within, and a moment later the door opened. A tall, wiry man, clad in a long, thick, leather apron appeared in the doorway. His golden hair was pulled back from his face in a scraggly braid and his face was covered in a short beard that looked as though it had recently been on fire.

His hazel eyes sparkled as with the light of heated iron as he gazed upon his visitors. "Thorben! Have you come to inspect the monster Daegan and I have been working on?"

He reached forward and pulled Lord Adelfried into an embrace. Dalmir watched, a bemused expression on his face. It was hard to imagine someone so thin wielding a forge hammer with any amount of strength, but he had a sneaking suspicion that the man's wiry frame hid a body corded with lean muscle.

"Nadia, Drengur!" The man grinned and pulled off one long leather glove, taking Lady Adelfried's much smaller hand in his own and bending over it. "But who is this?" He turned to Dalmir, a welcoming but puzzled look crossing his features.

"This is Dalmir," Thorben replied. "He has a new project for you, Keene. One that I think will challenge even your skill."

"Ah." Keene's gaze swept over Dalmir, taking in every aspect of his appearance in a single measuring glance. "Welcome to my humble forge, Master Dalmir." He opened his arms wide. "I look forward to working with you on whatever it is you have brought me. Come in, come in." He stepped aside and gestured for them to enter the cavern beyond.

The interior was not what Dalmir had expected. The room on the other side of the door was large and comfortable, with a high ceiling. Tapestries lined the walls and a large iron chandelier hung from the ceiling in the center of the room, its candles burning brightly and giving a warm and cheery light to the room. The furnishings were simple and worn.

"I've told you that a beard is not practical for a man of your profession," Nadia teased.

"Beards are the pride of the Routhmin clan," Keene said in injured tones.

"But yours is continuously catching fire."

"It's easier than trimming it." Keene chuckled, and Nadia laughed, her voice ringing off the walls.

Beyond this room several hallways stretched away. Keene led them down one of these. The ceiling above their heads curved into a gentle vault, and from the far end of the hall emanated a rumble of light and warmth. Keene did not take them all the way to the forge, however, turning instead to a door on the left that opened into a small workroom. Shelves stacked high with papers and notebooks lined the walls. A high table was shoved up against a wall, a tall stool before it. On this stool sat another man, bent over the papers on the table, studying them intently.

"Daegan!" Keene's voice boomed into the room.

Dalmir squinted in the dim light. Daegan was short and had broad shoulders. Where Keene was thin and looked as though he could not even lift a forge hammer, Daegan looked as though he could lift a mountain. His face was clean shaven, and his much shorter hair was white and streaked with what looked like ink stains. Upon hearing Keene's voice he whirled around on the stool.

"Keene! How many times have I told you..." He trailed off upon seeing the rest of the group in the doorway. He hopped down and stood awkwardly, wiping ink-stained hands on rumpled trousers.

"Lord and Lady Adelfried!" he exclaimed in surprise. "To what do we owe this honor? Have you come to inspect the device? We are not quite finished..."

"No, we are not here for that," Thorben assured him, "though I would like to see it, if you and Keene are willing. We are here for a different reason. This is Dalmir." He gestured and Daegan glanced at Dalmir with a vague and disinterested expression. Thorben Adelfried continued, "He has a device that I think you will find interesting. We are hoping that with his guidance you can recreate it in such a way that allows anyone to use it."

At these words, Daegan straightened, his eyes narrowing with interest. "What sort of device?"

"If you don't mind?" Adelfried turned to Dalmir.

Drawing the refiner from his robes, Dalmir strode across the workroom and placed it on the table. Daegan stared at it for a long moment. Then he glanced up at Dalmir.

"May I?" He reached his hand toward the device.

"Please."

With infinite care, Daegan picked up the refiner and turned it over in his hands, exploring every angle, every facet of the device. After a few moments of study, he set it back down on the table and turned to Dalmir. No longer did he bear any trace of vagueness or disinterest. His eyes were sharp with an eager hunger.

"What is it? What does it do?"

"In the Igyeum they call it a refiner," Dalmir replied. "It is the device they use to fill cynders so that they can power airships."

Daegan's lips parted slightly and his expression grew excited. "How does it work?"

"With this." Dalmir pulled out the shimmering blue orb and placed it in the refiner. Instantly the device began dripping a shining blue light over the brim and onto the table. Dalmir removed the orb swiftly and the liquid light paled into a dark mass. "You need to have the ore shaped and ready to catch it," he explained, "otherwise it's useless."

"Fascinating," Daegan whispered. He plucked the dimmed orb from Dalmir's hand and held it up, examining it closely. "We have speculated about how the cynders are made, but this design has eluded us. It's not"—he glanced up at Dalmir, pausing briefly as he handed the orb back—"natural, is it?"

"Not strictly speaking, no," Dalmir replied.

Daegan's eyes shone. "I thought not. That is why we could never figure out the formula. How did you learn the secret?"

Dalmir shrugged. "Quite by accident."

Daegan's face shone with a conspiratorial light of understanding and he winked. "All the best discoveries happen by accident, do they not? Whatever you need, I am at your complete disposal. I am assuming you will want to recreate a larger version of the refining device?"

"And I will need your help with something else, as well."

Daegan rubbed his hands together, the ink stains on his fingers spreading. "Excellent. This is perfect timing." He glanced at Adelfried. "You wanted to see the device? It isn't quite ready, yet, but I believe you will be sufficiently impressed with our progress. I was nearly done with my latest round of schematics, so having a new puzzle to work on is a great boon."

"I do wish to see it. And I have something else I need you to take a look at."

Daegan glanced sideways at Dalmir. "Not to be rude..."

"Dalmir is trustworthy," Adelfried assured him.

"Good, what do you have to show me?"

"Just this." Thorben handed Daegan a stack of papers and waited while the man's quick eyes darted back and forth. Daegan's expression started out curious, turned to sharp interest, and then astonished disbelief as he riffled through the pages faster and faster. When he had finished, he looked up, his eyes wide.

"Where did you get these?"

"You won't believe it."

"Tell me!"

"One of our initiates turned that in for an assignment. A cadet by the name of Wynn Drexel."

"The assignment I developed for Mathis?"

Thorben nodded.

"But that…" Daegan looked down at the pages. "It doesn't seem possible. All this time and an initiate comes up with this? It is brilliant."

"I thought you'd be interested."

"Thank you for showing me," Daegan replied. "This design isn't as elegant as what Keene and I are working on, but even just glancing at it I can see there are aspects of this idea that will add stability to what we have already built. We're not so far into the process that adjustments cannot be made."

"What are you making?" Dalmir asked, curious in spite of himself.

Daegan moved to the door and beckoned, his teeth gleaming in a knowing grin. "This way, come and see the marvel we have created."

29

The *Valdeun Hawk* soared through the air, its wings and sails slicing through the wind like the bird for which it was named. Marik stood at the wheel, his dark hair ruffling slightly. He closed his eyes and took a moment to simply enjoy the sensation of flying. This was freedom. This was what he lived for. Marik could never explain it to the rest of his crew, but it was this beautiful siren call that drew him to the skies again and again. More than necessity. More than greed. More even than his need for vengeance. It was the freedom of flying that truly made Marik feel alive. It was what he believed redemption might feel like, though a man like him could never hope to attain that level of forgiveness. He had done too many things he was not proud of.

"So, where to first, Captain?" Oleck asked, appearing at Marik's side.

Marik opened his eyes and let out a long breath, releasing the moment of peace with a wistful pang. Those moments were too short, too precious. But he was the captain, and as such must shoulder the responsibilities that came with the position.

"First to the hideout," he replied. "We stashed our supply of cynders there, and I would like to have a few extras on board if we need them. I'd also like to contact some of our friends and see if they can shed any light on the information we've been commissioned to find. From there, I'm not sure yet. The missing troops are a concern, but I have a feeling our main goal should be trying to get close to the Ar'Mol."

Oleck scratched his cheek. "That sounds like the beginning of a plan. But we've spent the past few years doing our best to be the taste of sand in the Ar'Mol's food. Chances are good he knows our names, if not our very faces. Getting close enough to spy on him could be difficult."

"I'm working on that," Marik said.

Oleck grimaced. "I hope you come up with one of your crazy ideas soon. I've missed them."

"We've been stuck in the middle of my last crazy scheme for lunats. I didn't think anyone could handle more than one at a time." Marik's face split into a wide grin.

Oleck guffawed loudly. "Words of truth, Captain."

With Oleck's laughter, a tension that had been invisibly present on board the *Hawk* snapped and relinquished its hold on Marik. He joined his friend laughing, his hands ever steady on the wheel. It felt good to laugh again.

As though summoned by the spontaneous mirth, Raisa and Mouse emerged from belowdecks. Raisa's eyebrow arched elegantly as she took in the scene before her. Mouse's head swung back and forth between Oleck and Marik, his lips stretching into a puzzled grin.

"What's so funny?" he inquired, chuckling in spite of having no idea what the joke was.

"Marik's latest crazy scheme," Oleck barked, laughter erupting from the big man.

Raisa smiled and shook her head. Marik met her gaze and held it, his laughter calming to a chuckle. Marik savored the moment of merriment, soaking in this moment with his crew, the most important people in his world.

———

NIGHT RAIN PELTED Malei as the airship swooped down into the canyon, hidden by the double blanket of darkness. Marik had taken them to their hideout on a meandering, roundabout route, and as a result the crew was tired and a little stressed. The rain didn't help their moods, either. As water dripped down his face, plastering his hair to his head, Marik deftly steered his beloved *Hawk* into the large cavern that was the closest thing to a home he possessed on land. He carefully positioned the lithe airship above the docking apparatus and set her down with a light touch that would have awed most other airship captains. It did not matter that the *Hawk* was lighter and nimbler than most airships in use, Marik's command of her steerage was impressive by any standard, and he knew it. Elation filled his spirit as he shut down the cynders and let his ship fall asleep, an elation that he always experienced after a successful run and return home, an elation that was tinged with the shadow of melancholy that pierced his soul at no longer being airborne. Whistling a jaunty tune to cover the creeping melancholy, he slid down the railing of the steerage, his boots clumping loudly on the main deck as he landed with a heavy thud.

"We're home," he announced, to no one in particular.

Being home and out of the wet improved the crew's countenance. They all helped pull in the sails and wings, lashing them tightly to keep them safe from sudden gusts of wind that could come whipping through the cavern. Together, he and his crew mopped the deck, soaking up the extra water the storm had deposited there. Then Oleck headed down to the cynder room to make sure everything was in working order. When they had finished checking over every inch of the airship to Marik's satisfaction, they lowered the rope ladder and clambered down to the cavern floor. Outside, the storm had intensified.

"It's a bit stormy to try to get into town tonight," Raisa commented, staring out at the sheets of rain pouring down to the canyon floor several spans below their cave. "I don't relish trying to cross the canyon floor in this weather." As if to punctuate her statement, lightning arced through the sky, followed by a deafening crack of thunder. Raisa put her hand on Mouse's shoulder and Marik noticed that the young boy did not shrug it off. He turned his back to conceal his grin. As hard as Mouse tried to portray himself as being street-smart and tough, he was still young enough to appreciate a modicum of comfort during a thunderstorm.

"It is a good thing we have plenty of supplies here, then," Marik replied. "We can wait out the storm tonight and head into town in the morning."

Marik and Oleck disappeared into a small, concealed side cavern to retrieve some of the dry wood always stored there. They returned with armloads and quickly put it to fire. Raisa and Mouse went back on board the airship and returned laden down with food and bedrolls. Shaesta hovered in the shadows, her expression haunted. Marik glanced at her out of the corner of his eye and then turned his attention back to helping Oleck with the fire. It would be so easy to invite her back into his circle, to welcome her wholeheartedly to his crew. It would feel right to have her back amongst them as companion and friend. It might even begin to heal the hole she had ripped in his heart with her betrayal. But it was because of that very betrayal that Marik could not welcome her back yet. He did not know if he ever could.

"Do you care to give us a hint as to that plan you said you were working on?" Oleck asked as he stirred the fire.

"First, I want to get some information in town. Find out what has happened since we left," Marik replied, tossing more kindling into the baby flames, which leapt higher and began licking at the logs.

"Was it only a few lunats ago?" Raisa wondered out loud. "We thought we were plotting the impossible then."

Shaesta moved a bit closer, but stayed out of the ring of light cast by the growing fire.

"This is no more impossible than that was," Marik

murmured. "It is just going to require a lot of careful planning. And we're going to need to do some work disguising the *Hawk*."

Oleck rubbed a hand behind his neck. "I think I can guess where this is going."

Marik tossed him a reckless grin. "Lots of merchants in Melar."

"A few more wouldn't hardly be noticed, now would they?" Oleck replied evenly.

"But what will our cargo be?" Raisa asked.

"That's another thing I want to ask about in town," Marik replied. "Find out what things are scarce or expensive these days. Whatever it is, that will be our cargo."

"And how will we get our hands on such expensive or rare items?" Raisa demanded.

Marik's grin grew wider and his eyes darted to the back of the cave and then back to Raisa's face, which paled.

"No," she breathed. "Marik, you wouldn't!" Her voice contained a pleading note.

Mouse looked back and forth between them. "Wouldn't what?" he asked.

"We have a large stockpile of cynders." Raisa's words came out through teeth that were clamped tightly together, as Marik's grin grew fierce. "Worth a fortune. Enough to see us settled in comfort for life. And he"—she threw the words at Marik as if they were daggers—"wants to use them to buy trade goods so we can pose as merchants and maybe... maybe get close to the Ar'Mol." Her eyes danced with a dangerous light and she rose, hands on her hips. "Marik," she growled, "this might be too far."

"Too far? Too far for what?" Marik asked, his tone calm. "Too far to secure the freedom from tyranny we've always dreamed of? Too far to stop the Ar'Mol from his raids on our own people, forcing our young men into his army, forcing the people to work to feed and outfit that army and reap none of the benefit themselves? Too far to stop the burning of villages over minor infractions? Have you forgotten so quickly that we've been granted a gift, Raisa? We've been given citizenship in Telmondir and a chance to actually make a real difference in the coming conflict with the Ar'Mol. We've attached our ship to their star and it's too late to turn back."

Raisa scowled.

"Raisa." Marik's tone grew gentle. "When did it become all about the money? Piracy has always just been a means to an end, never the end itself. I thought you of all people understood that."

Raisa shrugged, her expression twisting. "I did. I do. I just... You know I'd follow you to the depths of the ocean. But tying us to the Council... are you so sure it makes a difference who is in charge? Are you sure that the Council is any better than the Ar'Mol and his commanders?"

"I think your father would tell you they are." The words came out of Marik's mouth softly, but Raisa reeled back as though he had struck her. "After all, the freedom that the people of Telmondir enjoy is the exact thing he died for. You remember the injustice he suffered at the Ar'Mol's whim. Are you really telling me it makes no difference? Have you become so much of a pirate that you can't remember why we took on this life in the first place?"

A heavy hush permeated the cave, broken only by the percussion of the rain drumming at the entrance. Raisa's face paled with emotions Marik could not decipher.

"How do you know about my father?" The question came out in a strangled whisper.

Marik did not answer.

In a single, fluid motion, Raisa stood before Marik, staring up at him, her eyes brimming with pain. "I have never spoken about my past, not even to you. How could you know anything about my father?"

Marik glanced at Oleck, hoping he might find an excuse that she would accept, but Raisa shook her head, a defiant, angry motion. "No. Oleck promised me. He would never..."

"He didn't," Marik said heavily.

"Then… how?"

"Because I…" Marik's voice came out hollow and hoarse, and then failed him altogether. He stared down at his boots and then drew a knife from its sheath at his side. Solemnly, silently, he handed it to the woman standing before him. She stared at it in confusion. Marik raised his gaze and stared directly into her eyes. Helplessness overwhelmed him, regret piled on regret in a vast and unending sea of decisions and paths he wished he could take back and do differently. But he never could. Time only marched forward, to his everlasting shame. He swallowed. "I was there, Ray."

Raisa gazed at him, her expression blank, uncomprehending. His words did not seem to touch her at first. Then he saw her fist tighten as her fingers clenched the dagger's handle. Her eyes hardened into an expression of pure hatred as she raised the dagger, her mouth opened in a wordless cry of rage.

"Raisa!" Oleck jumped to his feet.

Mouse let out a shrill cry of terror.

Marik simply gazed into Raisa's eyes. He said nothing. His hands remained at his sides. He was defenseless. As defenseless as Raisa's father had been. If she let the blow fall, it would be no less than what he deserved.

"I'm sorry," he whispered.

Whirling, Raisa flung the dagger at the fire; it bounced off a log, sent up a shower of sparks, and clattered onto the stone floor. She turned, her eyes wild.

"Oleck," she demanded, "did you know?"

"Raisa…" Oleck stared at her and extended his arms slightly, palms out. "I…" His voice was gruff and hoarse. He did not continue, but sat down by the fire, pulled a dagger from his belt, and began cleaning it vigorously.

Raisa's eyes flashed in the firelight, gleaming with anger and unshed tears. Without a word she spun and stalked out of the cave and into the storm.

"Raisa!" Marik called out after her. "Raisa, wait!"

"Best let her alone for a bit," Oleck muttered, keeping his eyes on the dagger in his hands. "She may need some time to process this."

Marik's jaw twitched as he considered Oleck's words, but a flash of lightning followed by an immediate clap of thunder settled the matter. "It's dangerous out there. I don't care how mad at me she gets, I'm not going to let her wander around out there alone," Marik snarled. He scooped up an extra cloak, pulled his own hood up, and dashed out into the rain.

———

RAISA HAD NOT GONE FAR. Marik found her huddled under a ledge, her arms wrapped around her knees, staring out at the water pouring down from the sky. He did not say anything, merely squeezed under the ledge beside her and draped the extra cloak over her shoulders. She did not turn to him or acknowledge his presence, but neither did she flinch from his touch or the proffered cloak. Together they sat for a long time watching the storm as it battered the landscape around them. There was a beauty in the wildness of the rain and the way the wind caused a fine spray to blow into their meager shelter and across their faces. There was an artistry to the way the lightning split the sky, rending the clouds and spidering out in all directions. The rumble and crash of thunder that followed pounded its way into Marik's heart, stirring his soul. A part of him wanted to leap out into the open and stand in the downpour, arms outstretched, welcoming the tempest and all its fury. Another part of him was content to just sit next to Raisa, despite the awkward silence and the anger and hurt he could feel radiating from her, mirroring the weather.

"You were a soldier in the Ar'Mol's army." When Raisa finally spoke, her voice was flat. "How could I have missed that? All these years at your side, flying the *Hawk*, everything we've done together. How could I have been so stupid?"

Marik heaved a sigh. If only he could take back his words in the cave. The secrets he had held for so long huddled tightly in his chest, angry at being discovered and reluctant to be dragged into the light.

"Why didn't you tell me?" A sorrowful note tinged Raisa's words that made Marik's heart ache strangely.

He worked his jaw for a moment before words would come. "It's not a period of my life I'm exactly proud of." Marik did not turn his head as he spoke, but kept staring out into the storm. Perhaps this would be easier if he did not look at her.

Raisa glanced sideways at him, her lips set in a thin line. "Tell me now."

"I had just joined up." Marik found the words difficult to say, but he forced them out anyway. It would serve him right if he choked on the story. "I hadn't even been given a real assignment yet, just marching with my squad. We were ordered to meet up with another unit where we would get our first mission. We stopped in a town for the night. Just another town. Like any other town, really. I remember it seemed peaceful. Then something struck me. I remember it came out of nowhere. It knocked me off my feet. There I was, lying in the dust, groaning, nearly blacking out from the pain. I didn't even know what hit me. We were completely caught unawares." Marik closed his eyes, the unwelcome memories flooding through him. His temple throbbed as though he had just been struck again by the flying rock.

The air was thick and hot, smelling of dust and sweat. They had been trudging along the parched road under the intensely pounding sun since dawn, with barely a rest for water. The commander of the squad was a wizened, cruel man who seemed to enjoy witnessing the misery of his underlings. Reaching the town just before dusk had been a relief. Here they would find water, food, a cool place to sleep. Marik had no idea anything was wrong until the moment that pain exploded along the side of his face, burrowing its way into his skull. He did not remember falling, just blinking up at the hazy purple of the sky in the twilight. Blood pounded so loudly in his head that it took him a few moments to realize that some of the roaring he was hearing were the shouts of his squad and the tramp of their feet as they scattered toward whatever cover they could find. More rocks pelted the earth around him. He heard the cries of his comrades as several rocks found their marks. Rough hands seized him under his arms and his body was dragged painfully across the ground. Another rock grazed him and he was bumped onto the ground as his rescuer had to let go to dodge the projectile that had been flung at his head. Marik was too dazed to do anything but lie there. The hands appeared again and he was dragged behind a nearby barn where someone pressed a rough piece of cloth to the side of his face and helped him sit up. It was then that Marik noticed the wet trickle of blood running down his cheek.

The ambush had possessed the element of surprise, but the squad had been well-trained. They gathered themselves together and then sallied forth into the town. With the swift hand of justice, the perpetrators were discovered and placed in the town stockade, awaiting their sentence: hanging.

The next morning, however, it was discovered that the young men who had been imprisoned for the night had somehow escaped. Further investigation had led the squad commander to the home of a mason, who had freed the young men in the wee hours of the night. The commander dragged the man to the town square and executed him on the spot. A teenage girl, little more than a child, had run into the street begging them to let her father live, that he was all she had left. Marik remembered all too well the sickening sound of his commander's hand across the girl's tear-streaked face. The empty horror he felt as she fell to the ground, stunned and weeping as the commander killed her father.

That incident had been the first in a series of drumbeats that had changed the course of what Marik would march to.

Marik opened his eyes. "You know the rest."

Raisa's face was wet, but Marik knew it was not from the rain. Her shoulders shook. The insides of his stomach churning with trepidation, Marik put a tentative arm around her shoulders. He half-expected her to turn and snarl at him, or at the very least shrug off the unwanted comfort. Instead she turned into him and pressed her face against his shoulder, sobbing. He adjusted slightly, wrapping his other arm around her and patting her hair awkwardly as one might comfort a child.

There was no tracking how much time passed as they sat there, Raisa's sobs drowned out by the pelting rain and the receding rumble of thunder as the storm rolled over their heads and continued on its journey across the sky. As the rain grew lighter, Raisa quieted, reduced to long, shaky breaths. When at last she pulled away, she wiped a damp sleeve across her face and then looked at the ground.

Marik was not sure what to say or do. In the dark, he could not read Raisa's expression.

"Well," Raisa said at length. "Oleck and Mouse will be wondering what happened to us."

"They know you're more than capable of taking care of yourself," Marik assured her.

"That's true. But they might be worried about you." Raisa forced a laugh.

Marik smiled at the jibe, but gazed at her solemnly. "We don't go back until you're ready."

Raisa took a long, slow breath. She lifted her chin. "I'm fine." Her voice was steady.

"Are you sure?"

"Yes," she replied softly, "I'm sure."

Without a word, Marik stepped out from under the little ledge that had provided them shelter and offered his hand to Raisa. She took it and he helped her stand. Together, they traversed the canyon path back to the cave, their boots sloshing through the puddles. Marik was not certain that all was well, but Raisa was no longer radiating hurt and anger. She seemed tired more than anything else. Only time would tell how much this new revelation would affect their crew.

30

The days of sparring and classwork and learning all began to blur together as the lunats marched by. Winter held its frosty ground as Edrian ended and Tella began. The trees stood barren and stark, but since their orienteering mission, there had not been any considerable snow and the temperatures had grown much warmer. The days marched by with bleak sameness. There were no festivals or holidays to celebrate at the Academy as there would be back home, so there was little way for them to mark the passing time.

"Does it snow much in Telsuma?" Wynn asked Beren one day during a rare moment when all three of them were studying in their room together.

"We get a veritable mountain of snow each year," Beren replied easily, making a mark on his paper and then putting his quill down to look out the window, a grin lighting his features. "The passes are closed and the sounds of mining cease. Every home is filled with the smell of baking bread and pastries and smoked lamb. The families gather together and read books or tell stories. We have outdoor games that we cannot play without the snow and ice. And on the dark evenings my brothers and I exchange our bouts of outdoor wrestling tournaments for indoor games such as tranga and urbel."

"We play those games, too," Wynn said, his voice wistful. "I wanted to bring my tranga board and pieces to the Academy, but my brothers and sisters begged me to leave it for them to play."

"Do you get much snow in Dalsea?" Beren asked.

"Some." Wynn shrugged.

"A lot more than here," Grayden said. "We don't get mountains of it, but it usually gets deep enough to cover all the grass. We've had a few snows that came up to my knees. On my father's orchards, we always knew that the more snow we got, the better it was for the trees."

"It's nice not to have to deal with that here." Wynn stretched his arms over his head and yawned.

"I miss it." Grayden's voice was soft. "Never thought I'd miss something like that."

"I miss it, as well," Beren added. "Though perhaps I miss the games and the camaraderie more than the snow itself. It is nice to spend the winter lunats not wrapped up in furs attempting to cling to some semblance of warmth. The air gets bitterly cold in Telsuma, and often we have sennights where it is dangerous to venture out of doors."

A knock sounded. Wynn, who was closest to the door, opened it. An older student stood outside with a bored look on his face.

"Headmaster Freidzen wants to see all three of you directly."

The three young men exchanged puzzled glances.

"Did he say why?" Beren asked.

"No," the older student replied. "But you're to go right away. Not to his office; he's waiting in the Pit."

Wynn looked at the other two and shrugged. Grayden and Beren rose and together they made their way across the Academy grounds to the large building that housed the Pit. "The Pit" wasn't its official name, but it was what the students called it. Very few people even remembered the building's proper name, or where the nickname had first originated. The building was a large, squat, wooden framework with a low roof. It appeared circular, though upon closer examination one would see that the building boasted a myriad of thin, straight walls which abutted each other with the slightest of angles. The reason for the low roof was apparent as soon as one stepped through the door, as the floor dropped away immediately in a series of wide stone steps. These steps led down to a large, sandy arena that was an indoor practice and training ground, used mainly for the Experyus students and the occasional company that was periodically stationed at the Academy. The Conspectus cadets rarely used the Pit, except for some of the larger classes that needed extra space for lectures.

The headmaster was not alone. There were several other students standing before Headmaster Freidzen already. They turned and watched as Wynn, Grayden, and Beren entered the Pit and descended the steps to join them. As they reached the sandy arena floor, the door behind them squeaked. Grayden turned and saw Koen entering the building. He leaped nimbly down the steps to join them.

The headmaster nodded. "I believe we are all assembled."

Grayden took a moment to glance at the other students. Most of them were familiar: Enric, Zarek, and Arven were present. There were two other students standing next to Enric. Grayden did not know their names, but he recognized them as being of the older, Experyus ranking. Despite the accelerated program this year, the students still saw themselves and each other by the rank or year they were supposed to be according to the old order. Grayden could see that even in front of the headmaster, they had arranged themselves in order of age and rank. A little apart from the group stood a man Grayden had never seen before.

Koen hurried across the sandy arena, coming to a stop near Grayden. A flicker of admiration made Grayden give a tiny grin. Koen ignored the old ranking system, preferring to accept things the way they were: everyone on an equal field. Koen raised an eyebrow at Grayden's smile, but made no comment.

Headmaster Freidzen clasped his hands behind his back. "You men will be assigned the Storvas Outpost come spring."

Beren's head jerked up. Grayden peered at him with a questioning glance, but his friend did not look his way. Grayden frowned, puzzled, and shifted his weight slightly to one side. What did this mean? Obviously the words "Storvas Outpost" meant something to Beren. He trained his attention on the headmaster.

"The nine of you are ready for this assignment, and it will serve as a better test of your abilities than any we could devise. Instead of a mission or a test, then, we are giving your team command of this remote outpost. You will train for the harsh, rustic conditions with Captains Tomasson and Petrescu, journey to the outpost on your own, and serve for a lunat. Upon successful completion of this assignment, you will graduate from the Academy as full defenders." The headmaster paused to let those words sink in. He unclasped his hands from behind his back, gesturing toward the man standing next to him. "Your training begins now. The captain will explain the particulars."

Captain Tomasson raised his chin and his piercing blue eyes swept across the recruits before him. His gaze rested the longest on Grayden and Wynn. "For those of you unfamiliar with the Storvas region, this is what you can expect: it is a mountainous and rocky terrain, both rough and wild. The wildlife is plentiful and there are many predators. The Storvas region is also near the Telsuman-Pallan border, and that is where we have already encountered several incursions from Igyeum soldiers. Your mission is to take over the outpost and hold it so that older defenders can be sent to the front, but there is no guarantee that you will not encounter enemy forces who make it past our defenders. Your absolute best will be required of you. Before we begin, are there any questions?"

Grayden chewed on the inside of his cheek. He had a hundred questions, but he couldn't put any of them into words.

Wynn stared at Headmaster Freidzen with narrowed eyes.

"Sir, if I may be so bold, can I ask why I and my friends here have been included in this group?" He nodded at Grayden and Beren. "I know we have been performing well in the arena and classes, but if this exercise is so difficult, why would you allow first-year initiates to undertake it?"

Grayden watched Captain Tomasson as Wynn spoke. The man was solid as a mountain, though his eyes did appear to grow the tiniest bit wider as Wynn said the words "first-year initiates." So, the defender hadn't known just how much younger than usual these recruits were.

"Your performance has been impressive," Headmaster Freidzen replied evenly. "You are more than capable of undertaking and even excelling at the Storvas Mission. However, if you feel that our judgment is in error in any way, you may of course pack your bags and head home."

Wynn gave the headmaster a calculating look, but said no more.

"Any other questions?" the captain asked. He was greeted by stony silence. "Very well. For the next three lunats, you cadets will be training with me. You will no longer be staying in your usual quarters."

"Where will we be staying?" Zarek dared to ask.

"Follow me."

The defender strode through their ranks and up the stairs, not bothering to glance back and see if they obeyed. Without a word, each of the young men fell into line behind him, following Tomasson out of the Pit and across the various training yards. Their feet crunched through the frosty grass. When they reached the edge of the forest that bordered the eastern side of the Academy grounds, Captain Tomasson stopped. He pointed at a pile of canvas.

"These are your new quarters for the time you will be training with me."

The cadets looked at each other in dismay at the idea of sleeping in tents for the next three lunats instead of their own beds. Grayden wondered just how rustic the living conditions would be at the Storvas Outpost. He was well aware that some outpost locations were little more than simple bivouacs, while others were actual forts with indoor barracks. He did not know enough about the Storvas region to know which one this was, and resolved to ask a few questions of Beren when they had time.

Zarek looked as though he wanted to complain, but he kept his mouth firmly shut as they began working on setting up their tents. As they worked, Captain Tomasson began pacing about, barking orders.

"Two men to a tent. Each morning you will be responsible for taking down your tent and packing up all your supplies and belongings. Each evening you will set up your tent once more. You will take turns preparing meals for the entire group. During the days you will be with me foraging and hunting. You will continue your weapons training and attending all your regular classes. Each day I will test you on the knowledge you should have acquired by now that will help us survive the coming exercise. If you fall behind in any respect, you will be removed from this special assignment. For the next three lunats, you will not receive any rest days. Am I clear?"

"Yes, sir." Their voices echoed out into the trees as one. Grayden could see his own dismay reflected in all their faces. And yet, he felt a spark of determination ignite in his heart, as well. This was why he had come to the Academy, after all.

"Good. With my training, you will be ready when we depart for the Greyklasp Mountains this coming Paute." The defender's mouth quirked in an expression that might have been a smile. "Now, as I assign you to your tents, you will pick up the packs and prepare yourselves for our first day of training. In a sennight or two we will be joined by the other defender who will be participating in leading you on this mission, Captain Petrescu."

Beren raised his chin. "Ioan Petrescu?"

Captain Tomasson gave him an odd look. "Yes, are you familiar with the defender?"

"I am," Beren replied.

"That is good to know. Do not believe he will do anything to make your life easier simply because of some previous friendship. Defender Petrescu knows that it is in your best interests to be prepared, not coddled."

"I do not expect any special treatment," Beren said, his voice rumbling into a growl.

"Good," Tomasson barked. "Now, get back to your classes. Return here when classes are finished and your first assignment will be waiting."

31

I t was late when Regeont Roshana arrived home after the long journey from the Arxis. The sun had long since set, and she felt a weariness deep in her bones as the carriage clattered to a stop before her home. She rested in the carriage for a moment, waiting for her porter to open the door. She was too old to be making such a journey three times a year; her bones ached, and her head swam with weariness. The day-to-day rigors of the job she could still manage, but these long voyages by airship were growing more and more difficult, the recovery time lengthening with each journey.

She pulled herself out of the carriage with a bright smile pasted on her face. It would not do to worry her attendants. A misty quality permeated the air beneath an overcast sky of tumultuous gray stormclouds. Roshana entered her home through the front door and set down her things in the hall, heaving a deep sigh. Making her way through the house, she collapsed into her favorite chair and leaned her head back, closing her eyes. The warmth of the fire in the hearth before her was a welcome change from the chill that had permeated the air at the Arxis. She had no idea how anyone managed to survive the harsh winters of her northern neighbors.

"How was your trip, Grandmother?" A familiar, deep voice behind her made Roshana's eyes open in surprise. Joy welled in her as she twisted in her seat, stretching her arms out toward the young man.

"Ioan!" she exclaimed. "I did not expect you to be here when I returned. What prompts this treat? When did you arrive? Are you staying long? What of your duties with the defenders?"

"I just arrived. And I am here because of my duty," he replied, bending down to embrace her and then taking a seat on the couch next to her chair. "I have been assigned as one of the guides for this year's Storvas mission."

Roshana's lips puckered slightly. "Have you met the candidates?"

"Not yet." Ioan grinned. "I have a few sennights of leave, which I planned to spend with you before I join their training. I want to make sure Captain Tomasson has time to establish himself as the group leader. I heard that Beren was one of the recruits involved this year. Don't worry, I won't play favorites. But I'm not going to pretend our friendship never existed, either."

Roshana threw him an annoyed look. "I would never worry about that." She rose from her chair and paced over to the window, absently patting Ioan's cheek as she passed him. Further from the hearth she could feel the little bit of chill creeping in from around the window pane. Outside, it was dark, no light from moon or stars penetrated the cloud cover. As she stared out the window, she fancied the darkness creeping closer to the window, scrabbling at the pane to get inside, to overwhelm the pitiful light of hearth and candles within her home. If she would but throw open the window, it would dart in and overwhelm her in an instant. She shivered and wrapped her arms around herself.

Ioan was next to her in an instant, his arm around her shoulders. "Are you feeling well, Grandmother?"

She patted his hand on her shoulder. "Quite well, Ioan. I just don't feel right about the decision the Council came to regarding the Storvas Mission. I think it is too dangerous for initiates, no matter how qualified or brilliant they appear to be. There was a reason we structured the Academy the way that we did, and I am concerned that we are being too quick to toss our cautions aside."

"That is exactly why the students undergo so much training specific to the mission before they go," Ioan reassured her. "Three lunats gives them plenty of time to prepare. It's also why two defenders are always sent with them. We won't let anything happen to these students, Grandmother. I promise. The territory around the Storvas Outpost is harsh and wild, but it's never been truly dangerous. Besides, Headmaster Freidzen has been doing this for many years. It might seem hard to believe, but if he says a first-year is ready for the Storvas Mission, then I trust him to know what he's talking about."

"It may not be that easy. Not only are these students younger than usual, but we are at war, Ioan. Even if there is no front line, it was made clear at the Arxis meeting that war has begun. We have tried to predict it, to prepare for it, to prevent it if possible, but in spite of our best efforts, it has come to us. I never wanted to see this happen. Not in my lifetime, not in yours."

"Nobody wanted this," Ioan replied. "Not on our side, at least. But we will not back down from it, either. We will defend ourselves and those we have vowed to protect."

Roshana gazed up into her grandson's eyes with deep gravity. "Never believe I would expect or do anything less. I just worry, that is all." She attempted a smile. "Just the fears of a feeble old woman who has no wish to see her grandson come to harm."

Ioan pulled her into a tight hug. "You're not old," he whispered, kissing the top of her head.

"Never lie to your elders," she shot back at him, pulling away gently.

"You're not feeble, anyway," Ioan protested, laughing.

She did not turn back to the window. "If you only just arrived, then you have not had time to see your cousins."

"Ilya and Elan?" Ioan raised his eyebrows. "I haven't seen them. I would enjoy catching up with them."

"If you can stay the night, I am sure they will be joining me for breakfast."

"I would enjoy that," Ioan replied. "I don't have to report to the Academy until tomorrow evening."

Roshana gave him a weary smile. "I am glad to hear that you will stay for breakfast. I miss having you about the house."

"At least Ilya and Elan are here to keep you company. Has it been pleasant visiting with them these lunats as your houseguests? Do you know how long they plan to stay in Doran?"

Roshana shrugged. "Ilya and Elan are butterflies, never staying in one place for long. They have already stayed longer than they meant to. I doubt they will be here more than another sennight, maybe two. They seem restless. But it is no matter." She fluttered a hand. "I have survived on my own for many years already. But for now, I am tired."

"Get some rest, Grandmother," Ioan said, leaning down and kissing her wrinkled cheek. "I will see you in the morning."

———

BREAKFAST WAS JUST ENDING when a servant appeared at Regeont Roshana's elbow with a note on a silver tray. She wiped her mouth with a delicate pat of her napkin and then retrieved the note. Her eyes scanned it and she looked up swiftly, meeting Ioan's eyes across the table. Ilya and Elan had stopped eating and were staring at her with interested curiosity.

"Please, show him to my office," she said, glancing up at the servant and taking a long sip of water from her glass.

"What is it, Grandmother?" Ioan asked.

"I have a visitor requesting an audience. Nothing to worry about." She finished the few bites of food that were on her plate and then pushed her chair back from the table. She did not wish to worry him. "Please excuse me, this won't take long."

She touched her lips with the napkin once more before exiting the dining room, ignoring the questioning glances from her family. With calm, measured steps, Roshana strode down a hallway that led to her main office where she conducted the business of her position as Regeont of Ondoura. Inside the room, her visitor waited. The man's elegant clothes and impeccable taste heralded his status as a nobleman: black boots polished to a glossy shine, gold buttons on his long jacket, the gold embroidery at his cuffs and collar, every thread sparkling in the light of the morning sun pouring in through the window.

He rose as she entered and bowed his head. "Regeont."

"I am surprised at you, Ericole." Roshana kept her voice chilly as she moved around her desk and took a seat across from the man. "It is not like you to do something so foolish."

"Foolish, my lady?"

"I am speaking, of course, of your attempt to abduct and hold for ransom the son of a dear friend of mine last fall. And now you have entered my home and placed yourself within my power. Very foolish, indeed." She stared at him through slitted lids.

Ericole Niveya's handsome face showed no hint of surprise or alarm. He bowed his head again. "A grave misunderstanding, my lady. I am no kidnapper. My people rescued the boy from air pirates who were bent on his murder. Our only desire was to see young Adelfried returned safely home."

"And yet, it was these same so-called air pirates who actually did return him safely." She straightened a document sitting on one side of her desk and adjusted the placement of her inkwell.

"Yes." Ericole spoke fluidly, without a single hesitation or pause. "Well, my people may have miscalculated just how many players were involved. It seems that there were two sets of pirates, one only interested in the cargo cruiser, and the other bent on assassination. I have people working to discover who exactly was involved."

"Is that so?"

"Yes, it is." Niveya met her gaze steadily, one eyebrow raised slightly, his head cocked at a jaunty angle, daring her to disbelieve him.

"You expect me to believe that after five lunats you have anything less than the names of every person involved in this scheme?"

Niveya coughed politely. "My lady, you do me great honor. However, in this case, I must confess, the other players are evenly matched to my cunning."

"I see." Roshana smoothed her hands across her desk. "Then I suppose I must ask why you have requested an audience with me today?"

"I have come to offer my aid in the coming war."

"And what aid do you think you have to offer?"

"Weapons, information about troop movements and patterns, supplies, manpower... I have many useful resources at my command that I would be happy to lend to Telmondir in the approaching conflict." Niveya spoke smoothly, entirely unruffled by any part of the conversation.

"What makes you think we would trust anything offered by a Niveya?"

"Come, come, Roshana, we have been neighbors for many years, have we not? Do not tell me that you have forgotten our mutually beneficial dealings of the past."

The Regeont regarded him dispassionately.

Ericole shifted in his chair and waved a hand. "If you would rather I sell my aid to the Ar'Mol, that is your decision, of course."

Roshana narrowed her eyes, studying the man before her. He leaned back slightly in his chair, appearing to be completely at ease. He met her gaze with unflinching confidence, a slight smirk on his lips.

"I am not qualified to accept or dismiss any offer such as yours on behalf of Telmondir," she said at length. "But you already know that. Your offer would have to go through the Council for consideration."

Ericole leaned forward on the desk, resting his elbows on its edge. "I am aware of how politics on your side of the world operate. But surely we could make a deal just between the two of us?

Just like we have in the past. Come, come, dear Regeont. Your dear friend's son is well, no harm came to him, and now that I know he is precious to you, he is under my protection as well. Forgive me my lapse in judgment and at the same time do what is in the best interests of your people. Think of the influence you would wield in the coming days. If you had beneficial information to offer or a surplus of weapons and supplies for the troops, Ondoura would become invaluable to the rest of Telmondir."

"I have no interest in political posturing or in becoming ruler over all Telmondir. We are not the Igyeum." Roshana waved a hand dismissively. "And I am not inclined to make a deal with you outside of the agreement of the entire Council. It is a pity you did not bring me this offer a lunat ago; I just returned from a Council meeting, I could have presented your ideas to my fellow Councilors and a decision would already be made. There will be no further meetings until Urin."

"That is a pity," Niveya replied smoothly, leaning back. "However, messages can take a long time to traverse the country, and I am sure that the other Councilors will have questions. It could take lunats before a decision is attained. That is your prerogative, of course, and if you wish to delay until Urin, I will abide by your decision. However, in that time, the Igyeum could have troops positioned all along your borders. Many of your young defenders may have already lost their lives by the time the Council reaches a decision about my offer. You would not wish to be responsible for that, would you? Their deaths would be a stain on your own hands, and I would hate to see you have to deal with such guilt."

Roshana could not help herself, her eyes darted to one side, in the direction of the dining room where Ioan was finishing up breakfast. Fear wrapped its bony hands around her throat and for a moment she found it hard to breathe.

"A partnership with me does not have to mean political posturing if you don't want it to." Niveya's voice was quiet, gentle. "You can send those messages to Duke Langston and Lord

Adelfried if you wish, but there is no reason to wait for their answers in order to begin receiving my aid."

"Why come to me?" Roshana asked, her eyes narrowing.

Ericole held out his hands to either side. "I am merely attempting to continue my status as a good neighbor. Our dealings together may have been rare, but I have enjoyed them."

Roshana paused, calculating the odds of his sincerity. They had managed to be business partners in the past, though she had made certain that their deals remained entirely above-board and slightly more advantageous for Ondoura than they were for Niveya. She knew she had bested him in their every encounter, though only barely, and that the losses chafed at Ericole. Could he be attempting to use flattery to get even for her successes? Could he be lazy enough not to wish to travel further into Telmondir to find a more malleable partner for his latest scheme? Could he truly wish to help her? She summarily dismissed that last notion. Ericole Niveya never did anything altruistically. "Why not go to Dalma or Telsuma first? I know you have people everywhere, and your airship makes the excuse of distance seem ridiculous."

Ericole grinned and traced a random pattern on her desktop with his finger. "You are as astute as everyone says, you know. Very well, I will be honest with you. I came to you first because I believed you would be more open to a deal, more willing to do what needs to be done, even if it means associating with people of low repute. I know about your background, you see. Of all the Council members, you are the most like me. You were not born into this luxury you are now surrounded by. But you did not let being poor stop you. I admire your tenacity, your willingness to do what had to be done to get to where you are. And I have always found your integrity to be inspiring." He glanced up at her as though struck by a sudden thought. "I wonder if your fellow Councilors know your history as well as I do? They are younger than you, newer to the Council than yourself, if I am not mistaken?"

"Is that supposed to be a threat?" Roshana maintained a

placid mask, but inside she laughed. If it was a threat, it was a poor one. She had risen from poverty, a nobody with no heritage, that was true, but she had done nothing underhanded to earn the election of Regeont. Her conscience was clear.

Ericole jerked back, his nonchalant mask slipping as his expression revealed actual surprise and confusion. "No... my dear Regeont..." He sputtered, making a twirling motion with his hand, and Roshana realized to her astonishment that the man before her was at a genuine loss for words. He paused for a moment, staring at her, and then leaned forward. "You misunderstand my intent," he said in a low, earnest tone. "I meant that as a compliment. I hold you in the highest esteem. Your wits are as sharp as my own, and I have truly enjoyed our few encounters. You are one of the few people in the world who can best me at my own game." He leaned back, his mask firmly back in place. "My comment earlier about the young men who will die soon if you do not accept my help, that was my threat. By the by"—he paused as though suddenly remembering something—"I heard that your grandson recently graduated from the Academy. Congratulations." He smiled pleasantly, as if they were two old friends idly discussing the weather or reminiscing, and not as if he had just thrust a dagger into her heart.

Roshana felt a great pressure building inside her skull. Her heart drummed in her head and she counted the beats. One. Her face felt warm. Had she truly seen through Ericole's mask? Was he in earnest, or was this another of his games? Two. Niveya smiled pleasantly at her, unaware of the distress he had caused. Three. Or perhaps he was completely aware of her inner struggle. Four. She did not trust him, could never trust him. Five. Her heart betrayed her as her thoughts turned to her grandson. Ioan. Six. She could not let Ioan charge blindly into danger, not if there was anything she could do in order to give him even a moment of warning. Her love for him was as deep as the uncharted depths of the ocean that lapped her country's shores. Seven. Eight. Nine. The heartbeats stretched between them, the smirk firmly fixed on Ericole's face.

Ten. Eleven. Twelve. If she made this deal, what would she end up losing? Did anything else matter if she did what she must to keep her loved ones safe? Roshana let out the breath she had been holding. Thirteen. Fourteen. Ioan.

"Very well." Her voice was crisp as it broke into the air. "What is your price for this aid?"

If Niveya felt triumph at her words, his expression reflected none of it. His smirk faded and his eyes grew intense. "I will provide weapons and supplies to you for half the price you can buy them at any marketplace in Ondoura. The information will be a bit more costly."

Roshana merely lifted her eyebrows, not saying a word.

"I need to be able to cross your borders without being harried by your defenders. I am not uninformed. I am aware of the fact that you already have spies in the Igyeum. There is information I want that my spies have been unable to glean about the innermost workings of the Ar'Mol's most intimate movements and orders. I believe your people may already have this information, or will soon gain access to it. The information will be useless to you, but for me it will be invaluable."

"If the information is useless to me, then how will I recognize it to pass it along to you?" Roshana's question held a note of wry humor.

"I will not expect you to recognize it," Ericole replied, "I want your permission to ask questions of your information-gatherers upon occasion. That is all."

"Oh, is it? That's all?" The Regeont was half-tempted to laugh and dismiss him out of hand. But then she heard Ioan's voice in the hall as he spoke to his cousins and her mind was made up. With a single, sharp nod of her head, Roshana rose. "Very well, Lord Niveya. I accept your terms. I will have the necessary papers drawn up directly. Where can I reach you to deliver them once they are signed?"

"I will come get them." He extended his hand.

Roshana pressed her lips together, but she offered him her

hand in return. Instead of shaking it, Ericole raised her fingers to his lips and brushed them with the barest trace of a kiss. She resisted the urge to pull her hand away and wipe it clean. He grinned up at her, his eyes twinkling as though he guessed her thoughts.

"I believe this is going to be a most advantageous arrangement for us both. As always."

The Regeont retrieved her fingers with as much haste as was polite and rose from her seat. "I believe you know your way out?"

Ericole threw her a jaunty wink. Somehow the childish gesture did not detract in the least from the refined and elegant persona which clung to him like a luxurious cloak. With a flip of his hands a hat appeared on his head and before she could wonder where it had sprung from, he was out the door and had disappeared down the hall.

After he was gone, Roshana relaxed back into her chair, a fond smile on her face. She was aware that Ericole was always a few moves ahead, and playing a grander game than he thought she knew. His next move would most certainly be to make a similar deal with the Ar'Mol, or one of his higher ranking officers. She would have to be careful to ensure that only the information she wanted Ericole to have was placed in the hands of her couriers. Oh, she would have to allow him some useful intelligence, but she would pick which tidbits he received. And in return, she had just procured an excellent deal on weapons and supplies for the defenders. She allowed a small laugh to escape her lips. Dealing with Ericole was always a challenge, but it was one of the few aspects of her job as Regeont that she truly enjoyed.

32

Daegan's device was impressive, impressive and worrisome. Dalmir eyed it askance whenever he happened to be in the forge. It was not yet ready, but every day Keene made progress on its construction. As promised, Daegan was implementing modifications based on Wynn's designs, and the older man was so excited about the process that he practically hopped from his work room to the forge and back. In spite of himself, Dalmir could not help but admire the feat of engineering being constructed; it was similar to a device Palte had designed once. That had been a long time ago, and Palte's creation had been more sophisticated. Still, it was frightening how much Daegan's contraption resembled that ancient device. Dalmir shuddered, remembering the destruction Palte's achievement had caused.

Theirs had been a tiny kingdom, all those many years ago. Not much more than a fiefdom, really. Nestled in a large river valley, their lands had been green and fertile, desired by all their surrounding neighbors. Their father had sent his seven sons on a quest to discover a way to defeat the much larger army that had threatened their homeland. Dalmir's thoughts stuttered as the memory of their quest, their discovery, their failure, and the consequences flooded through him. His brothers... all dead. His fault. His fault!

He squeezed his eyes shut, as though that could banish the pain, and focused again on Daegan's ingenious creation.

Palte had designed many mechanical marvels, and together, his devices had provided the answer they sought, but at a horrific cost. In the aftermath, Dalmir had left his home. Reeling from the cataclysm they had wrought on their home and the surrounding fiefdoms and vowing to be done with war forever, Dalmir had wandered away, traveling west until he came to the end of all the land there was. Palte told him later that he had destroyed his devices and every shred of vellum with even the barest hint of his notes about it, but the decision to use the things had driven a wedge between them for a long time.

Thankfully, the contraption in Keene's forge resembled one of Palte's defensive devices, rather than any of the terrible weapons he had designed. It was not only Uun who had been capable of dreaming up such horrors.

"Dalmir?" Nadia's voice interrupted his thoughts.

He blinked and looked up at her, rubbing a hand across his eyes. Ink stained his fingers and the side of his hand; try as he might, he never could get the hang of writing without getting ink on his fingers. It was the curse of being left-handed, he supposed.

"Is something wrong?" Nadia peered over his shoulder, standing on tiptoe to do so. Compared to her husband and Keene, she was so slight of frame he could almost forget she was a full-grown woman—until he looked at her face: the wisdom therein was impossible to deny.

"No." Dalmir dipped his quill back into the inkwell. "I am just a little tired, that is all. This is taking much longer than I expected."

"You have been at it for quite a while."

"How long have I been down here? It is hard to tell the passage of days with no windows."

"Several sennights, now," Nadia replied. "You should make it a point to go outside every now and then. Fresh air will help you think and function better. Hubert has been missing you."

Dalmir smiled. "I will make a point to come to dinner soon. Tell him I would be happy to build something with him."

Nadia's sharp eyes took in his mood. "What is wrong?"

Dalmir shrugged. "I vowed long ago never to have anything more to do with war. And here I am."

"There are some things worth fighting for," Nadia said, her voice gentle. "But you should try to get some rest, too."

Dalmir nodded. "You are right, of course. I just hate feeling that the minutes are ticking away. Time is a slippery thing, you know, you cannot grasp hold of it, no matter how you try. It continually leaks through your fingers..." He trailed off, staring at his ink-stained fingers and frowning. Then he glanced up, an apology in his eyes. "Forgive me, what was I saying?"

"You were talking about time." Nadia rested a gentle hand on Dalmir's shoulder. "Why don't you come outside with me for a bit? The sun just set and the stars will be out soon. Have you ever seen the stars in Telsuma? They are brighter than the veins of ore running through the mountains."

A faint smile flickered around Dalmir's lips. "In a moment, perhaps. I want to finish these notes, first."

"Do you think you can figure out how to make the refiner work?"

"Of that I am certain. I need a few more days. Perhaps a sennight. Then Keene can begin forging it."

"How long will that take?"

"Another sennight, perhaps. I'm afraid it won't be as elegant as something Palte would design, but it will get the work done."

Her brown eyes brightened. "You know of Palte, the founder of Palla?"

Dalmir hesitated, his fingers hovering over the quill. "Yes," he said slowly, his voice soft. "How do you know of him?"

"My family came from Palla. We fled to Telsuma after the Ar'Mol ordered the execution of my father."

"I thought you looked a little out of place here in the mountains." Dalmir's expression grew gentle. "I'm sorry about your father. That must have been terrifying for you. These rising tensions must be dredging up unpleasant memories."

"I was just a child then." Nadia picked up one of Dalmir's abandoned sketches and studied it. "The Ar'Mol who ordered the execution is long dead. And we all escaped, my father included. My story has a happy ending, though many don't."

"Still..." Dalmir trailed off. "Have you been back to your homeland?"

"I haven't been back to Palla since my parents brought my brother and myself here, but I remember some things. The dry heat of the air, the empty plains, the beautiful melodies of the songbirds, the aroma of the sun on the sand... and the stories my parents told me about Palte, the creator of our homeland."

"Palla was always a rather unique blend of harshness and beauty," Dalmir murmured. "Palte liked beautiful things, but he was more interested in their usefulness. He had very little patience with anything that was simply beautiful for its own sake. He and Avaleun were complete opposites in that way."

Nadia's eyebrow quirked slightly. "You speak of him as though you knew him. As though he were a real person. At the Arxis, you spoke of Edoran in the same way."

"He was a real person," Dalmir replied. "And he didn't create Palla, not really. He cultivated what was already there. None of us truly created anything new, in spite of the power we were granted. We were sculptors only. Tools in the hands of Emri, the true Creator."

Nadia peered at him. "If anyone else heard you talking that way, they might mistake you for being mad. Few are those who remember the Builder."

Dalmir gave a shy chuckle. "Perhaps I am mad." But a thrill shot through him at her mention of the Builder. So perhaps not everything had been forgotten.

Nadia stared at him for another long moment, as though

debating whether or not to reply. She gave a little shake of her head and glanced down at the paper under Dalmir's hands, comparing it to the older sketch she held in her hands. "It looks like you're making progress."

"We will soon see if that is true. I just hope that once the new refiner is built it works the way it is supposed to."

"I am sure it will."

"I hope so," Dalmir replied. "I do not wish to spend much more time here. There are other important things to be done."

"My husband said you had given him a few ideas. Thank you for your aid with all of this. Telmondir is strong, but I fear that the Igyeum is far better prepared for this conflict." Nadia's gaze grew distant. "I worry for my son, for all the young defenders who will be asked to risk so much for us."

Dalmir grimaced, but did not respond. Instead, his fingers grasped the quill and he began once again to draw marks upon the page, tweaking the design, adding notations. Nadia stayed at his side for some time, watching quietly. Her presence was at once comforting and unbearable, reminding him with every breath, every pound of his heart, that the world teetered on the edge of a war he might have prevented had he been more diligent.

The oil lamp on the table burned steady and true, but at last Dalmir passed a hand over his eyes. He carefully wiped his quill and put the lid on his ink pot and then blew on the lines he had just drawn. With a weary sigh, he turned to Lady Adelfried.

"I think I will take you up on that walk now."

She opened the door and waited while Dalmir blew out the lamp. Together, they ambled down the hall and out the door that led onto the side of the mountain. The air had a crisp bite to it that was pleasant after the warm, stale air in the workroom. Though Tella was drawing to a close, and with it the standard winter lunats, a thick blanket of snow still covered the ground here in the mountains. Dalmir breathed in deeply and leaned back against the icy, solid rock of the mountainside, gazing up at the stars twinkling brightly in the black canopy overhead. They did not speak. There, under the stars, the silence of friendship was enough. The door behind them opened and Thorben Adelfried stepped out into the darkness, his boots crunching in the snow. His wife turned to him with a glad smile and they embraced.

"Daegan and Keene are making fine progress," Thorben whispered into his wife's hair.

Dalmir felt a pang in his chest. His thoughts sprang away from Telsuma and flew to another time, another lady. She had been one who captured his heart with her gentleness and kindness. A woman with a staunch heart and a keen mind, her smooth, porcelain face framed by long, sleek black hair floated before his memory for a moment then blurred and faded as his eyes filled with unwelcome tears. He passed a hand across his eyes with an angry swipe. How dare thoughts of her invade his mind? He was no longer worthy of her love, not even worthy to remember her face, let alone speak her name. And yet, unbidden, her name formed itself on his lips and rested there, trembling, like a frightened bird. With a whisper he could loose it into the night, send it winging on its way to wherever she was. The temptation grew until Dalmir clamped his lips tightly shut. Nay, he would not utter her name. Not until he had redeemed himself. Silent as the mountain itself, Dalmir slipped back inside the door, leaving Nadia and her husband to their private conversation. With slow steps he made his way to the chamber Keene had rearranged for him to sleep in and fell into his bed. In the morning, he would return to his work. But for now, he wished only to sleep, and, for the short hours of the night, to forget.

33

The days grew long and arduous. Grayden had lost track of just how many days had passed since he and his companions had begun this exercise. How long had it been since Captain Tomasson spoke to them and changed everything about the routine they had grown accustomed to? The days blurred together into a foggy haze of misery. No longer did he look forward to the next day as he fell into his bunk; instead, he crawled into his tent each night with the last dregs of his strength, too weary to care if he ever woke again. Each morning began with the sound of Defender Tomasson's voice bellowing that it was time to rise. The waking hours were filled with his voice shouting orders at them. Each evening, as he dragged himself onto his bedroll and closed his eyes, Grayden wondered if he would ever get the ringing in his ears to cease. He had nightmares that he was being given more orders: frustrating demands that made no sense, which made his nights on the cold ground anything but restful.

They packed up their camp every morning, ate cold rations, and hiked through the wild all day. They foraged along the way and hunted as they could, but for the most part they performed navigation exercises and always had to be ready and able to point to their precise location on the map if the defender asked it of them. In the evenings they sparred until Grayden was certain his arms would fall off. He often thought with longing of the classes he had once considered difficult, or of the long days out in the orchards with his father pruning trees or picking the fruit. He had once considered those chores to be taxing! Now he would have given anything to take on those tasks once more and luxuriate in the restfulness of them. He used to have free time! Never again would he take for granted the concept of rest. None of the men dared complain, though. There was an unspoken fear in each of their minds that if anyone raised his voice in objection, he would be sent home in disgrace.

They had crossed the forest in the first few days and begun climbing up the base of the mountain that loomed over the Academy grounds. Though tall enough to have a bit of snow at its peak most of the year, this mountain was, in truth, quite small compared to its brother and sister peaks that rose up behind it and stretched out into the Randeau Mountain Range. Grayden tried to focus on the trail before them, but his thoughts kept betraying him, winging away from the work at hand. The Niveyan Fortress lay somewhere beyond those peaks. He wondered if they would take sides in the war to come, or if they would sit back in their stronghold and watch to see which side would emerge victorious.

"Strange to think that the Niveyas aren't that far away," Wynn panted, coming up next to Grayden on the trail.

"I was just thinking about them," Grayden replied. "I wonder what they're up to right now?"

"Probably helping the Ar'Mol get ready to invade." Wynn shrugged.

"Maybe," Grayden mused. He was quiet then. The trail was steep and talking required an energy he did not possess. But his mind continued to whirl, thinking of that great fortress from which they had barely escaped and the people who lived within. Ericole Niveya did not strike him as the sort of man who would bow in servitude to any man, even the Ar'Mol. But what would he do, then? Would he attempt to manipulate events to his benefit, or hide away in his fortress until he was sure of the outcome? Grayden was inclined to believe the former. Niveya struck him as the sort who could not sit idly by; he would want to manipulate events to his greatest advantage.

As he was mulling over these thoughts, the group reached a mountain stream and Captain Tomasson called a rare halt.

"Fill up your waterskins, lads. We still have a long way to go before we reach our campsite for the evening."

The students all groaned in unison, though none too loudly. Grayden plunged his waterskin into the sharp, cold water. He just had time to take a handful of dried berries and nuts from his pocket and shove them in his mouth before the order to continue was given. A little further along the trail they came to a sheer cliff face. Defender Tomasson commanded them to scale it and all thoughts of the Niveyas fled from Grayden's mind as he needed all his mental energy focused on the task before him.

"I thought I would eventually stop being sore," Grayden muttered to Wynn over a bowl of porridge one morning. They took turns at the cook fire, but their shared exhaustion was so great that meals had ceased to be anything they took pride in; whatever could be thrown together the fastest and in large amounts tended to be their default. This evening's porridge was lumpy and tasteless, and it was also the best thing Grayden could ever remember eating. That was the only benefit he could see to the rigorous training that left him feeling constantly exhausted and famished: everything they cooked over the fire tasted incredible. Grayden Ormond the Orchardist—the Grayden of just five lunats ago—with his mother's excellent home-cooking to compare to this simple fare would have shuddered and turned up his nose at every meal. But Grayden the Cadet hungrily devoured every morsel of food on his plate and still felt an ache in the pit of his stomach wanting more. He finished the last scrapings of porridge and fell onto his bedroll, too tired even to climb under the blanket.

The next day held more of the same, finishing with a race back to the camp. Grayden and Beren finished well ahead of the others to find Defender Tomasson waiting for them with a stranger sitting next to him.

"Ioan!" Beren's voice rang out across the camp. He strode toward the newcomer, arms outstretched.

"Ah," Grayden breathed. This must be the other defender who would be joining them on the Storvas Mission.

Defender Tomasson leaped to his feet and strode to Beren, placing a hand against the burly Telsuman's chest. "I believe you meant to say 'Captain Petrescu' and salute, isn't that right, Cadet?"

Beren's footsteps faltered and a look of confusion chased its way across his face. Grayden glanced over at the newcomer, who had half-risen from his seat on the log and now stood, hesitating. The defender sat back down, his expression unreadable. Grayden shifted his gaze to his friend and walked up next to him.

"Good evening, Captain Tomasson," he said with a salute. "I believe it is my rotation to cook supper tonight?" He nodded toward Defender Petrescu. "Is our guest the other defender you said would be joining us on our mission?"

Tomasson turned his glare upon Grayden. "It is your rotation, Cadet, but Defender Petrescu has graciously brought food to share from his grandmother's home. If she were anyone but the Regeont herself I would turn it down; such fare isn't fitting for a group on an arduous training mission..." He trailed off and grimaced. "But I have no wish to offend Regeont Roshana. You can help Captain Petrescu unpack the meal he brought."

Grayden saluted sharply and threw a sympathetic glance at Beren, who gave him a brief nod of thanks in return. As he had hoped, his friend had taken the moment of distraction to recover from his surprise. As Grayden made his way across the campsite, he heard Beren's clipped voice apologizing for his lack of respect for protocol. Beren did not follow Grayden, but set about dismantling his tent.

As he approached the newcomer to their camp, Grayden took a moment to look him over. Ioan Petrescu was obviously Ondouran by birth. He had a round face, but high cheekbones and a square jaw served to make him look regal rather than pudgy. His black hair fell about his ears but in a well-kept, pristine sort of way. His skin was lighter than Beren's, but darker than Grayden or Wynn's. He stood slightly shorter than Grayden, but his shoulders were as broad as Beren's. His eyes were dark and troubled, but seemed to hold a glimmer of good humor, as well.

"Captain Petrescu," Grayden introduced himself with a sharp salute, "I am Cadet Grayden Ormond."

"That was quick thinking just now," the man replied, stretching his hand forward in a friendly gesture. Grayden clasped it, slightly caught off-guard by the captain's amiable and relaxed tone. He raised an eyebrow. "I am glad to see that this team is pulling together and looking out for one another. Isak is a bit of a thick-headed mule when it comes to following protocols and rules, wouldn't you say?"

Grayden stared at him, uncertain of how to respond. To disparage an officer out loud could get him in serious trouble.

Petrescu chuckled. "Of course you would, but not to his face, and never behind his back. An honorable man, as well as one who looks out for his teammates. Don't worry, I won't tell him you're thinking it. But really, Isak's a good sort, when you get to know him... or if you can get him on an even playing-field. He's making your lives an absolute misery, I'm sure, but you'll never find anyone who will prepare you better for the mission you're about to undertake. He's not doing any of this because he's mean-spirited or because he hates you, even if it feels like it. He just takes his job extremely seriously, and that's a good thing. Trust me when I tell you, anything the Storvas Pass can throw at you will seem like a summer breeze compared to whatever Isak dreams up for your training."

"I believe you." Grayden couldn't help but grin ruefully as he thought over the training they had endured so far.

"Good. Now, Cadet Ormond, why don't you help me with this." Ioan indicated an enormous basket from which emanated a myriad of smells that made Grayden's mouth water.

"I would be honored, Captain Petrescu."

"None of that, now." The man waved a hand. "I'm Ioan to you and your comrades, and if Isak doesn't like it he can sit on a nettle. He can be the strict one if he wants, but we have to form some sort of camaraderie between ourselves if we're going to make it through the Pass with everyone in one piece." His eyes darted toward Tomasson. "Even Isak. That's why I'm here. He's good at preparing you, but I'm the one who will build this group into a team."

"That is good," Grayden replied. "Because right now, we're not much of one."

"Perhaps you can tell me who trusts each other?"

"Well, Wynn and Beren and I have been rooming together this year at the Academy, and after our encounter with the pirates and the Niveyas, I'd guess we all pretty much trust each other with our lives."

"You were one of the initiates with Beren during that encounter?" Ioan's tone grew interested. He pulled a large, steaming ham out of the basket and began slicing it.

"Yes." Grayden lifted out a fine piece of crockery. The smell of glazed sweet potatoes emanated from around the sides of the lid and he couldn't keep back a grin as he took a deep breath and savored the delicious scent.

"Can you tell me about it?"

Grayden started at the beginning and as they unpacked the food, he told the defender all he could about the incident. The other cadets began to come panting into camp, but they perked up at the sight of Grayden and Ioan setting out the wooden trenchers in preparation for dinner.

"That is quite a story." Ioan shook his head as the cadets began to congregate around them, each wearing an identical expression of longing as they filled their nostrils with the scent of real food.

"Attention!" Captain Tomasson's voice echoed through the clearing. "This is Captain Petrescu. He will be joining us for the rest of your training and accompanying us to the Storvas Outpost. I expect you to show him the respect and dedication you have shown me. Today he has brought a feast; don't get used to it. Defender, would you like to say a few words?"

Ioan stood and brushed off his pants where he had been kneeling on the ground. "My name is Ioan Petrescu. I would prefer it if you would call me 'Ioan.'" He held up a hand to ward off Tomasson's protests. "No, Isak." He lowered his voice slightly. "Your job is to prepare them for the harshness of the mission. Mine is to build them into a team. As the leader, it is your right to insist on a level of formality toward yourself, but it is mine to dismiss that formality if I feel the need. And I do." He turned back to the group of cadets. "I see before me a group of men. But I do not see a team. I know that it probably feels as though the Board of Instructors have turned your orderly world upside down, and I can understand any resentment you might feel about it. But it is time to put all that aside. No longer are you Initiates versus Cadets, or Conspectus versus Experyus. You are all here, training for a mission that your instructors believe you are each eminently qualified for, so we need to start working together. I've been watching you for the past few days, and I can see you have organized yourselves into neat little groups. I'm going to change that. We will become a single team. Every one of us will trust our very lives with any one of us or this mission is forfeit before we even begin. That, gentlemen, is the purpose of our training."

They shuffled a bit and nodded their heads.

"Now, line up and get some dinner. Captain Tomasson is correct, this is the last good meal you will have until our mission is complete."

———

GRAYDEN GRITTED his teeth and tried not to flinch as he listened for Enric's instructions. He was blindfolded, and Enric was leading him through an obstacle course set up by Captain Petrescu. In spite of Ioan's friendly demeanor, none of the students found it easy to call him by his first name. Grayden stumbled over a root and caught himself as Enric called out to him, telling him to step a bit more to his left.

At least he had been paired with Enric. He already knew that he would not be paired with Wynn or Beren for any of these exercises. Trust and camaraderie already existed between them, and Petrescu had made it clear that such trust needed to exist between all members of the team before they could begin their mission. Enric was not exactly friendly, but he did not give off an aura of disdain the way that Hamil did. Hamil, like Koen, was in his fourth year at the Academy, but unlike Koen, Hamil had made it clear that he resented the presence of "initiates" on such a significant mission. Peder was less hostile, possibly because he was only in his third year, but kept pretty much to himself. What he thought of the new order of things at the Academy, Grayden could not quite determine. He was not sure if Peder's aloof behavior was born of bitterness, or if he was merely reserved.

He slammed into something hard and reeled backwards with a grunt of pain.

"Grayden!" Enric shouted, his voice echoing across the obstacle course. "Are you all right? I said you needed to turn left!"

Grayden rubbed his hand across his nose and winced at the pain, mentally kicking himself for his lack of focus. "I'm fine," he called back. "That was my fault, I let my mind wander for a moment and missed hearing your directions."

He felt the blindfold being lifted from his eyes and found himself staring into Enric's dark, serious face. "Well, you're not bleeding," Enric said, relief evident in his tone. "But I think maybe we should take a break and come back to this exercise later."

"Really, I'm fine," Grayden argued.

"You walked full-force into a tree."

"I wasn't going that fast. I didn't break anything, I'm not bleeding."

"Still, I think we should stop for the day. It's getting late."

Grayden chuckled. "Are you really worried about me? Or is it that you don't want to take a turn wandering around in the dark while I shout directions at you? There's enough daylight left for me to see which way to tell you to go, and the lack of light shouldn't affect you under that blindfold."

Enric made a face and reluctantly tied the blindfold over his own eyes. "Direct away, oh leader mine," he announced in a confident tone. "As long as your instructions are clear, you won't find me letting my mind wander like a bleating initiate."

"We'll see about that," Grayden retorted. "Walk straight ahead ten steps."

Enric complied and Grayden continued to call out instructions. Enric executed each direction with precision, and at the end of the course, he had not walked into any trees or stumbled over any roots. As he came to the end of the course, Ioan joined them.

"The two of you are doing well," he commented. "The whole team is coming together better than I expected."

Grayden nodded and gave a slight, involuntary shrug.

Ioan looked at him sharply. "You don't agree, Cadet?"

"Forgive me, Defender, but some of the members of our team resent the new accelerated program. They don't believe anyone younger than a fourth-year Experyus cadet should even be allowed to train for this mission, let alone raw first-years. And I can't really say that I blame them. The Storvas Mission has been a ceremonial standard of graduation for a hundred and thirty years. For those of us who have only been at the Academy for half a year to be included on a mission of such significance must feel like a slap in the face to those who have spent the last four years working as hard as they can. I'm not saying I question the headmaster's decision; I think he's right to accelerate the training, we are going to need all the defenders we can muster soon. But I also understand why some of the older students are having such a hard time with it."

"You've been here eight lunats," Ioan replied.

"I was rounding down. They do," Grayden retorted.

"I see." Ioan rubbed his fingers across his mouth. "I can't say I'm completely surprised by your assessment. Nor can I say that you're entirely wrong. But it is a soldier's job to follow the orders he's given, so long as they don't bring harm or dishonor to himself or his fellow defenders. And regardless of whether or not they like the reality of their situation, it continues to be reality. You are all about to become defenders of Telmondir, and there is a war brewing. A war our leaders do not seem to think we can avoid any longer. A war that—in many ways—has already begun. That is more important than petty rivalries made in the Academy. The sooner you all learn that, the better off we'll all be."

"I understand, sir."

Ioan glanced at him. "I know you do. I'm trying to figure out how to explain it to the members of this team who are having a hard time grasping the same truth."

Enric, who had taken off his blindfold and come over to join them, narrowed his eyes. "It may be something they just have to learn for themselves. Either they can dwell on their resentment and drown in it, or use it as a stepping stone to motivate themselves to work even harder, to achieve more than they thought possible."

Ioan turned to Enric. "And is that what you have done?"

Enric might have gone red in the face, but it was hard to tell under his dark complexion. He stared at the ground. "Yes, sir."

Ioan nodded slightly. "Good for you. That will be all for today, time to turn in and get some rest."

Grayden and Enric strode away from the obstacle course and walked back to their campsite where Peder and Wynn had been assigned to take care of the evening meal. The fire danced merrily under an iron pot from which emanated the smell of something that might be edible. Over the past few sennights Grayden had learned not to trust the smell of Wynn's cooking; sometimes it meant the meal would be delicious, and sometimes it meant the opposite. However, Peder's cooking was consistently delicious, and Grayden was hungry enough that he wasn't sure he cared how the food tasted, as long as it filled his stomach.

As they arrived at the campsite, Grayden noticed that Peder was chuckling, and Wynn had a mischievous glint in his eye.

"That's not good," he muttered.

"What do you mean?" Enric asked. "Whatever they're making smells good, at least."

"Not that. I meant Wynn. He's up to something."

"How can you tell?"

"The look on his face," Grayden replied. "I've seen it a few times. Wynn's not usually a prankster, but he can be talked into helping with them, and that's the expression he gets when he does. I haven't seen it since we got to the Academy, because he doesn't tend to think them up himself, and I've been too busy trying to stay on top of my studies to pull him into a scheme."

"Peder's got a wicked sense of humor," Enric said. "If he's pulled Wynn into a prank, I think we should keep a wary eye out."

"Should we tell Ioan or Captain Tomasson?" Grayden asked.

"Tell us what?" Ioan's voice behind him made Grayden jump.

"Oh! Sir, I didn't realize... you... I thought..."

"Calm down, Cadet. What were you wondering if you should tell me?"

"Wynn... I mean, the look on his face... I mean"—Grayden stumbled over his words for a moment—"I think he and Peder have some trick or antic brewing."

"I see." Ioan narrowed his eyes, then he gave a little jerk of his head. "Perhaps we just keep that bit of information to ourselves, shall we?"

Grayden nodded wordlessly, his mind racing to understand Ioan's instruction. As he headed to his tent he comforted himself by reminding himself that Wynn would never agree to something harmful. He didn't always have the best discernment, but he would never do anything to hurt someone, even if a friend urged it and called it a prank. He didn't want his friend to get in trouble, but surely Wynn couldn't get in too much trouble if Captain Petrescu knew about the possibility of a trick in advance and allowed it to happen anyway, could he?

Grayden was still mulling over this question as the rest of the cadets arrived from their various activities and assignments. With a great amount of ruckus and noise, they each retrieved a wooden bowl and approached the pot of stew where Wynn and Peder were waiting. Stew was ladled into each bowl, and the cadets took their seats around the fire, digging into the meal with the fervor of men who have been working hard all day and are famished. Grayden settled himself on a log between Enric and Beren. Like the others, Beren fell about gulping his stew down, making appreciative sounds as he ate. Grayden and Enric were a bit more cautious. Grayden took a careful bite of his stew. Thick and warm, the stew filled his mouth with a delightful mix of flavors. He tried to savor the taste but Wynn and Peder were now openly snickering together and Grayden felt a hand clench around his stomach. Could he trust Peder to watch out for Wynn? Or had he set up a despised first-year to take a massive fall? He met Enric's questioning gaze and returned it with one of his own. What had Peder and Wynn done?

He did not have to wonder long. As Ioan, the last one in line, accepted his bowl of stew, Wynn and Peder sat together, their own bowls in hand.

"Well, Peder," Wynn said, his voice just loud enough to carry across the campfire, "I wonder which one of our comrades got a surprise in his stew."

The sounds of hungry men slurping up stew slowed and halted.

Peder gave an exaggerated shrug. "There's no way of telling until it's all gone. I swear, I had no idea Captain Tomasson was washing his laundry in that pot of water. I thought he was just helping us get ready for dinner."

An eruption of gagging and choking sounds immediately filled the camp. One of the cadets dropped his wooden bowl on the ground with an exclamation of disgust. Grayden peered suspiciously at the thick stew in his own bowl. Beren looked up from his nearly empty bowl, spoon hovering halfway to his mouth as though unsure about which direction it should go.

Across the fire Tomasson and Petrescu continued eating as though they had not heard. Hamil leaped to his feet and stormed over to where Wynn and Peder were sitting. He loomed over them, hands clenched into fists at his sides.

"Did I hear you right, Cadet?" he demanded through clenched teeth. "Did you just say that you cooked our dinner in a pot of boiling socks?"

Wynn and Peder stared up at him, their faces bearing identical expressions of innocence. Wynn looked at Peder.

"Did I say that?"

Peder shook his head slowly. "I don't think you did."

Wynn looked up at Hamil. "You must have misheard. I did not say anything of the kind."

There was a long pause as Hamil glowered down at him.

Then Wynn tilted his head to one side with a casual shrug. "But Peder did."

Hamil shouted something inarticulate and lunged at Wynn, hands outstretched. Zarek and Arven did not move from their spots, but they glared at Peder, daring him to move. Enric glanced at Grayden, a question written in his eyes that Grayden did not know the answer to. As Hamil reached him, Wynn let out a yelp and started hollering. Grayden and Beren jumped to their feet and ran into the fray to defend their friend. To his surprise, Zarek and Arven were right behind them, dashing to Wynn's rescue. By the time they reached him, Hamil had Wynn on the ground, but his expression had changed from anger to uncertainty, for Wynn was not yelling in distress, but was laughing so hard tears poured from his eyes. Peder shook with laughter as well, so hard that his broad shoulders were shaking. Ignoring all the others, Peder stood up and shoved Hamil off of Wynn, then reached down and helped Wynn to his feet.

"It was just a joke," Peder managed to choke out between bursts of laughter.

Wynn chortled. "Just a joke, and you all believed it!"

And that was all either of them could manage for a long while. Hamil's face first turned red, then a strange shade of purple. His mouth opened and closed a few times as he stared hard at Wynn and Peder. Then, like the sun coming out from behind a cloud, his expression smoothed and he began to chuckle as well. Grayden could not blame him, it was hard to stay angry in the face of Wynn's laughter; he knew that from experience.

"You two had me believing you had cooked our supper in the laundry pot." Hamil chuckled and tromped back to his place by the fire. He retrieved his empty bowl and marched back to Wynn and Peder. "Another helping of your excellent sock stew, if you please."

This set Wynn and Peder roaring with laughter even harder, and Hamil was forced to dish up his own second helping. He met the gaze of Enric as he passed by.

"Best eat up," he recommended. "Wynn's cooking only tastes this good half the time. Next time he cooks for us, we'll probably be wishing he had put some socks in it."

This set everyone to laughing. The cadets finished their stew and everyone lined up for a second helping. Grayden did not return to his spot between Beren and Enric, but rather went over and sat down next to Captain Petrescu.

"Excellent stew, wouldn't you say?" Ioan winked at him.

"How did you know?" Grayden asked.

"How did I know what?"

"What Wynn and Peder were up to?"

"I didn't," Ioan replied.

"Then why let it happen? It could have been a worse prank, it could have gone too far."

"It could have. But I know both Peder and Wynn well enough

by now to know that they wouldn't do anything truly harmful. Especially not with myself and Isak sitting right here. Besides, not much builds camaraderie between soldiers better than a good practical joke."

Grayden blinked at him. "So you let it happen because you believed it would turn us into a team?"

"Not completely." Ioan took another bite of stew. "But it eased a few of the remaining tensions. Didn't you notice how everyone jumped to Wynn's defense? Next time Wynn is threatened, Hamil will be the first one to jump in front of him. Tonight's prank worked better than any of the exercises I've come up with. I believe you are almost ready for the Storvas Mission."

"And a good thing, too," Tomasson muttered. "We leave in less than a sennight." He softened his gruff words with an expression that on anyone else's face might have been called mischievous. "This really is the best sock stew I've ever tasted. I believe Peder and Wynn should be put on cooking duty together more often."

34

Strains of music and barks of laughter reached Marik's ears as he approached the unmarked entryway of the Lantern Inn. He put one hand on the rough wooden door covered in peeling paint and pushed it open, slipping inside. In the dim light, he saw a crowded common room. The dreary weather had chased many inside for some warmth and entertainment. Near the blazing hearth a young woman stood, playing a lively tune on her fiddle. Her red hair glinted in the firelight and her mouth quirked up in a mischievous grin. She was unfamiliar to Marik, but most of the other faces within the tavern were well-known acquaintances. He relaxed slightly, wringing his cloak out a bit, and sauntered over to the bar. His boots squelched as he walked and his toes were numb, but he ignored these minor discomforts.

"Ale," he drawled lazily to the barkeeper, a tall, muscular man not much older than Marik.

"Yes, sir," the man replied affably. He glanced at his new customer and then paused, blinking in disbelief. "Marik! Is that really you?" The man reached across the counter and gripped Marik by the shoulders, peering at him through dark brown eyes. Under his neat, well-trimmed beard the man's teeth gleamed in the firelight and he pulled Marik into a tight bear hug.

"It's me, Valen," Marik assured him.

"Well!" The man rested his elbows on the counter, then reached below it for a tankard which he filled and pushed toward Marik. "Well, now." He whistled, wiping his hands on a rag and then handing it across the counter to Marik. "Nobody's seen scale or claw of you in lunats! Word had it you had been captured, killed, or hightailed it to Telmondir for good. It's been, what, how many lunats since you've been seen in your old haunts? Seven or eight? I'm guessing you have a story or two to tell."

"A few," Marik admitted. He accepted the dishrag gratefully and wiped the rain from his face. "And I'll tell them to you, I promise. But right now, I'm needing information and supplies."

"A new job?" Valen gave him a conspiratorial wink. "What do you need to know?"

"First of all, what sorts of trade goods are in demand these days?"

The tall man squinted and frowned. "Hmm. It depends. You looking to acquire a new trade, or commandeer a valuable cargo?"

Marik shrugged. "Maybe both."

Valen chuckled. "Well, the big demands right now are boots and seeds. Winter was harsh and it isn't nearly over, the snows here have lasted longer than normal, so the farmers are getting nervous and stocking up on seed. Shoes and boots are also in high demand, but even you might not be able to steal what you need. There was a scarce supply of leather for cobbling this year."

"Regular scarcity or the Ar'Mol?"

"The Ar'Mol," Valen replied, his voice growing grim. "His soldiers were everywhere, requisitioning leather for their armor, claiming it was their due for protecting us citizens."

Marik made a guttural sound in his throat. "I'll bet they were."

"Requisitioning, ha!" Another man sat down next to Marik and took a long swig from his own tankard. "Stealing's what it was. Outright stealing. They practically peeled the shoes off our feet... off our children's feet, no less." He scowled then gave a contrite grin. "My 'pologies. My tankard was nearly empty. I couldn't help but overhear your conversation."

"No worries, friend," Marik replied easily. "Let me buy your next round."

The man's eyes lit up with gratitude. "My thanks, my thanks." He held out his mug and Valen filled it up.

"Valen, any idea where a man might find leather that has managed to stay out of the Ar'Mol's greedy fingers?" Marik asked. "My family is in need of some shoes."

"All our families are in need of shoes." Valen shook his head, a mournful expression pulling the corners of his mouth down. "The Ar'Mol's men took everything, lad. And even if they hadn't, such leather would be truly priceless right now."

"What if I had the right currency?" Marik asked.

The big bartender pulled thoughtfully on his beard. "I couldn't rightly say. You know me, usually I know a direction to point you, but this time..." He raised his hands helplessly.

"I know where you could get some leather. Quite a bit of leather," the stranger next to Marik muttered harshly into his tankard, not raising his eyes from his cup. "But it would cost you."

Valen turned and looked at the man in surprise.

"What would it cost? And how did you come by this information?" Marik asked.

The man jerked his chin up and stared at Marik with defiant, hopeless eyes. "I know a man who has a stockpile of leather. I come by the information as honest as I can: he's the one what stole my entire trade out from under me."

"Who?" Marik stared down into his tankard, trying not to seem too eager.

"If I tell you, and you use the information to acquire some of it for yourself, I want something in return." The man scowled, his dark eyes hard as flint in his dark face.

Marik eyed the man. Tall, thin, and wiry, with unkempt curly black hair, at first glance he appeared disheveled and untrustworthy. However, despite his belligerent tone and the flashing fire in his brown eyes, something about his scowl seemed uncomfortable. This was not a face used to intimidating others. His eyes were not focused on Marik, and his eyebrows were slightly raised. Through his attempts to appear forceful, Marik read something deeper in the man's eyes: desperation and fear prompted him to speak, not the anger on display. Marik took a lazy swig from his own tankard, doing his best to appear unthreatening.

"And what might that be?"

The man's scowl slackened, then intensified. "Enough leather to make three small pairs of shoes." His voice was gruff, but Marik caught a glimmer of tears in the dark eyes before the man took another angry swig from his tankard and then wiped his mouth roughly on the back of his sleeve.

Marik squinted into his own tankard to hide the wash of sympathy that flooded over him. "I think I could be persuaded to make that deal"—he kept his voice soft—"provided I can actually acquire the goods."

The man peered at him, his eyes narrow and hard. He tossed a querying glance at Valen.

"Marik's a pirate and a rogue," Valen said. "But he's true to his word. If he makes a bargain, you can always count on him to keep his end of it."

The other man considered for a moment longer. Then he stuck out his hand. "Name's Teo. There's a merchant who lives over in Temin. Name of Warrick. The soldiers left him and his merchandise alone. He comes through town every now and then, but nobody here can afford his prices. He knows it, too. It's like he comes just to gloat." Teo slammed a fist down on the counter.

Marik took a long drink. "Why did the soldiers leave this Warrick alone? That isn't usually their style."

Teo's lips thinned into an angry line. "He's a cousin or something of the Ar'Mol. Couldn't have His Majesty's relatives wandering around in the winter with holes in their shoes, their children's toes suffering from frostbite, now could he? Oh yes, our great Ar'Mol is the picture of a kind and caring heart. I heard he even gave some of the leather he didn't need to Warrick. Stole it from us and then handed it over so we would have to buy it back. Not that any of us can afford to with the winter as bad as it's been." He wiped a hand across his mouth with a low mutter.

The old, angry fire roared to life within Marik's chest. It took all his strength to keep his voice steady. "Can you get me directions to this Warrick's shop?"

"I can," Teo said. "It's fairly easy. Follow the river up to Temin, just across the Palla border. Once you reach the city, look for the largest shop in the middle of town. His emblem is an emerald airship."

"How do you know so much about this Warrick and his shop?" Marik asked, his suspicious nature rising.

"I traveled there," Teo replied, his voice dropping to a whisper. His eyes darted about guiltily. "Made the trip so I could beg for leather and wool." His hands clenched around his tankard. "Warrick's lad laughed at me. Said my money was no good, wouldn't even be enough to buy scraps." He slammed the tankard down on the counter, sloshing some of the liquid out in great drops over the rim. "When I refused to leave, Warrick himself came out and told me to get out of his store and make room for serious customers."

Marik felt his face harden. He tossed a few tavs on the counter. "For myself and Teo here," he said.

Valen began to protest, but Marik raised a hand. "If it's too much, then use the extra to give this man some food to take home to his family." He turned and clasped a hand over Teo's shoulder. "You've got yourself a deal, friend."

Teo stared up at him, eyes wide, a look of hungry gratitude filling them for an instant. Then the expression faded back into bleak despair. He shrugged his shoulder out from Marik's grasp. "Well, if you manage it, you can find me at the farm on the north end of town. But I won't be holding my breath."

Marik strode out of the tavern, back into the rain. He had

what information he needed, and perhaps more than he had expected from a single inquiry. Now it was time to return to the hideout. Plans were beginning to spin in his mind. A grin tugged at the corner of his mouth. His crew would approve of these plans.

35

As he passed through the doors of his fortress, Ericole's grin faded. The bargain he had struck with the Regeont of Ondoura was only a single piece in the puzzle he was assembling. If he wanted the picture to reflect his vision, there was far more work to be done. He could not yet afford to relax his guard.

He snapped at a servant. "You there."

"Yes, my lord?"

"Tell my men to get ready a shipment of weapons and armor from storehouse three. They are to be delivered to Regeont Roshana with my compliments. She will pay the messenger an agreed-upon amount."

"Right away, my lord. Also, my lady asked me to inform you the moment you returned that a guest has arrived and is waiting in the South Parlor."

"Thank you."

The servant scurried off. Ericole strode down the hall, his boots clicking in a smart rhythm against the marble floors. His heart hammered in his chest. He knew who waited for him in the South Parlor. He had set the wheels in motion himself. But he could not quite calm his breathing. It was a dangerous and exhilarating game he played. He paused before a mirror in the hall, checking to be sure his coat was straight. He ran a hand over his hair and gave himself a feral grin. Then he pushed open the door and entered the large room.

The man waiting for him did not rise as Ericole entered. The snub would have rankled had this emissary been sent from anyone lower than the Ar'Molon himself. It was both irksome and intriguing that the Ar'Molon had sent an emissary at all. Ericole would have preferred not to deal with the Igyeum, but until he had all of his plans in place, he needed them. He was surprised the Ar'Molon had reached out to him, but he was grateful, as it saved him some effort. Ericole had been prepared to play out a longer line, reeling the Igyeum in with pretty promises, but they had practically leaped into his boat. Idly, he wondered what he could glean from their seeming desperation.

Ericole crossed the room, an ingratiating smile plastered on his face. He was thankful that Dianira and Kale were not in the Fortress at the moment. Neither one of them would understand this meeting, and they could easily have made things awkward for him had they been present. The last thing he could afford at the moment was to be unprofessional. He loved his sister dearly, but far too often she let her emotions drive her actions. Arrio's death could not be undone. Working with the Igyeum would not bring him back. It might help him exact the family's vengeance, however, if he could be left to work out the details precisely. No. Dianira and Kale would not understand. They would later, though; he would see to that.

"Lord Niveya." The man at the other end of the room finally rose as Ericole drew nearer. He extended his hand, and Ericole took it, shaking it without the slightest trace of disgust. For all he knew, this was the man who had carried out the orders the Ar'Molon had given to have Arrio murdered. In fact, it was more than likely. Ettore had managed to dig into the De'Anan's past. Roald held the prestigious and highly secret role as captain of

Ar'Molon Uun's secret guild of assassins called the Kotai. Of course, he could not let Roald know he knew such precious information, but he would find a way to use the knowledge to his advantage.

"Sir Roald, I presume?" Ericole replied. "My wife told me of the message you sent. You implied that the Ar'Molon had a proposition I might be interested in."

"Quite so," Roald replied.

The De'Anan took his seat once more, and Ericole joined him, sitting across a low table from the man and studying him. He was of a medium height and bulky, with thick muscles winding their way up his arms and across his shoulders. Even sitting down, Roald looked ready to spring into action. There was an alert look to his hazel eyes, which darted about, never seeming to rest. His dark hair was sprinkled with silver and gray that caught the light and glinted when he moved his head. Gray was also scattered throughout his well-trimmed goatee and mustache. His clothing was nothing worth note at first glance, though upon closer inspection it was apparent that his garments were well-made and of fine, if plain-colored, materials. The man had been a soldier once, Ericole decided; perhaps he still considered himself to be one. He wore no weapon, but Ericole would have bet his only son that the man carried multiple daggers expertly concealed beneath his clothes. If the situation called for it, this man would not be caught off guard or defenseless. His boots were of a soft leather, the kind that would make little noise as he walked. The deep tan of his skin placed him as a native of Vallei, though his accent put his origins at the north-east end of the country, influenced by the lilting tones of Malei, not as harsh as Niveya's own accent. Ericole took in all of this information in a glance. He leaned forward, elbows resting on his knees.

"What sort of proposition does the Ar'Molon have in mind?" he asked, dispensing with any small talk. He would work with the assassin, but no rules of engagement dictated the requirement of politeness.

"Lord Uun is well aware of your resourcefulness," Roald began. "Due to rather unfortunate—and unforeseen—setbacks last year, the Ar'Mol has been forced to expend his resources differently than he had intended. This leaves our military with an insufficient stock of the supplies that may be needed."

"I see." Ericole's mind began to spin. In his interactions with the Ar'Molon, Ericole had found the man to be both brilliant and cunning. They had not crossed paths often, but Ericole had often found himself thinking that Uun would make for a challenging opponent in a game of tranga. He frowned up at the ceiling, pretending to consider the proposition. It was not possible that the Ar'Molon could think so little of him that he believed a business deal would distract him from the murder of his beloved nephew. Could he? No. But perhaps that was exactly the question he was supposed to be asking. Perhaps the Ar'Molon hoped he would ask that question and grow so busy trying to figure out what he was up to, that he would be distracted and not cause any further troubles or—as Roald himself had put it—"unforeseen setbacks." Niveya grinned. "What is the Ar'Molon willing to pay for such a business deal? Weapons are not easy to come by these days. And supplies..." He let his words trail off with a meaningful look at Roald. "Surely the Ar'Molon is aware of the serious shortage in leather and seed afflicting the Igyeum at the moment."

Roald did not even blink. "The Ar'Molon will pay one and a half times the going rate. And he will receive first pick of all your customers."

Ericole Niveya pressed his lips together in annoyance. "First pick? I have many others who would be willing to pay three times the going rate for such a privilege." Ericole waved his hands in a gesture of dismissal. "No, if the Ar'Molon is not ready to make a serious offer, then I suggest you go tell him that such a proposition is an insult to my good name as a businessman. Come back when your master is ready to offer something worth my time."

Roald gave him a hard look. "This is not a negotiation. This is not a request. The Ar'Molon told me to urge you to think of the welfare of your family before attempting to haggle."

Ericole tried not to show the shiver that raced down his spine at the threat. "You might think I am not in earnest, friend. But it is no small matter for me to let these supplies go at a loss. I have to pay my contacts for finding them, and then I have to pay for the supplies themselves. And then there are the details to consider: where am I to deliver these supplies? How long must I hold them for the Ar'Molon to get around to sending someone to pick from them? I have others interested in these supplies and weapons, people willing to pay what they are worth."

"The Ar'Molon will take care of all the logistics of transportation. You will not have to worry about that. And I promise you, there will be no need to hold on to the shipments for long durations; the Ar'Molon has already arranged for someone to come inspect your stores and choose the first batch."

Oh, had he? Ericole raised an eyebrow. *That was an interesting tidbit of information.* He sighed. "This business is my livelihood."

Roald's face hardened. "Shall I make an example of how Lord Uun deals with imbeciles who cannot understand their place?"

Ericole paused for a heartbeat longer than he felt was truly safe. Then he rose and extended a hand. "Your terms are acceptable. One and a half times the going rate, and Ar'Molon Uun gets first pick." *Of whatever is left after I send Roshana her supplies,* he thought smugly, but kept his expression placid.

Roald ignored Ericole's hand. "My master will send someone in a few days to inspect the weapons and supplies you have and transport them to the troops. You will not be troubled with such details."

Niveya kept his disappointment well concealed. Information on where the Ar'Mol's troops were located would have been valuable. He would just have to discover those details on his own. "Very well. I will have the shipment ready for inspection by tomorrow morning."

"I will inform His Lordship."

"A pleasure doing business with you, De'Anan."

The man narrowed his eyes but said nothing as a servant entered.

"Please show De'Anan Roald out," Ericole said. The servant bowed and in a well-practiced way ushered Roald out of the room in a manner that gave every semblance of courtesy and respect, while still being a pointed dismissal.

36

As the group of young men filed onto the airship, Grayden found himself inundated with memories of the last such journey he had taken. Had it only been eight lunats prior that he had set foot on board the Crimson Eagle on his way to the Academy? He had been so full of the spirit of adventure and wonder—so certain of the long years of study stretching out before him. So confused about what he would do at the end of those years. He paused just before stepping aboard the airship, one hand on the frame of the hatch, and looked over his shoulder. The Academy lake below him glistened in the late winter sun. The trees near the shore were beginning to blossom in the early Urin warmth, a full lunat earlier than would the orchard trees back home. His thoughts turned to the Ormond family farm. Did snow still blanket the ground? In his mind's eye, he could see his father, tall and strong, headed out to the barn to begin the day's chores. His cloak would be pulled around him tightly, his breath steaming as he tramped his way from the house to the barn. In the kitchen his mother would be putting away the breakfast things. His memory lingered over the beloved features of his mother's face, seeing the ever-present gentle kindness in her eyes and the way her hands moved steadily from task to task. Seren would be finishing up her own chores, cleaning her room, pulling on her shoes, heading off to school. This had been her first year in school. Grayden smiled at the thought of his impetuous, carefree little sister skipping along the road, sitting quietly on a bench and reciting her lessons, hands and legs squirming to be off and outside the moment the teacher dismissed the class. He patted his breast pocket, feeling the much-crinkled and worn envelope there. He had not yet read the letter his father had given him before he left home. He wasn't sure what he was waiting for, but there was something holding him back, keeping him from opening it, some lingering reluctance, as though reading the letter might make his departure from home more complete, and in spite of all he had been through so far, he was not quite ready to let go so fully.

"Cadet Grayden, step along." The gruff voice of Tomasson pulled him from his reverie.

"Aye, sir," Grayden replied smartly, adjusting his pack and pulling himself up the final rung of the rope ladder and onto the airship. As he stepped onto the deck, he felt a flutter of misgiving deep in the center of his being. Was he truly ready for such a mission? He could not deny the intensity of his training, the arduous hours of sparring and studying, the grueling physical inuring that had been pressed into him. And yet, he still felt eminently unqualified to be partaking of the honor upon which they were embarking. It seemed impossible to fathom that his instructors and the Council would have made such a mistake, and yet, here he was, boarding this airship and about to be carried off onto a mission that no first-year initiate had ever ventured. The immensity of what was being asked of him and his comrades was not lost on Grayden as he made his way across the deck of the airship.

The vessel that would be carrying them to Telsuma was nothing like either the *Crimson Eagle* or the *Valdeun Hawk*. It was a stout little ship, with a rounded hull and a single tall mast in the center. No hint of decoration or elegance graced this ship. It was neither beloved schooner nor valuable cruiser; everything about the *Darrow* bespoke a utilitarian, austere mentality. It was a tool, utilized by the defenders as one of their few military vessels. Its value was without measure, being one of the few warships Telmondir possessed, but none of its worth was measured in sentiment.

Defenders crewed the airship. The cadets had been informed before their departure that they would be spending the journey to the Greyklasp Mountains putting their learning to use. What they knew of airships, navigation, and sailing would be put to the test. Grayden soon discovered that, due to his classes, he was the only cadet aboard who had put in any time behind the wheel of an airship.

As the rest of the cadets and crew assembled on the main deck, the captain stood before them. "Welcome to the *Darrow*," he bellowed. His stern features showed no hint of good humor or compassion. "She's not the fastest airship, but she is reliable. We will make good time getting to the Greyklasp Mountains. If all goes well, our journey won't take more than a sennight. Each of you will be paired with one of my wind-riders and assist him with his duties. I've set up the roster so you will gain experience in every aspect of aeronautical travel. You won't learn everything you need to know in such a short time, but you'll make a good start. Are there any questions?"

The man's tone did not invite questions, and nobody dared to speak.

"Good. My name is Captain Steiner. My first mate, Master Phelps, will get you started."

The captain turned and strode away, climbing the ladder up to the helm where he began barking orders to his wind-riders. The wings of the airship unfurled with a fluttering snap.

"You there," Master Phelps barked, pointing at Grayden. "What's your name?"

"Grayden Ormond," he replied.

"I thought so," the first mate said. "Captain wants you to get as much time at the helm as possible this trip. Get to the wheel."

Grayden leaped to obey, climbing up the ladder behind the captain where he stood at the wheel. His hands on the controls, Grayden watched for the signal to take off. His heart pounded with nervous excitement as he eased the lever forward and the *Darrow* gave the now-familiar lurch as it left the water and skimmed its way into the air. Over the wheel, Grayden grinned at his friends. Their training, short and swift as it had been, was about to be tested.

Master Phelps called each of the cadets forward by name and assigned them to a wind-rider. A short, stocky defender came up and introduced himself.

"Name's Cain," he said. "Seems you've been assigned to me."

"Nice to meet you," Grayden replied, focusing on his job of climbing the airship into the sky.

"You handle the wheel well," Cain commented. "Like you were born to it."

"Thank you," Grayden replied.

Cain squinted down at the other cadets, now following their wind-riders about. "Your group seems a bit young to be taking over an outpost."

"We are," Grayden admitted.

Cain scratched at the stubble covering his dark chin. "Well, I guess that outpost is fairly remote. Shouldn't be too difficult of an assignment. Still..." He shook his head. "I'd heard rumors coming up through the ranks that the Academy had made some changes to their program this year." Cain spoke in an easy, rolling manner and matter-of-fact tone. "Didn't believe 'em, to be honest with you. Tell me, are you truly a first-year?"

Grayden nodded.

Cain whistled through his teeth. "Shew. Then the truth is even stranger than the word we'd received. And just as troubling."

"Troubling?"

"Has to mean that the Council thinks we're closer to open war, don't it? Why else would they start to accelerate students through the Academy if it didn't mean we're soon going to need every able-bodied defender we have?"

Grayden's hands tightened on the wheel. It was the conclusion he had come to, as well. The words weren't all that different from ones he had discussed with Beren and Wynn. But hearing them spoken by someone else, someone who was already close to the front lines, made the realization that much more palpable. He could ignore his own suspicions, or eschew them entirely. Confronted by the simple declaration that his conjecture was accurate made the truth suddenly impossible to ignore and terrifying.

"Have you seen any other signs that war is imminent?" he asked.

"There have been signs for lunats," Cain replied. "But we weren't certain how serious we should be taking things." He blew a sharp breath out through his mouth. "The Council needs to communicate with the armies if they think we're coming to the brink of matters. But I'm sure they don't want to be seen as making the first move. War with the Igyeum won't be popular, or pretty. I can understand why the Council is doing all they can to maneuver us into readiness without openly declaring what our position is." Cain stopped abruptly. "You're veering off course a bit there, best correct a bit to port."

Grayden made the adjustment.

"Good. You'll have this duty until third bell. Then we'll check the rigging. After that, we head below for our time in the mess. Fourth bell, we're on watch duty, which will consist of keeping an eye out for other airships, weather patterns, and faulty equipment. Tomorrow we'll take a turn working in the mess, as we don't have a full-time cook on this voyage. After that, you'll get a turn at the helm again. I skimmed your file, looks like you've had a little more training than your companions, so you let me know if I'm telling you something you already know. Don't want to waste any of the time we've got, eh?"

Grayden listened attentively, nodding his understanding as

Cain continued speaking, pointing out things that were important or demonstrating a technique. Grayden took him at his word and stopped him whenever the defender began to explain something he already knew. Cain took the interruptions with good humor and moved on, letting Grayden consume the information as fast as he liked.

The days stretched out into endless hours of duty rotations. Their work with Tomasson had already prepared them well for the difficult pace of working alongside Cain and the wind-riders. Flying an airship was just as much about mental energy as it was physical. The work was arduous, but effective as Grayden did his best to force his body to perform the tasks his mind already understood from his classes. By the third day, Grayden was scrambling up the rigging to help unfurl and reposition sails without needing any guidance from Cain. By the fifth day, he had mastered astronavigation on the move, and could pinpoint their location above a map with accuracy. It was harder on a moving vessel than on the ground outside the Academy, but Grayden found it an exhilarating puzzle.

On the sixth day, their path was blocked by a sudden storm front that spanned the horizon. The air whipped stinging shards of ice into Grayden's face as he and Cain hurried to furl the sails of the *Darrow*. Billowing dark clouds hemmed them in on all sides, making it impossible to get their bearings. Grayden forced his numb fingers to tie the knot he was working on as securely as possible, but Cain yanked on it for good measure.

"Can't be too careful in a squall like this!" the defender shouted. "Captain will be trying to bring us down out of the clouds so we can set our course."

As they clambered down to the deck, the captain came out of his cabin.

"Short shifts round the clock," his voice boomed out into the raging wind. "Every man tied securely by a lifeline when he's on deck. This storm is going to delay our arrival a bit, but it's nothing we haven't flown through before."

"Best get a quick bite and turn in all standing," Cain instructed Grayden, leading him belowdecks when their shift ended. "Short shifts don't give you a lot of time for sleeping."

Grayden frowned at him. "What?"

"Stay fully dressed," Cain explained. "We don't have the luxury to change in and out of our clothes. Take off anything that's soaked through, but that's it."

Grayden nodded his understanding and trudged to the mess hall where he got his bland porridge and sat down heavily at a table, eating as fast as he could with his body still partially numbed with cold. Beren came in and slumped onto the bench across from him.

"I wonder if making it through this storm is going to factor into our marks at the end of the mission." Beren's words were lighthearted, but his face was grim.

"You heard the captain, it's nothing his men haven't flown through before," Grayden replied. "Besides, this is nothing compared to being attacked by pirates and kidnapped."

Beren managed a small grimace that might have been an attempt at a smile. "Maybe they'll add that consideration to our marks."

"I think they already have, or we wouldn't be here right now," Grayden reminded him with a low chuckle.

"Do you think we would be here if there hadn't been any pirates?"

"What do you mean?" Grayden asked, scraping up another spoonful of porridge.

"I just..." Beren stirred his spoon in the grayish-white lumpy mixture and paused. "I'm not sure. It feels as if we got a lot of extra attention that maybe we wouldn't have if we'd had a normal flight to the Academy. I can't help but wonder if it's truly our skills that put us here, or just our perceived heroism in the face of an uncommon trial."

Grayden put his spoon down. "Do you think we've been tested or graded any less harshly than any other cadet?"

"No."

"We've gotten high marks in all our classes, held our own on the sparring grounds, even against much older students. If anything, it always felt as though I was being watched more closely, pushed harder. Being on this mission is something each one of us earned. And the three of us aren't the only initiates here, either. Zarek's only a second-year, and he wasn't even aboard the Crimson Eagle."

"That is true." Beren studied his porridge intently, gathering a final spoonful. "I just want to be judged on my merit alone. I don't want special treatment."

"I can understand that." Grayden shrugged. "You're probably used to wondering if you're being valued for yourself or your title."

Beren nodded.

"Beren." Grayden gave an exasperated little chuckle. "Who are you kidding? You're the strongest student at the Academy, and the best fighter I've ever seen. The only reason my record in the ring was undefeated for so long was because you refused to meet me there—for inexplicable reasons of your own. We both know who would win in a contest between us: it would be you, handily. Your marks in class are every bit as good as Wynn's, and he's the smartest person I know. I'm pretty sure you're not here because of your father. I think you're here for the obvious reason that you will make certain the rest of us survive this mission."

The gloom lifted from Beren's face for a moment. "Truly?"

Grayden reached across the table and clapped Beren on the shoulder. "I wouldn't say it if I didn't believe it."

The corner of Beren's mouth quirked up. "Thank you, my friend."

―――

THE STORM CONTINUED to batter the stocky little *Darrow*. The tumultuous winds tossed them across the sky, and the murky clouds spread nearly all the way to the ground. The only way for the men aboard the airship to see where they were heading was to fly dangerously close to the ground, and then they had to set extra watches to keep a lookout for trees, hills, and various other hazards that might endanger their stalwart vessel.

Though he had been trepidatious of their ship at first, comparing it to the sleek nimbleness of the *Valdeun Hawk* and the overwhelming might of the Crimson Eagle, Grayden had learned to respect the *Darrow* for what it was: a game little airship with little elegance but plenty of heart. The flying vessel lurched with ungainly fits and starts, now avoiding a tree, now pushing through the wind and the sleet that continued to pour down on them from the clouds, but she did so with nary a creak or complaint. There was no concern in anyone's mind that the airship might come apart at the seams.

It was bitterly cold. Even in the belly of the airship and out of the wind, it was impossible to get warm. The men suffered through the nights, wrapped tightly in their wool blankets and shivering until the bell sounded for them to return to their duties. Grayden felt as though he was moving in a haze somewhere between the waking and sleeping worlds. Every movement became an effort as he forced his body to perform the tasks assigned to him, stamping his feet and flexing his hands in an effort to keep himself warm and moving while above deck.

"I don't know," Wynn gasped to him as they passed each other on the stairs, "how much more of this I can take. And if Captain Tomasson is to be believed, this is the sort of weather we'll be dealing with in the Greyklasp Mountains, too."

Grayden could only muster a discouraged nod.

Three days passed. Three endless, exhausting, bone-chilling days of being on constant alert. And then, as quickly as it had blown in, the storm blew itself out. The clouds parted and the sun shone down upon them from a brilliant, sapphire sky. The men swept the snow and slush from the deck and set to work scrubbing it down and mopping it with towels lest the water turn to a sheen of perilous ice.

Wynn was assigned to shoot the sun and determine their precise location. He attended to the duty with earnest speed and announced his answer to the captain, who grinned broadly.

"Only a day away from the drop-off point," he boomed with pleasure. "I am proud of all of you, men. A lesser crew would have found itself blown far off course by such a storm, but your steady nerves and diligent hands have served us all well. Good job."

It was the first and last time Grayden heard the man utter a compliment to anyone.

37

Oleck's arms strained at the oars as he rowed the large boat they had chartered up the river toward Temin. Raisa sat on the other bench next to Marik, staring out at the darkened shores, keeping an eye out for anyone else who might be on the water. The night was clear, but moonless, the only sound the gentle swish of the oars as they dipped in and out of the gentle waters of the Temnia. The warm, dry wind brushed their faces as it swept in from across the desert. Even in the midst of winter, there was little snow and the temperatures were mild enough that light cloaks were all that each traveler required. The misty darkness above the riverbank grew lighter, a golden glow emanating from just beyond their vision.

"The city." Oleck's whisper came to their ears as he lifted the oars and let the boat coast soundlessly. The watercraft slowed, unable to continue its gliding path against the current without additional propulsion, but silence was needed as they strained their ears to listen.

"Row." Marik whispered the all-clear, and the oars dipped once more into the water, making small splashing noises like that of fish leaping from the water to catch hapless bugs flying too near the surface.

For many long strokes he rowed, pulling the nimble craft closer to the torchlight of the city, until they reached an abandoned dock. Oleck and Marik tied their boat securely to the more sturdy-seeming posts of the dock, and then Oleck cautiously tested the boards to see if they could make their way across.

"I think it'll hold," he breathed, pulling himself up onto the weathered planks and creeping over it to the shore. When he was safely on the other side, the others followed, picking their way across the rickety bridge.

"You're certain the boat will still be here when we return?" Raisa hissed as she stepped onto the grass.

"The dock is old and abandoned, but it's not falling apart yet," Marik murmured, adjusting the heavy pack over his shoulder.

"I still think we should have brought Mouse along to watch the boat." Raisa placed her hands on her hips. "And Shaesta would play my role better."

"You heard what Shaesta learned in town. The Ar'Mol is well-aware of our return, and has men out watching for us. There's a price on our heads. Someone needed to stay behind and get started on disguising the *Hawk*." Marik kept his voice low and even. They had already had this argument, multiple times.

"I could have stayed behind," Raisa said. She did not add that she would have preferred that. She did not feel comfortable in the role of wealthy patron, nor did she feel entirely comfortable around Marik since his revelation that he had been one of the Ar'Mol's soldiers, but she kept those thoughts to herself.

"Shaesta's still earning back my trust," Marik replied.

As you are earning mine, Raisa thought.

"Does the Ar'Mol know who you actually are?" Oleck asked.

Marik shrugged one shoulder. "Shaesta's informant didn't say. We've kept our heads down in the past, not made too much of a name for ourselves with the authorities. I would guess that all he knows about us is contained to our part in the abduction and rescue of young Adelfried."

Raisa huffed and removed the rough cloak she had been wearing to protect the finery beneath. She busied herself smoothing the wrinkles from her elegant dress with her hands. The fancy dress felt wrong, and she worried she would trip over the long, billowing skirts. Shaesta had always been far more at home in such get-up.

"You think this will be convincing?" she asked, twirling from one side to the other. The long skirts swirled around her high-buttoned boots.

Oleck and Marik squinted at her, and then at each other.

"You look fantastic," Oleck drawled. "Of course, it's pitch black, so how would we know?"

Marik let out a snort of laughter that he cut short as Raisa's head whipped toward him. "Oleck's got a point," he said.

Raisa made an exasperated sound in the back of her throat and strode away haughtily. She climbed up the bank with dainty, careful steps, making sure to keep her skirts held high so they would not catch on any lurking thorns, until she reached the road. There she waited, the toe of her boot tapping impatiently.

As shadows, the three companions made their way across the grassy riverbank toward the city gates. Temin boasted a good-sized wall with sturdy gates and an actual guardhouse attached to it. As they approached, a single guard exited the guardhouse.

"Your business in Temin?" he asked, his gaze alert despite the early hour.

"Merchants here to do business with Warrick," Marik replied smoothly.

The guard's eyes roved over them, taking in their well-tailored, elegant clothing and landing with brief interest on the heavy pack Marik had slung over his shoulder. He nodded. "It's a bit early to be opening the gates."

"We got an early start," Marik replied. "But we made better time than we expected."

The guard narrowed his eyes. "Which way did you come from? I didn't hear the riverboat sound its gong yet."

"We came overland," Marik said, no hesitation in his voice, even as Raisa's skin prickled with nervous apprehension.

"Please, good captain," she interjected. "We have come a long way."

The guard's expression softened a bit. "My apologies, lady. But the gates have to remain closed until sunrise, and Warrick's won't even be open for another couple of hours."

"I know, you are just doing your duty." Raisa gave an admiring sigh. "I am merely exhausted and eager to finish my business here. I know it is early, but we have traveled long. I would like to find an inn and rest for a bit, perhaps bathe before our appointment with Warrick. My feet are sore and my dress is simply filthy with dust." She shook her skirts and made a disgusted face. "Couldn't you let us in a bit early? And can you recommend a good place to rest and get some food?"

The guard's lips quirked in a slight smile. "The best place in the city is Mem Osala's bakery and guest house. It's about a mile up the road, and a few blocks past Warrick's Mercantile. Best breads in Temin, and mighty fine mead, as well. She'll be opening her shop up by the time you get there." He bowed. "I am afraid I cannot open the gates just yet, but you are welcome to come through the guardhouse: there's a door on either side."

Raisa fluttered her eyelashes demurely and let a tiny smile grace her lips. "You are far too kind."

The guard ushered them through the little guard station. On the other side of the wall, he gave them directions to Mem Osala's, and bade them fair deals in their trading with Warrick. The three pirates made their way up the road until they reached the first row of buildings. From what they could see by dying torchlight and fading starlight, the city sprawled before them in quiet slumber. Buildings towered above them, many boasting a second level, while a few rose as high as three or four. Old trees lined the street, their boughs arching overhead in an interlacing tapestry. Raisa could only imagine what it would look like in the warmer lunats, when each tree sported its full foliage.

In spite of the size of the buildings, it did not take them long to reach the center of town, or to spot the hanging sign with an emerald airship soaring across it. Above the door in gold letters was printed: WARRICK'S GOODS AND MERCANTILE.

The horizon grew lighter, and a stirring of motion began to creep across the town. A dog woke up, noticed them, and began to bark, but its din was halfhearted, as though the creature knew it had been asleep as they approached and was ashamed of itself. A door opened nearby and a woman stepped outside to draw water from a nearby pump.

"The shop won't open for a couple of hours," Marik said in a quiet voice. "Let's go find that bakery and guest house."

38

As the sun rose overhead and the rest of Temin began to bustle about its normal business, Marik, Raisa, and Oleck finished up the pastries they had bought at Mem Osala's. They were unlike anything Marik had ever tasted before, flaky and buttery and filled with cinnamon sugar. Raisa had tried one that was filled with chocolate, and Oleck's had a sort of apple pie filling. Such a flavorful experience was not one any of them would soon forget. They thanked Mem Osala and Marik left an extra handful of stin on top of the glass case that contained the freshly baked goods. Mem, a tall, willowy woman with dark hair pulled back into a tight bun on the back of her head, tried to wave away the coins, but Marik ignored her protests as they exited the little bakery.

"That place alone would be worth living in this city," Marik commented, capturing the last few flakes of delight from his fingertips. "We might have to scout the area and see if there's a place big enough to hide the *Hawk* nearby. A new safe house might be in order soon. But for now, to business. Let's pay a call on Master Warrick."

When they arrived at the mercantile, the door was open and a flurry of activity filled the shop. A few lads were busily folding cloth and rearranging goods on shelves. Several customers perused the merchandise. Near the back of the store stood a long counter, and behind that, resting one elbow atop the counter, a quill in hand and eyes intently fixated on a large tome, stood a short, balding man. Marik watched for a moment as the man's expression turned thoughtful and he dipped the quill into a small jar of ink and then made a notation in tiny, precise strokes. Handing Oleck the heavy pack and muttering for him to stay near the door, Marik took Raisa's arm and together they meandered through the store. They walked casually. Raisa would point out some item and Marik would sniff at it as though it wasn't worth the effort of opening his pocketbook. Eventually, one of the busy lads made his way over with a sort of hopefully helpful expression on his face. Marik executed a graceful step that effectively turned both their backs on the lad with a haughty air of one who can't be bothered to acknowledge anyone but himself.

He raised his voice so that the boy would hear him, speaking as though replying to a question Raisa had just asked. "No, no, no! You see, my dear, the problem with these droll little villages is that even their largest shops are but a paltry, country equivalent to the much grander and more well-stocked mercantiles of the cities. Why, if I were to buy you something here, it is beyond doubt that we would be overcharged and the item would not last through the sennight. Please, come, my dear, I do not believe you will find anything to your liking in such a"—and here he paused and sniffed disdainfully—"quaint little shop."

"Excuse me, sir, my lady." The lad who had crept up on them interrupted. "Is there anything I can help you find?"

Marik stared imperiously down his nose at the boy. He gave another slight sniff. "I strongly doubt it."

"We have the finest selection of goods this side of the Temnia," the boy pressed on, undeterred by Marik's contemptuous frown. "If there's anything you desire, I'm sure my master either has it or can get it for you. Our prices are quite reasonable, as well, or so I'm told."

Raisa tugged on Marik's arm. "Why don't we just ask?" she pleaded, her tone wheedling. "You promised to buy me something nice in every town we traveled through." She looked down at the boy and batted her eyelashes. "We've just been married, and this trip is part of his present to me." Raisa's lips turned into a pout and she twisted back and forth slightly, causing her long satin skirts to swish around her feet. "I need a memento from every place we pass through. You promised."

Marik looked down at her and let his expression soften. "Well..." He turned to the lad. "You heard the lady. How can I deny my bride such a little thing? Very well, take me to your master and we shall see if he has anything suitable to catch this beautiful woman's fancy."

The boy beamed up at them and trotted back to the counter where the short, bald-headed man stood.

"Master Warrick, these customers are looking for something unique," the boy reported.

The man looked up and his gaze took in Marik and Raisa from head to toe in a single, sweeping glance. His dark eyes narrowed as he noted the fancy silver stitching on Marik's sleeves, the elegant dress, and the subtle, but expensive, brooch at Raisa's collar. He met Marik's gaze, which came at him down a nose raised high in the air. Warrick smiled, white teeth gleaming in his dark face, as he closed the book and gave them his full attention.

"My good sir, my dear lady, please tell me, how can I be of service to you?"

"This lovely creature here is demanding a memento from every place we journey through," Marik began. "She absolutely insists upon it. What am I to do? I cannot refuse my new bride anything her heart desires. But the lady is intolerably picky, and it cannot be just any item, it must be something exquisite, unique, just like herself."

Master Warrick's dark face folded into thoughtful wrinkles. Then he brightened and reached under the counter. With a flourish, he placed a tray filled with ropes of jeweled necklaces and intricately braided chains of the most delicate silver and gold.

"Perhaps the lady would fancy one of these?"

Raisa glanced sideways at the tray and her expression grew bored. She waved a hand. "What need have I for more jewelry?" she asked. "Another necklace, another ring, how will that serve to remind me of the picturesque setting of this quaint village?"

Warrick frowned, bristling a bit at the "quaint village" remark. "Quite true," Warrick muttered, putting the tray of jewelry away. "Let me think, ah! This way!" He led them across the store and gestured at a painting hanging on the wall. It was a likeness of Temin, and a good one. The artist had captured the sun setting behind the town, the last rays flickering on the water of a river so realistic it looked as though the paint were still wet.

Marik had to resist the urge to reach out and touch the thin blue squiggle. He let out a delighted sigh. "Ah, yes, my dear. This would go perfectly in your drawing room, don't you think? Look at how the artist has captured the city like a living picture. Every time you gazed upon it, you would be transported back here."

But Raisa merely shrugged. "The artist has done a fine job," she said, "but such a cumbersome thing would surely hinder our travels. In the end, it's just a picture. Not something I can truly show off to my friends."

Marik let his face fall in disappointment, and he gave Warrick an exasperated stare. "You see what I have to deal with?"

Warrick nodded sympathetically, warming to the challenge. "I see what you mean, indeed. Well then, perhaps you might find this interesting..."

They followed him around the store as he pointed out one trinket after another, each one more exquisite and unique than the last. Marik allowed himself to grow more enthusiastic with each item, but Raisa turned her nose up at all of them, claiming some different imperfection with each of them. At long last, as Warrick was panting a bit from running back and forth across the store, and looking defeated, Raisa put a gloved hand on Marik's arm.

"Forgive me, my love," she said in a haughty and not-at-all contrite tone, "it seems that we shall just have to carry our memories of Temin with no trinket at all. I shall let you out of your promise to me. It turns out you were right, I did not find anything to my liking in this... quaint... little shop."

Warrick's head rose up and his eyes flashed at her words. "One moment," he gasped, "one moment more of your time, my lady, sir. I might have something in the warehouse that would be to your liking. I do not put everything on the floor, you see. There are a few things I like to keep in the back room, for customers of such discerning tastes as yourselves."

Marik turned to Raisa. "What do you think, my dear?"

Raisa tossed her head in a disdainful gesture. "Very well," she huffed. "Though I have no idea what the man could have in a dusty storeroom that would be any better than what is out here."

Warrick led them to a small door at the very back of the store and pushed it open as Raisa flounced behind him. The door opened up into a room much larger than the store itself. Inside, neatly piled in stacks and on shelves was an overwhelming amount of merchandise. Raisa gave the room a cursory glance and then turned impatiently to glare at Master Warrick.

"Well? Are you going to show us what you have, or are we supposed to hunt for it?"

Warrick eyed her with a calculating smile. "Why don't you tell me what you're really looking for?"

Marik tensed. Had the man seen through their ruse?

Raisa folded her arms across her chest and raised her chin. "I'm sure I have no idea what you're talking about."

"You clearly came here looking to trade," Warrick said. "The man you left standing at the doorway? He's carrying something heavy; I'll bet it's valuable, and you want to trade it for an item of equal worth. So"—he spread his arms wide—"now that you have made it into my storeroom, what is it that you wish to trade for?"

Marik relaxed slightly and gave a low chuckle. "You do have an eye for a business deal. Forgive us the charade, but we had to make sure we were dealing with someone as shrewd as we had been told. Word is you have a large supply of leather."

Though it was obvious that Warrick was a man unaccustomed to revealing his true feelings, his eyes widened and his face grew pale under his deeply tanned skin at Marik's announcement. He shook his head mournfully. "No, my friend, I am afraid you are mistaken. I only have a small supply of leather, and it is quite dear these days. I've been selling it at a colossal loss because the need for shoes has been so very great. The Ar'Mol and his men took every bit of it they could find. I did not like lying to my liege, but I managed to keep a bit for myself." His face took on a pained expression of woe. "The children who live here need shoes, you see. No, even if I could be persuaded to sell what I have, I do not believe you have the funds to pay for such a commodity. You are well-dressed and you bear yourselves with a certain flare, but if I am not mistaken, much of what I see here is nothing more than an act."

Marik pushed the door open a bit and made a gesture. A moment later, Oleck slipped through, setting the large sack carefully on the floor. Warrick glanced from the sack to Marik to Oleck, his eyes darting this way and that as if searching for the answer to some riddle. Marik opened the sack to reveal a crate. With an effort, he pried the lid off the crate and let Warrick see what was inside.

As he peered into the crate, Warrick's facade crumbled to dust.

"Cynders." The word came out in a reverent breath. "Where did you get these?"

"Been saving them for a drought," Marik quipped. "Now, how many of these would it take to purchase all the leather you have?"

The man looked up and made a visible attempt to regain his

composure. "Are you implying you have more than what is here in this crate?"

"Quite a few more," Marik replied.

Warrick stared at the crate for a moment, his head nodding up and down slightly as he counted. Then he paused. "Three cynders in a crate. How many crates do you have?"

"Three more besides this one."

Warrick's eyes gleamed. "For all four crates, I'll give you all the leather I have. Let me show you my supply and you can tell me if you think it's a fair deal."

He ushered them to a table near the back of the storeroom. An enormous supply of leather in various colors and thicknesses stood in rolls piled high on and under the table. There was enough material amassed to keep half a dozen cordwainers steadily employed for a year.

"Small supply, hmm?" Raisa whispered.

"Hush," Marik hissed.

Raisa stepped up to the table and touched the leather with a gentle hand, lifting a few of the rolls and examining them. She took her time and Marik waited, letting her complete the inspection. At length she turned and nodded to him.

"It is good quality."

"Good quality?" Warrick blustered. "It is the finest quality."

"Very well," Marik replied, his tone abrupt. "I will leave the lady here while I and my man go fetch the rest of the crates. It may take us some time, so we won't be back until nightfall."

Warrick squinted. "Why leave the lady here?"

"To make sure you don't go misplacing any of these goods in an attempt to cheat us on the fair deal we've made."

"I would never..." Warrick gasped in horror, but Marik ignored him.

"Look for us at nightfall." He turned to Oleck. "Leave that crate here. No sense dragging them with us only to return."

The two men strode out of the storeroom. As they made their

way down the road toward the dock where they had left their boat, Oleck looked back over his shoulder.

"If ever a man deserved to be flogged, that one does," he muttered. "He'd better leave Ray alone."

"He will, or he'll learn his lesson quick," Marik chuckled. "He may still be under the impression that she's a highborn lady. Don't worry, Oleck, Raisa can take care of herself. She's likely got more than a dozen daggers hidden in that dress of hers, and she knows how to use every single one."

Oleck snorted, but seemed to relax at Marik's words. "What are you planning on doing until nightfall?" he asked. "Won't take us that long to get the crates from the boat."

"We'll need to rent a horse and cart; I don't fancy hauling each one of those crates this whole way ourselves. But mostly I figured we'd just let him stew a bit, let his greed simmer. We need him to be impatient by the time we get back. He needs to think he has the upper hand. He's cheating us, remember?"

"I know the plan, I just wanted to know what we were going to do while we waited."

"Lie low, mostly. Just in case Warrick sends someone to look for us."

The two made their way back to the boat by an overly circuitous route, doing their best to make sure they hadn't been followed. Leaving Oleck with the boat, Marik headed down the road to a farmhouse he had spotted along the riverbank and paid the farmer handsomely for the use of his pony and cart for the day. The amount of tavs he pressed into the farmer's hand made the man's bushy white eyebrows soar to the sky. Bidding him wait a moment, the farmer ran inside. He came back out with two meat pies and a small barrel of ale, which he insisted Marik take for the road, while his wife leaned out the door and beamed at him in adoring gratitude.

Marik made it back to where Oleck waited and together they made short work of the meat pies and the ale while the pony grazed, contentedly lipping up the sweet grasses that grew on the banks of the Temnia River. At long last, dusk approached. The men loaded up the heavy crates into the cart and then led the pony up the road back into Temin, where Raisa and Warrick awaited their return.

Night had fallen by the time they reached the sign of the emerald airship. Master Warrick was waiting in the doorway of his shop as they drew near. With an impatient gesture he waved them around the side of the shop to the back door, which he opened with surprising alacrity. Inside, Raisa lounged against the table piled with leather, idly inspecting the edge of a dagger. She looked up as the door opened. When she saw Marik and Oleck the dagger disappeared into the folds of her dress.

"Took you long enough," the merchant snarled as Marik and Oleck positioned the cart. "The missus will be waiting on me with supper. I hate eating cold stew." He eyed them suspiciously. "Let's just check and make sure you brought the correct crates, shall we?" Picking up a pry-bar, Warrick opened each of the three crates, revealing the glowing cynders within. Satisfied, he closed them up again. "Hurry up, just put the crates over there, right there under the table." He waved his arms, directing Marik and Oleck as they strained under the weight of each crate, sliding it into position with laborious movements. When they had finished, the merchant began piling the leathers into their cart, eager to do everything he could to speed them on their way. He grinned and hummed to himself as the goods were slowly transferred from the table into the cart. When they were finished, he brushed his hands against his pants and then reached out with the offer of a handshake.

"Pleasure doing business with you," he said. "If ever you are back this way, I would be pleased to barter with you again."

"Well, you came highly recommended," Marik replied, unable to resist the jibe.

"Oh? Who recommended me? I like to remember my patrons who pass my name along, maybe give them a discount now and again."

"Man by the name of Teo."

Warrick's forehead wrinkled. "Teo... Teo..." He shook his head. "Doesn't strike my memory." He shrugged. "Well, if you see Teo again, give him my thanks."

"We will," Marik replied. "Now, we really must be going. It is getting late, and your supper will be growing cold."

Warrick straightened and clapped a hand to his head. "Yes, yes, of course. Many thanks." He closed the doors to the store-room, locking them with a key on a large ring, and then the merchant bobbed off into the night, coat tails flapping in the breeze behind him.

"Gee-yup!" Marik slapped the pony on the rump and the three of them hurried into the darkness back to the river.

It took them an hour to load the leather into the boat and return the pony and cart. The farmer's wife insisted on giving them more food once she saw that Marik had a young lady with him this time. Raisa accepted with a grateful smile. As they climbed into the boat and shoved the much heavier craft into the current, Raisa let out a little cough.

"How soon, do you think, before he realizes he's been cheated?"

Marik glanced behind them, his heart racing with trepidation. "He shouldn't discover the ruse until morning."

"He'd be hard pressed to find us. We never gave him our names, and we'll be home before he can pick up our trail," Oleck said.

"Unless he remembers Teo," Marik muttered. Why had he said that? He should have kept his mouth closed.

"That was brilliant, using the crates of unrefined cynders you and Dalmir found and painting them with nightvine sap," Raisa said.

Marik gave her a half-smile, glancing back again. "It only worked because we made the exchange at night. The sap only glows in the dark."

"You played your parts perfectly," Oleck said, chuckling. "He kept getting angrier and angrier the more things you turned your noses up at."

"I hope we didn't make him too angry," Marik said.

Raisa gave him an odd look. "What are you worrying about?"

Marik shook himself. "I don't know. I think we got away clean, but I can't help worrying. Warrick didn't get to his position just because he's related to the Ar'Mol, he's a shrewd grymstalker, and I wouldn't put it past him to make some retaliatory effort."

"He can't know who we are," Raisa replied.

"I gave him Teo's name," Marik groused. "I shouldn't have done that."

"Marik, stop worrying," Raisa said.

"I just wish we hadn't had to turn over a crate full of real cynders," Oleck lamented.

"Well, at least now we have a cargo that will get us into Melar," Marik replied.

"Do you think we got enough to pass as real merchants?" Raisa asked.

"We got enough to become real merchants." Marik grinned. "Even after we pay Teo and donate a good amount to Elben."

"Elben?" Oleck frowned. "Why would we donate any of this to Elben?"

"The Ar'Mol took their leather." Marik's voice turned hard. "And we're still caught in the grip of winter. Teo's not the only man in Elben trying to keep his children's feet warm."

Oleck muttered under his breath something uncomplimentary about the Ar'Mol. Marik glowered into the night behind them, his arms pumping the oars with long, steady strokes. His jaw jutted out as he ground his teeth together, thinking of the long list of crimes he planned to hold the Ar'Mol and his Ar'Molon accountable for someday. His eyes fell on Raisa as the moon peeked out from behind a cloud and bathed their little group in its silver light. Her expression was filled with a softness he had rarely seen on her face since the day she had joined his crew, just a little wisp of a thing then, but already with fiery eyes and a quick tongue that could cut a body to ribbons with its sharp wit. Was it his imagination, or were her eyes filled with the mistiness of tears? He dropped his gaze before she could notice that he had seen her in such a moment of weakness. He wondered if he would ever be able to explain to her that such emotion was not a weakness at all, but their greatest strength. That same compassion, that desire for justice that she hid so ferociously, those emotions burned in his heart, often the only things that prodded him on, that kept him going when it would be so much easier to just go back to Telmondir and take up a simple life as an honest farmer or captain of one of the mighty cargo cruisers.

"Captain." Raisa's voice was soft.

"Yes?"

"Thank you."

"For what?" Marik asked, mystified.

"For reminding me..." She broke off. "It's not just hatred of the Ar'Mol, is it?"

"What do you mean?"

"Why you're doing all this." She made a broad gesture with one arm. "Why you've always done the things you do."

"I hate the Ar'Mol," Marik said cautiously, not sure where she was heading with this line of thought.

"I know. I do, too. But I just... I mean... you love our people. I forget that, sometimes. We fly so high above it all, living on an airship, hiding out, making our own rules. I forget that we do all of this for them. So thank you, for reminding me what this has always been about."

Marik nodded in the darkness, feeling ashamed. How often had he forgotten the exact same thing? If not for Dalmir, would he have ever remembered?

39

The design was complete. It was not a work of beauty or a great marvel of engineering, but it would work. At least, Dalmir hoped it would work. Keene still needed to finish his task of forging the pieces together and soon they would discover whether or not the past two lunats had been a massive waste of time. Weariness coated him down to the bones, and he knew that if the device did not work, there was no way he could fix it. If Palte were here, he would have at least three different ideas already spilling out of his mind and onto sheets of paper for how to make the device better, but Palte was not here. And Dalmir knew of his own shortcomings when it came to this sort of work. Give him a vast mountain to work with, or a building to design, or a farm to plant. This working with small, mechanical pieces that needed to fit together in a tiny puzzle had never been Dalmir's strength.

All morning, men lumbered in and out of the forge, dropping off loads of rock that had been mined and cut into the cylindrical parameters Dalmir had specified. Even after two lunats, they did not have a thousand of them, but five hundred was a good start, and if Dalmir's device worked, it would fill these empty cynders slowly enough to give the miners time to keep up with the pace.

Lady Nadia paced in front of the forge doors, her arms crossed, her posture rigid. Dalmir stood still in an alcove, waiting.

"How can you be so calm?" Nadia demanded.

"It will work or it won't," Dalmir replied. "Fretting won't affect the outcome."

Nadia opened her mouth, either for a reply or a retort, but Keene came swinging through the doors, his arms wrapped around the device as he wrestled it into the hallway. It was vaguely pitcher-shaped, with the original refiner that Dalmir had discovered held above the top of the pitcher by thin bands of iron. Near the bottom, a secondary spout jutted from the pitcher, poised to pour into a small container just big enough for one of the cylinders to be placed. The whole contraption was rough and somewhat ugly to look at, but it was the best they could do in such a short time. Palte would have managed beauty, as well as function. But Dalmir was not Palte.

"It is complete," the wiry smith announced. "Shall we test it?"

"Where would you like to set it up?" Dalmir asked.

"Preferably somewhere I won't trip over it when I'm working on other projects," Keene grunted. "But I need to be able to keep an eye on it, as well." He looked up thoughtfully. "I have just the space."

With painstaking steps the tall man lugged the device down the hall and kicked open a door Dalmir had not been through yet. Inside stood a mostly empty chamber, with some shelving along two of the walls. Assorted odds and ends lay upon the shelves as though they had been carelessly tossed there. Nothing about the chamber indicated organization. This struck Dalmir as strange, for everything he had seen of the rest of Keene's abode and forge was meticulously tidy. Keene situated the device in the center of the room, and then darted back up the hall. He returned with a crate full of the cynder-shaped ore and raised an eyebrow at Dalmir.

Dalmir heaved a sigh. "You will need someone to stay with the device and move the cynders under it." He gave an apologetic grimace.

Keene waved a hand. "That's no matter. I have a few apprentices who can do that work. You haven't met the lads?"

Dalmir frowned. "I haven't even seen them."

Keene grinned. "Well, you and Daegan keep yourselves so intently focused on your work." He shook his head. "I'll go get them now so you can show them what to do. They are careful and capable."

"If it works," Dalmir muttered.

"It will work," Nadia whispered.

A few moments later they heard the tromp of Keene's heavy footfalls, accompanied by a patter of lighter steps. The smith appeared in the doorway and ushered in three young men, who were a sight more than "lads." Dalmir felt more at ease as he looked at them, glad that his definition of "lad" and Keene's seemed to be vastly different. The tallest of the men was thin and wiry and resembled Keene closely, definitely in his twenties, already with a full beard. The other two were perhaps a year or two younger and more burly, and bore no similarities to their master.

"My son, Ilvan, bound for his own forge at the end of this lunat. And my two apprentices, Gunnar and Conrad," Keene introduced them briefly. "Lads, this here is Master Dalmir. He designed that device you see there. It's going to help us in the war."

Dalmir winced at the matter-of-fact tone in which Keene said the word "war." Such an ugly term should not be used so casually. But he remained quiet, keeping his thoughts to himself.

Keene showed the men the crate of ore and explained that they would soon become cynders, if everything worked the way Dalmir expected it to. The apprentices cast appreciative glances at Dalmir, seemingly impressed by the ingenuity of the device.

Keene grunted. "Master Dalmir? I think we're ready to test it out."

Dalmir nodded and pulled out the blue gemstone. He set it carefully into the tiny cup at the top of the device that was part of the original refiner. At first, nothing happened. Then the orb's glow intensified to a brilliant beacon of light, and a steady stream of blue liquid began to pour out of the refiner and into the machine Keene had built. The fluid was not like water, but appeared thicker, more like the molten rock that spills from the mouth of an angry volcano.

Fair shores, but it was beautiful! Dalmir kept finding himself holding his breath. He forced himself to inhale and exhale normally. This part should work. The next bit was the question.

"This could take a while," Dalmir said. He bent down and pointed out the lever above the opening at the bottom of the pitcher. "See this?" He looked up at the young men, who all nodded at him. "Good. One of you hand me one of those cylindrical stones from that crate."

The shortest of the men moved swiftly to obey. Dalmir showed him how to position the cynder into the slot.

"Then you just push this lever up so the liquid can flow out of that spout." He demonstrated, and the glowing blue liquid spilled out into the waiting cynder. The ore absorbed the liquid. Dalmir restrained himself from showing any flicker of the triumph he felt as the cynder filled. Instead, he busied himself showing the boys how to adjust the flow to make it come out faster or slower. When the cynder was full, Dalmir pulled the lever back down, cutting off the flow, and removed the now-glowing blue cynder from the slot.

"This is the part when you have to be the most careful," Dalmir intoned, his eyes boring into each of the men standing before him. "Once the cynder is full, it has the potential to power an airship. What do you think will happen if you drop one?"

Keene's son stared him straight in the eye. He grinned, but his tone was serious. "Same thing that happened when Gunnar here forgot to keep the bellows going steady and gave them a good yank. Coal gas had built up inside and fire just poured out into the air. Loud noise, too." Ilvan clasped his hands together and then pulled them apart in a wide motion, making a rumbling noise with his mouth. "He's lucky he only singed his eyebrows off. Pa took the strap to him for being so careless; he couldn't sit down for a sennight."

Gunnar, the middle-sized man, flushed scarlet but kept his mouth shut. The smallest of the young men gave Keene's son an exasperated glare.

"And he learned his lesson and has been extra careful ever since," Conrad retorted. "We all have. Could'a been any one of us made that mistake, even you, Ilvan. Besides, that was over ten years ago, aren't you ever gonna give it a rest?"

"Nope." Ilvan grinned.

"That explosion of fire? That's exactly what would happen here if you dropped one of these cynders, but much worse, and much bigger," Dalmir said, heading off the argument he could see brewing. "It wouldn't matter if anyone was close by or not, it could bring the entire mountain down on top of you."

Everyone's eyes widened, even Keene's. They glanced at the cynder in Dalmir's hand with apprehension and a new respect.

"Right," Keene interjected. "How long until the device is full?"

Dalmir squinted thoughtfully. "Probably a few days at the rate it's going."

"We'll leave it for now, then," Keene replied. "Lads, this is going to be your main responsibility once Dalmir leaves. Until then, you have your regular duties and chores. Understood?"

"Yes, sir," they chorused in unison, nodding their heads.

"Skip to, then," Keene barked.

"The big trick is to see what happens when I remove the orb," Dalmir said, once the boys had left.

"We should test that now," Nadia suggested. "Better to know now than to be disappointed after waiting for several days for the device to fill up."

"Words of truth," Keene rumbled.

Dalmir nodded and rubbed his hands together slowly. With painstaking care, he lifted the orb from its setting. As he did so, the flow of liquid ceased and the orb faded to its normal pale glow. The three adults held their breath as Keene placed another piece of ore beneath the spout and pushed the lever. The stream of blue liquid flowed once more until the ore shone with living brilliance. Keene turned the lever, halting the flow, and lifted the glowing cynder, holding it up for Dalmir and Nadia to see.

"It works," Nadia breathed.

Dalmir glanced at her, an amused expression dancing about his face. "You sound surprised. I thought you were the one who was certain we couldn't fail."

Nadia's cheeks flushed and she dusted her hands together briskly. "I was. But it's still gratifying to see that I was right."

Dalmir and Keene laughed out loud. At that moment, Daegan entered the room, looking as disheveled as always. His gaze darted from one face to the other.

"I wondered where you had all gone off to." He glanced at the device in the center of the room. "Ah. Well? Does it work?"

"It does," Keene exulted.

"Excellent," Daegan replied, rubbing his hands together eagerly. "That is excellent news. I am glad to hear it." He looked to Dalmir. "I suppose you are taking your leave of us soon, then?"

"Not for several days, perhaps a sennight," Dalmir said. "It will take some time to fill the device." He placed the orb back in its bowl and the process began again.

Daegan approached the device and watched it work, his gaze studying everything about what was happening. When he finally stepped back, his expression was puckered in a strange thoughtfulness.

"I was wondering if you might be willing to take a look at what I am working on." He did not turn to address Dalmir, but it was clear to whom his words were directed. "I would be glad to hear any thoughts or ideas you might have in the way of improvements."

A coldness settled in the center of Dalmir's stomach. Suppressing a grimace, he gave a short nod, concealing the reluctance he felt as best he knew how. "I'm sure there is little I can add to your design. What I saw the first day I was here was quite impressive. But since I have to wait a few days, I can certainly take a look at it."

"My thanks." Daegan stared at Dalmir's device for another moment, his gaze probing. Then he shook himself and turned to leave. They could hear him muttering to himself as his footsteps echoed down the tunnel.

Keene snorted. "I've never seen Daegan ask anyone for help like that before. Usually he is the one taking everything upon himself, trusting no one else to be as detailed as he is."

Dalmir did not reply. A weight crushed down upon his chest and it was all he could do to take normal breaths. War. Another war teetered before him, ready to fall like a tree struck down in a storm. It would crash through everything in its path, leaving only destruction and death, so much death. He could not face it again. His past whirled before his eyes, the faces of everyone he had ever lost accusing him for every mistake he had ever made. Was this a portent of things to come? Was it to be his lot in life to repeat history again and again, making similar mistakes in each generation?

"Daegan's a man who doesn't like things he doesn't understand. And there's not much in Turrim he doesn't understand," Keene continued with a low chuckle. "But your contraption here seems to have rattled him. For that alone, I think I should take you over to Goodie's and buy you a drink. Or, if you're not a drinking man, they have the best cream custard tarts in all Telsuma."

Dalmir allowed a smile to spread across his face. "I could use a tankard after the long days of work, and a cream custard tart sounds especially good. I believe I will take you up on your most generous offer."

Keene clapped him on the back with a rumble of approval.

"Good man. Let me just clean up the forge and we will both take the evening off to celebrate our success."

Nadia smiled demurely. "I will leave you gentlemen to your celebration," she murmured. "My husband needs to hear this encouraging news as soon as possible." With another brilliant smile and a word of congratulations, Lady Adelfried took her leave of them.

Keene turned to Dalmir. "Shall we, then?"

Dalmir nodded. "Lead the way, my friend."

40

The *Darrow* hovered above the glistening white ground as the cadets made their way down the rope ladder. The snow was only a few inches deep here, but after the more temperate climes of Ondoura, it felt like they had stepped into a different world. Great pine trees rose up like dark sentries standing guard here in the little cleft valley deep in the heart of the Greyklasp Mountains. When the last of the cadets had reached the ground, the shadow of the airship swept over them in a final wave and then they were left alone in the silence of the snow.

"Why couldn't we just land at the outpost?" Zarek asked, stomping his feet in the snow and grimacing.

Neither Tomasson nor Petrescu deigned to answer. Grayden assumed it had something to do with the outpost being difficult to access via airship, which made sense since the Igyeum had the advantage of air-power over Telmondir.

"At least it's warmer down here than it was during that storm," Wynn commented as they assembled themselves and shouldered their packs.

"Let's get moving," Tomasson barked. "We need to reach our campsite by nightfall."

Without a word, the cadets fell in behind him in a steady, disciplined line. Their boots crunching in the snow, they took their first true steps toward their destination. In the shadow of the mighty Greyklasp Mountains, Grayden could not help but feel his spirit soar. He felt a sense of accomplishment that they had made it this far. It was a fine thing to be here, on the threshold of what they had been training relentlessly for over the past lunats. Any misgivings he may have had about his place here disappeared as he began the trek up the mountainside with his comrades. The crisp, late morning air sparkled through his lungs as he breathed it in. A hunter's cry drew his eyes heavenward and he saw a great predator bird circling lazily, the sunlight glinting off its feathers. He could taste the pure freedom it was enjoying as it soared overhead and he answered its fierce cry with a wide grin. He found that he was glad of the hike. Ahead of him, he could see that the beginning of their mission had affected the others in much the same way. His fellow cadets strode through the snow with their shoulders thrown back and a bounce to their steps.

Behind him, Captain Petrescu chuckled. "It is amazing what getting out of the classroom and conquering the elements can do to a body, no?"

Grayden didn't answer. He did not have to. His agreement wrote itself into the very footprints he was placing on the mountainside and leaving behind.

After a few hours of hiking, they took a short break to eat before continuing their march. As they walked, Grayden jogged up the line to walk next to Beren.

"What do you know of the guard post at the Storvas Pass?"

"Not much," Beren admitted. "I did spend some time in the library looking for references. It sounds like it's fairly rustic. I don't think there's any permanent building, but it's more than just a campsite, which would explain a lot about our training these last three lunats. The actual fortress would be the Storvas Fort at the mouth of the Storvas Pass, which is one of the few ways through the mountains into Telsuma from Palla, without airships, of course. But even air travel over the mountains can be hazardous, as we recently experienced for ourselves."

Grayden nodded but did not reply, content to walk wrapped up in his own thoughts. He wondered what it would be like to run an outpost on their own, even a rustic one. How would they respond if Igyeum soldiers suddenly appeared in the Pass?

As night fell, Tomasson led them into a copse of pine trees. "We will set up camp here for the night," he announced. "Captain Petrescu and I are expected to check in at the outpost this evening to let the defenders there know we have arrived. We will return. Meanwhile, you men know what to do."

The defenders left them, marching north-east. The cadets busied themselves accomplishing the tasks of setting up camp. Enric and Arven volunteered to go hunting. Wynn and Hamil set up the shelters while Zarek and Peder got a fire going and then set off into the woods to gather more firewood. Grayden helped Beren gather snow to melt in a pot over the fire. Grayden found himself amazed at how much snow it took to produce a good quantity of water, and Beren laughed at his astonishment.

Beren pointed him to a log piled high with snow. "Get that," he said.

Grayden carefully scraped the top layer of snow into the pot, but paused at Beren's sudden grunt of laughter. He looked up to see Beren rolling his eyes.

"City boy," the Telsuman rumbled. "Let me show you." He grabbed the pot and forcefully scraped the log clean, heedless of the flakes of bark that came with the snow.

Grayden took the jibe in the good nature it was meant. He shrugged and continued to help gather snow. It took a while, but by the time they had finished refilling all the waterskins, Enric and Arven had returned with a large deer hanging between them and triumphant grins on their faces.

They cooked their feast on spits over the fire and enjoyed an evening of shared victory. In the absence of the defenders, the atmosphere grew lighter and more carefree. It was an unexpected evening of near freedom, and as the moon began to rise and the sparks from the fire danced up to greet the stars, Grayden found himself filled with an unmitigated contentment that he had not experienced in many lunats. The tangy, sweet scent of the pine branches burning in the campfire flooded his nostrils and the heat radiating off the flames bathed his face in warmth. The voices of his friends whispered through the air as the other cadets talked and joked, producing an aching sensation somewhere in Grayden's heart as the comfortable companionship tugged his thoughts once more toward home. He leaned his head back on his hands and stared up at the stars, wondering if his parents and sister might be outside looking up at the same sky. He closed his eyes and held the memory of their faces in his mind's eye, lingering over their features.

Someone kicked his boot and he opened his eyes. Enric stood over him, holding out a hand to help him up. "You and I drew first watch," the older cadet informed him.

"Oh? How did that happen?" Grayden asked, allowing himself to be lifted to his feet.

"Apparently we were the only ones not paying attention." Enric chuckled and Grayden joined him. First watch was more to his preference anyway. He would rather stay up a bit later than have his sleep interrupted in the middle of the night.

As the others turned in for the night, Grayden and Enric sat up on the perimeter of the camp in companionable quiet. The fire crackled behind them and a night owl hooted in the trees above. Somewhere below their position a wolf howled and then a chorus of wolf-song soared into the air, haunting and sad, but also proud and free in its melody. The air grew colder as the night wore on, and Grayden found himself fighting to stay awake.

"What's your family like?" Grayden asked as he stood up to throw another log on the fire. He swung his arms back and forth, asking the question to help himself ignore the cold and his own exhaustion.

Enric stamped his feet in the snow. "I have an older sister and two younger brothers. My pa is a rancher."

"What did they think of you going to the Academy?"

"They were proud. I think Ma was a bit saddened by it, but she couldn't deny the honor of it, nor the opportunity. What about you?"

"Just one younger sister, Seren. She's six. My family has orchards." Grayden rubbed his hands together. "My parents were proud, as well. Though I'm not sure they'd have been so eager about it if they'd known how close we really were to war."

"Words of truth," Enric replied. "At least I always planned to become a defender anyway. It's been harder for others who still dreamed of going home and starting up a profitable trade with the compensation they were expecting to receive."

Grayden grimaced. The headmaster's announcement had been a shocking dose of cod-liver oil to swallow as an initiate. What would it have been like to be headed into his final year of Conspectus, dreaming of going home with a good amount of coins in his pocket, only to be told that his new option was to become a defender or go home empty-handed? It was a wonder there hadn't been open riots and rebellion among the students. And yet, he remembered what Ailwen had said. Fewer and fewer of the men who entered the Academy chose to go home after completing their Conspectus years. More and more of them in recent years had found themselves grown beyond what they had left behind, instead opting to continue in the trade they had been trained for: as warriors.

Standing in the dark, their backs to the fire, Grayden and Enric continued their conversation. They talked about little that mattered. But when it was time to rouse Peder and Hamil for their watch, Grayden had lost some of the apprehension he had always felt around the older student. The shared trials they had already passed through and the unknowns they now faced had done a bit to soften the scowl that always lingered about the corners of Enric's mouth. Perhaps they would never be friends, but Grayden now believed that they were comrades who could rely on one another if the need arose.

———

MORNING BROKE and Petrescu and Tomasson had not returned. The cadets had their breakfast, packed their gear, and made ready for the final trek to the Storvas Outpost. An air of expectancy hovered throughout the camp like a low-lying fog. Still, the defenders did not return.

"Maybe this is a final test," Wynn suggested. "Finding the outpost on our own."

Koen tapped a finger to his chin thoughtfully. "That's not a bad guess," he remarked. "Good thing it didn't snow any more last night. We should be able to follow their trail well enough."

Zarek paused a moment, then asked, "Do you think that's wise? They said they would return."

"We are training to become defenders of our nations," Koen argued. "Not to sit around on our hands waiting for someone else to tell us what we should do. If they're not back, there's probably a good reason. They expect us to be able to think on our own and find our way around; it's what we've been training for."

"That makes sense," Zarek agreed. "If they were coming back, they would have returned by now. Wynn is probably right, and this is some sort of final test before we take over the outpost from the defenders."

"Then I say we show them how quickly we can pass the test," Hamil said.

The others nodded and a rippling sound of agreement flowed through the young men. Grayden glanced around and saw that every one of them was as eager as he to get underway and accomplish whatever mission was set before them.

"Best we break camp, then," Koen said.

They had been trained well. Within minutes, the camp had been struck and each cadet had his pack strapped to his back. Their gear was heavy, but they were used to the load after Captain Tomasson's demanding regimen of the past two lunats. As a group they fell into line behind Koen and began following the footprints left in the snow by their mentors. The trail was easy to follow: the snow had a crisp crust of iciness across its top, so even the winds had not been able to completely fill the tracks. As they traveled eastward, the peaks rose up on their left and a dark army of trees stood silent and strong on their right. The day was overcast and a bit of a wind blew the occasional dusting of snow into their faces, but it was not as cold as Grayden had believed it would be. Spring was on its way, even here.

Despite the fairly even terrain, it still took several hours to spy their destination. The outpost was not much to look at, more like a permanent bivouac than a proper guard station. The signs that it was even there were slight: evidence of multiple sets of footprints in the snow, broken branches and a couple of felled trees that showed men had been here with axes and made camp, a thin wisp of smoke signaling a campfire. Koen held up a hand and hunkered down in the snow.

"Something's wrong," he whispered. "I'm not seeing any movement in the camp at all."

"Do you think it's all part of the test?" Peder asked.

Koen frowned. "I don't know. I'm not sure what's going on. I think we should swing well into the tree line and approach from the cover of the forest." The other cadets nodded their assent and they made for the trees in a stealthy, crouching run.

Grayden's heart beat fast with the exhilaration of the game. He felt as though he were back at home playing Cat and Mouse with his friends. Of course, whatever test the defenders had devised would not be dangerous for the cadets, but it still held a thrill of excitement. At any moment, someone might jump out at them, or descend from the trees. At any moment, they would see the legendary skills of full-fledged and battle-ready defenders on full display and they would know what to strive for in the coming years. But as they reached the safety of the trees, all remained silent. No cry of warning pierced the air. No crunch of booted feet in the snow gave any sign that they had been spotted. They paused for a moment, breathing hard. Then Koen led them deeper into the trees, skirting the campsite with a wide berth, stopping to listen every few steps. Still, no sound came from the camp.

"What do you think?" Koen whispered to the others, a light in his eyes that mirrored the thrill Grayden felt. "Waiting ambush?"

"Possibly." Beren grinned.

"Probably," Wynn whispered back. "We should keep half our team back."

"Good idea," Koen chuckled. "We'll show them they've trained us well. Wynn, Beren, Zarek, Arven, and Hamil stay here. Everyone else, with me."

Grayden and the others followed Koen, slowly creeping through the snow, keeping the trees between them and the camp as much as possible. No movement stirred in the camp. Grayden began to feel as though the trees were closing in on him and he stopped short with a gasp.

"Hssst!" Koen hissed at him, waving a hand in an impatient gesture that said Grayden should stay quiet. But the sensation persisted and Grayden shook his head adamantly.

"Wait," he whispered. "Something's wrong."

"What is it?" Enric asked.

"I don't know. I can't explain it. I get these... hunches, I guess you could call them."

Peder narrowed his eyes. "Sure you're not just feeling jumpy before a fight?"

"I'm not..." Grayden trailed off. If Wynn were in the group he would be able to explain it better, but it was not something Grayden could put words to. He had never understood this ability, himself; how could he explain it to someone else? There was nothing he could do but stay extra alert and give warning if it was needed.

However, it was not Grayden who cried the warning, but Koen, who stopped abruptly and let out a harsh hiss of dismay. The others had their weapons at the ready in an instant, but Koen did not stop to explain, he bounded through the trees and into the clearing, heedless of their frantically whispered urgings to pause. As they followed at a more cautious pace, Grayden saw what Koen had already noticed and his sword arm dropped to his side in helpless horror.

This was no final test. No celebration awaited them. No life awaited them at all. The outpost was littered with the aftermath of some dreadful attack. Defenders lay motionless in the snow, stains of red creeping out around them. A few of them had weapons out, but most appeared to have been taken unawares. Off to one side, they found the body of Captain Tomasson. His sword was out, his face frozen in a look of wild terror.

Peder stumbled back into the trees at a run and brought the rest of the group to join them. They stared around in bewildered trepidation as the awful truth of what they were seeing began to fully sink in.

"What happened here?" Beren growled.

Grayden shook his head, a numb daze overwhelming him. "I don't..." He paused. "Did you hear that?"

Beren's sword leapt into his hand as if of its own accord. "No... what did you hear?"

"Sounded like... There it is again!" Grayden scrambled through the snow, skirting the bodies with as much respect as he could muster. The painful noise came again, a low whining groan like that of a wounded animal, or perhaps a man. His heart leapt with hope: could someone have survived? He made his way over to the woodpile—the only real barricade of any kind in the defenders' bivouac—and gave a shout of surprise.

"Over here, it's Ioan, he's hurt, but he's alive!"

The other cadets came running as Grayden and Beren knelt

down in the snow at the defender's side. Ioan's eyes were closed and his face was flushed. He clutched his side, his face a mask of pain. His leg was bent at an odd angle. He let out another pitiful moan and Grayden rose.

"We need to get him warm and treat his injuries. Quickly!"

"It might not be safe to move him," Peder cautioned.

"It definitely isn't safe to leave him lying here in the snow," Grayden replied, pulling his pack from his back and rummaging for a clean cloth. He found one and pressed it to the wound in the defender's side to stanch the blood. Due to the cold temperatures and the snow, the wound was not bleeding much, but there were flecks of ice in the wound that concerned Grayden.

"Where will we take him? Is it safe to stay here? Should we move to a different site?" Zarek asked.

Koen glanced around. "I don't want to stay here," he muttered. "But whoever did this left because they thought their work was finished. I think it's safe for a little while."

Beren, who was carrying one of the tents, began to set it up behind the wood pile, away from the bodies of the slain. "They'll need to be buried," he growled.

"The ground is too hard," Hamil replied, lending a hand with the tent. "But we can build a pyre or a cairn."

"Here in Telsuma we prefer cairns," Beren said. "Very well. When we get this tent up, we'll begin gathering stones."

Once the tent was up, Wynn and Zarek built a fire near the entrance while Grayden and Peder gently lifted Ioan and placed him inside. The rest of the cadets gathered the bodies of the defenders and lined them up, then began the difficult work of gathering stones for so many cairns. There were six dead men to bury, and the work took the rest of the day while Grayden and Peder worked feverishly over Captain Petrescu, trying to coax the little flame of life flickering within him into a greater flame.

"His leg is broken," Peder said grimly. "We'll have to set it and bind it so it heals properly."

"Do you know how to do that?" Grayden asked.

Peder nodded. "I've been focusing my studies on medicine. But I'll need you to hold him down."

"He's unconscious."

"Even so, this is going to hurt, and I can't have him flailing about while I try to do this. Kneel on his shoulders and hold his arms down." Peder reached into his bag and took out a leather belt. "Here, put this between his teeth." Then he poked his head through the tent. "Beren!" he shouted. "Get over here, I need your strength."

Beren entered the tent. He took in the scene before him and knelt by Ioan's good leg, pressing it down with his hands without needing to be told what he had been called in to do. Peder gave him a tight, appreciative grin. Then he took the bad leg in both his hands. Grayden closed his eyes. He heard a popping, grinding sound and felt Ioan lurch under his hands. A roaring scream filled the tent as Ioan tried to writhe in pain. Grayden pressed the other man's shoulders and arms down with all his strength, but even in his weakened state the defender had an amazing strength to his movements. Grayden feared the man would toss him to the side like so many scrapings of leftovers, but his violent convulsions only lasted for a few heartbeats as Peder set the broken bone. Then Ioan lay still once more, his body shuddering.

"That's done it," Peder gasped. "Quick, Beren, I need you to bind the leg."

More moments passed. Grayden still could not bring himself to open his eyes until he heard a pair of sighs.

"There," Beren said, breathing heavily, "that should hold it."

"Good," Peder replied. "Now we just need to keep him warm, and tend to that cut on his side. Grayden, you can let go of him, I need you to make him a tea with these herbs." He tossed a packet over. "They will help with the pain."

Grayden set about boiling water over the fire. He mixed in the herbs and let it simmer for a few minutes before pouring it into a cup. It took them quite a bit of effort to get any of the tea down Ioan's throat, but they managed to force a few swallows into him.

Peder inspected the gash on Ioan's side and declared that it was not as bad as it looked.

"I thought maybe it had gotten some frostbite, but it looks like he had just the sense to pack some snow into the wound to help stop the bleeding before he went unconscious," he said as he cleaned the wound out and sewed it shut with a needle and thread.

"I'm glad you know what you're doing," Grayden told him. "We've only gotten basic training in treating wounds."

"Medicine has always been my interest," Peder replied. "But these are classes that are getting skipped in the accelerated program." He gave an angry shake of his head as he tied off the thread. "Nobody should be out here without this sort of basic knowledge."

Grayden could not help but agree. Suddenly the accelerated program and his position on this mission seemed a foolish thing. Seeing that Peder had the situation well in hand, Grayden ducked out of the tent and began helping the others with the cairn. The sky had darkened and the moon shone high in the sky before they finished. The cadets stood in a solemn group before the cairns they had built; nobody seemed to know what to say over the fallen.

After an uncomfortable silence stretched over them like a leather hide being readied for shaping, Koen took a small step forward. "Captain Tomasson, you were a harsh taskmaster, but your harshness was more necessary than even you realized to prepare us for what we would face in the coming days. Thank you for your dedication." He shifted in the snow. "I did not know the rest of the men who lie fallen here, but what I know of them is enough for me to respect them. They worked hard to protect our people, and they died heroes. May their courage inspire us to a fortitude and bravery of our own." His words hung in the air as the group shuffled away from the cairns, drawn away from the cold tombs and toward the beckoning warmth and life of the fire.

"Who do you think did this?" Wynn asked, walking between

Grayden and Beren. "Who would attack an outpost of defenders this far inside Telsuma?"

"The answer to that question worries at my mind," Beren replied. "A normal attack from wild animals might claim the life of a single defender upon occasion, but not an entire outpost. This can only mean one thing: a well-trained and intelligent enemy has penetrated our borders to an alarming degree."

As they joined the others around the fire, it became obvious that the rest of the cadets had reached the same conclusion as Beren. Koen and Hamil stood before them as the oldest and highest-ranking cadets.

"We need to form a plan as to what we should do next," Koen declared. "This incident changes everything about our mission. We were meant to stay here and man this outpost, but it is now critical that we take the news of what happened here to the fort at the Pass. The defenders there need to know about this attack. Enemies have breached our border, and our men must be warned."

Peder emerged from the tent, a weary expression on his face. Beren strode over to him, his face a mixture of apprehension and hope.

"How is he?" Beren asked.

Peder's shoulders slumped. "He is stable. There is no fever, which is a good sign, and his wounds have been tended."

"Is he awake?" Beren asked.

"No, but I think he may awaken in the morning."

"Will we be able to move him? We cannot leave him here alone."

Peder raised his arms in a helpless gesture. "There is no way that he can be moved from this site for at least a sennight. Maybe more."

A somber silence fell.

"Some of us can remain here with him," Hamil said. "While the rest take the news to the Fort."

"That might be the best course of action," Koen replied. "We should not leave the outpost unmanned. And Ioan's wounds are serious. He must be our first priority." He shook his head. "We can make more definite decisions about our next moves in the morning. For now, we need to eat and get some rest. I want four men on watch at all times tonight."

41

The attack came without warning, which was the highest compliment anyone could pay the ensuing siege. One moment Master Kiefer was sitting at his desk jotting down notes about which students were doing well in his class and which ones needed a bit more pushing, and the next there were armored men racing down the hall brandishing weapons and shouting. Kiefer leaped to his feet and snatched up his sword. He emerged into the hallway at the same time as several of his colleagues and shared a confused glance with them.

"The students!" Mathis shouted, pointing the way that the group of warriors had disappeared.

Together, they charged down the hall in the direction of the wing where the living quarters were held, pursuing the intruders. Somewhere behind them, the alarm bell sounded. It appeared that the headmaster had been alerted to the situation.

"What is going on?" Kiefer muttered under his breath as they rounded a corner and caught up with the group they had been pursuing. He gave a wordless, blood-curdling cry, which caused a few of the intruders to halt and turn.

"To arms! To arms!" Mathis' voice rang out down the corridor as he joined Kiefer, his own weapon a hefty quarterstaff. Together, they charged into the group of men and began laying about with their weapons. The cramped nature of the corridor made it difficult to move the way he would have liked, but Kiefer still managed to fell two assailants, and he saw out of the corner of his eye that Mathis was enjoying good success as well.

Doors on either side of the hall burst open as students, armed with their own weapons, charged out to defend themselves. Moments later, the skirmish was over. The intruders lay on the ground, some dead, some moaning and holding their heads where Mathis had knocked more than a few with his staff.

One of the students stared around in confusion. "Master Kiefer, was this a test of some kind?"

"No," Kiefer replied, wiping his forehead with the back of his hand. "It was an attack. I do not know if more of them are coming, or what their goal was, but we should take the ones that are still alive and get to the dining room. It is the most defensible place in the building. Let us see if we can get some information from our captives." He glanced around at his colleagues. "Mathis, take the students to the dining hall. Cormac, see if you can find some rope and help me tie these two fellows up." He indicated the two groaning men at his feet. He pulled aside two of the oldest students he recognized. "Everett and Ellis, are you willing to try to make it to Freidzen and see if you can get more information? And tell anyone you see along the way that we're barricading ourselves in the dining hall."

Cormac disappeared into a room and came back holding several lengths of cord, which they used to tie the hands of the two semi-conscious intruders. Then, roughly slapping them awake, Kiefer forced them to stand and walk down the hall before them. They reached the dining hall about the same time as Headmaster Freidzen. The students were arranged in lines, their weapons at the ready. Kiefer spared them a tight, approving smile.

"Did Everett and Ellis find you?" Kiefer asked the headmaster.

"Yes, I sent them to the training rings and the library to round up anyone who might not have been alerted by the bell," Freidzen replied.

"Sir, what is happening?" Cormac growled. "How did these men even get inside?"

"I am not certain," Freidzen answered. "It appears to be a coordinated attack, several areas of the Academy were infiltrated at the same time, but so far all of the intruders have been beaten back." He nodded at the two men with their hands tied behind their backs. They were staring at the ground with sullen expressions. "I see you took prisoners. Let's see if they can tell us what is going on." He strode over to one of the men and forced him to sit in a chair. "Who are you and who are you working for?"

The man glanced up and then away, a growl emanating from his throat.

Freidzen grabbed the man's hair and jerked his head back. "Try that again."

"I don't need to tell you anything," the man snarled.

Kiefer kept an eye on the other man and saw his eyes darting about the room as though looking for an escape. He sidled up next to the man.

"You don't really want to be here, do you?" he asked in a low voice. "Perhaps you were told it would be an easy job, attacking students, since they're not real defenders yet, right?"

"Y-yeah." The man gulped. "We were told it would be an easy job, just get in, cause a little havoc, and get out. They didn't say nothing about..."

"Shut up!" the other man hollered. "Don't say anything else!"

The man Kiefer had been talking to turned white and clamped his lips shut.

"More are coming," the first man shouted. "Your Academy will fall!"

Freidzen's foot lashed out and the chair the man was sitting in toppled backwards. The man's head thudded on the hard floor.

"He's out for a bit," Freidzen commented. He turned to the other man. "You were saying?"

The man stared at the headmaster, his eyes wide. "I sh-shouldn't say."

"If you want to get out of this without having to spend the rest of your life in a cell, you should say," Kiefer snapped.

The man paled. "They said..."

"Who said?" Kiefer asked. "You were hired?"

The man nodded. "I don't know who they were, we never saw them directly, everything was through written missives."

Kiefer jerked his head toward the man lying on the floor. "He said more were coming, is that true?"

"If it is, I don't know about it." The man shrugged. "I thought it was just us, but I'm not the leader, so there might be things I don't know about."

"What was the goal? To overthrow the Academy, like he said?" Freidzen asked.

"N-no!" The man's eyes went wide. "I swear, we weren't even supposed to hurt anyone, just cause a ruckus. Whoever hired us offered a good price, and it seemed like an easy job, no real risk, see? Some of us thought that you professors might even be behind it, hiring us as a sort of test for the students. We didn't... well... not all of us... you see... we just... I thought... didn't want to hurt nobody... it's just... times are hard, see... and..." The man's words came fast and thick and stuttering, with no real point or purpose as fear caught hold of him.

Freidzen gave the man a piercing glance and then gestured at Kiefer to join him by the window.

"None of this makes sense," Freidzen muttered, keeping his voice low.

"I was just thinking the same thing," Kiefer replied. "Tactically, I can understand the desire to attack the Academy: it makes an appealing target since it houses the future of our defenses. But practically it just isn't a sound idea. The location of the Academy makes it impossible to besiege, and taking out the next generation of defenders doesn't seem worth the effort of such a long game. Besides, anyone with strategic understanding would know that as soon as an attack fell upon the Academy the defenders from all the nearby outposts would be called to our aid."

Freidzen pulled at his beard. "Maybe that is what they are after."

"But why?"

"Perhaps this was merely a diversion. The attack was well-coordinated, but there aren't enough men here to pose a serious threat. And I am not inclined to believe that other fellow, I don't believe more are coming. It almost feels like this was just a token attack, designed to pull attention to this location."

Kiefer nodded his agreement. "Then what is the true target?"

Freidzen scowled. "I don't know. I can think of a few likely targets nearby. I think we had best warn the Regeont first."

BELLS WERE RINGING THROUGHOUT DORAN. Ulia darted up the stairs, her heart fairly leaping out of her chest. Thankfully, the oil lamps had already been lit for the evening, making it easier for her to find her way through the corridors. Her post was at her mistress' side in such a crisis. How could this have happened? Of course the bells would sound during her first break of the entire day. How could she have known it was coming? The warning bells rarely sounded in Doran. Something terrible must have happened. Or perhaps it was just a drill.

Please, please let this just be a drill, Ulia thought as she raced down the hall.

The door to the Regeont's study stood open a crack, and Ulia slowed, taking a deep breath and trying to compose herself. Then she caught her breath in dismay. Through the door, she heard strange sounds: a gasp, a thud, a sound like snapping wood, a grunt, more thuds... Ulia rushed into the room and stopped, choking back a scream.

The Regeont stood on the far side of the room, her hair disheveled, one sleeve torn and hanging in tatters. A strange man stood facing her, a dagger in one hand. Two bodies lay stretched on the floor, dark stains spreading out around them.

Ulia whimpered.

Roshana's eyes turned toward her and in that instant the assassin lunged at her.

"Regeont!"

Roshana ducked and spun as the dagger slashed into the space where she had stood a moment before. The Regeont came up behind the man, using his own momentum to propel him forward as she pushed him off balance. His arms flailed wildly, and he managed to maintain his balance. The Regeont used his momentary inattention to tear her sleeve completely off and swiftly wrap the fabric around her hand. She darted toward the hearth, snatching something up from within the smoldering embers. Ulia stared, confused, when a thudding of footsteps sounded behind her. The door crashed open and then Lord Elan was inside the room.

He stood in the doorway, breathing hard. "Aunt Roshana!" he shouted, his gaze quickly taking in the entire scene. "Look out!"

The assassin attacked again, but Ulia couldn't follow the movements. Her head spun and her vision blurred. She should do something. She ought to be able to help the Regeont. But what could she use as a weapon? What could she do to help? She wasn't trained in combat like the Regeont, but she was her personal maidservant, and she ought to be able to do something, anything other than just stand here like a dazed mouse.

She opened her mouth and let out a hysterical, piercing shriek. Her voice flooded the room, and everyone halted to stare at her, shaken by the ghastly wail emanating from her mouth.

The assassin glowered at her and raised the dagger.

"No!" Elan shoved Ulia out of the way as the dagger whirled past her head, thudding into the wall behind her. "Run!" His hand took her by the shoulder and roughly spun her around.

"But..." she tried to protest.

"Run!" Elan shouted in her ear, shoving her through the door. "Run!"

Ulia obeyed. Her legs pumped of their own accord, her feet pounding against the polished floor. She ran into Lady Ilya, who came rushing from the opposite direction.

"Ulia?" Ilya shouted, grabbing her by the shoulders. "What's happened?"

Ulia gave a great gasping sob. "The Regeont! Assassins! Elan..." She gulped. "I must run! Run! Must find help!"

And then she was past, away from Ilya's grasping hands that tried to stall her flight. But she could not stop, could not be stopped, she must run. All Ulia knew was the deep need to get away, to somehow outrun the sight of the two dead bodies, of the Regeont's tattered dress and wild hair, of the sound of a dagger whooshing past her head. She needed to get away, as far away as she could. Shame and terror coursed through her in equal measure, and so she fled. Elan would take care of the Regeont. He was far more suited to a battle than she. Ulia could go for help like she had told Lady Ilya.

Her mind seized on the idea of something useful she might do. She could get help! She would race to the guardhouse. The Conscripts must be alerted to this attack! The Regeont must be defended.

She darted out through the front doors, down the majestic path, and out onto the street. Dimly, she wondered what had happened to the guards around the manor; where had they all gone? Shouldn't someone have been alert to the assassination attempt? Why had she not passed any of them on her way out of the house? It did not matter. What mattered was that she bring back help as swiftly as possible.

Down the road she ran, her feet slapping on the cobblestones. The bells had ceased ringing, and even through her frenzied flight, Ulia wondered what the bells had signified. In light of the attack on the Regeont, she had completely forgotten the sound that had sent her seeking her mistress in the first place.

Ulia arrived at the guardhouse out of breath. "Tirbodh!" she called out in a gasp, hoping that one of the higher ranking conscripts occupied the building. "Tirbodh!"

Then she noticed how quiet the guardhouse was. She stepped over the threshold tentatively. "Tirbodh? Akhin?"

A young conscript appeared from a side room. He eyed her warily. "Yes, lady? I am Akhin-rank. What do you need?"

"Where is everyone?" Ulia asked. "I need help!"

"The Academy is under attack," the young man replied. "We got word of it and everyone ran off to help. They left me behind." He scowled.

"What?" Ulia pressed a hand to her chest. Why couldn't she catch her breath? "The Academy? Under attack?"

"Didn't you hear the warning bells?"

"Yes, I did, but..." Ulia felt her nerves unraveling. Tears leaked out of the corners of her eyes. "You must come. You must! The Regeont is under attack. Assassins!"

"What?" The man stepped toward her, moving in the direction of the Manor before she had stopped talking. "Where are her guards?" he called out over his shoulder.

Ulia shook her head. "I don't... I don't..." Her breath caught in her throat and suddenly the world rolled around her. Her vision tunneled and went dark. Vaguely, she heard someone shouting at her, but she couldn't think to answer. She couldn't breathe. And then, nothing.

Daegan's design was a masterpiece of sheer brilliance. As Dalmir inspected it, he could find no flaws. The man's genius could not be denied. He also had an eye for detail.

"I really don't think there is much I can offer," Dalmir repeated after Daegan had walked him through the design schematics and allowed him to handle the model prototype he and Keene were constructing. "It is both an impressive feat of engineering and a work of art." It was, too. Deadly art, perhaps, but there was an undeniable beauty to what Daegan and Keene were building. Dalmir placed the unfinished device back on the table.

Daegan's eyes crinkled at the corners, a sign that he was pleased by Dalmir's words. He accepted the praise with a humble bow of his head. "I thought it finished lunats ago, but we've still got the major problem of propulsion. And I'm not happy with the wheels, yet. They are going to have to be much stronger if they are to stand up to the terrain."

"I wish I could help," Dalmir said. "But I'm not an engineer. If my brother, Palte, were here, he would be the one to ask."

"I know I can find a solution," Daegan replied. "I just don't know if I'll have enough time."

"Time is the enemy of all artists"—Dalmir smiled faintly—"and the truest friend of innovation."

Daegan glanced at him curiously. "That is an interesting expression."

"I was quoting." Dalmir gazed away, staring off into nothingness, a fond expression on his face. "Edoran used to say that, whenever Palte and Avaleun began arguing."

"Is the refiner working as expected?" Daegan asked.

"The container is more than half-full. It is taking a bit longer than I expected, but perhaps that means Keene will be able to get more cynders than I first estimated. It will still be a few days before I can take my leave, though."

"You must be anxious to be away."

"In part," Dalmir admitted. "There are things I must attend to. But Keene has plenty of interesting projects. I've kept quite busy."

Daegan nodded, his quill scratching away on the parchment. "What do you plan to do once your device is full?"

Dalmir rubbed a hand across his mouth and down his chin. The bristles of his beard itched; it was time to shave again. "To be honest, there is so much to do, I am not certain where to start."

Before Daegan could reply, Keene burst into the room, a wild look on his face. "Have you heard? The Academy is under attack!"

Dalmir and Daegan stared at the big smith, uncomprehending.

"Did you hear what I said?" Keene adjusted the spectacles on his nose. "The Academy is under attack, word just reached us."

"What do you mean, under attack?" Daegan asked, his voice low. "Who would dare attack the Academy?"

"I don't know any more than that." Keene frowned, taking off his glasses and rubbing an arm across weary eyes, smudging soot across his face. "The word just arrived, Gereon informed me."

"Where is he now?" Dalmir asked.

"Probably about to head back home," Keene replied.

Grabbing his cloak from where it was draped over a nearby chair, Dalmir dashed from the room and down the winding corridors. He reached the main door and pushed it open. A young man with sandy brown hair and broad shoulders trotted away down the road.

"Gereon!" Dalmir called out.

The lad halted and turned around, a questioning look on his face. Though stocky and broad of shoulder, Gereon was only ten summers. He bore some resemblance to his older brother, though he favored his father more, while Beren favored his mother's finer features.

"Dalmir?"

"Are you heading home?" Dalmir asked as he pulled his cloak around his shoulders.

"Yes, sir."

"May I walk with you?"

"Of course."

They trekked up the path to the large house of Chieftain Adelfried. Dalmir asked a few more questions about the attack on the Academy, but Gereon didn't know any more than what he had told Keene. When they reached the front door, Gereon bounded through it, shouting for his parents.

Dalmir hung up his cloak on a hook. He had been staying with the Adelfrieds for so long that their home had taken on a familiar feel for him. It felt like home to him, too. They had been so kind in extending such hospitality to him, and he always looked forward to coming back to Nadia's cooking and building forts with young Hubert each evening.

"Dalmir." Lady Nadia's soft voice behind him made Dalmir spin around. Nadia and Thorben stood together, observing him with solemn intensity.

"You've heard about the attack?" Thorben asked with a heavy sigh. Gereon scurried over to his parents and looked up at them, his gaze worried. Thorben tousled his son's hair and looked down at him with a gentle smile. "Everything will be well, Gereon, don't you worry. Why don't you go see if Elma and Freja have finished their experiment in the kitchen? I think they were baking tarts; if you ask nicely and offer to help them clean up whatever mess they've made they might let you sneak one."

Gereon's concerned expression dissolved into a brilliant grin and he skipped away, sliding recklessly around a corner and disappearing down the hall.

Dalmir hesitated. "Do you know any details?"

"Not yet." Thorben swallowed with difficulty. "Word only just reached us, and the message was short." He turned to Nadia and put an arm around her shoulders. "I'm sure Rahmund is well. He has plenty of experience, and will be doing everything he can to keep the students safe."

"Rahmund?" Dalmir asked.

"Headmaster Freidzen," Thorben explained. "He is my wife's brother."

"Ah. What about the students? Did the message say if there had been any casualties?" Dalmir's tongue was thick. Should he have stayed? Could he have been meant to protect them somehow? What was his purpose? If only he could call out to Emri... but would the Creator even listen if he called out to him? Surely Emri had given up on him by now.

Thorben held up a hand in a gesture of helplessness. "The information I have told you is all that I have."

"Well, what are we going to do about this?" Dalmir demanded, his voice growing strained with anger. "How could anyone attack such a place? A place filled with children? How dare you stand here as though nothing needed doing? Are there any defenders nearby who can be called upon? Is there a... a... an airship we can get on? I could lend aid if cynders are in short supply. And why be concerned about the headmaster when your own son is at this moment in danger?" He tripped over his words as emotions he had long-thought dead obfuscated his thoughts.

Thorben gave him a strange look. "The students at the

Academy are hardly children..." he began, at the same time Nadia gasped out, "You don't know about Beren?"

The words came out together in an indistinguishable jumble and Dalmir took a reeling step back, his shoulder blades slamming into the wood-paneled wall. He put a hand over his eyes. No, it couldn't be true. Angry tears filled his eyes as visions of death filled his mind.

"Forgive me, I did not mean to bring accusations. I can see you are grieving. Please accept my condolences."

"What?" Nadia's voice exploded with a high-pitched squeak.

"I think you misunderstand," Thorben said. "Please, sit, let us explain. We did not mean to give the wrong impression."

Dalmir took a few stumbling steps into the room and collapsed into a chair. Thorben and Nadia sat down on a sofa across from him. Dalmir leaned forward, elbows on knees, and gazed at them with a mute appeal.

"Beren, Wynn, Grayden, and a handful of other cadets left the Academy a sennight ago," Nadia explained. "They were to receive their first mission manning the Storvas Outpost. They were not at the Academy when it was attacked two mornings ago."

"The news of the attack only came to us this morning," Thorben added. "But we are confident that the students and faculty have the situation well in hand. There is an outpost of defenders stationed not far from the Academy and I am certain that my brother-in-law will have wasted no time calling for their aid. As for the rest of the 'children' as you termed them, they are all of them training to be warriors in defense of our nation. They are not without recourse, I assure you."

Dalmir let out a breath and sat back, rubbing his hands across his face. "I see... Forgive me for my outburst. I confess my concern did eclipse my common sense."

Thorben raised an eyebrow at him. "Ahem. Well. You are forgiven if you need to hear it, but an apology is not necessary. No parent can begrudge any person so concerned for the welfare of their child. In any case, we need to address the situation and determine our course of action. For that, I believe my presence is needed in Ondoura and I mean to leave as quickly as possible." He gave Dalmir a penetrating glance. "Would you like to travel with me? I know it will delay your own plans; Nadia said that your device is nearly full, and I know you had other business you hoped to attend to."

"No, my concerns can wait. I would be most grateful if you would allow me to travel with you to the Academy. Perhaps I can be of some assistance in whatever is happening there."

———

DALMIR CHAFED as he waited for Thorben Adelfried to make the arrangements that would speed them on their way to the Academy. He did not bother trying to explain his impatience to the Chieftain. It was not a thing he could explain, this writhing discomfort in the pit of his stomach, the restlessness in his legs and feet that urged him to swifter action than was being taken. The first blows of this war had been gentle, subtle. The kidnapping and attempted assassination of Beren Adelfried had been orchestrated to feel more like a warning arrow fired over the heads of the army. But something deep in the recesses of Dalmir's subconscious told him that this attack was the true first strike. After this, open war would swiftly follow. He could not help but feel that it was, in some ways, his own fault. If Uun had not been alerted to his presence, or if he had not loosed the chains that bound him, perhaps he would have continued to bide his time. Perhaps not. Uun never had possessed much in the way of patience. Either way, it appeared that Uun was done with subtlety.

Despite Dalmir's impatience, it was a full day before they could board the airship, and then two days of monotonous travel before they glimpsed the Academy grounds. What they saw from the air appeared calm. Where Dalmir had been expecting to see an army camped outside the Academy's gates in a siege position, there was only the pale tan of the grass still dormant from the winter lunats. No smoke rose from the buildings, no cries of battle echoed from below.

"It is not what I expected," Dalmir said to Thorben.

Thorben stared down at the Academy. "Perhaps the report was sent in haste. It appears that the attack has already been dealt with. At any rate, it looks safe to land. Let us see what we can discern of the situation."

The airship touched down on the still waters of the lake, and Dalmir and Thorben made their way to the shore. Headmaster Freidzen waited for them there, his face grim.

"I see you got my message." Freidzen spoke without preamble. "Thank you for coming."

"It appears the attack is over," Thorben replied. "I was half-expecting to find the Academy besieged."

"It was a small force. The attack was well-coordinated, but not large enough to do any real damage... at least, not here." Freidzen's tone was sober. "I apologize for not being clear in my message, but I felt that this news would be better in person. It appears the Academy was not the true target of this attack."

Adelfried shot him a sharp glance. "What do you mean?"

"I mean that the Regeont is dead."

Thorben stared. His brow furrowed. "What?"

"The Regeont is dead. Killed on the same day as the attack at the Academy. I believe the attack here was meant as some sort of diversion, while she was the true goal."

Thorben did not appear to have heard or understood his brother-in-law. He gazed past him, staring into nothing, with a disbelieving expression on his face.

"Thorben." Freidzen reached out and grabbed his upper arms. "Thorben, I'm so sorry. I know she was a dear friend to you and Nadia. I know Ioan and your sons are like brothers. I deeply regret having to be the bearer of such news."

Thorben blinked, his massive hands clenching and

unclenching into fists at his sides. "Do we know how it happened? Who was responsible?"

"Not yet. Everyone has been in a bit of an uproar since the attack and the news from the Regeont's home. I haven't been able to coordinate an investigation. And I thought you might want to be involved in some way."

Thorben nodded. "Thank you." He took a long, slow breath and held it for a moment before letting it loose again. "And here at the Academy? Is everyone well? Was anyone hurt in the attack?"

"Everyone is well. Nobody was harmed." Freidzen gave a tiny shake of his head. "Except the attackers. We did take a few of them prisoner, though we haven't been able to get any information out of them. From their lack of coherent replies and the panic in their eyes, I am growing more convinced that they know nothing useful."

"Very good. Keep trying. I will be back to question them myself shortly."

"You are going to the Regeont's?"

"Yes." Thorben turned to Dalmir, who had remained silent throughout the exchange. "Will you come with me? I could use another pair of eyes and ears as I question the servants and guards."

"I would be honored," Dalmir said. Though he had only met the Regeont once—and in that time she had been skeptical of him and his motives—he had found her to be a pleasant sort of combatant. Her sharp questions had impressed him, as well as her willingness to listen to reason and admit when she might be biased.

"Let me get one of the cadets to hitch up the carriage, it will be but a moment," Freidzen said.

"My thanks," Adelfried replied. "We will wait out front." He sighed. "This is a deep blow to our Council. With all that is transpiring, it seems that this tragedy must have been designed by the Ar'Mol himself. What better way to tip the scales in his favor than to throw an entire nation into chaos?"

"And if that is the case, then it is best you be on your guard, as well," Dalmir replied. "And word should be sent to Duke Langston immediately. If it is useful to your enemies to bring about the death of one Council member, then why not all three?"

Thorben's stride did not falter as they rounded the building. "That was my thought as well."

———

THEY DID NOT HAVE to wait long for the promised carriage. The horses were fresh and lively, and they made the trip to the outskirts of Doran in good time. Leaping from the carriage and tossing the lines to a stable hand who came out to greet them, Thorben marched up the stone steps and rapped smartly at the door. A moment later, the door opened and a young woman stood before them, her face drawn and tired, her eyes red. She stared up at Thorben and fresh tears began to stream from her eyes.

"You're too late," she sniffled. "Aunt Roshana is dead."

"So I heard," Thorben said gently, taking her by the arms and pulling her into a gentle embrace. "Dear Ilya, may we come in?"

She nodded, raising an already soaked handkerchief to her face before stepping aside to admit them entry. The two men stepped over the entryway. The mansion had not changed in the short lunats since Dalmir had met with Nadia there. And yet, there was a stillness to the air, a sorrow that seemed to cling to the edges of each shadow, making the halls seem a bit darker, the doorways and alcoves a bit more ominous. Even the candles in their sconces appeared pale and listless, their lethargic flickering appearing to require an inordinate amount of effort. The entire mansion seemed to mourn: "Our mistress is dead. Our mistress is dead!"

Lady Ilya closed the door behind them. "You will want to see where it ha-happened?"

"Yes," Thorben replied.

"The bodies have all been removed," Ilya warned them, her eyes welling up with tears. "But we touched nothing else. The guards explained about the investigation."

"Bodies?" Dalmir inquired.

"There were two of them," Ilya replied. "Assassins, I mean. Three if you count Aunt Rosh..." She sniffled and could not finish. "Oh, oh!" Her voice came out in a sudden wail.

"Hush." Thorben's tone was quiet. "There is no need for you to say any more, we can look at the room where it happened and ask questions later. I will want to speak with her guards. Is your brother here, as well?"

Ilya nodded. She ushered them to the room and gestured at it with a shudder. "If you don't mind, I'd prefer not to enter. I will go inform Elan of your arrival."

"That would be most helpful," Thorben replied.

Lady Ilya padded off down the hall, her slippers barely making a sound against the richly stained oak floors. Thorben took a deep breath, glanced at Dalmir, and then pushed the door to the den open. Together, the two men entered the room.

43

Ioan woke the following morning, but nothing useful could be gleaned from what he had to say. He stared about wildly and spoke of the forest attacking the camp, of trees coming to life and walking, of the screams of his fellow defenders. None of his ravings made any sense. Eventually, Peder decided that Ioan should be asked no more questions, and mixed up a tea to help calm the man. Ioan drank the tea and drifted back into fitful unconsciousness.

Grayden stayed nearby the tent in order to offer his aid wherever it might be needed and found himself pouring tea and a thin gruel down the defender's throat throughout the day.

It was a gray, dreary day. No snow fell, but a bite in the air made them all loath to stop moving. The tent was warm, but Ioan kept waking, and when he did, he babbled incoherently to anyone who sat with him, making that duty far less appealing, despite the additional warmth to be gleaned from being out of the wind.

"I don't understand this raving," Peder confided to the others halfway through the morning. "There is no sign or hint of fever."

"Maybe he got bashed on the head and it addled his brains," Zarek suggested.

"I would have noticed," Peder said drily. "I'm surprised he's awake at all, honestly."

"So who is staying with Ioan and who is going on to the fort?"

"I've been thinking about that," Koen replied. "Peder is the most experienced with medicine, so I believe he should stay here with Captain Petrescu. But I don't want to just assign tasks." Koen's face creased with uncertainty. "Who wants to go with the scouting party to try to find the other outposts and tell them what happened?"

Grayden frowned slightly as everyone began speaking at once. Everyone argued for a different group, or why they should be involved in one party or the other. Grayden remained silent, waiting for Koen to take charge, until he noticed the helpless look in the older student's eyes and realized the truth: Koen didn't know how to take charge.

Putting his fingers between his lips, Grayden let out a shrill whistle that made everyone stop and turn to look at him. Inside, he quaked beneath their stares. He hoped that his sudden apprehension did not show on his face.

"Arven, Hamil, and Zarek should stay here with Peder and Petrescu," Grayden said.

Koen narrowed his eyes. "Explain."

"As you said, Peder needs to stay with Ioan. Arven and Enric are our best hunters, so they should be split between the two groups, and Enric has more experience finding his way around in the wilderness. Wynn is the best of all of us at navigation by stars, which we will need as we cross the mountains, so he should go with the group to the Pass. Beren, Zarek, and I are the best fighters, and Zarek is the oldest and most experienced of us three and should stay with the group here at the outpost to keep everyone safe until Ioan is better."

"I don't think any of us relish the tasks before us," Hamil said. "But this is a good plan. Koen, you go with the party to the Fort as their leader. Peder and I will lead here and keep watch over Ioan and fulfill the mission we were originally tasked with."

"Very well," Koen replied. "My group, pack your things and be ready to leave at first light."

It was a somber group around the campfire that evening as the thought of splitting the group weighed heavily on all their minds.

"Do you think there's anything to Captain Petrescu's ravings about the forest coming to life and attacking the camp?" Arven asked as he brought an armful of firewood to the campfire.

"How could there be?" Koen asked.

Arven stared down the hill at the tree line, a faraway look in his eyes. He sniffed in the cold air. "You're right."

"Still," Hamil spoke up, "no sense in letting the fire go out. There are sure to be wild animals in these parts, and we need to keep Captain Petrescu warm. I'll help you gather another load of wood."

Arven shot him a grateful glance and the two young men marched back into the forest together.

"I'll be glad to be moving on from here tomorrow," Wynn said, coming up to Grayden and stomping his feet in the snow. "Something about this place sets my teeth on edge."

Grayden nodded, his gaze locked on the forest where Arven and Hamil had disappeared. There was an ominous looming nature to the trees in the pale twilight. "I don't think we should stay here this evening," Grayden muttered.

Wynn turned his head sharply. "You sensing something? Should we try to convince the others..."

Grayden shook himself and rolled his shoulders slightly. "No, it's nothing like that. I just... something about this place gives me an eerie feeling. I knew something was off when we first approached the camp, I feared we might be ambushed like we were in Dalton, but I was wrong. The danger had already passed."

"Or it had just begun," Wynn commented. "Whoever did this may have moved on, but that doesn't mean we're clear of them. We have a long way to go before we get out of these mountains."

"In any case, whatever attacked was not natural. The others

are dismissing Ioan's words as feverish ravings, but I am not so sure," Grayden said.

Wynn rubbed his gloved hands together and gave his friend a wary sidelong glance. "Trees that walk? A forest attacking? You know that's ridiculous."

Grayden shrugged. He didn't understand half of what Ioan had shouted in the moments when he was conscious, but he couldn't shake the feeling that he ought to listen carefully. Something in his own thoughts screamed at him to pay attention, even though it didn't make sense. Even though it seemed impossible.

"You're not serious?" Wynn asked.

"I don't know," Grayden admitted.

"Don't let the others hear you putting stock in that kind of talk. They already think Ioan's half-mad."

Grayden shot his friend a wry grimace. "Words of truth."

"Looks like the hunters are back, which means everyone will be wanting supper soon," Wynn said, nodding at the tree line. He paused, lowering his voice. "You know I trust your instincts. If you believe the forest attacked, I believe it, too. But until we have proof, let's not say anything to the others... right?"

"Right. I should check on Peder and see if he needs any help with Ioan," Grayden replied. He gave his friend a tight smile as they returned to their duties. But Grayden kept an ear cocked toward the forest until he heard Arven's and Hamil's voices mingle with the others once more.

———

THE NIGHT PASSED without event and the morning dawned with a thick fog obscuring the sunlight breaking over the horizon. Captain Petrescu woke as well, and to everyone's great relief he seemed to be past the raving of the previous day. He still seemed confused and dazed, but he could feed himself the tea and broth they brought him for breakfast, and his eyes were clearer and more focused. When the cadets told him that some of them would be breaking camp and heading east, he said nothing, but nodded. Whether it was a nod of agreement or mere understanding was more than anyone could guess.

Grayden could not deny that he was eager to get away from the camp where so many defenders had fallen. The cairns stood as a dark stain against the fog, an eerie reminder of the horror they had unwittingly stumbled upon. The others stood in a semi-circle around the fire, watching as their comrades began the long hike away from the outpost and into the wild.

Koen led the way as they set out, breaking the trail and picking out the easiest terrain he could find, with the others following him in a long line. After an hour, Koen moved to the back, and Enric took over the job of leading so that Koen could get a rest. In this way, they proceeded, sharing the burden so that nobody used up too much strength.

The snow grew deeper the higher into the mountains they went, and their pace slowed. Grayden thought of those left behind and was glad that they had not attempted to carry Ioan with them.

As night fell, they found a sheltered spot to make camp. Though all he wanted to do was fall to the ground and sleep for a sennight, Grayden helped the others setting up the tents and searching for something with which they could start a fire.

"We'll be up past the treeline soon," Enric said. "We should each gather firewood before moving out tomorrow."

Though already weary, they all agreed that this was a good plan and took the time to gather enough for each of them to carry a good bundle on their backs. This chore accomplished, they ate a cold dinner of rations, assigned watches, and turned in to their tents for the night.

A SENSE of urgency lay upon them all as they struggled along. They were exceedingly aware of the importance of their mission.

Something dangerous prowled the Greyklasp Mountains and the defenders needed to be alerted. However, if direct routes existed between the Storvas Outpost and the Fort Pass, they were buried beneath the snow and hidden from their view. They often ran into insurmountable obstacles and had to spend precious hours backtracking the way they had come. What cliffs they could scale, they did, but when they couldn't, they lost time they could ill afford.

Grayden ached with effort. He watched his companions falling more and more into a despairing sort of drudgery, but he did not know how to break it. The snow continued to deepen the higher they went into the mountains, making their progress ever more difficult.

On the fifth day since leaving the bivouac where the defenders had been attacked, they came to yet another impassable cliff wall. Beren came back down the trail from where he had been scouting ahead of the group and told them the news, and the cadets sank to their knees in the snow.

"Koen," Beren rumbled. "We can't keep on like this. We keep wasting our energies on these fruitless paths. I'm afraid we're getting so turned around that we're not even going in the correct direction anymore. Wynn says he needs to wait until nightfall so he can fix our position by the stars. And I'm worried about Ioan. We need to send help back to him as much as we need to warn the defenders about the threat."

Koen ran a hand over his face, his eyes wild. "What would you have me do, Beren?" he barked sharply. "I've already split our group in two against my better judgment. Even if we travel as swiftly as we can and encounter no further obstacles, it will be days before we can get help back to the captain. Do you have a better plan than the one we've been following? Because I'm open to suggestions!" Koen's voice rose in volume and bounced around the high cliffs, echoing back to them in waves of sound.

"Koen," Beren began, but Koen ignored him.

"This isn't how our mission was supposed to go!" Koen

continued, shouting now. "This isn't what any of us signed up for. Dealing with whatever happened at the camp back there, leaving behind the man who was supposed to be our guide. Let me tell you something, Beren, I'm not even sure I'm going the right way! How am I supposed to make the right decisions when I'm not even certain I know what the right decisions are? But I'm the oldest, so everyone is looking at me like I have all the answers, so I keep trudging along, heading east, because that's the best thing I know to do. But if you have a better idea or plan, then tell me. Tell me now!" Koen's voice rose in pitch and volume with every word. The other cadets, gathered around in a sort of half-circle on the narrow ledge of semi-flat ground they had found to rest upon, stared at him, a mixture of emotions on each of their faces.

"Koen," Beren said again.

"What?" Koen snarled. "What wisdom do you have to share, oh son of the Chief of Telsuma?"

"I was merely going to caution you to keep your voice down," Beren replied evenly. A muscle in his cheek twitched and Grayden knew that he was seeing a rare sight: his easy-going friend furious.

Koen stared at him.

"There are many predators in these mountains," Beren explained, his voice calm but his words tight and clipped, "and I noticed the tracks of grymstalkers and cliff lizards earlier today. I believe we face enough adversity at the moment without drawing the attention of one of those beasts to ourselves."

Koen's face turned red, and then deepened to a dark purple. His eyes darted up to the glistening white peaks high above them, but nothing on the mountainside moved. Slowly, he sank to the ground and sat with his head in his hands. The others stood around him, shifting awkwardly, unsure what to do next. The trees rustled in the light breeze, unperturbed by the trials of the young men standing beneath their boughs. Dark clouds sped across the sky far above them, threatening a storm. When Koen rose to his feet, his demeanor was calm once more.

"Forgive me," Koen said, his voice soft. "I am at a loss."

Before anyone could reply, the sky ripped open with a bright flash, followed by a low rumble. Rain began to patter down through the canopy above them. Koen stared up at the sky, his face filled with a mixture of frustration and despair. He shook his head once. "No time to discuss it now, we need to get to shelter."

"I passed by a good-sized cavern while I was scouting ahead," Beren said. "It is not far."

With Beren leading the way, they made it to the cavern just before the drizzling rain turned into a downpour. The sheets of rain pounded down over the entrance to the cave like a waterfall while the cadets huddled miserably together. Wynn set about lighting a small fire with some of the dry branches they had been carrying, but they all knew the meager warmth it provided would not last until morning. It was enough to get them warm and dry out their clothes a bit, however, and Enric set about brewing a weak tea to warm them.

The rain continued through the night, but tapered off as the first glimmer of dawn emerged, turning the clouds a lighter shade of gray. The fire died long before morning, but the rain had come following after a sudden wash of warmth that brought with it the humid scent of spring. Grayden woke before his companions. Quietly, he rose and went to the cavern entrance, surveying their surroundings. The air outside clung to his skin with muggy sticki-ness but there was still an underlying bite of cold to it, though he could hear a bird chirping somewhere, like the promise of flowers and warmth and all things green.

A strange rasping sound made Grayden wheel about and then stand staring, blinking his disbelief. A tall figure pulled himself up the narrow trail they had traversed the night before. He walked slowly, leaning on a wooden crutch.

"Ioan?" Grayden whispered. Then he sprang forward with a glad cry. "Ioan!"

"Grayden?" Ioan blinked up at him.

"What are you doing out here?" Grayden asked, bewildered.

"We left you with the others at the outpost. You had a broken leg…" He trailed off, glancing down at the bandage around the defender's leg. "How did you follow us? Why?"

Ioan grimaced. "I wasn't injured as badly as you thought," he said. "When I came out of the fever, Peder explained what had happened. I left them guarding the outpost and came after you."

Grayden eyed the defender. "You just… got up and left? On your own? And caught up to us in less than a sennight? Your leg was broken. I saw it. I helped hold you down while Peder set it."

Ioan waved his free hand. "Not broken. Just sprained. I'll be walking without this crutch in a few days."

A strange prickle rippled its way up Grayden's spine. He frowned, but before he could say anything more, the others emerged from the cave. They gaped at Ioan for a moment, and then they welcomed him with much jostling and excitement, which Ioan took stoically.

"What do you remember from the attack?" Beren asked, handing him a waterskin.

Ioan winced. "Isak and I went to the outpost. We were preparing everything there for your arrival. There was going to be a little ceremony, and the defenders were going to give you a bit of a hard time. But in the middle of the night, the camp was attacked." He fell silent, staring blankly at the cave wall.

"Who attacked you?" Wynn prompted.

"More like what attacked us. This is going to sound insane, but I swear the forest itself came to life. I've never seen anything like it." He took a sip from the waterskin and turned to them, his gaze intense. "The trees walked. We were no match for them. I don't know what they were, but they were unstoppable. And there was something else…" He trailed off with a shudder.

"What?"

Ioan shook his head. "I can't remember."

Grayden shivered. It was one thing to dismiss the ramblings of a man in a fever, but to scorn this earnest account told in simple, measured words was far more difficult.

Ioan sighed. "I'm glad I caught up with you. You're a little off in your directions."

"We know," Koen said. "We've run into a few obstacles."

"I can show you the right path," Ioan said. "There is a hunting trail between the Outpost and the Fort. You just missed it under the snow."

"And Peder was all right with you leaving his care?" Grayden asked, still feeling that something was not quite right with Ioan's story.

"He couldn't argue with the fact that I was well enough to get up and about on my own. And when I told him how difficult the terrain is to navigate and that I was worried you would all get lost, and that, frankly, I outranked him, he couldn't stand in my way."

"We're glad you're here," Koen said.

They ate a quick breakfast and then headed out again, this time with Ioan leading the way. He spoke soberly to all of them as they hiked out into the mountains once more, and soon they were on a much easier path than the one they had been forging.

By late afternoon, they had climbed high into the mountains. The rain and warmer air had melted much of the snow on the lower reaches of the paths they had been following, but now they found the ground covered in a gray blanket of partially melted snow and ice and the climb grew difficult once more. Their boots crunched and slipped on the snow as they searched for better purchase over the rocky terrain. Enric had the hardest time of it, being from Ondoura and the least used to the snow and icy climate. He slipped often and as the sun sank in the sky behind them Enric took a bad fall and wrenched his arm painfully trying to catch himself.

"Perhaps we should stop and rest for the evening," Ioan panted, his face pale in the waning light.

"I agree," Enric said, rubbing his shoulder and glancing at the defender with concern. "Koen, I think we should find a level spot and call this day over."

"Very well," Koen replied. He glanced up at the glistening

peak above them, still covered in snow despite the heavy rain of the night before. "Trying to get any higher as we lose the light would be too dangerous, anyway."

They spread out until they found a level area a couple hundred paces farther along that provided an almost perfect campsite. An outcropping of rock and some scrubby, mostly dead trees made a partial shelter, and a good helping of dead brush gathered around the base of the trees served as kindling. Dinner was a bland affair as there had been little time to hunt. Dried rations from their packs was all they had, but after a long day it tasted delicious. A trickling fall of water nearby offered them the ability to refill their waterskins. As the sun descended, so did the temperature, and soon they were huddling around the fire for warmth, their breath visible in the chilly air. The moon rose, perfectly round and with an impossible brightness of silver light shining down through crisp winter air and reflecting on pure white snow.

Grayden joined the others in rolling out his bedroll when an enormous sound like large wooden balls all being dropped on a stone floor at once rang out across the mountain. Grayden sat up and saw that his comrades had reacted to the sound. Their heads shot up and they gazed about, confusion and fear written on their faces. For a moment all was still, and then they heard, far away but getting louder, the distant rumble like that of thunder.

"Avalanche!" someone hissed. In the dim light of the fire, Grayden could not determine who had spoken, but the word struck like lightning in a parched forest.

"Everyone under the rocks, now!" Grayden spoke without meaning to. Enric began to wrestle with his bedroll and Grayden grabbed him by the shoulder and propelled him toward the rocks. "Leave your gear, get beneath the rocks," he barked.

There was no time to think, only to react. Following his own instructions, Grayden raced to the outcropping and crouched low, staring down the mountain. His heart roared in his ears, echoing the rumbling bellow of the avalanche as it drew closer, growing louder with every heartbeat. Across the dying campfire he saw that Enric and Wynn had not yet made it to the shelter. He shouted at them, but couldn't even hear his own voice in the roar of the avalanche. Koen and Beren were on either side of Ioan helping him toward safety. The defender was hopping on his good leg, hobbling to safety as fast as he could. A trickle of snow skittered down over the rocks above Grayden's head, foreshadowing the impending waterfall of death chasing on the heels of this harbinger. Without thinking, Grayden leaped out and grabbed Ioan, adding his own strength to the effort and pulling him into the tiny shelter. As they tumbled into the small haven, the deadly wave of ice and snow poured down, sweeping across their campsite and carrying away everything in its path.

Grayden breathed quickly, counting the seconds that passed as the barrage of snow swept down and poured over their heads. Snow spray splattered across his face, stinging with its icy force. In less than a minute it was all over. The cadets picked themselves up and cautiously listened, hardly daring to breathe. Snow piled around them on all sides, but their shelter had not been completely buried. Wynn poked his head through the opening left behind and peered around.

"Seems clear," he said.

Grayden glanced at his companions, then frowned. "Where's Koen?"

The others exchanged worried looks. The older cadet was nowhere to be seen. Ioan and Beren stared at him in alarm.

"He was helping me," Ioan said. "When you pulled me in I thought he was still holding on, we all tumbled to the ground together."

"We have to look for him," Enric said. "The avalanche can't have carried him far."

Grayden stared out at the frozen sea of snow below them and dismay threatened to overwhelm him, but he gave a sharp sound of agreement and headed to the spot where he had last seen the older cadet. If they were to save Koen, they did not have much time. Living in Dalsea, in the shadow of the mountains, Grayden had often listened to the older men and miners tell stories about snow slides and avalanches, and he knew that anyone buried beneath would not have much time. If they could not find Koen quickly, it was likely they would be doing little more than rescuing his body for burial.

44

Marik grimaced as he surveyed his beloved *Hawk*. He and his crew had labored over the disguise for days, and their efforts had turned the sleek, elegant little schooner into a convincing merchant scow. They had built a framework around the prow of the airship, changing its shape into something far more boxy. The wood had been polished to a fine sheen, the triangular sails replaced with square ones, more befitting a merchant ship. A fresh coat of gold paint rimmed the *Hawk's* hull just below the railing on the outside, marking her as a member of the merchant guild. And royal purple lettering now declared her to be *The Gilded Petunia*. It was enough to fairly break Marik's heart, seeing his beloved *Hawk* transformed into something unrecognizable, something bulky and lumbering and hideous, but it was necessary to the plan, and he comforted himself with the knowledge that everything that had been done could eventually be undone.

Belowdecks the airship brimmed with fine leather, as well as all the tools necessary to a cordwainer's trade. Shaesta had assured them she had the necessary skills to make shoes if they needed to demonstrate in order to maintain their cover as merchants and shoe-makers. Marik had heard her story with a certain amount of skepticism and then asked for a demonstration. Much to everyone's amazement, and Marik's consternation, Mouse was now fitted with a handsome pair of soft leather boots. The boy's delight with his new apparel rang throughout the ship as he exclaimed with surprise that he could still feel the ground beneath his toes. Mouse's broad smile made Marik think of Teo, and a warm glow rested in the pit of his stomach as the memory swept over him of the night they had returned from their excursion to Temin.

––––––

MARIK MOUNTED the rickety wooden steps of the farmhouse and knocked on the faded door. Footsteps sounded within and a moment later the door cracked open. Teo peered out at him with suspicious eyes. From behind his legs, three small faces appeared, staring up at Marik with unabashed curiosity. The man pushed them back a little, then, slowly, recognition dawned.

"Marik?" He pulled the door wider and extended his hand. "Didn't think I'd see you again... so soon."

Marik did not miss the pause in the man's words. The farmer hadn't thought to see Marik again at all.

"I've made good on my promise, Teo," Marik replied. He swung a bundle down from his shoulder and held it out. "That should be more than enough leather to put shoes on your family's feet. Maybe even enough to repair a harness or two. Whatever's left, maybe you can sell. I know it's not what we agreed upon, but your information was more helpful than we first thought."

Teo accepted the heavy bundle and peered inside. "What of Warrick?" he asked, his voice gruff.

Marik rubbed a hand across his mouth. "Well, right about now he's probably having a rather bad day. You see, he may just have made a very foolish deal with a band of pirates who decided that his fee was a mite too high and left without paying it."

Teo gave a rough guffaw and then raised his head, looking

straight at Marik. There was a faint gleam of tears in his eyes. "I thank you," he managed in a choked voice.

"My pleasure." Marik grinned fiercely. His gaze flicked to the three children behind Teo's legs. "You take good care of your pa, now, you hear me?"

Three small heads nodded, and a pair of chubby arms wrapped around one of Teo's legs from behind.

"Good day." Marik nodded at the farmer.

"And to you," Teo replied. He reached out and gripped Marik's arm in his rough hand. "May the ancestors grace your path and bless you."

A flicker of surprise ignited in Marik's chest. To speak of any god besides the Ar'Mol was dangerous, if not outright suicidal. The Ar'Mol taught that he was divinely appointed, wielding the power of the heavens, and it was the only acceptable religion of the Igyeum, though the older beliefs were sometimes secretly observed by some. Marik did not hold to the Maleian view of the ancestors, for how could the dead care for the living? He stayed silent, though, merely bowing his head respectfully and with a small amount of hope; perhaps the Ar'Mol did not command as much devotion as he believed.

Marik turned and made his way down the steps, his heart lighter than it had been in sennights. Raisa and Oleck had taken another load of the leather they had acquired into town. Valen would make sure that it was given to those who needed it most. Despite their generosity, there was still more than enough leather for them to take on the guise of merchants. Of course, the hardest part of their subterfuge had only just begun. The Hawk's disguise was well underway, but it would take a few more sennights to finalize their plans. Nevertheless, Marik's heart and steps were light as he made his way down the road.

———

SHAKING his head to banish the memory, Marik raised his voice. "It is time," he announced to his small crew. Like the airship, they each wore their own disguise. Dressed in the traditional garb of merchants, they wore colorful vests laced up the front over tunics with billowing sleeves and capes fastened at the shoulder. Mouse had on a jaunty cap. Oleck had shaved off his beard and wore a white wig that contrasted strangely with his deeply tanned skin. Shaesta had drawn faint lines on his face, making him appear quite a bit older than he was. Enormous hoop earrings dangled from Shaesta's ears and her forearms were covered with thin bracelets. Streaks of gray threaded their way through her own gold-tipped dark curls, and artfully applied makeup made her face appear older as well. Marik's outfit was the most drab in comparison with his comrades, with its soft browns and various other muted colors. He wore a pair of wire-framed spectacles and had stained his fingers with ink, as he would be posing as the unassuming clerk for the merchant family. But Raisa's outfit put them all to shame. Over her soft gray leggings, knee-high black boots, vest, and tunic, she also wore a jacket of varying shades of blue that flowed around her knees and was held in place by a black leather belt adorned with an ornate silver buckle in the shape of a crescent moon. The entire ensemble was designed to bring to mind the night sky, and it did its job well. Anyone glancing at their crew would immediately pick out Raisa as the wealthy leader of the merchants.

As the sun crept above the horizon, the *Gilded Petunia* lumbered its way out of the cave and took to the air. The new boards surrounding its hull creaked and groaned, giving it a whiny sound that Marik felt was appropriate. His airship sounded the way he felt, apprehensive and a bit discontented with his disguise, and yet also somewhat smugly confident that his plan would succeed.

"How's she flying, Captain?" Marik asked once they had risen up into the clouds. Marik insisted they adopt their new roles during the journey so that everything would seem natural by the time they arrived in Melar.

"She's listing a bit starboard, but not enough that anyone looking at her would notice, I reckon," Oleck said, one hand on the wheel, the other on the lever that adjusted their speed. "Her handling is a bit ungainly. Nothing I can't navigate, though. How are you coming on those records I told you to recheck? We need to know exactly how much our shipment is worth so we can get the best price from those swindlers in Melar."

Marik ducked his head. "Sorry, Cap'n. I'm almost finished. Just needed to come up and rest my eyes a spell. I can't do figures when my head feels liable to split open down the middle."

"So be it," Oleck barked. "But there's no call to be up here at the helm irritating me with your pestering questions. Go rest your eyes elsewhere."

Marik nodded, satisfied that Oleck had both his role and his charge well in hand. He slipped down the ladder, grinning at Oleck's muttered tirade about "clerks who got headaches while doing figures not being worth their pay," which followed him all the way to the deck.

The voyage took less than a day, and soon the *Gilded Petunia* rested comfortably in her dock while her captain and crew descended the long staircase to stand on the streets of Melar. The two men pulled behind them a large cart filled with their wares. They made their way down the road toward the open-air marketplace not far from the Ar'Mol's palace. The cart wheels squeaked and groaned beneath the weight of its cargo, but despite its loud complaining, it rolled smoothly over the dusty ground.

"Do you think this is actually going to work?" Raisa hissed between her teeth.

"A large quantity of leather should be just what we need to attract attention," Shaesta replied. "The information Marik got from his contacts was the same as what I received from mine. Don't worry, the plan is sound and everyone knows their role."

"I always worry," Raisa muttered.

Marik grinned behind her, wondering if she knew that the crew thought of her fondly as their "mother." Despite her youth, Raisa tended to be the one who kept them on task, together, and took care of the various details in any given venture. She did not enjoy being at the front; he knew that playing a role in front of Warrick had been uncomfortable for her, despite the fact that she had a gift for acting.

It was a few miles from the docks to the market, but Marik had arranged with the dock master for a booth as close to the palace as possible. The "merchants" arrived at their assigned location and began dismantling the cart and reassembling it into a small store. Once their shop was arranged to his liking, Marik nodded at Shaesta. The woman smirked and then turned her attention to the people passing by.

"Leather!" she shouted in a strong voice that creaked slightly with feigned age. "The finest tanned hides on the market! Good enough for stout shoes to keep your feet warm and dry through the entire year. Leather at fair prices!" Her call rang out across the marketplace again and again and soon began to attract customers.

"How much for enough to make a pair of shoes?" a wizened elderly woman asked of Marik. Her demeanor was hesitant and despondent, as though she already knew she could not afford whatever they were asking.

He eyed her feet and flipped open his leather bound notebook. "Ten stin," he said after a long pause.

The woman's eyes widened with a sparkle of renewed interest. "And do you fine folk have the skills of a cordwainer to make the shoes for those who cannot?"

Marik looked down at her with a gentle expression. "For that, we would charge five stin extra."

The woman's mouth fell open slightly, then her eyes narrowed with suspicion. "Are you having a laugh at my expense, boy? Has no one ever taught you respect for your elders?"

"No, dear mother," Marik replied, his tone earnest. "That is our price. Is it…" He paused, considering her shabby appearance. Perhaps he had misjudged the situation. "Is it too much?"

"Too much!" The woman's creaking voice exploded from her mouth. "You're practically giving away your wares. And these are precious wares. What is your game, here?"

"No game, good mother," Marik said, making a placating gesture with his hands. "We are simply honest merchants with wares to sell. We hope to make a small profit to take home with us when we have sold all we have. Do you wish to purchase a pair of shoes? You may pick out the leather yourself and my mistress will set to work making your shoes directly." He pointed to Shaesta.

The elderly woman, her face alight with wary joy, nodded to Marik. "Show me your wares," she ordered.

Marik led her to the table and let her peruse what they had to offer. She picked out a nice piece and paid the fifteen stin in advance, while Shaesta measured the old woman's feet and sat down on the ground and began cutting the pieces she would need. When the old woman disappeared after Marik promised that her shoes would be ready on the morrow, Shaesta looked up at him.

"Do you know how long it takes to make a good pair of shoes?" she demanded. "I cannot make shoes for the entire city, not if we are also supposed to be gathering information."

"Don't worry." Marik grinned at her. "I'll spare your sore fingers. But we needed that first customer."

"Why that one?"

"Couldn't you tell? She's the city's informant. If anyone wants to know anything, they go to that dear woman and she tells them all the important things they need to know. She's probably a healer of some sort, as well."

"And how could you possibly know that? From a short conversation about leather prices?" Shaesta asked, beginning the process of punching holes in the leather so she could stitch the pieces together.

"First, I saw her earlier when we were setting up. She was

watching our booth rather closely. Second, I watched several people approach her. And third, she has a pouch of healing herbs hanging from her belt." Marik ticked the points off on his fingers. "Also, there was a woman just like her in the town where I grew up. There always is at least one. She'll tell everyone she knows about our shop and our amazing prices, and just like that we'll become the biggest attraction in this marketplace. If that doesn't get the attention of the Ar'Mol, then nothing will."

45

The former Regeont's den was dim. One curtain hung over the window, partially obscuring the light and preventing it from penetrating further into the room. The other curtain lay on the floor in a heap, a dark stain spreading out from beneath it and covering the polished wood floor. The window itself was broken, jagged edges of glass hanging from the frame of the window, but most of the glass had poured out onto the ground outside. The furniture lay in broken fragments as well. A large ring lay in the middle of the room, as though tossed there, a charred black smudge on the floor beneath its tip. Thorben leaned over to examine what he could of a shattered chair, while Dalmir strode over to inspect the window.

"We believe that is how they entered the room."

Dalmir turned from the window at the sound of the unfamiliar voice. A young man stood in the doorway, his face solemn. He gestured at the window.

"We believe that is how the assassins gained entry." He strode over to stand by Dalmir. "She put up a good fight." He shook his head, his expression one of awe. "She took two of them with her."

"Then there were three attackers?" Thorben asked, standing. He held a chair leg in his hand.

"Three, yes." The young man chewed on his lower lip, his expression one of distress.

"You must be Elan," Dalmir said. "Roshana's nephew?"

"Yes," Elan replied. "And you are...?"

Dalmir did not reply, but walked over to Thorben. "What is that?"

"There is blood on it," Thorben replied, showing him the finely turned piece of wood.

"The guards think that was the weapon they used to..." Elan broke off, his voice cracking.

"The third assassin escaped?" Dalmir asked. "Did anyone catch sight of him?"

Elan grimaced. "I saw him briefly, but he knocked me out before I could be of much use."

"Nobody heard the breaking of the window?" Thorben questioned. "It must have made quite a loud noise, shattering like that. I would like to speak to the guards who were on duty at the time."

"Certainly," Elan replied. "I will send for them."

Dalmir crouched down and examined the ring while they waited for Elan to return. He gestured at it without touching it. "Why do you think this is in the middle of the room?"

Thorben shook his head. "We will ask the guards."

Elan returned with the three guards who had been on duty the day of the murder. Thorben asked them where the bodies had been found and in what positions.

"Where were you when the attack took place?" he asked one of the guards.

"I was circling the grounds," the man replied. "I was on the far side of the house when it happened."

"And you heard nothing? No sounds of struggle, no glass breaking?"

"No, sir. I couldn't have, especially with the city in a bit of an uproar due to the attack at the Academy. Seemed everyone was shouting and running that night."

"What about the Regeont's seal ring?" Thorben asked the

second guard, who had been stationed at the front door. "Why is it in the middle of the room?"

"We don't know. Maybe she was holding it when she was attacked, or maybe it got knocked off her desk and kicked across the room in the scuffle," the second guard answered.

After nearly an hour of questions about the night of the assassination, Thorben released the three guards. When they had gone, he turned to Dalmir.

"What do you make of this?" Thorben asked.

"The guards' stories are consistent," Dalmir said. "Nobody heard anything, the bodies of two assassins and the Regeont were discovered by Elan, and the chair leg was the weapon used upon the Regeont. From listening to them just now, I would hazard a guess that they are telling the truth as they know it."

"You do not sound convinced that it is the truth, though," Thorben said.

"Neither do you."

"A few things do not seem to connect." Thorben turned and pointed at the window. "If the assassins came through the window, why is there no glass on the floor?"

Dalmir strode to the window and carefully stuck his head through the hole. "There is plenty of glass on the ground outside, which indicates that this window was broken from the inside. Not a method of entering the study, then, but the means of escape. Out through the garden and over the wall."

"Which would make sense, except..." Thorben joined Dalmir at the window. "It is only the top half of the window that is broken. Not a convenient way to escape a room. And what did he break the window with? There is no furniture over here."

"The chair leg?" Dalmir asked.

"Then why not take it with him? Why would he pause to put it back beside the body where Elan said he found it?"

"What about the servants?" Dalmir's voice was thoughtful.

"What do you mean?"

"Surely there were some servants nearby. We've talked to the guards, but none of them saw or heard anything. Whoever did this knew where the guards were and how to avoid them, but servants are more easily overlooked. Perhaps we should talk to them, as well."

Thorben nodded slowly. "Yes. But we should be subtle about it. If the person who did this indeed had knowledge of where the guards would be and when, then it is possible that the assassins were hired by someone within the house."

Dalmir nodded. "Can you think of anyone in this house who would want to hurt the Regeont?"

Thorben shook his head. "As far as I knew she was beloved by her staff. She paid fair wages and took good care of the people in her employ."

A small cough made them both turn around. Lady Ilya stood in the doorway.

"Forgive my intrusion"—her voice was soft—"but dinner is ready."

"Very good," Thorben said. "We were just about done here."

Ilya's eyebrows gave a barely perceptible lift. "You have finished the investigation already?"

"I believe so," Thorben replied.

"You know what happened, then?"

"We may never know all of what transpired in this room. But the evidence appears to be consistent with the testimony of yourself, your brother, and the guards. Unfortunately, there is no way to find the killer since nobody saw him... or her."

Ilya lowered her chin a bit and a tear dripped down her nose. "Then Aunt Roshana's killer will go free?"

"It appears so." Thorben laid a gentle hand on Ilya's shoulder. "And if that is the case, we must all be wary."

Ilya's eyes widened in a startled expression. "Why is that?"

Dalmir spoke. "Because we have no way of determining the motive. It could be that this was a warning to the Council, or a murder paid for by an enemy of the Regeont, or an enemy of your family. It could be that this was a scheme by the Ar'Mol in an attempt to weaken Telmondir before he launches a full-scale offensive at our borders. There could be any number of other reasons for your aunt's death, but without knowing, we must assume the worst. Come, we will walk with you to the dining hall."

"I see." Ilya stared down at the floor. "Then you believe my brother and I could be in danger, as well?"

"And Duke Langston and Lord Adelfried, and anyone close to them," Dalmir replied, his voice low and earnest as the three of them headed down the hallway together.

Ilya gave a single, slow nod. "I will inform my brother. Perhaps it would be wise to hire a few more guards."

"Perhaps so," Thorben agreed.

Ilya's footsteps faltered and she stopped. "What of the sending?"

"Sending?" Dalmir asked, stopping as well.

"The Ondouran ritual for the dead," Thorben replied. "Ilya, is that something you would feel up to arranging? I am afraid the investigation will require my full attention." He motioned for them to keep moving.

"Of course." Ilya nodded and resumed walking. "It seems almost indecent to ask, but what of the Regeont's title and position? A vote will need to be held soon. Already word of Aunt Roshana's murder has spread."

Thorben rubbed his palms against his temples. "In my grief over the passing of my friend, I had not given thought to her position as Regeont of Ondoura and her seat on the Council. There will need to be an election. Ondourans have often elected to give the position to a family member of the previous Regeont. As far as I know, you, Elan, and Ioan are the only living relatives Roshana had."

"Yes," Ilya murmured.

"There will probably be a few other high-ranking officials who may be candidates as well," Thorben continued. "I wish Ioan could be here for the sending, though I am certain he has no interest in the position of Regeont. He is too committed to his role as a defender. Spread the word to the available candidates that we will hold a vote two sennights after the sending. It is too quick, but also not quick enough. It is critical that the position of Regeont be resolved and filled as swiftly as possible."

They arrived in the dining hall and sat down to eat. The long, elegant table held a spread of foods. They took three chairs around the foot of the table.

Thorben looked at Ilya in concern. "Where is Elan?"

Ilya slid a roasted tomato onto her plate and carefully cut a tiny bite. "He went for a walk. He has been going for many walks these past few days. Being cooped up in the house where our aunt was murdered has been... difficult... for both of us. Elan copes by walking. I cope by"—here Ilya's face flushed—"crying."

Thorben patted her hand. "I am not looking forward to taking the news to Ioan."

Ilya sniffled. "They were so close."

Dalmir stared thoughtfully at his plate. "You know, Thorben, I've been thinking about the attack on the Academy."

"Yes?" Thorben asked, spearing a slice of meat and depositing it on his plate.

"Why was there an attack on the Academy the same day as the assassination attempt?"

"To draw attention away from the assassination, I suppose," Thorben said, waving a hand as he glumly stabbed a slice of potato and put it in his mouth.

"It worked," Ilya muttered. "That night was chaos."

"But why attack there? The Academy is located too far away to truly be a distraction from anything happening here in the center of Doran. And what would have happened if word of the attack had reached the Regeont before the attempt on her life?"

"The guards would have been doubled around the house and the city gates would have been barred." Thorben put his fork down, his expression filled with interest. "You're right, the attack on the Academy doesn't make sense. Do you think the two incidents are not related, after all?"

"Perhaps," Dalmir replied. "But the attack on the Academy was so clumsy, it seems the only reason it was even attempted was to draw attention to itself. Honestly this all feels more like a child playing at a game of war, attacking places that seem important with no real understanding of what a winning strategy requires."

"What are you driving at?" Ilya asked, then she blushed and looked down. "Forgive me, it is not my place."

"What are you thinking?" Thorben asked.

"I'm not sure."

Thorben took a bite of his meat and chewed it slowly. "You're right, though." He sighed. "But that doesn't make the job of finding the culprit any less difficult. They might have bumbled about in their strategy, but it did work. The Regeont is dead, and at least one of her murderers survived." Adelfried's brow furrowed and his face darkened.

"I am sorry. I know she was a friend," Dalmir said.

Thorben glowered, then his expression relaxed from anger into sorrow. "What am I going to tell Ioan when he returns?"

"He was her grandson, correct?" Dalmir asked.

"And our cousin," Ilya added. She looked up, her eyes filled with tears. "Though Aunt Roshana raised him. He was more like a son to her than a grandson." She rose and came around the table, placing a hand on Thorben's arm. "It will be difficult for Ioan to accept that she is gone. Elan and I will stay to help break the news as gently as we can."

Thorben patted her hand. "Thank you. I would appreciate it if you stayed and looked after the house for a while. But Ioan is on a mission in Telsuma at the moment, so it is likely that I will have to tell him before he returns here."

46

───────

I t seemed the entire city of Doran was draped in deep purple, the color of mourning, in honor of their beloved Regeont. All the shops and marketplaces were closed on the day of her sending. As soon as the sun touched the western horizon, enormous crowds of people, all wearing purple and bearing wreaths of various sizes, lined the streets as the Regeont's honor guard bore her body through the city and down to the harbor. The bearers walked slowly, reverently carrying their charge down to the water. The Regeont lay in a shallow, cushioned box with poles on either side so the guards could carry her easily. She was dressed in the ceremonial robes of her position, robes she had rarely ever worn in life. On her head rested an intricately woven headdress of white and purple violets. The flowers twined their way down on either side of the Regeont's head and draped over her shoulders. More violets had been woven around her wrists, and a bunch of them had been placed in her hands, which were folded over her heart.

When they reached the harbor, the guards placed the box into the small boat that had been prepared and waited near the shore. Vertical poles at the head, foot, and one on either side of the little craft held torches that flickered brightly in the twilight air. A hush lay over the massive crowds. No words were spoken, but those closest to the Regeont came forward and placed small wreaths of flowers in the boat around her body. The reverent silence lasted another moment and then the voices of all those gathered rose up in a soft chant as the guards pushed the boat out into the water. The onlookers watched as the six torches flickered in the gentle breeze. The little craft bobbed up and down on the black waves tipped with white foam that glowed in the torchlight.

Ilya's clear, soprano voice rose into the night air in a song of remembrance, and after the first line rang out into the air, a thousand voices joined hers, weaving a tapestry of melody across the beach and out over the water. The craft bobbed away from the shore, carried on the constant current that swept from this particular beach out between the ancient isles on which stood the ruins of the great structure that it was believed had once stood as a beacon of Ondoura, its feet spanning across the harbor in massive arches. The people stayed, singing song after song until at long last the shining lights of the little boat bearing its solemn charge winked out of sight beyond the last of the isles.

Dressed in an elegant purple jacket, a tall, handsome man stood on a high, empty pier that extended from the beach out over the ocean. His vantage point allowed him to watch the little boat bob up and down on the waves long after the last of the mourners had departed for home. In his hands he clutched an elaborate wreath he had purchased earlier that day. His fingers tightened on the circlet of greenery and flowers while he observed the proceedings below. The Regeont's assassination had come as quite an unwelcome surprise to Ericole Niveya, and he was not quite certain about what to do next. The Regeont had been true to her word, the signed papers had been waiting for him before night had fallen on the day he had sauntered into her palace. The arrangement was made, and there was no need to inform the Council. In fact, if the information he had gathered was correct, it would be most unwise for a known criminal such as himself to be seen anywhere in Doran right now, as it seemed that one of the Regeont's assassins had escaped justice. And yet, in his few interactions with the Regeont over the years, Ericole had come to respect and admire her as a leader, which was not something he could say about many people. And beyond that, as a buyer and seller of information, the question of who might be behind this attack caused a burning itch within his brain. As the sending boat passed beyond even his sight, Ericole sighed and tossed the wreath out onto the waves.

"Fare thee well, Regeont," Ericole whispered, watching the wreath sidle over the waves and disappear into the darkness. He straightened his jacket and turned back to the shore. "Time to find your killer and make him pay."

47

Thorben looked down at his notes where they were spread across Roshana's desk and rubbed a hand over the back of his neck. The past few days had been disappointing. He had interviewed most of Roshana's staff, but the exercise had yielded very little in the way of new information. His time was growing short, as well, for he would have to hand the investigation to the Doran Conscripts. He was due at the Storvas Outpost soon to greet the cadets there and speak over their graduation. He needed to leave soon; he could only put off the journey back to Telsuma for another day, maybe two.

The door opened and he glanced up as the last of the servants entered the room. The young woman approached him timidly and he gave her what he hoped was an encouraging smile as she sat down on the other side of the desk. She fidgeted with her skirts and stared down at her hands.

"I just have a few questions about the day of the Regeont's death," Thorben began.

The young woman nodded, still staring at her hands resting in her lap as she clasped and unclasped her fingers.

"Where were you at the time of the assassination?"

"In the kitchens," she mumbled.

The kitchens, on the other side of the estate. Thorben sighed inwardly. There was no way she could have heard or seen anything.

"Do you remember anything strange or out of place on that day?"

"No." She glanced up at him, her eyes wide, and he was startled to see tears begin to pour down her face.

"What's wrong?" he asked, concerned.

"What will happen to us, now?" She choked out the question. "Lady Petrescu rescued me from the streets. She took me in, gave me a good paying job, practically raised me. Where am I supposed to go? What can I do, now that she's gone?"

Thorben stared at her. The question had simply never occurred to him. In his search to discover what had happened on the day of Roshana's murder, he had not given much thought to what her death would mean for her servants or even for Ondoura. A pang of remorse twinged in his soul. His single-minded pursuit of the killer seemed suddenly selfish. He cleared his throat.

"I am sure you will be able to find a good job," he assured her. "Having served the Regeont, many doors will be open to you. Or perhaps you can go on serving whomever the people elect to be the new Regeont."

The young woman sniffled and produced a handkerchief from the pocket of her skirt. She wiped her face with it and then looked up, her eyes big and sorrowful.

"I don't know that I could stay here with Lady Petrescu gone," she whispered. "It just... I just... I couldn't." She leaned forward, her face in her hands, her shoulders shaking with sobs.

"I understand," Thorben replied, his voice gentle. "She was my friend, too. Like a sister to me."

The young woman wept into her handkerchief, and then she took a long, shaky breath and sat up. "Have you spoken to Ulia?" she asked.

Thorben scanned through his notes. "No," he replied. "Who is Ulia?"

"One of the servants. She hasn't been to work since the Regeont died. The only thing I remember from that day is that Ulia stopped by the kitchens before she went home. Most of the servants have homes outside the estate. Only a few, like me, live on the premises. Anyway, we had all heard about what happened and Ulia came downstairs, and she looked awful, white as a sheet. She told Cook that she was sick and might be gone for a few days, and nobody's seen her since. It might not matter or be important, but you asked if I remembered anything odd or out of place... and I remember this: Ulia didn't look sick. She looked scared."

Thorben's brow furrowed. "Scared?"

"Mm-hmm. I didn't think much of it at the time, she was pale and a little shaky, looked like she might have a fever. I'm fairly certain she was attending the Regeont that day." The young maid paused. "You know, she might have been the first one to see the bodies." She shuddered. "I wouldn't want to come back to work either if I'd seen that."

"Perhaps," Thorben replied. "I'd like to speak with her, in case she did see something important. Do you know where Ulia lives?"

The woman nodded. "I can give you directions."

Thorben wrote down the directions she gave him, a rising sensation of mingled excitement and dread welling within him. It was the first and only lead he'd gotten, but what would it reveal about the circumstances of his friend's death?

———

THORBEN WENT ALONE to call on Ulia. If she did know anything about the Regeont's death, he did not want to frighten her. She lived in a small house several streets over from Roshana's palace. The place was neat and well-kept, though Thorben would have expected nothing less. Roshana always had looked for certain qualities when hiring her staff. He climbed the two short steps and knocked on the door. He waited. Nobody appeared to answer the door, so Thorben raised his hand to knock again.

"She isn't home," a voice from the corner of the house said. A lean man stood leaning against the dark siding. He moved over to stand before Thorben, as lithe and graceful as a cat. "I assume you are looking for Ulia?"

"I am," Thorben said stiffly. "And who might you be?"

"I was looking for her, too," the man admitted. "I needed some information that she has, but she was gone before I arrived. It appears she left in a hurry."

"And how do you know that?"

"I broke in and looked around," the man said with a smirk. "Looks like she packed up everything of value and left a few days ago."

"Why would she do that?" Thorben asked.

"Why indeed," the man replied. He gave Thorben a long, measuring look. Then he extended his hand. "This might be a mistake, but I'd like to introduce myself. Ericole Niveya."

Thorben slowly began crushing the man's hand reflexively and he felt his jaw tighten as his teeth clenched together. "You had my son kidnapped."

Ericole let out a single sound that was somewhere between a laugh and a cough. "I did. That... I did. And you have my sincerest apologies. If it makes any difference, I intended no harm against you or your family. I was merely attempting to steal a prize from the Ar'Mol. He had ordered your son's assassination."

Thorben growled, the sound rumbling from deep in his throat. "That does not make a difference."

"I... ah... thought not," Ericole replied. "But perhaps this will." He held up a rolled-up piece of paper and offered it to Thorben. "The Regeont was able to look past our differences and come to an agreement with me."

"If you expect me to honor some agreement you made..." Thorben's face darkened with rage.

"No! I expect you to allow me to find her murderer," Ericole gasped out as Thorben's grip tightened, crushing his hand.

Thorben's eyes widened in spite of himself and he released

Ericole's hand. "What?" He snatched the rolled-up paper and opened it, his eyes scanning the document. Then he looked up, the anger fading from his face to be replaced by suspicion and curiosity. "But if this is correct, you already have everything you bargained for with the Regeont. So why would you care about finding her murderer?"

"I play dangerous games for a living," Ericole replied, his voice regaining some of its accustomed smoothness. "And it is easy to sit up in my mountain fortress and play chess against the world. I'll admit, it isn't often I get involved for personal reasons. But in my few dealings with the Regeont, I came to respect her. She had a strength and intelligence that was admirable. There were even times when she outwitted me, though it is painful to admit. I grew to regard her as an equal, if you will. Not many earn that from me. And as a man who plays dangerous games and understands strategy, something about this entire situation strikes me wrong. There is something missing, and it irks me that I cannot figure out what it is."

"I know the feeling," Thorben muttered. He eyed the man thoughtfully. "I warn you, if you double-cross me or if I find that you had anything to do with Roshana's death, I will throw you in the deepest, darkest hole I can find, and then I will blissfully forget your entire existence."

Ericole's lips twitched into a wry smile. "Ah. Then we shall work together?"

"I suppose we must."

48

"Listen," Grayden told the others as they began their search. "If Koen is alive, he may be calling for help. Be quiet and listen, it may be our best chance of finding him."

The others nodded at him, accepting his leadership in this matter. Grayden quickly cut several branches off the dead tree, which surprisingly had not been carried off by the avalanche, and passed them out. "You can use these to push into the snow, gently, and see if we can find him that way. Work steadily, but don't spend too much time in any one area. Time is not our friend. Look carefully for spots where it looks like the snow has been disturbed, as that could be a signal of Koen trying to move underneath the snow."

Grayden now stood on the snow, his head cocked to one side, his entire focus on the sounds around him. He paced quietly below the spot where he had last seen the older cadet. The full moon sent down a brilliant, silver light across the mountainside. Around him and down the mountainside even further, the others had spread out and were making a similar search in the direction the snow had been moving. Enric poked his stick down into the snow periodically, but so far none of them had found a trace of their missing comrade. Ioan had been left in the shelter of the rock outcropping, though he had chafed at not being able to provide assistance with the search.

The precious minutes ticked by, and with each passing breath, Grayden felt a rising despair. He pushed it to the back of his mind, using it to add urgency and strength to his efforts. It was not time yet to give up hope, several minutes still remained. He continued on, his gaze scanning the ground, his ears straining to hear anything, his long branch ready to probe down into the snow.

Wynn gave a sudden shout and Grayden dropped his stick and rushed over to him. Wynn knelt on the ground, using his hands to dig into the loose powder. A hand and part of an arm stuck out from the snow, sending a jolt of hope through Grayden's heart. The others dove in to help but Grayden stopped them.

"It's better to work in shifts, two at a time. If we all try to dig at the same time we'll just get in each other's way. Thankfully he's not too far below the surface, but it will still be a difficult undertaking without shovels. We need to get his head out first so he can breathe. Wynn and Beren, you start. When you get tired, Enric and I will take over. Then we'll switch."

"I'll get a fire started," Ioan said. "We'll need some way of getting Koen warm after you rescue him."

Wynn and Beren began digging in the area where they believed Koen's head was most likely to be. The work was tedious and difficult and they soon had to rest and change places with Grayden and Enric. The snow was loose and powdery, but shot through with large chunks of ice that interrupted their progress and slowed the rescue efforts. It seemed like hours, but was only a few minutes, before they uncovered Koen's head. His face was red and he was unconscious, but breathing.

Beren took over again when Grayden began to tire. The young giant did not grow weary through the long effort of digging the rest of Koen out of the snow and ice that were packed solidly around him. Koen remained unconscious as they worked, and Grayden knew that if he had been buried any deeper, their efforts would have been in vain. By the time they got him disen-tombed, Ioan had a blazing fire going. When they returned to the campsite, they were greeted by more good news: Ioan had spent his time and what little strength and mobility he had and managed to unearth two of their packs with their bedrolls and waterskins still attached. They wrapped Koen in the blankets and set him as near to the fire as they could without putting him in danger of being burned. Within a few minutes he had regained a semblance of consciousness and was moaning about his face and feet being on fire.

"That's a good sign," Ioan told them, getting the waterskin and holding it to Koen's lips so he could take a drink. "It means the blood is beginning to move again. I don't think it is serious frostbite. He was lucky."

"In many ways," Grayden agreed.

Once they were certain their friend would be all right, they took stock of the supplies they had left. It was a discouraging venture. In addition to the two blankets wrapped around Koen, they had two packs, each containing a coil of rope, a waterskin, three sets of clothes, four pairs of socks, two packs of rations, a bowl, a spoon, and a knife. One pack contained the rude map they had of the area, as well as flint and steel and a bottle of oil for tending their blades. The other had two rolls of bandages and a pack of medicinal herbs, as well as a pot for cooking over the fire. They all had the weapons they had been carrying, and each of them was already wearing several layers of clothes because of the return of the colder temperatures that morning.

"We aren't in dire straits," Beren said, his voice cheerful.

"Our top priority for now is keeping the fire going," Ioan said. He quickly assigned shifts for keeping watch through the night and sent the cadets down the mountain to gather firewood. "Better to have too much and not need it," he directed.

They made several trips down the mountain to the closest stand of timber until they had more than enough firewood.

Wynn threw himself down on the ground near the roaring

fire. "I'm starving," he exclaimed, "but I'm too tired to eat."

"That's a good thing," Beren said, "because there isn't anything to eat."

Wynn groaned. "I would offer to go hunting, but we didn't see a single sign of any animals while we were chopping wood. It's eerie."

Grayden frowned. "Come to think of it, I haven't even heard any birds since we left the cave this morning."

"Think a storm is coming?" Enric asked.

A horrified silence greeted this question. They all knew their current chances of surviving a storm were slim.

"I'm not sure," Grayden replied. "It could be that we've climbed high enough there just isn't any wildlife, but the tree line isn't that far down the mountain."

"Says the man who didn't make twelve trips to get firewood," Wynn grumbled, but his lips quirked into a teasing grin.

"You need more exercise than me," Grayden quipped back.

Wynn scooped up a handful of snow and made a halfhearted attempt to throw it at Grayden. The snow mostly missed, though a few drops of mud spattered across Grayden's face. He laughed.

"If we can still laugh, we can't be doing too poorly," Beren remarked. "But if we can't find something to eat, I predict that our cheerful mood won't last much past tomorrow morning."

Grayden sighed and looked up at the sky. The moon had fallen much closer to the horizon since the avalanche. "We'd best turn in," he said. "I have first watch."

Ioan passed out the extra clothes and socks that had been in the recovered packs, and the young men all set about doing their best to wrap themselves in the additional layers and setting their bedrolls as close to the fire as they dared in an effort to keep from freezing while they slept.

Grayden stared into the flickering flames as the others around him drifted off to sleep. He rose and paced around the camp, trying to keep himself awake, stomping his feet in an effort to warm his toes. Worry for Koen filled his mind. Then his thoughts turned to home and his parents and he wished his father were there with him to tell him what to do or to give him a word of encouragement. With fingers trembling from more than the cold, he pulled the letter out of his pocket and contemplated it. He desperately needed words from his father.

"You can go lie down." Enric's voice startled Grayden and he nearly dropped the letter.

"What?"

"It's my turn to take the watch," Enric said.

"Oh." Grayden stuffed the letter back into his pocket. Perhaps this was not the moment to read it, after all.

The extra layers of clothing did little to keep the cold from seeping into Grayden's bones as he lay on the ground once his turn at watch was complete. If he had not been exhausted from the long day of travel and the subsequent arduous task of digging Koen out from beneath the avalanche, he might not have been able to sleep at all. During the night another blast of warm air rolled over the mountains, and Grayden awoke to the sound of trickling water.

Though the ground was still cold, the late morning sunshine had a definite warmth to its rays. That warmth was the most welcome thing he had experienced in sennights, ever since they had begun preparing for this mission. Memories of their training made Grayden's mind turn to thoughts of Isak. A strange sorrow and regret settled itself like a cloud above his shoulders. He rose and went to check on Koen, but the cloud hovered along with him.

The fire had fallen to embers. One of the small pots that had been recovered with a pack sat on the coals, containing a small amount of Ioan's broth. Ioan himself was at Koen's side. He looked up as Grayden approached.

"How is he?" Grayden asked.

Koen pushed himself up on his elbows. "I'm alive." His voice came out in a rasp. He forced a grin and was seized by a fit of coughing. Ioan put a steadying hand on Koen's shoulder, concern written across his face. He offered Koen the waterskin, but Koen waved it away weakly. When he finally stopped coughing, he looked up at Grayden. "I understand I have you to thank for that."

"Everyone did their part," Grayden replied, uncomfortable taking credit for the group effort.

"Well, I'm grateful." Koen began coughing again as Ioan brought the pot of broth and poured it into one of the two bowls they had. When his coughing subsided, Koen accepted the broth and sipped it slowly.

"We need to get out of these mountains," he said between sips. "Ioan filled me in on what we lost in the avalanche. With only two packs we do not have the supplies we need to survive up here. The weather has gotten warmer for the moment, but there's no telling how long it will hold. It could still get cold and snow a dozen times before spring is here to stay. We should..." Koen was interrupted by another round of coughing. At last he was able to take a deep breath, and then he took another sip of broth. Around them, the others were beginning to stir and rise. Koen set the bowl on the ground and lay back down, exhaustion written across his features. "I honestly don't know what we should do next," he mumbled, his eyes closing. "You need to get us out of the mountains, Grayden."

Ioan rose and motioned to Grayden to follow him. When they were a little distance from where Koen lay, he spoke to Grayden in a low undertone. "He came through the ordeal surprisingly well, but that cough..." He shook his head. "He's right, we need to get out of these mountains."

As the defender spoke, Grayden shifted uncomfortably. He had not missed the expressions of his companions the previous night as they took stock of their supplies and discussed their options. Wynn and Beren had looked at him like that during their ordeal with the pirates. It was the sort of look that carried with it expectation and hope, seeking answers and guidance. He had not been prepared for it on the airship, and it was even more unexpected now. There were older, wiser options here to turn to with their questions. Having Captain Petrescu include him in the discussion of what to do next felt wrong. He felt as though someone had placed a yoke on his shoulders, weighted down with the expectation of the others to help get them through this ordeal alive. He wasn't sure he was strong enough to bear this burden, and yet, it had been given to him anyway.

"How far to the Pass?" Grayden asked.

Ioan scratched his jaw just below his ear. "I've been trying to figure that out since yesterday morning," he replied. "In spite of the slower pace at which you've been forced to travel, you have made good choices. If we are where I think we are"—he nodded up at the towering peak above them—"and if that is the mountain I think it is, then we are very near Deer Valley. I was on a training exercise here last year and we spent a fair amount of time there. We should be able to find game in the valley, and possibly some ration-packs. There is a hunting cabin that the defenders use often. Sometimes we leave supplies behind for the next rotation. Once we're over that next rise, I'll know for sure."

As he spoke, Grayden peered at the defender, feeling that something about the man had changed. He wasn't sure what it was, though. But Ioan looked different. Something about his eyes seemed strange and feral. And could it be that the tall defender had grown taller? Grayden blinked. The exhaustion of the journey must be hitting him hard for his mind to start playing such tricks.

"And how far is Deer Valley from Fort Pass?" Beren asked.

"About a three-day hike," Ioan replied. "Though with my leg and Koen's injuries, it will probably take us six."

Grayden shouldered one of the packs. "Best get going, then. We'll make camp early so Enric and Beren can go hunting. Perhaps they will have better luck finding game this evening." He did not give voice to his fears about the desperate situation they would soon find themselves in if there was no game.

Slowly, they set off across the side of the mountain. Their pace was impossibly slow, and although neither of the two injured men uttered a word of complaint, it was evident in every movement how much pain they experienced with each step. The team did what they could to help ease the passage, but there was little aid they could offer.

The sun hovered low in the sky by the time they crested the next rise. They stood at the top looking out at the view before them. Directly in front of them plunged a steep cliff that dove straight down. To their left was more of the mountain they were traversing, with a jagged path cutting across its midsection like a belt. The path curved across the mountain as far as they could see and then ended where the line of another mountain rose up into the sky.

"I remembered correctly," Ioan said. "We are on the correct path, this cliff is familiar." He paused, a line puckering between his brows. "But we should be able to see Deer Valley from here." He gestured at the mountain. "It's a hidden valley between these mountains, but from here I remember being able to see the opening." Ioan shook his head, his green eyes puzzled. "There must have been a rockslide."

"Perhaps we should set up camp now," Enric suggested.

"I agree," Grayden said. "We're losing the light and I don't like the idea of trying to follow such a narrow and winding path in the dark. It would be better to tackle it in the morning when we've had rest."

Beren and Enric tramped off down the mountain to hunt while the others tried to create a place to camp. There were no trees, but there were plenty of scrubby bushes in the area that Grayden and Wynn set about pulling up and chopping into pieces. It wouldn't be enough fuel to keep a fire going all night, but it might provide them with a cook fire should the hunters return successfully. At the very least, it might give them a modicum of warmth once the sun went down.

"It's a good thing it warmed up," Wynn commented. He grabbed a bush at its base and worked at wresting it from its shallow hold in the rocky soil. "This isn't what I imagined when I dreamed of going to the Academy. How about you?"

Grayden stared at him over the top of another bush. "Let me think. Did I dream of camping out on a wintry mountainside, having lost all my gear in an avalanche, with no food and everyone looking to me to lead them, days away from the nearest outpost?" The absurdity of the question struck him like a well-timed blow upon a length of iron in a blacksmith's forge. In spite of all his worries and the weight of responsibility that pressed down on him, Grayden could not hold back the flood of humor that washed over him. He doubled over and roared with laughter. He laughed until tears rolled down his face, and then the laughter began to subside, turning into short bursts of chuckling. Resting one hand on his knee, he wiped his eyes with the back of his other wrist and looked up at Wynn. "No." He shook his head, hysteria causing his shoulders to shake. "No, this isn't what I dreamed of at all."

Wynn stared at his friend, his expression perplexed, his fingers beginning to tap against his thigh. "We are in trouble, aren't we?"

Grayden's laughter died, cut off by the weight of Wynn's question as though it had never existed. "Yes," he replied soberly.

"Do you think the group back at the outpost is all right?" Wynn asked.

Grayden tugged on the bush in front of him. "I'm sure they are."

"What aren't you saying?"

Grayden silently cursed his friend's keen attention to detail. "Deer Valley isn't where Ioan said it would be."

"He said there could have been a rockslide. Something like that could easily have covered up a small entrance to a hidden valley."

Grayden shrugged, breaking branches off the shrub. "You're right."

"You think we're lost."

Grayden did not meet his friend's eyes, instead he studied the shrub before him, laying the branches in a neat pile and striding over to the next one. "That is my fear, yes," he muttered.

Wynn's eyes narrowed and he tossed his shrub down. "But that's not all. Gray, what is it?"

"It's nothing."

"I've known you too well for far too long to believe that. Tell me."

Grayden leaned closer to Wynn, lowering his voice. "Have you noticed anything odd about the captain?"

Wynn began tapping the fingers of his right hand against his knee as he pulled up another scrubby bush. "Maybe."

"Wynn?" Grayden eyed his friend. "What have you noticed?"

"His eyes." Wynn's fingers tapped faster. "They are a different color than they were. And... he's taller."

A chill swept through Grayden. "People don't get taller at his age."

"I know. But he did. And... there are some strange lines on his arms and neck..."

"Scars from where he was attacked?"

Wynn shook his head. "Not like that. More like... tattoos. Thin ones. Hard to see, but they seem to be getting darker." He looked Grayden directly in the eyes, something that did not happen often. "What do you think it means?"

"I'm not sure. But his injuries healed too quickly. I saw his leg when Peder set it, bone was sticking out. And now he's walking without any assistance at all. It's like one of my hunches, but different. I don't like being exposed on this ridge, either. There's just this..." He paused and stared off beyond the edge of the cliff. "I don't know."

"Do you think whatever attacked the defenders is nearby?"

"I'm not sure," Grayden replied. "But keep your eyes open."

Wynn looked around. "It would be pretty difficult for anything to sneak up on us here."

"Like I said, keep your eyes open."

Wynn nodded and they continued to work in silence.

49

It did not take long for the newly arrived leather merchants to gain the type of attention they desired. By the fourth day, Raisa spotted soldiers watching their booth. She surreptitiously pointed them out to Marik and Oleck, but the soldiers did not approach; they seemed content to watch from a distance.

Raisa smiled and greeted customers who came to their booth in a steady flow. Her cheeks ached and her throat grew hoarse as she showed off their wares. Shaesta and Mouse glared at her from their hidden seats behind the booth every time she sold a pair of shoes rather than the unfinished leather, complaining about their pricked and aching hands and fingers. Even Oleck had to join them as the commissions piled up. And still they did not seem to attract any additional attention from the guards.

However, on the eighth day there a commotion erupted down the street. The setting sun heralded the end of the market day and Marik and Oleck had begun closing up shop, but the tramp of footsteps coming their way made them pause. A man dressed in the resplendent attire of a member of the Ar'Mol's court and accompanied by a flock of servants approached their booth with no small amount of pompous ceremony. Raisa gestured for everyone to pause as the man walked about the tables with a leisurely sedate air, rubbing the leather between his fingers, picking it up, bringing it close to his face, and examining every aspect of their wares.

Raisa approached him with a broad smile, taking in his finery and noting the ring on his finger that heralded him as a noble lord of a high-ranking house. "Good evening, De'Anan," she purred, loading her voice with deference. "Are you interested in purchasing some of the finest leather this side of the Temnia River? Or perhaps your excellency would be desirous of commissioning a fine pair of shoes?" She ignored the hateful glare Shaesta shot her from behind the table.

The man simpered. "Nothing so banal as that, I assure you. I come from the palace, where I serve at the Ar'Mol's pleasure. Word of your delightful shop and your copious supply of goods has come to my master's attention. He is in need of leather to cover the feet of his soldiers so that they may better protect us from our enemies. I am afraid I must confess that I was suspicious as to the quality of your goods. Leather of any quality has been in short supply for several lunats. In fact, an argument arose between myself and another courtier about it. The Ar'Mol sent me to inspect your goods. He said that if I found them to be of the high quality they were rumored to be, I was to invite you to the palace for an audience with the Ar'Mol himself."

Raisa allowed her expression to convey surprise, widening her eyes momentarily before dropping them respectfully in a show of humble gratitude. "You are far too kind to simple merchants," she murmured. "We are simple folk, just trying to make a living. Surely the Ar'Mol does not have time for such as us and our poor wares."

"Please, I have been authorized to extend the invitation to you if your leather was of any sort of quality, and I can see in just these few moments that it is very fine, indeed. It was the terms of the deal should I be in the wrong of the argument. The Ar'Mol does not issue such invitations often, and to refuse would be taken with great offense." He stared at her meaningfully. "Great offense."

Raisa gave the man a long, measuring glance. Her entire being was focused on resisting the urge to glance to Marik or Oleck for assistance. Her role as the owner of this shop meant she answered to no one.

"Very well. I am at the Ar'Mol's disposal."

The man beamed and offered his arm.

"Right now?" Raisa stared at the offered arm, trepidation surging within her. She did not love this plan, and she had hoped to talk with Marik before being dragged off to the palace. Trying to stem the rising tide of panic welling within her, she gave a brilliant smile that she hoped exuded confidence. "Should I bring a sample of our goods?"

The De'Anan smiled and made an expansive gesture. "Of course. Have one of your men bring them along."

Raisa turned to Oleck. "You there, gather up a sample of our very best for the Ar'Mol." She turned to Marik. "Mind the shop while we're gone."

Behind her, Oleck shouldered a bundle of leather. She met Marik's gaze as she took the De'Anan's proffered arm. It was all she could do to keep the panic out of her expression, but she took a long, slow breath and reminded herself sternly that this was part of the plan. Getting into the palace had always been the goal. With strides that implied far more confidence than she felt, Raisa walked calmly down the dusty street toward the lair of one of the most powerful men in the world. She tried not to let herself dwell on what would happen if the Ar'Mol were to discover their true identities.

As they passed through the doors of the palace, Raisa was nearly knocked to her knees by the splendor that assailed her senses. The door opened into a hallway lined with columns made out of dark opal. Veins of red and green glimmered within the glossy black pillars like living fire dancing inside. They passed room after room filled with beauty. From one room gentle music poured out into the hall. Though she did not have time to stop and listen to the words, the aching sweetness of the music brought tears to Raisa's eyes. An aroma of expensive spices filled her nostrils: cardamom, thyme, nutmeg, and several others she couldn't place. The De'Anan turned into another room and Raisa and Oleck followed. Soft cushions littered this space, which was also adorned with tall windows to let in the light of the sun, which glittered against the walls. Raisa gasped slightly when she realized that the walls had been decorated with various blue gems.

A servant entered the room with a tray of delicate crystal chalices, filled with a dark brown beverage that smelled of cinnamon and cloves. Raisa took one, holding it carefully, afraid that if she gripped it too hard it might shatter. Oleck gave the tray a suspicious glower and waved the servant away, declining the offer.

"Any two of those gems could feed the people of an entire village for a year," he muttered in Raisa's ear. "And yet the Ar'Mol's people go shoeless and hungry through the winter."

She shot him a scowl. It was unwise to whisper such things here, of all places. But she was grateful for his words. They reminded her why they were here, and who they were dealing with.

A door on the far side of the room opened and a young man strode in, a red velvet cape swirling around him. The man who had led them inside bowed, as did the guards still escorting them. Raisa and Oleck followed suit, though Raisa dared to lift her head slightly so she could study the man who had just entered the room.

So this was the Ar'Mol. He was younger than she had expected, only a few years older than herself. His bearing was arrogant, but his brown eyes held a hint of uncertainty as he studied his guests. Blond curls escaped from beneath the large crown that covered most of his head. He caught her gaze and Raisa quickly lowered her eyes once more, her breaths coming in short gasps as she tried in vain to control the racing of her heart. This man was the reason her parents were dead and her village starved. He was the reason they had been forced into lives of piracy and hiding. He was at the heart of every painful memory in her life. Although she had not spent much time dwelling on the past or the Ar'Mol, in that moment, she felt she understood the ghosts of rage she often saw lingering in Marik's gaze.

"De'Anan Haldor." The Ar'Mol spoke, and his voice released them from their obligation to bow. "Are these the leather merchants we have heard so much about?"

"Yes, milord."

"And are we to interpret this incursion into our throne room as evidence of your loss in the matter of the argument between yourself and Tu'Anan Janson?"

"Yes, milord." De'Anan Haldor hung his head.

"You will pay Tu'Anan Janson the ten tavs you wagered, and the matter will be settled."

"Yes, milord."

"Thank you for bringing them to me." The Ar'Mol waved a hand. "You are dismissed."

"Yes, milord." The man backed out of the room and disappeared.

The Ar'Mol studied Raisa and Oleck, his gaze thorough and unnerving. Raisa fought the urge to fidget. Then he gave a slight smile and sat down in the throne-like chair. He raised a finger and beckoned them closer. He extended his long scepter to them and Raisa and Oleck took a few steps closer so they could touch the gem at the end of the scepter, as was the custom.

"Did Haldor explain why we wished to meet with you?" the Ar'Mol asked, his omission of the honorific speaking volumes to how high above even a noble lord the Ar'Mol found himself to be.

Raisa took a tiny step forward. "Something about Your Excellency being in the market for leather?" She did her best to appear nonchalant, but it was not easy.

"Your prices are most extraordinary." The Ar'Mol ran his forefinger in a circle around his chin. "Particularly since what you are selling is so scarce."

"Is it?" Raisa asked.

"Surely you cannot be so naive as not to notice. You are leather merchants, are you not?"

"I am a merchant, milord. I buy and sell and trade in many things. Leather happens to be what we are selling today."

"Clever," the Ar'Mol mused. "But we find it hard to believe that you are so unaware of the market as you seem. Unless you are a very terrible merchant."

Terror clutched at Raisa. It was all she could do not to glance at Oleck or turn and run from the room.

"I must admit, we haven't seen many others selling leather lately," she replied evenly.

The Ar'Mol's eyes narrowed. "And yet you keep your prices low, which would seem to indicate that you acquired your wares at an inordinately low price. And here I thought my men had been most thorough. Tell me, where exactly did you acquire such a substantial quantity of leather?"

"If we merchants told everyone where we acquired our goods, we would soon be out of a job, milord."

An angry flush rose in the Ar'Mol's cheeks. "We are the Ar'Mol, the ruler of the Igyeum, not a common patron of your shop. Or do we look like a rival merchant to you?"

"I am sure you could never appear so pedestrian as either of those things, milord," Raisa bantered. "But you must forgive me, it is habit that speaks, nothing more. We acquired our goods in Renoix."

"Ah, up north." The Ar'Mol leaned back, his demeanor relaxing. "And is that where you and your family are from?"

Raisa simpered. "My family has been of the wandering merchant guild as far back as my great-grandparents, milord. I haven't the faintest idea where they originated."

"Interesting. We are certain that you have many fascinating stories to tell about your life on the road."

"It has its moments," Raisa said modestly. "Perhaps milord would like to hear a few of the tales I could tell."

"We would like that," the Ar'Mol replied. "We would like to issue an invitation to you, Lady...?"

"Sandvik." She gave him her falsified surname.

"Lady Sandvik, to dine with us tonight. You can amuse us with a few stories about your life, and we will settle on a fair price for your wares."

———

"I DON'T LIKE IT. Everything is going too smoothly," Marik said from the doorway. It was the twentieth time he had said those exact words since Raisa had returned from the Ar'Mol's palace with an invitation to dinner and she wished he would stop repeating himself. Her nerves couldn't take it.

"I won't go if you think I shouldn't," Raisa replied. She had no desire to go to the dinner, and hoped Marik would come up with a believable reason she could not attend. However, just as he had done nineteen times already, Marik let out a sound that was part exasperated sigh, part annoyed growl.

"No, it is the plan," he replied. "We stick to the plan. Things are going smoothly because the plan is solid. I just don't like the idea of you in there by yourself." He gave a shake of his head. "The guards will be here any minute to escort you back to the palace. Be careful."

"Always," Raisa promised, trying to sound equal parts confident and flippant. She didn't want him to think she was worried. She could do her job and play this part, but desperately wished Shaesta were going in her stead. Shaesta didn't have to pretend, the woman's confidence was nearly tangible. Raisa envied her ability to slip into her roles and perform them without a flutter of nerves.

As he turned to leave he glanced at her over his shoulder, his eyes twinkling. "You look good."

A few moments later, Raisa, dressed in Shaesta's very best dress, was stepping into the carriage sent by the Ar'Mol. The ride from the docks to the palace did not last long, and Raisa barely had time to think about the evening ahead of her as she stepped out of the carriage and followed a guard into the palace and down a long hallway. They reached a door and the guard pushed it open for her. She paused, taking a few deep breaths and trying to get her nerves under control. She wished one of the others could have been there with her, but the invitation had been extended to her alone. This was her part to play.

Taking one final deep breath, Raisa entered the dining room. It was as lavish as the rest of the palace. A mahogany table gleamed in the candlelight and was covered with dishes filled with delicacies from all over the Igyeum. The Ar'Mol and a man she did not recognize stood at the head of the table. As she stepped into the room, the Ar'Mol smiled at her and beckoned her over to the chair next to his own where a servant waited. She hastened across the room and stood at her chair, feeling awkward and not knowing exactly what to do next. She knew only that it would be considered a breach of etiquette to sit before the Ar'Mol. Thankfully, she did not have to stand there waiting for long. The Ar'Mol took her hand in his, kissed it lightly, and then sat, beckoning for her and the man on his left to do the same. Terror and hatred mingled in the depths of her being and she wondered vaguely if she would be able to make it through the meal without gagging or stabbing him in the heart. Her eyes flicked down to her place setting and the knife resting there next to her plate, so innocuous, so innocent. It would be so easy...

She slid into her chair with a demure smile.

Servants came and filled their chalices with a dark red liquid, and the Ar'Mol raised his glass. "To new friends, and profitable enterprises."

Raisa held up her glass and then took a cautious sip. The taste of the beverage was unfamiliar: a sweetness like honey coated her tongue, followed by a nearly overwhelming bitter aftertaste. She refrained from wrinkling her nose, and replaced the goblet on the table. She was suddenly very thirsty, and wondered how rude it would seem if she requested a glass of water.

"The Ar'Mol informed me of your visit this afternoon," the second man said, taking a sip from his own goblet. "He was quite enamored with you."

The Ar'Mol grinned, looking boyish. "This is Ar'Molon Uun," he said, his tone conspiratorial. "He absolutely insisted on meeting you."

The Ar'Molon! Rumored to be the true power behind the throne, perhaps he was even more culpable than the Ar'Mol himself for all that was wrong and unjust in the Igyeum. Raisa twined her fingers together below the table to hide their trembling and she pointedly avoided letting her gaze flick back to the knife. Instead, she looked down at her plate.

Food had appeared on it while she wasn't looking. She frowned in confusion, not recognizing any of it. She wished Shaesta were here. The other woman was good at this sort of social maneuvering, and Raisa never knew what to say or how to respond to things. Put a rapier in her hand and give her a mission and she would accomplish it. She was at her best when sneaking into places under cover of darkness, her nimble fingers were well-suited to picking pockets and locks, and she liked the background, directing the others, helping iron out any wrinkles in Marik's crazy plans. Darting in and out with a dagger was her forte. Doing so with words was harder. Dressing up and playing a part was the hardest, but it was what was required on this mission. She glanced up through her lashes the way she had seen Shaesta do when flirting.

"Milord is too kind," she said demurely. "I am just a simple leather merchant. I do not merit this sort of royal attention."

"There is nothing simple about you, my dear," the Ar'Mol replied.

The warmth in his voice made her relax slightly. Perhaps this was going better than she thought. Raisa giggled flirtatiously and took a dainty bite of her food. "This is delicious," she said. "Though I must confess, I do not recognize many of these foods."

"They are delicacies from all over my empire," the Ar'Mol said. "Only the finest for my honored guests."

Raisa smiled and glanced away.

"Have you considered my offer?" the Ar'Mol asked.

Raisa looked at him out of the corner of her eye. "Yes, milord. I have."

"And?"

"And I am willing to sell you my entire stock at the same prices I have been offering to the good people of Melar."

"That is quite generous," Lord Uun said.

"Indeed it is," the Ar'Mol agreed. "The matter is settled, then."

Raisa grinned openly and took another bite.

Lord Uun suddenly broke the silence. "Tell me, my dear Lady Sandvik, have you ever been to Temin?"

Raisa forced herself to show no visible reaction, though her insides all turned to ice at his words. "Temin, milord?" She looked up thoughtfully. "I can't say that I have ever had the pleasure. That's in... Palla, isn't it? I don't spend much time in Palla."

"A shame, it is a beautiful part of my empire," the Ar'Mol said, his tone disappointed. "I have a distant relative who lives in Temin."

"Oh?" Raisa took another tiny sip from the goblet, but her heart quickened, throbbing in her ears, and her face grew warm.

"Yes. Word reached me that he recently suffered a loss."

"My sympathies. Who died?"

"Not that kind of loss. His mercantile was robbed."

Raisa's hand flew to her mouth and her eyes grew wide, though she was certain the entire gesture looked as feigned as it was. "Robbed! How dreadful!"

"Yes, isn't it?" Uun said.

"His entire supply of leather was stolen," the Ar'Mol said, his voice quiet.

He knows. Raisa looked straight into his eyes. "How unfortunate," she said, keeping her tone casual. "It will be difficult for him to recover from such a loss, especially if leather is as scarce as you claim."

"Perhaps." The Ar'Mol sipped at his wine and a chill swept through Raisa's body. She risked a glance at the closed door and wondered if she had any chance of making it out of this dinner alive.

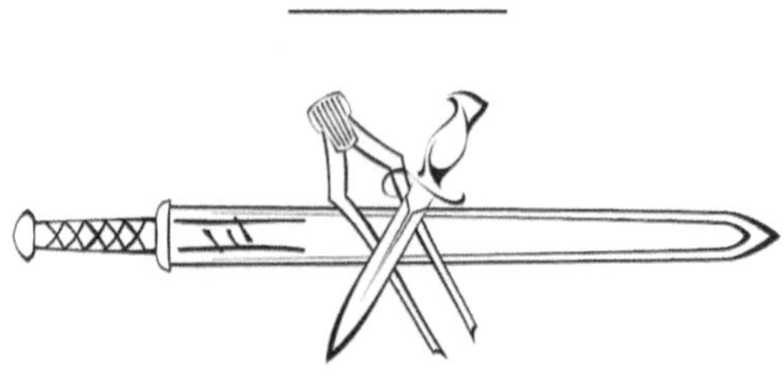

50

Enric and Beren finally returned, each bearing a brace of mountain hares. Grayden saw the tense expressions begin to relax as everyone began to realize there would be more than their meager rations to eat that evening. They were able to cook the meat and make a fairly tasty broth, but even this was not enough to truly defang the hunger gnawing in their bellies. They divided up the watches and bedded down for the night. The pile of brush burned down, and by morning everyone was stiff and cold in addition to being hungry. There was no breakfast except for a little bit of broth with cold meat and some herbs thrown in, and nothing to do but rise with the sun and begin the journey along the perilous cliff-side trail.

The trail widened a bit more and they found it not as treacherous as they had anticipated from that first glimpse, but the periodic rains that plagued their journey made the trail muddy and slick in places, so they had to pick their way along the trail slowly and carefully. They stopped frequently to rest, and every stop made Grayden chafe with worry. Koen was the worst off of all of them, and needed help to walk. He didn't have a fever, but his eyes held a worrisome glassy sheen.

As the sun crested above them and began its journey to meet

the western horizon, Grayden felt the familiar prickling sensation he used to get playing childish games with his friends. It was the feeling of being watched, but this time it contained a malevolence he had never before experienced. At the same time as this awareness rolled over him, Ioan straightened.

"This is where the entrance to Deer Valley used to be."

Grayden and the others peered at the spot he was indicating. There had not been a rockslide. Two trees, about thirty or forty spans tall, grew up from the path so close to the mountainside that it looked as if their bark had melded with the stony cliff. Their thick trunks stood side by side, at places with barely an inch's worth of gap between them, and their branches twined together up above. In places, it appeared that the branches of one tree had grown into the trunk of the other.

Ioan stared up at the trees, a strange expression on his face. After a long moment, he looked at Grayden. "Your family works with trees," he said. "How fast do they grow?"

"My family works with fruit trees," Grayden replied. "These are oaks, so I'm not as familiar with them. But I mean, one— maybe two—spans a year?"

"These trees weren't here a year ago," Ioan whispered. The color drained from his face. "This is all wrong. We have to get out of here, now!"

The prickling sensation on the back of Grayden's neck intensified. He remembered what Ioan had said about being attacked by trees, and he had seen the result of that attack. Suddenly, that story did not seem quite so far-fetched. Without questioning Ioan's statement, he motioned for the others to continue up the path, gesturing for them to be silent. They edged past the trees, when suddenly Enric let out a gasp.

"There is a valley through there," he said.

"Shh!" Ioan hissed, but it was too late.

A heavy limb slammed down on the ground, landing between them. Koen shouted with surprise as the trees creaked and separated. Grayden was never able to explain exactly what happened next. They heard a rustle of leaves and a creaking of wood and then a heavy beat like someone pounding on a door. Shouts of terror. Confusion. Running. His breath coming in short gasps, hot blood coursing its way through his temples, throbbing a painful rhythm. The sound of crashing branches pursued them, and then faded. Grayden slowed, daring to throw a glance over his shoulder. Nothing chased behind. He stopped, and the others slowed to a halt as well.

"What was that?" Enric asked, panting as he tried to catch his breath.

Koen, supported between Ioan and Beren, released his hold around their shoulders and dropped to the ground, grimacing painfully.

"Those... things... they are what attacked our camp," Ioan said. "I almost didn't believe it myself. I had half-convinced myself it was a dream created out of my fever." A shudder coursed through his body.

"Trees attacked the defenders?" Koen asked, his voice incredulous.

Ioan gave him a serious look. "You saw them moving with your own eyes just now."

Koen opened his mouth and then closed it.

"We have to go back," Beren suddenly announced.

They all stared at him in horror.

"What?" Koen burst out. "Those things killed an entire camp of defenders. We don't stand a chance against those... those... whatever those things are!"

"The defenders were taken by surprise," Beren argued.

"What if there are more of them?" Enric asked.

"What if there are?" Beren countered. "Why are we here?" He gazed around at each of his companions in turn. "Are we just cadets on a training exercise? Or are we here to prove that we are ready to defend Telmondir? There are many who would say that most of us shouldn't even be here, we are too young, we haven't had the proper amount of training. Well, we will prove them wrong. We're not here to do the bare minimum. Those creatures have already killed an entire squad of defenders. They have proven themselves to be a threat, and they cannot be allowed to remain in these mountains endangering our people. Even if we cannot defeat them, we can discover how many there are and bring that information to the commander at the Pass so that he and his men can deal with these creatures."

"Those things are unnatural." Ioan shook his head. "There isn't a defender alive who would blame you for turning away."

"I've faced unnatural things before." Beren glanced steadily at Wynn and Grayden.

Grayden, buoyed up by his friend's courage and solid assurance, gave Beren a firm nod. Of course, the unnatural things that Beren was referencing had been on their side in that fight, but he understood his friend's meaning.

Enric rubbed his hands together, pondering Beren's words. "I'm in," he said at length.

"I say we split up and enter the valley from two different angles," Ioan said. "Those trees that just attacked us seemed to be standing guard at the only easy access point."

"What do you think they're guarding?" Enric asked.

"I don't know," Ioan replied. "But we should find out as much as we can. I know of a few other ways to get down into the valley, but they are a little hard to get to."

Using a rock, Ioan drew a rough map in the dirt and described as best he could what they should look for. Studying the directions and committing them to memory, the cadets shouldered their gear and set off in two directions: Beren, Grayden, and Wynn in one group, Ioan, Enric, and Koen in the other. The late afternoon sun caused the outline of the mountains to loom above them stark and ominous.

It did not take Grayden's group long to arrive at the base of the cliff. Wynn was the best climber, so they sent him up first to see if he could find the opening Ioan had described. Wynn scrambled up nimbly. After a few moments, he changed direction and disappeared entirely from their view. Several minutes passed before he came sliding back down.

"There's a ledge up there that leads into the valley, though we will have to climb down into it, and it's a bit steeper on the inside. Climbing up is pretty easy, but we will need the rope to get down. I wouldn't want to try it without one," Wynn reported.

"Could you see anything inside the valley?" Grayden asked.

"It's small," Wynn replied. "There's a whole copse of trees, and the slopes are covered in grass and flowers: blue and yellow, mostly. And there's a cabin. Made of logs, thatched roof. I couldn't see any windows, but there's a door facing the cliff. I don't know if there's a door out the back."

"Did you see anything moving?" Beren asked.

Wynn shook his head. "No."

"Let's go," Beren rumbled. "Before we lose what little daylight we have left. But be careful. We don't want to get into a fight with creatures that wiped out an entire outpost of defenders."

The others nodded, their expressions serious. With Wynn showing the way, they scrambled up the cliff face. When they reached the top, Wynn took the rope and secured it to the ground with a piton.

"It's a good thing we recovered those packs from the avalanche," Wynn whispered, "or this entire mission would be impossible."

Grayden volunteered to go down first. Using the rope, he lowered himself into the valley, making as little noise as possible. When he reached the bottom, he waved the rope a bit to let the others know he had reached the valley floor. He looked around as he held the rope steady for Beren, who came down next. It was warmer here inside the shelter of the cliffs which arced up overhead and formed a sort of ceiling with a large opening at the center. Thick green grass, dotted with wildflowers, covered the ground. In spite of the snow in the surrounding mountains, spring had inexplicably arrived in this valley. Large boulders covered in moss stood in clumps around the edges of the clearing, and a few trees stood nearby, large and still. He eyed the nearest trees warily, but they gave no appearance of being anything but ordinary. He could not see the cabin from the ground, but Wynn had pointed it out from above, so Grayden knew it lay to the south.

Once Wynn had made it down, Grayden turned to Beren.

"What now?" he asked.

"Scout a bit," Beren whispered. "Wynn, you go that way. Grayden and I'll go this way." He gestured. "Stay out of sight."

"Right. Stay out of sight of the trees," Wynn whispered sarcastically as he began to creep in the direction Beren had pointed.

Grayden and Beren started on their way south, toward the cabin. Though the valley wasn't large, the rolling nature of the terrain and the clusters of trees and boulders meant they could not see Wynn on the other side.

They neared the cabin and paused, crouching down behind a large boulder. They peered out, taking stock of the scene before them. The little house faced south, and an oak tree stood at each of the front corners. Smoke puffed from the chimney, and they could hear someone talking inside, though they could not make out the words.

"Those trees look a lot like the ones that attacked us at the entrance to the valley," Grayden muttered.

"I'm going to try to get over there and see who's inside the cabin," Beren whispered.

Before Grayden could stop him, the young giant had skirted the boulder and was stealing up to the cabin from the back. Grayden felt his heart racing as Beren poked his head up to peer inside the window. In the waning light, Grayden could not see his friend's expression, though he half-expected to hear a shout of alarm at any moment, but none came. Beren crouched back down and a moment later came creeping back to their hiding place.

"Who's in there?" Grayden asked.

"It's an old man," Beren said. "He's sitting inside at a table. At first I thought he was talking to someone else, but he's alone.

Then I thought he was talking to himself. But he's not. He's got one of those orbs, like the ones Dalmir has, but it's green. Kind of a sickly green. He's talking to it. Or... maybe not talking to it, just sort of muttering to himself while staring at it."

Grayden frowned. "What is he saying?"

"Mostly nonsense. Something about having generals and how he needs more of them. He seemed to think more had arrived, but he wanted to be careful. He said his power was growing, but that he's not yet strong enough to challenge the master."

A prickling dread crawled over Grayden's scalp. "He knows we're here."

"How do you know that?" Beren asked.

"Those walking trees are not natural," Grayden replied. "And we've seen what those orbs can do: things that shouldn't be possible. What if he made them somehow? What if the trees are his 'generals'?"

"And if he's talking about more generals arriving..." Beren trailed off, his eyes widening with horror.

"Trees don't arrive... but we did. What if..." Grayden stopped as a truly horrible thought occurred to him, freezing his blood even as he blurted it out without pausing to consider. "What if these moving trees used to be people?"

"Not possible," Beren replied, but his face turned ashen at the thought.

"Ah, but you see, it is possible. Your friend is quite right." A sly, silvery voice made them grab for their weapons. "Come, come, you will not need those," the speaker continued. An old man had approached the boulder they were crouched behind and now stood a few paces away, a benevolent smile on his face. Thin and wiry, his shoulders hunched slightly, and white-blond hair stuck up from his head in wild tufts. Grayish skin stretched tight across his face, as if he had never had enough food to eat in his life, but only just enough to keep him alive. Grayden could not tell how old the man was, he seemed at once both ancient and youthful. His expression invited them to relax, to remain calm, to remember that they were all friends, but the hard, calculating glint of his eyes shook Grayden to the bone.

"Who are you?" Beren asked, raising his enormous sword and leveling it at the man.

"Names are such a ridiculous custom," the man replied. "I am myself, and no one else. I may be called Lorcan, but so may others, but I am none of them, and none of them are me. So what point is it to know my name if by it you cannot determine anything of value? But let us not talk of such meaningless banalities, when a far more stimulating topic can be discussed. My generals. I understand that you have met them? Met them, have you?"

"If you are speaking of the trees that wander about attacking innocent travelers, then yes," Beren rumbled angrily.

Lorcan, if that was his name, rubbed his hands together and grinned, his dark eyes sparkling. "Yes, yes, those are my generals. I am rather proud of them. Proud of them, yes. They were merely a first attempt, you see. I hadn't worked with trees before. Well, no, that is a lie, I had worked with trees, but just normal ones, making them grow where they wouldn't have grown on their own." He chuckled. "Grown on their own!" He grinned a delighted, lopsided smile that showed slightly crooked teeth. "Spontaneous, unintended rhymes," he whispered, "one of the seven signs of true genius. But you can spot a genius better by his workmanship, and mine is evident in my generals."

"You said my friend was right about them," Beren said. "How is that possible?"

Lorcan smirked. "That was a supremely exceptional bit of brilliance," he replied. "I blended them."

"Blended?" Grayden asked, trying to keep the man talking. If it was true that this madman had use of one of Dalmir's orbs, then fighting was out of the question. But perhaps they could escape through a different means.

"Blended," Lorcan repeated himself. "Yes, I took a man and gave him all the strengths of a tree. Of course, in order to do that,

I also had to give the tree all the strengths of the man. But as I explained to him, it was a truly beautiful arrangement."

Beren's face drained of color. "That's monstrous."

"Is it?" Lorcan stared at him quizzically. "Perhaps it is. I suppose the trees might not enjoy the process, but I am giving them mobility."

Beren sputtered. "I meant for the people you trap inside the trees!"

Lorcan waved a hand. "People are everywhere. There are so many of them, nobody will even notice they are missing. Nobody noticed before, why should they now?"

"Before? I thought you said this was the first experiment," Grayden asked, feigning interest as his eyes darted about, searching for a way they could escape.

"I said it was the first time I'd worked with trees," Lorcan corrected him. "Trees were easier, oddly enough. I would never have expected that." He shrugged.

"Easier than what?" Beren asked, catching on to what Grayden was attempting to do.

"Leythan." Lorcan's face darkened as his gaze wandered. "Those experiments did not go well. No, I did not get what I needed then." His attention snapped back to them.

Grayden shivered. The dark eyes were alight with an intelligent gleam, but also wild with unfettered insanity. Lorcan's lips twitched in a smile.

"If you are so interested in the process, perhaps a demonstration is required." Lorcan reached into the pouch hanging from his belt and pulled out an object that shone with an emerald glow, reminding Grayden of hours spent lying in his family's orchards and looking up at the leaves with the sun shining through them. Lorcan raised the orb and there was the sound of hissing as two vines slithered across the valley floor and rose up behind him. Dangling by their feet from the vines hung Enric, Wynn, and Koen.

"Run!" Enric shouted, before a tendril of vine wrapped itself around his mouth.

"No," Grayden whispered. He frantically wondered what had become of Ioan. Clearly the other group had made it into the valley, but he dared not look for the defender, lest he give away Ioan's position.

"Shall I show you how it works?" Lorcan asked.

"No!" Grayden's voice erupted. "Let them go."

"I'm afraid I can't do that." The madness faded from Lorcan's voice and he spoke with precise, deadly calm. "I need more generals for my master. You understand." He waved the orb and roots crawled up out of the ground and began twisting up toward Enric and Wynn. They struggled in their bonds, straining to get away as the roots wound up the vines and then down around their feet and slowly worked their way down their legs.

Despair built within Grayden. With a loud, wordless cry, he leapt away from the boulder, sword drawn. He raced to his friends and hacked at the vines holding them prisoner. Behind him, Beren rushed to his aid, his great sword ringing as it sliced through vines.

Lorcan watched them for a moment, then gestured once more. Wynn shouted in terror. He had managed to get his sword arm free and he now hacked furiously at the roots, scraping them off, but they grew back as fast as he could chop them away. Beren and Grayden soon found themselves fighting a similar battle. Koen struggled against the vines and got one hand free, but he held no weapon. Grayden tossed him his dagger. Koen caught it and began digging it into the vines, which recoiled from the blade and began to loosen.

Lorcan's voice rose in a wail. "I thought you understood! Your questions... were you truly interested in my work, or was it all deception?" He sighed, shaking his head sadly. "It does not matter, I suppose. I will make of you such generals."

"And me?" A new voice filled with intense fury made Lorcan spin around. "What did you intend to make of me?"

Ioan stood silhouetted in the gathering twilight. His eyes burned with an intense fury. Lorcan stared at him, his expression mildly curious. Then his gaze sharpened and the corners of his mouth twitched.

"What have you done to me?" Ioan shouted. Without waiting for an answer, he gripped the boulder before him, his fingers digging into the stone and cracking it in half. With a bellow of rage, he lifted the chunk of stone and hurled it at Lorcan's head. The madman dodged to the side just in time, and the missile sailed past him and smashed against the side of the cabin. Grayden stared at the defender, unable to believe what he had just seen.

"Ioan?" Beren choked, slashing away the roots trying to climb up his body.

"I remember you!" Lorcan's eyes widened in awe. "I did not think it would work, but look at you. You are magnificent! A masterpiece! It worked! Finally... after all this time... I have done it!"

Koen and Wynn wriggled in their bonds, their eyes wide and terrified. The vines covered their mouths, but did not completely silence their muffled, panicked voices. The roots had crept up their bodies, completely encasing them up to their waists in wooden caskets. Their efforts with their blades became more frantic. Enric's eyes were closed and he hung from his vine with a worrying stillness. Without sparing a glance in their direction, Ioan drew his sword and advanced upon Lorcan.

"My generals!" Lorcan's voice pierced the air. "My generals, defend me!"

The valley filled with a deep rumble as eight trees converged on their location. The ones closest to the cabin roused and surged forward, one of them reaching out with an arm-like branch, sweeping a powerful blow at Ioan. The defender leaped nimbly over the branch and then spun, cleaving the branch from the tree with a single, powerful stroke of his hand-axe. The tree shrieked, a horrible, grating cry of agony that was all the more terrible for its being almost human in sound, and yet there was an otherly quality to it that sent a shudder through the valley. Ioan snarled back, his own voice altered in some inexplicable way, and plunged forward, his blade chopping into the tree's trunk. Chips flew and the tree shrieked again, lurching back, away from Ioan's axe. The tree creature lashed out, striking at Ioan with its branches, but the man evaded every blow, moving with impossible swiftness.

Grayden freed one of his legs, and then the other. He raced over to Wynn, who stared at him and made desperate sounds through the vines across his mouth. Beren wrenched himself free of his own bonds and raced to Enric, who hung silent, his eyes closed as the roots snaked their way up to his chin. Nearby, Koen dropped to the ground, having freed himself with Grayden's dagger. He tossed it back to Grayden with a grin and swept his own sword out of its sheath.

"Behind you!" Koen shouted.

Grayden whirled as the tree-creatures approached, his sword ready, but paused as they lumbered past him without stopping. He wondered why they had ignored him, but did not question this stroke of good fortune. He turned back to his friends just as Beren gave a mighty swing with his sword and severed the roots swirling around Enric from their source. With another blow, Beren chopped through the wooden chrysalis holding Wynn; he pried the roots apart and Wynn slipped out, free of his bonds. He fell to the ground, gasping for air. A moment later, Enric was also free, but unconscious. Wynn put his ear near the older cadet's mouth.

"He's not breathing." Wynn began pressing his hands on Enric's chest.

"No!" Lorcan's voice rang out in a scream of rage. "My new generals! They are escaping. You and you, capture them. The rest of you, protect your master."

"Time to go," Beren hissed.

"But Ioan..." Grayden began, turning to see the defender whirling his blade and running along the branches of one of the trees and into the next, slashing and chopping with the axe, and then diving through the air to land nimbly on the ground while limbs and bark rained down all around him.

"He has it handled," Beren shouted, his tone filled with awe. "We must run." He slapped Enric's face. "Wake up! Enric! Wake up!"

Enric did not move. Grayden stared down at the older cadet, the blood pounding in his ears. His vision grew suddenly narrow and dark, filled with a gloom that had nothing to do with the setting of the sun. A buzzing sensation like a score of wasps inside his skull throbbed in his temples. Wynn pounded on Enric's chest. Koen knelt at their prone friend's side, checking for a pulse. Beren's mouth moved as he shouted at the older cadet, but Grayden could not hear any of it.

Something collided with his back, throwing Grayden to the ground. Instinctively, he tucked his shoulder and rolled away as he had been taught, springing back to his feet with his sword up in a defensive posture just as the tree-creature swung another branch at his head. Grayden's sword sliced through the branch as he twisted away from the blow. As the limb fell to the ground, Grayden winced, wondering what that blow had just done to the edge of his blade and wishing he had a hand-axe, but Ioan was currently wielding the only one that had not been lost in the avalanche.

The other tree attacked his friends. Beren, Wynn, and Koen formed a protective half-circle over Enric's still body, holding the creature at bay. Their blades flashed as they cut at the roots and the branches indiscriminately, but nothing they did appeared to faze the monster.

Then Beren heaved forward, his massive sword driving into the trunk, plunging through the heart of the tree in a single blow. The creature groaned like a timber creaking in the wind and stood still.

Grayden evaded another branch and chopped again with his sword. This time, the blade bounced off the wood and he staggered back slightly, his palms stinging from the force of the blow.

The tree advanced and Grayden fell back, sliding his feet cautiously as he went. He was not sure exactly where he was in relation to the cabin, and did not want to find himself trapped up against it. He spared a glance to where Ioan was fighting and saw to his dismay that the defender was being herded up against the mountainside, hemmed in by five of the creatures. Despite the trail of branches and leaves on the ground, the monsters appeared no worse for the destruction Ioan had wreaked upon them. Grayden's spirits sank as he blocked another blow and parried, his blade connecting solidly with a branch and sinking into it. For a desperate moment, he could not free his sword, and he yanked at it urgently. A branch slammed against his head; his grip on the sword was the only thing that saved him from falling to the ground. He wrenched the blade out of the cut he had made and stumbled forward.

Then Beren stood next to him. He raised his sword high and plunged it into the tree. An inhuman scream rose up into the air, but Beren gritted his teeth and pushed harder, driving the blade further into the heart of the trunk. When the sword was buried to the hilt, the scream turned into a pitiful whimper, and then a hissing sound surrounded him, like a susurration of wind rattling through the last dead leaves clinging to a branch, and the tree ceased moving.

"Thank you."

The words, whispered near his ear, startled Grayden into nearly dropping his own sword. He looked up and saw an image carved in the trunk just above his head: the barest outline of a face. The carving pressed outward, becoming more identifiable: it was a man's face, twisted in agony. The eyes blinked a single, long, slow blink as they stared out, and then it receded, and there was simply a smooth patch where the bark had been worn away. The tree stood immobile.

"Did you hear... did you see that?" Grayden asked as Beren yanked his sword free.

His friend nodded grimly. "Come," Beren said.

"But..." Grayden stared up at the tree for a moment longer, then he stumbled after Beren, sickened by what he had just seen and heard. "Beren, what you did was incredible."

Beren shrugged. "My blade is of good quality."

Grayden did not have time to argue that even the best quality blade would not have allowed him to stab through an entire tree, for now they stood at the cabin door where Wynn and Koen had dragged Enric to a sort of relative safety. The four friends turned to watch the battle taking place in the clearing. Lorcan had advanced on Ioan, the glittering green orb held aloft in his hand as he commanded his remaining "generals."

"We need to help him," Beren said. "If we can take Lorcan out, perhaps the generals will stop."

The others gave him a nod and they stepped away from the cabin. Before they could move toward Lorcan, however, Ioan's voice rang out.

"No! Get out of here!" He waved a hand at them.

They hesitated, staring at the dark form of the defender. Ioan hefted his hand-axe and then swung it wide for a moment, pointing.

"What do we do?" Wynn asked.

"To the entrance," Beren barked. "Ioan has a plan. I'm not sure what it is, but I think he needs us out of the way."

"Right," Koen agreed.

Together they raced across the valley floor, making their way back to the rope dangling down the cliff-side. Wynn got there first and scrambled up, followed by Grayden, then Koen, and finally Beren came, carrying the limp body of Enric over his shoulder as the others helped haul him up. Behind them, they heard a sound like the swift rapids coming down out of the mountains during a spring thaw, a rumble not unlike the sound the avalanche had made. Wynn pointed across the valley.

"Look!"

Enormous pieces of the cliffside had suddenly come loose and were sliding down into the valley. They watched, breathless, as boulders and rocks crashed down through the trees in an unstoppable flood, knocking them over and sweeping them along in its flow like a waterfall pouring down the side of the mountain. A cloud of dust billowed up at the bottom of the slide, growing larger and larger until it had obscured the cabin and much of the valley floor from their view.

"How did Ioan manage that?" Wynn breathed.

"If he survived, he has quite a few questions to answer," Beren said, his voice firm.

51

Marik stood at the taffrail and gazed at the roof of the palace, just visible in the distance above the other buildings around it. They had packed up their merchant booth for the evening and retired to the *Gilded Petunia*, where they awaited Raisa's return. Oleck came up the companionway and stood by Marik. A thick humidity filled the air and a heavy cloud cover obscured the moon, making the night seem darker and more ominous than it had any right to be. Unease brimmed in Marik's thoughts as he watched the empty road coming from the palace.

"She should be back by now," Marik said.

"She'll be okay, Captain," Oleck assured him.

"I hope you're right," Marik began. Then he paused, his ears catching a faint sound that echoed with familiarity in his memory. He cocked his head, straining to listen. Why was that sound so familiar? Suddenly, his eyes widened. "Cut us loose," he barked at Oleck. "Now!" He spun on his heel, shouting for Shaesta and Mouse, who came scrambling up the steps at his call.

Oleck did not question the order, but pulled a small hand-axe from his belt and swiftly chopped through the lines securing the airship to its dock. Marik slid down the ladder to the helm and threw the lever that activated the cynders in the engine room. The trim sails on either side of the ship flared out, the gentle hum of the activated cynders throbbing through the deck beneath his feet. Marik pulled the ship's wheel toward his chest, expecting the surge of speed he usually got when they lifted off the ground. Instead, the little airship lumbered up out of her dock, complaining with loud groans. Marik cursed the added weight of the false hull.

He felt the familiar thrum of vibration as the cynder down in the engine room activated and sent power up into the sails and rudder. He glanced up at the mainsail battens. Two crimson ribbons fluttered there and Marik took note of the direction they were pointing.

By the time the airship had ascended a good fifty feet into the air, the sound that had caught Marik's attention could be heard by the rest of the crew: the rhythmic thumping of many feet marching together. A moment later, a regiment of soldiers came into view. They marched up to the docks with confident arrogance that turned briefly to confusion as they realized their quarry was no longer neatly docked and waiting for them to seize her. From where he stood at the wheel, Marik could not see what was happening below, but he did not need to.

"Oleck, trim the mainsail," he barked. "Shaesta, make sure everyone's anchor lines are secure."

His crew reacted to his orders with the ease and efficiency that came with years of familiarity. Marik allowed himself a tight grin of pride as he turned the wheel, adjusting the trim sails so that they would catch the wind across their bow. Their timing would need to be nearly perfect if they were to get away, but he had captured a few precious minutes of a jump start on their pursuers. He only hoped it would be enough. If they could catch the wind and make it into the safety of the clouds, he knew they could outrun any Igyeum ship in the Ar'Mol's armada, but the trick was getting there.

As they gained altitude, Marik spotted Mouse at the rail.

"Scout below," he shouted over the sound of the sails catching the stiff breeze. "What's the status of the troops?"

Mouse leaned over the rail, confident in the anchor line attached to his harness. "They're boarding a ship and powering her up, Cap'n!"

He had a few more minutes of open sky. Everything depended on those minutes. Marik adjusted their angle of ascent, heading for the thick cloud cover. The whistling sound of the other airship leaping into the sky caught his ears. At the same moment, he felt the *Hawk* leap forward as they caught the wind he had been aiming for. He aimed the prow of the ship with practiced ease, as though their lives did not hang precariously on the angle of their heading being exact.

"What about Raisa?" Mouse asked, his face pale in the darkness.

"We'll come back for her, lad," Marik said. Then he raised his voice and bellowed across the deck. "Oleck, ease the sheet slightly."

"Aye," Oleck shouted back.

"Shaesta, check the vang."

"Aye, Cap'n!"

"They're giving chase, Captain!" Mouse shouted.

But at that moment, the sails caught the wind and the *Valdeun Hawk* shot forward with the breathtaking speed of her namesake. Marik could not restrain the wild exultant laugh that billowed from his lips as his airship sped her way into the safe haven of the thick clouds, leaving the warship far behind.

52

Burdened with Enric's lifeless body, the cadets made their slow, weary way out of the valley. They had searched the rubble, but had been unable to find any trace of Ioan, so they trudged back to the hiding place they had started out from.

Miserably, they laid Enric's body to one side and started a small campfire.

"Do you think Ioan made it out?" Koen asked.

"Yes," Beren said. His glower made everyone loath to say any more on the subject.

"What are we going to do about Enric?" Wynn asked after a few minutes of silence. "It doesn't feel right to bury him out here, so far from his family and homeland, but we can't very well carry his body with us."

"We will give him a defender's burial." Ioan's voice startled them. He stepped into the glow of the firelight, his hands raised. They were empty. He was covered in dust and had a few scratches on his face and hands, but otherwise looked healthy. The cadets stepped back as he walked forward. They watched him warily as he knelt beside Enric and put a gentle, grimy hand on the cadet's forehead.

Grayden stared, uncertain as to whether he ought to be overjoyed to see the defender, or afraid. What Ioan had done in the valley... Grayden's train of thought stalled. What had Ioan done? How had he moved so swiftly? What had triggered the rockslide? What had Lorcan meant and why had Ioan seemed so certain that the madman had done something to him?

"Travel in peace, young warrior," Ioan whispered to Enric. Then he stood and surveyed the camp.

Scrape, scrape, scrape. Beren did not look up or stop his work on his blade.

"You survived, then." Beren's voice was rough.

"I did," Ioan replied.

"Took your time getting back here."

"I had a few things I needed to do."

The others backed away slightly, giving the two of them space.

"You have some explaining to do," Beren said. He lifted the sword from his lap and examined it, running his finger carefully along the edges. He laid it down again and continued working.

Ioan lifted his hands in a gesture of helplessness. "I'm not sure how to explain something I don't understand myself."

"Try." Beren's voice was hard.

Ioan sat down on the ground by the fire and motioned for the others to join him. He paused. "I knew something was wrong when I woke up at the outpost and found half of my charges had left. Peder expressed amazement at how quickly I had healed, but I found it hard to believe I had been hurt as badly as he said. I couldn't remember the attack at all, or even being injured in the first place. It wasn't until Grayden repeated the account of Peder and Beren setting my leg that I realized my injuries shouldn't have healed as quickly as they did." He pulled up the leg of his pants and showed them the spot where the bone had been sticking through the skin. They all gasped. The wound had healed completely. The only sign that the leg had ever been injured was a strange, rough appearance to the skin where a scar should have been. "It still hurt to walk on it, but I could tell it wasn't broken," Ioan continued. "I knew how easily even well-trained defenders could get lost in these mountains, so I left Peder in charge at the outpost and came after you."

"Why didn't you say anything?" Beren asked, wiping the blade with a cloth and picking up his whetstone.

"I didn't know what to say," Ioan replied. "I didn't know what was happening or why, and to be honest, I was a little afraid to find out."

Beren nodded, running the sword along the whetstone in a long, even stroke.

"When we were attacked at the entrance to the valley, some of my lost memories began to return. I remembered the attack on the camp more clearly. And I remembered a man, a strange old man with white-blond hair and an ageless face. I remembered lying on the snow with him bending over me. I remember looking into his eyes and thinking that here was a man locked in madness." Ioan licked his lips, his voice rasping. Grayden passed him a waterskin and he drank thirstily. "He did something to my leg, and then said, 'Let's try something new. If you survive, perhaps you will be the breakthrough I've been searching for. You probably won't survive, though. Pity.' And then he laughed and walked away."

"Lorcan," Beren said. He took out a rough cloth, poured a little water on it, and began wiping it down the edge of the blade very slowly.

"Yes." Ioan nodded. "Whatever he did to me, it was different from what he did to those poor creatures we fought. I don't know what he intended, or if the process is even complete."

"What happened after we left the valley?" Grayden asked. "We saw the rockslide."

"I set that off. I can..." Ioan hesitated. "Apparently, I can talk to plants and make them move a bit if I concentrate. I... I called to the plants. Well, to their roots, mostly. I asked them to help dislodge the rocks... and... they did."

They stared at him. Ioan shrugged. "Anyway, Lorcan fled into his cabin. The rocks buried his generals and the cabin with Lorcan inside."

"What's wrong?" Beren asked, putting away his polishing cloth and sheathing his sword.

"After the dust settled, I went down into the valley and tried to find Lorcan's body. I wanted to be certain," Ioan said. He scowled, and his hand clenched into a fist. "But what was left of the cabin was empty. I don't know how he escaped. But I'm sure he did."

"This is information the defenders need to know," Beren said. "Especially if Lorcan survived."

"I agree," Ioan replied. "Beren, I am sorry I did not say anything sooner. I'm sorry I let there be a wall between us since I graduated. We've been friends since we were young, like cousins, and that should have counted for something."

Beren stood. "There are barriers between the cadets and the defenders for a reason. I do not begrudge you that." He came over and stretched out his hand, clasping Ioan's forearm. "I just wish you would have trusted us more, that is all."

"I should have." Ioan clasped Beren's arm in return. "Forgive me, brother?"

Beren nodded soberly. "Of course."

———

STARVING, bedraggled, and heartsick, the five weary men finally stumbled through the gates of the Fort Pass. The captain of the outpost greeted them with some consternation that grew as he listened to their tale, his expression growing more sober with each word. When they had finished, he questioned Ioan further about all that had occurred, then sent a scouting party to Deer Valley to investigate their story and see if they could find any trace of the madman. He also dispatched a squad to travel to the Storvas Outpost and retrieve Hamil, Arven, Peder, and Zarek, who returned with two of the defenders to the Fort several days later, where they were greeted somberly by their comrades and informed of the loss of Enric.

They were a mournful group, despite the captain of the Fort's attempts to comfort them, and they spent many long evenings around their table in the mess hall reminiscing about their fallen companion and sharing stories about him.

On the twelfth morning after arriving at the Fort, Grayden, Wynn, and Beren stood on one of the high walls. The sky was still dark, but the horizon was rimmed with the early light promising dawn was on her way.

"I don't know if I'll ever get rid of this gnawing hunger," Wynn said, munching on a hard biscuit. "I can't seem to get full, no matter how much I eat."

"It will pass," Grayden assured him.

"Do you think they'll find him?" Beren asked.

"Lorcan?" Grayden replied, gazing out at the mountainous terrain beyond the wall. "I hope so. But something tells me they won't."

"Something tells me the same," Ioan said, coming up onto the walkway behind them. He continued to bear the marks of his ordeal, though it was unclear just how far the transformation would continue to progress. His skin had darkened a few shades more, and the strange tattoos were more noticeable, as well. "However Lorcan escaped from that cabin, he's long gone by now. But I doubt we've seen the last of him."

"How are you holding up?" Beren asked.

A shadow flitted behind Ioan's eyes, but he grinned. "I'm adjusting."

"Are you..." Beren walked closer to Ioan. "Taller?"

Grayden let out a low whistle as Beren stood side-by-side with his childhood friend. When they had met him at the Academy just a few lunats ago, Ioan had been quite a bit shorter than Beren. "Ioan's taller by an inch, now," Grayden said.

"I told you," Wynn said. "I told you he was taller."

Ioan shrugged. "That's just part of the adjustment. I need

new clothes." He tugged self-consciously at his too-short sleeves. The backs of his hands and his arms stuck out, revealing the dark lines that now adorned his entire body except his face and the palms of his hands. He flexed an arm. "The added strength is nice, but it's been hard to get used to."

"Your eyes are greener, too," Wynn added. "They're almost grass green now; before they were darker."

"Grandmother might have a hard time recognizing me," Ioan said with a rueful grimace. "They say being a defender changes you... but I'm not sure this is what they meant."

They chuckled softly together, but were interrupted by the tromp of boots below.

"Lord Adelfried has arrived and is waiting to speak with the cadets in the parade ground," a defender called up the ladder.

"Father!" Beren took a few running steps and swung down the ladder, the others following close behind.

"Dalmir!" Grayden called out as they entered the all-too familiar muddy yard where training happened inside the fort and caught sight of the two older men waiting for them. He started to run across the open square, then hesitated, wondering what the protocol for this moment was.

Beren, a few steps ahead of him, did not pause, but ran straight to his father and enveloped him in a hearty embrace. The other cadets emerged from the barracks, wiping sleep from their eyes and the crumbs of breakfast from their mouths. Adelfried held his son tightly, and then released him, hands on his shoulders.

"I am proud of you, my son," he said. He raised his eyes and swept them over the young men assembled before him and frowned. "Headmaster Freidzen said there were nine assigned to the mission this year?"

Beren nodded, his shoulders falling. "Enric Ghunrad was among the fallen."

Lord Adelfried's eyebrows climbed his forehead and his gaze sharpened. "Among the fallen? Tell me what happened."

Once again, the task of telling the tale fell to Beren. The others stood in an uncomfortable semi-circle in the cool air of the morning. As Beren spoke, each of them relived the worst moments of the past sennights all over again. The brutal scene at the bivouac. The avalanche. The fight in Deer Valley. The hunger. The pain. The injuries. The uncertainty. The loss of friends. Hamil, Arven, Peder, and Zarek shifted uncomfortably through the recounting; Zarek had confided in Grayden that all four of them felt guilty for staying behind at the outpost, wondering if they could have made a difference in the fight with Lorcan.

"Do you think Enric might be alive now if we had stayed together?" Zarek had asked.

Grayden tried to assure him that there was nothing they could have done, but he knew that all four of those left behind remained unconvinced.

Dalmir listened silently, not saying a word to interrupt, though his expression grew dark when Beren mentioned the glowing green jewel that Lorcan had employed.

As Beren's tale came to a close, Ioan joined them. He nodded to Lord Adelfried, who nodded back formally and then stopped, staring.

"Ioan? Is that you?"

The defender moved forward, and Grayden marveled at how smooth and silent his every motion had become. He glided forward with unconscious and unpracticed grace.

"Your son speaks the truth, as impossible as it may be to believe. I stand here as the proof," Ioan said. He stretched out his arms, showing the pattern etched in his skin.

"Son," Adelfried choked, clasping his hands to Ioan's upper arms. Sudden tears appeared in Lord Adelfried's eyes. "It seems unjust in the extreme to be the one to bring you this news, on top of all you have suffered already, but I come bearing sad tidings."

"Grandmother?" Ioan asked, his voice catching in his throat. "What happened?"

"Not here," Adelfried said. "I can give you the news in private."

Ioan gestured to the assembled cadets. "These men have become my brothers, Uncle Thorben. You may speak openly."

Adelfried looked around. "Perhaps it is best to hear it with friends, then," he agreed. "I am sorry, but your grandmother has gone on her final journey."

Ioan bowed his head, and tears streamed down his face. "How did it happen?"

"It was murder. Three assassins attacked her in her private library. She killed two of them herself."

Ioan looked up, his green eyes shining. "Grandmother always was fierce as a malkyn and tough as a leythan."

"That she was."

"What of the third attacker? Has he been brought to justice?"

"He got away and the trail has gone cold," Thorben admitted. "But we are not giving up."

"Good." Ioan bowed his head again and a moment of silence descended on the grounds. When he looked up again, his eyes were steely. "I believe you have a ceremony to complete, Uncle."

Lord Adelfried nodded and turned back to the cadets. "Ioan, sound the call."

Ioan let out a piercing battle cry, and all around the yard, the defenders who maintained the outpost appeared. Dressed in their full uniforms, they entered the parade ground and stood in a stoic ring around the cadets.

"Cadets, stand forth," Adelfried commanded, his voice ringing out in the crisp morning air.

As one, the cadets stepped forward.

"There is little glory that comes with accepting the mantle of defender, though it is a heavy responsibility, thus there is little pomp that goes with the ceremony of bestowing it," Lord Adelfried said, each word ringing with severe authority. "The mission you just completed is but the first of many such duties. There are many more days of hunger, cold, discomfort, pain, and loss before you. I warn you now, there will be little gratitude and little recognition for your sacrifice. But it is a worthy and honorable duty, and one I think every defender here would tell you comes with its own rewards." He paused. "As graduates—" And here Lord Adelfried caught the gaze of each cadet in turn. "As graduates from the Academy you are now bound for the duration of your vow, a minimum of two years of service from this day." His eyes scanned over their faces. "Kneel."

All eight cadets lowered themselves to their knees. Lord Adelfried surveyed them with a look of pride.

"Ioan." Lord Adelfried nodded.

The captain took his place before the cadets. He strode down the line, stopping to pin the iron chevrons on each of their collars. "As one of those tasked to train you for the Storvas Mission, I am confident that Captain Tomasson would tell Lord Adelfried that this group of young men has excelled and surpassed the hopes and expectations of the Academy, and I wholeheartedly concur. Our brother Enric—this year's first graduate—today stands tall in the brotherhood of heroic defenders gone before, all of whom stand proud with you today. All bear witness that you are worthy."

Lord Adelfried gave a solemn nod. "Kneeling as students, arise now as defenders. Well done, men. Well done."

53

His new uniform was uncomfortable. But Grayden had to admit the discomfort was mostly in his head. The dark green wool waistcoat bore gleaming silver buttons that went up the jacket in a diagonal line from his left hip to his right shoulder; it fit him perfectly. The light gray shirt and dark gray trousers were made of a soft, comfortable fabric and allowed for ease of motion. The shining black boots that came up to his knee and folded down were well-made from supple leather that both protected his feet and allowed him to feel connected to the ground. He stood before the mirror and frowned. Then his eyes lit on the dark iron chevron on his collar that marked him as a second lieutenant and the frown faded; he straightened, pride coursing through him.

"I've been told one gets used to the formal uniform." Beren stood in the doorway, smiling. He entered the room and gave Grayden a wink. "And that it only takes a few years, because you'll wear it so rarely."

Grayden chuckled. "It still doesn't seem real."

Beren polished a button with his thumb. "My head is still spinning, too," he confided. "It all happened so fast."

"I knew we were on an accelerated schedule, but I didn't quite realize..." Grayden was interrupted by the arrival of Wynn.

"The scouts that were sent to Deer Valley returned," Wynn reported. "They verified what Ioan said, Lorcan escaped. They found a tunnel hidden inside the house, but when they tried to go down and explore, there was a cave-in and the tunnel was completely filled." He fidgeted in his new uniform, pulling at the collar and looking miserable. "Just how required is the uniform?" he asked. "I've never seen Ioan wear one. It itches."

Grayden scowled. "That's not good. I don't like the idea of Lorcan out there somewhere, running his experiments on others and creating weapons to use against us."

"What makes you think that is his purpose?" Wynn asked, still wiggling his shoulders and tugging at his uniform. "I don't like these clothes."

"I spent some time speaking with Dalmir," Grayden replied. "He believes the Ar'Mol is using the orbs. Marik brought him to one of their cynder refineries. It seems an orb like Dalmir's was used to create the cynders, that's how they work, and that's why our engineers can't replicate them." He glanced at Wynn, who was undoing the buttons at his collar. "Wynn, not until after Lord Adelfried gives us our assignments."

Wynn wrinkled his nose, but let his hand drop from the buttons at his throat. Instead, he let his hands fall at his sides and nervously tapped his fingers against his thigh.

Beren crossed his arms and sat down in the room's one chair. "That explains rather a lot. Just how many of these orbs are there?"

"Seven," Dalmir answered as he stepped through the doorway.

"Seven?" Wynn asked, startled.

"For seven brothers," Dalmir replied. "We created them, my brothers and I, objects of great power keyed specifically to each one of us, that only we could use. When my brothers perished, I never dreamed I'd see their power at work in the world, never imagined their orbs could be used again. But Uun appears to have found a way."

The three men stared at him.

"You have six brothers?" Wynn asked.

"Had," Dalmir replied mildly. "Only one remains, and he betrayed us all. Now he works for the Ar'Mol, or perhaps the Ar'Mol works for him—that seems the more likely possibility. Uun never was content to be anywhere other than the top. It irked him no end that he wasn't firstborn. As for the orbs, I have two of them in my possession. From what evidence I have seen, my brother has two as well."

"Your brother works with the Ar'Mol?" Beren asked, still playing catch-up with this suddenly chatty Dalmir.

"Yes," Dalmir nodded.

"What evidence?" Wynn asked.

"The cynders bear the mark of my brother Palte. The tree-folk you described, while warped and twisted, bear the mark of Avaleun. And it is reasonable to assume Uun also has his own orb hidden away somewhere. That leaves two of them unaccounted for and I must search for them."

"Why?" Grayden asked. "What can you do with them?"

"Mostly, I can keep them out of Uun's hands," Dalmir said. "More than that... I do not know. I will most likely need your help figuring that out, young Grayden."

"Me?"

"Yes. It was you who first revealed to me that my knowledge of how the orbs work is incomplete. But not now. You will be getting your first assignments as defenders, and I must search for the missing orbs. I cannot allow him to twist any more of our brothers' legacies to his own foul schemes."

"How do you know the other two orbs haven't been destroyed?" Beren asked.

"They haven't," Dalmir said, his tone confident. "Nothing on Turrim could destroy them. Of that much, I am confident."

"How are you going to find something so small?" Wynn asked.

"I have a few ideas of where to begin." Dalmir did not offer any further information.

"Did you come to say goodbye, then?" Grayden asked, a sudden sadness welling up within him.

"For now." The older man gazed at each of them fondly. "I cannot help but feel a certain amount of pride in your accomplishments. I am certain that you will do well in all your future endeavors. I hope our paths cross again soon."

A trumpet sounded from somewhere outside the room and Grayden turned to the door. He glanced at his friends and gave Wynn a stern look when he saw him fidgeting with his buttons again.

"Well," Beren said, taking a deep breath. "This is it."

"We'll probably get relegated to some remote outpost," Wynn said with a forced laugh.

Beren gave him a puzzled look.

"Best not to get our hopes up too high for good assignments right out of the barn," Wynn explained. "We're the lowest rank they've got."

"Maybe," Grayden agreed. "But no matter where they put us, we're defenders now."

"Words of truth," Beren said, slapping them both on the back.

Together, they took their first steps toward the future. Enemies had breached their borders. A world in which they had always felt safe had turned out to be far more dangerous than they knew. The shadow of war hung over them like a bird of prey. But although their future seemed uncertain, the three men knew that whatever it held, they were not unprepared for it.

ACKNOWLEDGMENTS

It truly takes a village to raise a book. And I am so thankful for mine. As an author, I'm not used to running out of words, but there really are no words adequate to the task of saying thank you to everyone who helped bring this series to print. So I wanted to take a minute and just highlight my superheroes, the people who made this series possible, who helped me through all the different stages of book writing, editing, and production. Thank you.

———

My Editing Wizards:
Allan James, Nancy Walker, Deborah O'Carroll

My Cover Wizard:
Savannah Jezowski

My Book Formatting Wizard:
Declan Rowe

My Constant Moral Support and Encourager and World Builder and One Who Lifts Me Out of the Pit of Writer's Block Despair:
Derek Schmidt

My Narrator, Who Brings the Characters to Life With His Voice:
Benjamin Fife

My Launch Team:

DeeAnn S, Karyne N, Sarah P, Ashton R, Christine S, Miriam W, Nan W, Tyler S, Amy C, Marie E, Hannah K, Madeline R, Brianna W, Brittany W, Terry F, Priscilla P, Kenzie K

My Awesome Kickstarter Backers:

Kate A, LadyZabyth, Jamie F, Stephanie D, Maggie, Jen B, Kristen C, Suzanne M, Jeremy and Gabrielle G, Catherine C, Pris, Blaine W, Meghan S, Katherine S, Maida K, Hannah T, Adare E, Emily M, Bethany B, Megan, Kaycee B, Kelly H, Jessica B, Steve and Wendy L, Susan L, Tiffany R, Cathrine B, Kim L, Phil and Brandi C, Michele H, Leslie M, Trista S, Topper and Melissa C, Abigail C, Vicky G, James and Nancy W, Tara G, CJ M, Keino, Ed S, Echo, Ben L, Hannah D, Raf B, Kyle C, Ashton R, Paul M, Rodrigo W, Thomas B, Peggy K, Liz D, Tessa, Janeen I, Stephanie S, Jennette M, Daniel J, Brittany Jean, Brielle S, Karen T, Datta G, Danielle P, Larry P, Joe O, Rachel T, Jess S, Jason and LaBranda M, Michelle D, Rachael K, Noel Y, Katy W, Becky J, Sara L, Tia O, Caitlin, Loni G, Demus B, Grantland and Angelina W, Hunter and Sarah H, Fotios Z, Jill W, Courtney T, Christine S, David D, Ayla, DJ and Maria E, John S, Jason M, Deborah O, Callen B, Ricardo M, Amy B, Beverly E, Sarah P, Jeffrey J, Trevor and Gayle R, Micah W, Tiger H, Zach M, Lisa M, Heather and Spencer C, M.I, Elisabeth W, Casey, Hallee, John I, E. A. H, D. S. A, Elizabeth K, Pauline J, Riki, Kim and Jamie V, Rebecca J, Erin D, Marie L, Rafi S, Alex M, Chris K, Michael M, Evan and Claire W, Magnus C, Ho'okahi K, Tiffany G, Alan and Emily D, Mary S, Brian and Jeannie S

And a Special Thank You to My Younger Readers:

Leiana, Nathalie, Brantland, Grayden, Tyler, Caleb, Lydia, Benji, Ryker, Lauryn, Reagan, Kate, Kristina, Kira, Allainah, Rebecca, Talitha, Lydia - your enthusiasm for my stories means more to me than you will possibly ever know!